MEASURE
BY
MEASURE

a novel

Rebecca Fox
&
William Sherman

PEARLSONG PRESS
NASHVILLE, TN

Pearlsong Press
P.O. Box 58065
Nashville, TN 37205
www.pearlsong.com

ISBN-10: 1597190179
ISBN-13: 9781597190176

An earlier version of *Measure by Measure* originally was serialized
on the *Dimensions Online* website (www.dimensionsmagazine.com).
This version has been significantly rewritten for print publication.

Cover & book design by Zelda Pudding. Cover graphic is based on
the RADFAm logo originally created by Madonna Sullivan Wilkins.
Back cover author photo is by photographer/stylist Sali Farrell.

Quantity discounts are available to your business, institution or
organization for reselling, gifts, fundraising or educational purposes,
or incentives. For more information contact
Pearlsong Press • P.O. Box 58065 • Nashville, TN 37205
615-356-5188 • sales@pearlsong.com

Library of Congress Cataloging-in-Publication Data

Fox, Rebecca, 1954–
Measure by measure / Rebecca Fox and William Sherman.
     p. cm.
ISBN 978-1-59719-017-6 (trade pbk. : alk. paper)
1. Overweight persons—Fiction. I. Sherman, William, 1950– II. Title.
PS3606.O956M43 2009
813'.6—dc22
                                        2009006224

The Measure of Love
is to Love without Measure.

St. Francis de Sales

ONE
THE FIRST YEAR AND A HALF

PROLOGUE
FIVE MONTHS EARLIER

From the Feb. 9, 1996 "Weekend" section of The Trib:

Romance Blooms at Fat Dance
Plus-Size Patrons Step Out
by Tod Frente

JEFFERSON LOOKS OUT across the dance floor of the Figs 'n' Dates Lounge at the trio of full-figured ladies doing a line dance. To him, the sight is "the most beautiful view in the world."

All three women, young and in their late twenties, are larger than average. "Fat," as Dr. Dexter Logan bluntly puts it. Fat—and proud of it. For this is the Winter Wonderland dance of the local RADFAm (Respect and Dignity for Fat Americans) chapter. It is, chapter president Logan says, "a place where fat singles and their admirers can meet in safety."

The group holds these dances bi-monthly on the first Saturday of the month, and, according to Logan, "they're always well attended." Tonight, one can count fifty men and women of all shapes and sizes in the room. Everybody seems to be having a good time.

To Jefferson, a tall, black man of average build, this is heaven. Jefferson is a self-professed FA, a "fat admirer." A white-collar professional, he's been attracted to plump and bigger women since he was a teenager.

ACCEPTANCE

"Most big women have trouble accepting themselves," he notes. "They've been told all their lives that being fat is no way to get a man. So they can't hear any of the honest compliments you give them."

At RADFAm functions, he says, you meet women who've learned to accept themselves "as the lovely creatures they are."

Connie, a striking brunette of indeterminate age, echoes Jefferson's sentiments. While unwilling to give her weight ("Let's just say I'm beyond the range of most mainstream plus-size shops"), she appreciates the dances for the way they give fat women a chance to "dress at their most glamorous."

The owner of a downtown plus-size boutique, InFatuation, Connie has been both chapter officer and a regular at these events. "For years, fat women were denied the chance to wear truly beautiful clothes," she states. "These dances are long overdue. I particularly love it when I see a customer on the dance floor in one of my outfits."

To Jefferson, the dance is a chance for him to truly be himself, too. "Most FAs spend their lives hiding their preference from friends and family," he says. "Here, you can be open and honest."

Greg, an FA and insurance salesman, agrees. "There's a good deal of pressure in the business world for FAs to pick a thin partner," he observes. "Thinness equates with success. It takes courage to come to one of these dances, but once you do it, it becomes habit forming."

Habit-forming and maybe life changing. Ask Carl and Linda, a recently engaged couple who both cheerfully call themselves "fat."

FAT AND HAPPY

They first met six months ago at a RADFAm dance. Linda had been a member of the organization for over a year; for Carl, it was his first dance. He'd read about the event in a magazine devoted to appreciation of larger women and had come on an impulse. "Once I saw her, I fell head over heels," he says. "I never dreamed I'd meet a woman so big and beautiful who'd also find me attractive."

Linda was a self-described "casualty on the dating scene" for years before joining RADFAm. "I'd go to singles bars with the girls from work, and it was like I was invisible next to them. Here, the situation is reversed."

The couple rises and heads for the floor, where they dance their way through a slow song. Even from across the lounge, you can see the pleasure on both faces.

"It's really a shame," Dr. Logan says, "that there are so few places where fat people can go and be themselves without risking ridicule. But as long as that's the way it is, we'll probably keep holding these dances."

For future listings of upcoming RADFAm events, keep watching Friday's "Goin' & Doin'" Directory.

EPISODE ONE

"**SO, WHAT ARE YOU WEARING** to the Sweetheart Dance tomorrow night?"

Jenny Taylor glanced up to find her legal-eagle boss Lissa grinning down at her across the desk. "I d-don't think I'll g-go," Jenny stammered as she nervously shuffled the subpoenas she'd just finished typing. "I've got so much to do at home, and I really don't have a thing to wear, and—"

"Girlfriend!" Lissa interrupted. "You're not bailing out on me again. Hey, it's a dance, not a root canal."

Jenny inwardly balanced the agony of oral surgery with that of almost certain social suicide.

Lissa ran flawlessly manicured fingertips through her close-cropped Afro. "Jenny, when's the last time you really pampered yourself? A massage. Or a new outfit. And I don't mean something practical. We're talking stunning, sexy, drop-dead-gorgeous!"

"You can't get clothes like that in my size."

"Sure you can. You just have to know where. Look at me!" Lissa twirled coquettishly as her hands skimmed her fashionably voluptuous form.

"But you're a lot smaller than me!"

Lissa laughed. "How much do you think I weigh?"

Jenny blushed. "It's not polite to presume—"

"I pack 220 pounds in this compact chassis," Lissa replied, "and I've worked hard to make every single ounce of them beautiful. I'll bet you're not much more than that."

"Well, I wear size 26, but they've seemed tighter recently."

"And, I've also noticed, rather dowdy. How old are you, 28 or so? You look like your mother dresses you, for pity's sake!"

Remembering several recent motherly comments, Jenny had to admit it was probably true.

"Okay, so much for your wardrobe. What are you really afraid of?"

"I won't know anybody," Jenny admitted.

"Sure you will. I'll be there, and I'm sure you'll recognize others from the meetings I've taken you to."

Jenny's ambivalence wavered, but she protested one last time. "I'm not a very good dancer."

"So? Hell, with a body like yours, all you need to do is just stand in one spot and jiggle. The FAs will drool! Convinced? Good. Tomorrow morning we'll go spend some of those 'big bucks' I pay you on a visit to my spa, a stylish 'do, and some sexy rags. And then, Cinderella, you'll be the belle of the ball."

PAUL DAILY PICKED AT HIS HASH BROWNS, unsuccessfully trying to work up some enthusiasm for them. No good. His stomach was as jumpy as a fifth grade P.E. class.

Across the parking lot you could see the SkyAire Lodge. Every time a car drove up, he peered into the evening light to see if they were there for the dance. So far, he hadn't seen any likely candidates.

His waitress, a plump black woman with wearily concerned eyes, gave Paul a motherly look when she came to pick up his plate. "Anything wrong with the meal?" she asked.

"Not at all," he said. "Guess the eyes were bigger than the stomach." He gestured over his cup for a refill, which pacified the waitress somewhat. Not the best idea, getting yourself wired on Denny's coffee, but it beat the alternatives.

A large silhouette was stepping out of a minivan parked near the Lodge's entrance. An officer, perhaps, there to get things set up for the Sweetheart Dance. He couldn't make out any features, but from their size they had to be a member of the fat rights group.

It had taken Paul five months to get up the gumption to come to his first dance. Ever since he'd seen that writeup in the *Trib* ("Romance Blooms at Fat Dance"), he'd been garnering the courage to attend one of the bi-monthly events. He'd gotten this far; there was no point in backing out now.

He was a grown man, dammit. Why was he acting like a teen on his first date?

Because he'd never been to a dance where so many women looked like the ideal he'd been carrying with him all these years. Where women and men were the size they were and unapologetic about it. Where men who were attracted to a larger form were able to be open about this preference. Where he actually had a chance of meeting someone who was both physically and mentally compatible with him.

It was a lot to put on just one dance, Paul knew. But this was his first step into the size acceptance community, so who knew where it'd lead? He'd read that news feature to tatters, so he knew what he was called by people in the movement. An FA, a Fat Admirer—though "admiration" seemed like a pretty tame adjective for the fantasies he'd been having with increasing frequency.

His refill was cold by the time he actually thought to try some of it. In the meantime, at least a half dozen fat figures had made their way into the Lodge.

Paul took a look around the restaurant, scoped out the men's room, and rose to go straighten himself.

Now or never, he thought.

LISSA MANEUVERED HER LINCOLN TOWN CAR as close as possible to the front door of the SkyAire Lodge, where a knot of full-figured men and women waited to enter the hotel. It was a warm early summer evening, and more than one woman wore something sleeveless. The mix of attire was eclectic, from studded Western denim to cosmopolitan satin and sequins. Jenny had to admit they all looked lovely, regardless of size, like a vibrant garden bouquet.

In the company of so much bountiful beauty, Jenny felt her self-image slide. The delicious hedonism of the day-spa, coupled with her success at finding the perfect dress at the trendy InFatuation Boutique, had relaxed her body and buoyed her esteem. But now the doubts returned, and as Lissa pulled in to park, Jenny shrank into herself, physically and emotionally.

"Ready to wow 'em, kid?" Lissa reached over to pat Jenny's hand and felt her flinch. "What's wrong, Jen?"

Jenny sighed, then answered, "I'm fine, Liss. Just a case of jitters, I guess."

"You'll do just fine. These are not the enemy, you know. With very few exceptions, no one here will eat you alive. And in some cases, that can be pretty interesting, too."

With that, Jenny laughed and stepped from the car. The two friends joined the queue to the Figs 'n' Dates Lounge, where several RADFAm members took money and issued tickets.

Lissa stepped up to the table first and handed $5 to a 40ish redhead dressed in rather tawdry velour. "Hey, Delia, how's tricks?" Lissa chirped.

"Whadya mean by that?" the redhead shot back.

Lissa held up her palms to ward off her ire. "Nothing personal. Is it a good turnout?"

"Not enough fresh meat, if you ask me."

"Well, here's a new face for you," Lissa replied as she motioned Jenny forward.

"Wrong type," Delia grumbled. "Ten dollars."

"But Lissa told me it would be five," Jenny answered in confusion.

"You're not a member," Delia sneered.

"Get off it, Delia!" Lissa said. "Jenny is my guest, and she's attended several chapter meetings."

"Doesn't matter. Does it, Connie?"

The striking supersized brunette seated at the table beside Delia now entered the conversation she'd thus far observed with distant interest. "Aw, we can be big about this, so to speak," Connie replied with false solicitude. "Besides, she obviously has good taste, since she just bought that dress at my boutique today."

Jenny handed the $5 bill to Delia, who grudgingly placed it in the cash box and handed her a ticket and a blank nametag.

"Enjoy yourself," Connie leered.

And with that, Jenny and Lissa walked through the festooned entrance to the Sweetheart Dance.

PAUL GOT IN LINE BEHIND a wide platinum blonde in a beaded silk dress that hugged her voluminous hips provocatively. Ahead was the ticket table and behind it a poster with the group name (Rights and Dignity for Fat Americans) and motto: "Let us be measured by the size of our hearts, not by the size of our bodies."

In the short time it'd taken him to pay for his meal and make his way over to the Lodge, a small crowd had clustered in the hall outside the dance. He recognized one of them from the photo accompanying the newspaper article: Dr. Dexter Logan, the chapter president. Bearded and bearlike, in a 4X polo shirt and white slacks, Logan was talking to a Lodge clerk. He had a worried look on his face. When Paul got to the ticket table, he learned the reason behind said worried look.

"Deejay's stuck in Wisconsin," Logan said as he came up behind the two ticket sellers. "Probably won't make it down tonight."

The larger—and more attractive—of the two women made an exasperated face. "So what are we gonna tell people?" The look she gave Dexter made it clear that the "we" was meant to be translated as "you."

"The truth," he said. "If they want a refund, they can have it. The Lodge's offered unlimited use of the jukebox, though."

"It's your decision," the ticket seller said, shrugging. Then she turned to look up at Paul, and her expression did a full wattage turnaround. "Well, hello, " she purred. "Don't believe I've seen you here before."

"My first dance," Paul told her, grateful to hear his voice come out tremor free. The brunette had to be a few years older than he, but her round face was so lovely and artfully composed that he started to feel flustered.

"Connie Donovan," she said, holding out a plump handshake.

"Paul Daily."

"How many tickets?"

"Just one," he answered.

"Don't worry," the brunette said, giving him a knowing smile. "If I know the women in this chapter, you won't be coming to these gigs solo for long." She handed Paul a name tag and half a ticket stub. "Don't bother with the name tag," she said. "Nobody uses 'em. We've got door prizes for later, though, so save your ticket."

"Sounds like fun," he considered, pulling out a ten and handing it to her companion.

"See you inside," Connie promised.

EPISODE TWO

THE FIGS 'N' DATES LOUNGE was a typical hotel pub, smallish and crowded with tables and stools, cheap wood-and-vinyl bar running the length of the room, paneled walls covered with neon or mirrored brew signs. The dance floor, such as it is, was about the size of a card table—large enough, perhaps, to accommodate three supersize or four midsize couples, uncomfortably.

Yet the chapter had taken pains to create an attractive and pleasant milieu, with flowers and candles on each table. Posters with the chapter logo—a heart-shaped graphic with stylized full-figured couple reaching towards each other—and motto were placed strategically between liquor advertisements.

To reach the bar, Lissa sidled past a buxom blonde in cowgirl drag and a Hawaiian-garbed man. "What'll ya have?" the bartender inquired.

"A whiskey sour. How about you, Jenny? First one's on me."

"A rum and Coke, I guess."

As the barkeep turned to fill their order, Lissa scanned the room. "Not much of a turnout yet. Sure hope this isn't a dud, 'specially on your first time."

"I don't know how many more people we could fit in here," Jenny replied as a short man with a cane and receding hairline groped by her.

Lissa leaned over and whispered, "Be careful of that one. That's Rodney, and don't let his disability fool you. It's his favorite ploy—play a novice for sympathy and then it's all Roman hands and Russian fingers. Get your drink and follow me. There's someone special I'd like you to meet."

They made their way across the room to a relatively quiet corner. In this cozy pocket sat a table covered by a midnight purple cloth, punctuated with flickering candles, crystals of rainbow hues and a bowl of what looked like salt. Behind this arcane altar Jenny saw an angelic woman clothed in vivid robes and haloed in mahogany hair. A pile of cards lay beside her, topped by a large shimmering amethyst.

"Jenny, I would like you to meet RADFAm's resident bohemian, entrepreneuse and spiritual guide, Mystique Shores—Misty to her friends. Misty, this is Jenny Taylor. Now be nice and try not to scare her."

"Welcome, Jenny," Misty responded in a rich contralto. "I think I remember you from a meeting?"

Jenny smiled. "Yes, I've been to a couple, but I didn't do much mingling."

"Yes," Lissa agreed, "and we really have to do something to get this chick out of her shell. Have any voodoo spells you can cast, Oh She-Who-Must-Be-Obeyed?"

"Cut it out, you infidel," Misty chuckled. "You know it doesn't work that way. But if you'd like me to read the Tarot, Jenny, I might find some insight for you."

Jenny shifted uncomfortably in her seat. "I'd really like that, Misty, but I think another time would be better," she demurred. "Tonight I'm having enough trouble moving under my own steam, and goodness knows what the Tarot would have to say about me then."

A peal of laughter rang out behind her. As she turned toward its source she caught sight of herself in a mirror, and almost didn't recognize the woman glowing through the bronzed marbling.

She took her time getting acquainted with this vision—her shoulder-length blonde hair swept up softly in Gibson Girl style, makeup subtle and soft. A pale blue cotton gauze peasant bodice edged with creamy Battenburg lace, discreetly revealing luscious cleavage. Matching skirt cinched low on the waist with a macramé belt and falling below to a tea-length handkerchief hem. Hidden to the mirror yet known to Jenny, lace-up ecru sandals cradled her freshly pedicured feet.

Jenny realized this was a woman she would want to meet, which sent a flush radiating deliciously through her. For a moment she felt proud to be this woman. Then she smiled and rose to introduce her newfound self to her soon-to-be-friends.

THE ROOM WAS ALREADY FILLING with women and men in a variety of shapes of large. Back by the entrance, a short man with a cane was jostling up against a young girl in a painted top and satin skort. Over the jukebox speakers, the Gipsy Kings were bellowing their way through a Spanish-flavored tune. Nobody was out on the dance floor yet.

Looked like most of the tables were already taken, so Paul bee-lined it to an empty barstool. From there he tried to get his bearings. It wasn't easy with so many gorgeous full-sized women within reach.

"Careful you don't get whiplash there, fella," a male voice cautioned. "You can always tell the new guys at a Sweetheart Dance from the way they enter a room. Practically throw their necks out, trying to get a glimpse of all the wildlife."

Paul turned toward the voice.

Casually perched on the next stool was a tall figure in a colored T and sports jacket. Longish hair stylishly moussed, he had the look of someone from a Calvin Klein ad. He smiled at Paul sardonically and extended a hand. "Greg Dillman," he said. "One of the regulars."

"Paul Daily. New kid on the block."

"So I see. What're you having?" He gestured to the Hispanic barkeep, who was appreciatively watching a zaftig brunette as she perched herself on a barstool.

"O'Doul's," Paul ordered, once the bartender came within earshot.

"No 'Doul's. Sharp's."

"Okay," Paul said. "Why do I suddenly feel like I'm in an old Saturday Night Live sketch?"

"Relax," Greg advised. "Just enjoy the babescape. If you're an FA, this is Hog Heaven. No pun intended."

Then why draw attention to it? Paul wondered. But instead he asked, "This what folks are dancing to these days?"

"Only if you live in Mazatlan," Greg answered. "It appears our deejay's done a George Jones, so the Lodge has made the jukebox a freebie. Only problem is Speedy Gonzales here got to it first and punched up two albums worth of world beat."

Great. What he knew about world music could fit on a cocktail napkin—with space left over to mop up a bottle ring and not smear any of the lettering.

"So, what do you do when you're not ogling fat chicks, Paul?"

"Special Ed teacher," Paul told him. "Junior high."

"Must take a lot of commitment," Greg said. "My hat's off to ya. I'm in insurance myself." He tossed Paul a business card.

"I'm not looking for any extra coverage—" Paul began.

"Slow down, sport," Dillman interrupted. "Don't sell it all the time, but I do operate as a consultant on the side. For folks who have a hard time getting coverage. It's not easy buying health insurance if you're the size of some of these babes." He indicated the room with a cock of his head and straightened up suddenly. "Half a mo'," he said in a cheesy Cockney accent. "Here's someone new!"

Paul stared across the room over the sea of well-coiffed hairdos. They all were new to him, so he wondered what he was looking for.

"Blonde dish standing over by Madame Blavatsky's table," Greg indicated. "Haven't seen her before."

By a colorfully festooned table rose a lovely blonde in a pale blue gauze dress. The way the light diffused and hinted at her frame, she looked to be in the upper midsized range. She was talking to a smaller black woman and a berobed figure. Then she moved toward a neighboring table.

"Don't get any ideas, Paul," the insurance man said. "I saw this 'un first."

EPISODE THREE

AS JENNY ROSE TO MINGLE with the other dance patrons, she found the room had become far more crowded than she'd realized. Just getting to the next table involved much good-humored jostling. She squeezed by a laughing couple seeking an out-of-the-way spot and finally reached the table whose gaiety had first drawn her attention.

"Hi, I'm Lainie!" A 60ish silver-haired woman greeted her enthusiastically. "Welcome to Bedlam and have a seat."

"Thanks," Jenny replied as she slid into the proffered chair. "My name's Jenny. Quite a turnout. Is it always this—lively?"

"We could only hope." This from a striking woman with skunk-striped long black tresses. "Tonight the ratio is just about right—boy-girl, girl-boy. There's not much worse than a big crowd without the right 'mix.'"

"Oh, I don't know," argued a short, rather shabby blonde. "Remember that '40s swing dance a couple years ago? Plenty of guys, but most of 'em were probably around when that music was popular the first time. What a bunch of fogies!"

"Bite your tongue, Joyce," Lainie retorted. "That's my generation, you know. Forget Brad Pitt—give me Sean Connery any day."

A heated discussion raged briefly over male sex symbols, current and past. Jenny noted that several of the participants seemed to favor such hefty hunks as John Goodman and Luciano Pavarotti.

Lainie finally brought the huddle to a halt. "Enough testosterone for now, girls! Suffice it to say we all know how to appreciate a sexy man. It's just a shame that we don't receive the same appreciation."

Jenny seized this opportunity to ask, "Is it really true there are men who honestly prefer big women?"

Skunk-stripe laughed. "Hell, no! It's all a lie—just a figment of someone's sick imagination. So you'd better run along, little girl, and leave that bunch of phonies to us."

"Sometimes you are such a bitch, Valerie." Joyce giggled to take the sting from her words. "Jenny has every right to try her luck."

"Right on, sister!" Lainie chirped. "Yes, Jenny, there really are men who consider women like us sexy and desirable."

"Who are they, and where do you find them?"

"Well," Lainie replied, "surveys say five to ten percent of men are FAs, but not all of 'em have 'come out.' And when they do, they're afraid they'll be re-jected as weirdos. So they submit personal ads in magazines like *Dimensions*, or they dial up fantasy lines. Or they surf the 'net for topics like 'alt.sex.fat.'"

"Sometimes friends who know what they like steer them our way," offered Joyce. "And, of course, there are dances and other RADFAm get-togethers."

"Plus, if you believe in such things," Valerie sneered, lifting her chin as she scanned the room, "sometimes you just get lucky."

At that moment, a firm hand grasped Jenny by the shoulder and she jumped. "Well," a decidedly masculine voice spoke behind her, "where have you been all my life?"

THE JUKE WAS A ROCKOLA CD player—which explained the unceasing string of Gipsy (spelled with an "i," the teacher in him noticed) King tunes. Flipping through the selections, Paul sought something more familiar. There were plenty of contemporary dance albums on the machine, but again, this was an area where he came up short. Finally, he flipped to a quartet of Rhino oldies collections. Something familiar at last!

"Looks like you've ventured into my era," Dex Logan drawled as he ap-peared by Paul's side. "Wouldn't think you'd be old enough to appreciate this stuff."

"You kidding?" Paul said. "I'm a fanboy when it comes to '50s–'60s rock and roll." He moved aside to let the chapter president have access to the ma-chine. Logan ambled up to it, quickly scanned the choices and punched in five selections.

"Something I can dance to," he explained. "If I didn't choose any of your favorites, feel free to do so. We've got the juke free tonight." He paused, took a swig of canned Cherry Coke, then introduced himself. "Thought I'd check out any newcomers before taking over at the ticket table," he explained. "You familiar with our group?"

"Only what I read in the papers," Paul replied. Though he'd also read about RADFAm in a men's mag devoted to plus-sized models, this didn't seem the time to bring that up. Logan looked friendly enough, but why risk alienating him?

"It's a good group of people," Logan said. "A lot of them, this is the only place they can go without being hassled for the size they are."

"You want to make sure it stays that way," Paul said. "Can't say I blame you." Across the dance floor, Dillman was chatting it up with the beautiful blonde in blue.

"Couple months ago," Logan continued, "right after we hit the papers, we had a group of frat boys try to crash the dance. We kept them out, but since then, I've gotten a little more sensitive about keeping this place safe."

So that was it: Logan was telling him the house expectations. "Don't worry about me," Paul assured him. "I'm not here to ridicule or hurt anyone. I'm just here to dance."

"Then you've come to the right place," the fat man said. He smiled and patted Paul on the shoulder. In that moment, he looked like a domesticated Grizzly Adams. "Have a good time."

By the door, a matronly looking woman was gesturing to Logan. "Looks like it's my turn at the ticket table," he said.

As Logan sidled his way through the limited space between tables, Paul returned to the jukebox. At a nearby table, a trio of supersized women was giggling at the pronouncements of a serious looking black man in a three-piece suit.

"Hope you picked something good for us to dance to," Connie Donovan said, walking up and putting both plump hands on top of his.

EPISODE FOUR

JENNY TURNED TO SEE WHOSE HAND had captured her shoulder. The masculine voice seemed to belong to a poster-child for Models Anonymous—handsome in a Versace sort of way, with chiseled features and longish moussed hair, wearing fashionably casual threads and a barely-concealed leer.

The model spoke again. "Why's the prettiest girl here sitting when she should be dancing? With me."

Jenny swallowed. "Well, I don't even know your name."

"Dillman. Greg Dillman." His voice caressed each syllable. "And I'll bet your name is Venus."

Valerie spluttered with laughter, while Lainie waggled her finger and warned, "Your bullshit will getcha nowhere with Jenny. She's too bright for your type."

"Aw, Mom! All I want is a dance. So pull in your claws and let us show you how it's done." And with that he grabbed Jenny's hand, deftly lifted her to her feet and led her to the crowded dance floor.

The Toys' "A Lover's Concerto" was filling the room with its classical melody, and Greg held Jenny close. The scent of Polo combined with Binaca and something else, unmistakably male, tickled her nostrils.

Massaging her back gently, Greg asked, "First time, right? I'd have remembered someone like you, and I'm always here for the dances."

"Yes," Jenny smiled shyly. "My boss Lissa brought me."

"Oh yeah, the black lawyer." He looked appraisingly into her face. "You don't swing both ways too, do you? Not that there's anything wrong with it."

"What do you mean?" Jenny asked in confusion.

"Nothing," he hurriedly replied. "Just forget I mentioned it. Let's talk about us."

Jenny spoke a little about growing up in a small rural town and being a paralegal. The music switched to something more energetic, yet Greg continued to press her body against him. "But I'm sure you don't want to hear about my boring life. What about you?"

With that, Greg launched into a diatribe about his accomplishments (Tau Kappa Epsilon, MBA from Western, CLU/CHFC/CPCU/LUTCF—) and ambitions (insuring the uninsurable—i.e., fat people). Jenny's attention began to wander, and she was seriously wishing she were anywhere else when suddenly she was bumped from behind and thrust even closer into Greg.

"Well," he purred, "that's a lot better."

"Oh! I'm sorry," Jenny cried as she pulled away. "I've lost a contact lens."

"No problem, you can always get another," Greg replied as he tried to draw her close once again.

"No, no! I think it's still on my eye. Excuse me while I go to the restroom." Jenny extricated herself from his octopus grasp and quickly headed toward the exit.

"I'll be waiting for you," Greg shot after her retreating form.

Such a comfort. Jenny shuddered.

"How d'you call *your lover boy?*"

Bodies mashed tighter together on the dance floor, Paul maneuvered Connie through their limited piece of dance turf. It was hardly Fred and Ginger—

just the act of moving across the floor required the synchronous cooperation of every other dancing couple.

Still, it felt pretty damn amazing to even be doing this. Connie favored slow dancing even to the fast songs ("Keeps me on the dance floor longer"), but Paul wasn't complaining. The way her opulent forefront cushioned against him was almost overwhelmingly sensual. He should've done this months ago.

"Remember this song from—what was the name of that movie?—*Dirty Dancing*?" Connie cooed. Her round face was subtly made up to make the most of the lounge's lighting. In the dance wars, she was clearly a seasoned campaigner, even if she did claim to recognize Mickey and Sylvia's '60s hit from an '80s movie. "A pretty sexy scene," she continued. "Though I bet Jennifer Grey didn't do much for you."

"Not exactly," Paul admitted. "When I think period dancing, I think *Hairspray*."

"That figures," she smiled. "But even at her largest, Ricki Lake comes up pretty short compared to me!" She pressed a little closer to him, and the results were almost dizzying.

Paul wracked his mind for a suitable response, unsure whether to agree with or bypass that last statement. Over Connie's shoulder, he could see Dillman and the lovely blonde in the pale blue dress, and he momentarily wished for a dose of Dillman's confidence.

"I'd rather be dancing with you," he finally said, which brought a triumphant look on the supersized woman's face. "Ricki always seemed a little too young in that movie," he added. A twitch shot across Connie's full lips. Oops—another potential land mine! "But maybe that's just because I teach for a living."

"Maybe," Connie replied, recharging her positive face. "So tell me about yourself."

Paul obliged, starting with work and sliding into the discovery of his fat attraction. "I guess I've always looked towards bigger women," he said while Ben E. King crooned another cinemacentric oldie. "But for most of my life, I thought it was only fantasy."

He still remembered his first movie crush. It was from a Laurel and Hardy short, of all things—fat Oliver Hardy trying to elope in a compact car with an equally rotund young woman. The scene was meant as slapstick comedy, but he carried that actress's face with him into adolescence.

"Spent most of my twenties trying to keep my desire separate from my social life," he said. "It helped that I'd been raised Catholic."

Connie squeezed his hand, and he looked into her eyes. They were large and knowing, full of promise. She was the kind of woman who made self-as-surance supremely sexy. The sound of the jukebox seemed to recede, and in that moment, she was all there was.

"Oops! Sorry," a voice said as his hips momentarily connected with a small man carrying beers along the dance floor. Fortunately, nothing was spilled.

"Tell me about yourself now," Paul said once they returned to slow dance rhythm.

"Me?" Connie whispered. "I'm just your everyday supersize single gal. With a voracious sexual appetite and the ingenuity to satisfy it." She pressed Paul closer to her mouth, and he caught a whiff of her designer perfume.

The dance floor had emptied out by a third—room to breathe, at last—but who wanted it? On the juke, the Flamingos were softly assuring their loved one that they only had eyes for her. Dillman and his dance partner were nowhere to be seen.

"But enough talking," Connie said, stroking Paul's cheek with her pudgy fingertips. "Let's just dance."

EPISODE FIVE

THE WOMEN'S BATHROOM at the SkyAire Lodge was as drattedly in-convenient for people of size as every other "public" facility—even the handicapped toilet was configured by "normal" people with their own concept of accessibility. The TP dispenser was strategically placed to ensure that no matter how Jenny perched it would viciously poke her leg or sit-upon. Maybe that was a blessing in disguise, since she had to stay poised on the edge of the seat anyway, ready to grab the door, which threatened to fling wide whenever other customers shut theirs.

Unfortunately, this was a chronic concern due to an authentically Ori-ental wedding reception taking place across the hall. As brightly robed as butterflies, and just as delicate, wedding members and guests laughed and chatted as they performed their ablutions. Jenny emerged to jeweled swarms of tiny, elfin children. Ms. Gulliver to Lilliputian children. Three adolescent girls near the vanity mirror peered her way, then huddled to giggle.

The errant contact lens was nowhere to be found, and Jenny thanked her Girl Scout training for thinking to slip her glasses case into her purse. Her wire-rims weren't hideous or anything, but she knew she looked better sans glasses. Unlike Lissa, who looked beauteous in her vast wardrobe of prescrip-tion specs, Jenny knew her eyes were her finest feature, and even indulged in a little harmless "publicity." The blue-tinted lenses enhanced eyes whose depths ebbed from aquamarine to Wedgewood. Even her mother, who had very little positive to say to or about Jenny, never failed to comment on her eyes.

"Oh well," Jenny sighed, "at least I can see." She adjusted her peasant top, gave her hair a fluff, and prepared to do battle once more.

LIKE MOST MEN, Paul often wondered what women did when they hit the john. In his experience, guys typically dashed in and pissed as fast as possible, careful not to latch eyes with any of the other men in the room. Conversation with someone you didn't know? Not unthinkable—but pretty damn suspicious in the men's room. Which is why when he backed away from the porcelain and heard the voice to his side, he was sure the guy hadn't been talking to him.

He had been, though, and he repeated his statement to emphasize it.

"Hope I didn't mess you up on the dance floor," the voice said. "Wouldn't want Connie pissed off at me. That's one mighty mama."

It was the guy with the beers. A short, slightly stocky man with Hispanic features. He smiled amiably, moved to the sinks and started washing his hands, careful not to splash any water on his red silk shirt.

"No problem," Paul finally said. Clearly, this was a night for new experiences. "Hardly noticed ya."

"Haven't seen you at one of these before," the short man said. "I'm Joe. Been coming to this dance for months now, and I know all the regulars."

"You a member of RADFAm?"

"Naw," Joe said. "Just here to dance, find the right woman if I'm lucky. Lot of beautiful ladies here." He gestured with his hands, spreading them as far as he could, delineating a womanly figure that surpassed even the largest woman upstairs. "With plenty of potential," he said.

"Potential?"

"Like the song sez," Joe told him with a wink, "'I like 'em bulgin' from too much indulgin'.'"

Paul had read about guys like this, but he'd thought they only existed in the pages of FA fantasies. Now that he was face to face with one, he didn't know what to think. For some reason, a part of him was feeling guilty.

"Name's Paul," he finally said, wondering if he was jumping to conclusions. Joe had one of those boyish voices that made it difficult to imagine he could be so manipulative. Yet Paul's experiences in Behavior Disorder classes had taught him that even the most angelic seeming kid could be as maneuvering as the most experienced alderperson.

"Pleased to meetcha," Joe said, holding out a liquid-soap-scented hand.

"Excuse me if it seems like I'm butting in out of nowhere. But I don't know if you noticed—we guys are outnumbered at this dance." He pushed on the air dryer, saw it didn't work, then grabbed a paper towel off a pile by the edge of the sink. "I'm kidding," he said. "But one thing's sure—ain't a lot of guys willing to be open about this kind of preference. It's not something you can talk about to your buddies at work."

"So where do you work, Joe?"

Joe mentioned a downtown restaurant whose name Paul recognized from the dining pages of the *Trib*. The kind of place where you could blow a week's salary and still feel hungry afterward. "Pretty classy."

"I'm sous chef," Joe told him. "One of ten. Sounds more impressive than it actually is, but it's a good start." He headed for the door. "You seen that Misty yet?" he asked. "Spends all her time at the table with those cards of hers. Kinda hides her bod. But from the way she chews her popcorn, I bet she has a pretty good appetite. Wouldn't mind fixing a meal for her! And none of that nouvelle cuisine crap, either." He pushed the door open, passing two men in tuxes. "See ya upstairs."

AS JENNY TURNED FROM THE MIRROR, a pear-shaped young woman she recognized from the dance joined her. "Hi," the woman smiled. "I'm Patsy."

"Hi! Jenny. Quite a turnout—" implying not only the dance but the riotous horde around them.

"Yeah. Are RADFAm dances always so popular?"

"It's my first time, but I got the impression this is about par. Your first time, too?"

"Yes," Patsy nodded. "I read about it in the 'Goin' & Doin'' section of the *Trib* and thought it sounded like fun. How 'bout you?"

"My boss brought me." They were laughing at this delicious irony when Lainie and Joyce came in. As the room filled with bounteous flesh, the wedding party beat a hasty retreat.

Joyce flopped down in a chair and dramatically fanned herself. "Whoo, gotta catch my breath! Why, I ask you, does a bar put its bathroom so goddamn far away, and in the basement?!"

"Doesn't seem logical, I must admit," Lainie called from the handicapped stall. "But we have this discussion every time we come here. If you wouldn't drink so much—"

"—I wouldn't have to piss so much," Joyce concluded. "I also hear *this* every time," she stage-whispered confidingly.

Lainie finished her business and joined the others at the bank of mirrors. "Well, ladies, are we having fun yet?"

"Sure," Patsy replied. "I've met several people, and even danced a couple times."

Jenny blushed a little before answering. "Same here. There seem to be a lot of nice people."

"Don't kid yourself, kiddo," chirped Joyce. "There are some real stinkers, too. Saw ya dancing with Greggy-poo 'Dillweed.'"

"I thought it was Dillman," Jenny said in confusion.

Lainie smiled and said, "It is, honey. But 'Greggy-poo,' while a hunk, is also, let us say, one of our less 'desirable' members."

"Pussy-foot bullshit!" Joyce spat contemptuously. "He's an opportunistic asshole, and you know it."

"Only if you let him," Lainie countered diplomatically. "After he was censured last year, he's really been a lot more appropriate. But," she fixed her eyes on Jenny and Patsy, "don't you trust him any farther than you can throw him. Greg's not the only one—there are some real stinkers out there."

"I heard about 'The Gimpy Groper,'" Patsy giggled.

"Rodney? Aw, he ain't nuthin," Joyce slurred. "How 'bout Jefferson? All talk, and always 'I did this' and 'I saw that.' 'Nuff to give a girl self 'steem problems." Letting rip a decidedly unladylike belch, she continued to dish. "And how 'bout Ms. Connie Donovan and her toady, Delia? You be real careful—"

"Anyway," Lainie interrupted, "as my sainted mother used to say, 'If you can't say nothing nice about somebody—'"

"'Don't say nothing at all!'" Jenny chimed in. "So we both shared Thumper's mom."

Lainie laughed. "Well, inspiration comes from many strange places. You've just gotta be sure that particular inspiration is right for you. Now let's go back to the dance and 'get inspired!'"

PAUL RAN INTO DILLMAN on his way upstairs.

"Hey, buddy," the insurance man said. "You know that new blonde number you were drooling after on the dance floor? If I were you, I wouldn't bother. Looks like she doesn't swing that way. Not surprising, considering who she came in with."

"Am I supposed to know what you're talking about?" Paul asked.

"Suit yourself, Junior. Don't say I didn't warn ya," Dillman answered, pulling out a comb and running it through his glistening hair. "And watch out for that Connie, too. I won't say the woman eats men alive, but before her last boyfriend, the gal was close to midsize."

This was too much. "I think I can take care of myself," Paul said.

"That's how it works," Dillman said with a sharp laugh. "You think you can take care of yourself. But Connie knows different." He barked another laugh, leaving Paul in the stairway.

So these were his peers: Joe, who seemed to be into feeding, and Greg, who clearly was into being an asshole. Where'd that leave Paul on the continuum? No wonder Dex Logan had made a point of checking him out, Paul thought as he reached the top of the stairs.

"Thinking about me?" Connie said from the ticket table.

Outside Figs 'n' Dates he saw her fully for the first time. In her deeply slitted crimson sheath dress and matching see-through bolero jacket, her figure was accentuated dramatically. Back in the lounge, surrounded by so much bountiful womanhood, he hadn't realized how big-hipped she was.

She straightened herself and gave Paul a come hither gesture that put all of his thoughts on hold. This was one phenomenal looking woman. "C'mon in. They're getting ready to do the door prizes."

"Will do," Paul said, linking Connie's nearest arm. Through the long skirt slit her thigh jutted impudently against his as they returned to the lounge.

EPISODE SIX

WHEN JENNY AND HER NEW FRIENDS returned to the lounge, the music was silent and the crowd had vacated the dance floor. Chairs were at a premium, but fortunately Valerie, with what looked to be uncharacteristic altruism, had saved their seats. Jenny noticed a teddy-bearish man and a matronly midsized woman standing at the signup table shuffling papers and arranging things.

"I was afraid you wouldn't make it back in time," Valerie hissed. "Connie cornered Dexter and insisted that he start the drawing for door prizes now."

"Sounds just like her," Lainie sniffed. "Gives her a better chance at winning."

"Well," Joyce drawled, "I'd say she won the big prize already. Didja get a look at the stud she snagged?"

Valerie looked disgusted and took a deep breath to make some answer, but the teddy-bear cleared his throat and began speaking into a microphone. "Good evening! My name is Dexter Logan, and as president of this RADFAm chapter, I welcome you all to our June Sweetheart Dance. It's great to see such a big turnout tonight, and I hope you've all had a wonderful time. Now, let's give away some goodies!"

A spattering of applause rang through the room, and Jenny felt the height-
ened sense of excitement around her.

"As usual," Dexter continued, "several chapter members have generously
donated prizes, and there are some real treats here." He lifted what looked
like a Baskin-Robbins ice cream tub decorated with fat dancing cherubs and
dramatically swirled the contents. "So get out your ticket stubs and our vice-
president Eleanor Bollen will draw the first winner."

The matron beside him reached her hand in, pulled out a stub and announced, "The winning number is 2336. That's 2-3-3-6."

A moment of nervous anticipation was shattered by a shout from the bar.
"That's me!" The midnight cowgirl was the first winner.

"Well, come right up here, Denise, and choose your prize."

Sashaying up to the table, Denise picked out the largest item on the table
and held it up for all to see.

"Our first prize," Dexter intoned, "is a mini-boombox donated by Greg
Dillman. Congratulations, Denise."

Eleanor once again dipped her hand into the tub and pulled out the second ticket. "How about 2328? 2-3-2-8."

The crowd shuffled again, and this time a pudgy young man raised his
hand. "Here's our next winner. Come on down, Carl, and claim your prize."

Carl chose an envelope that revealed a year's subscription to *Dimensions*
magazine donated by Dexter, and returned to his seat with a huge grin.

The next winner received a certificate redeemable for a *Fat!So?* T-shirt donated by the 'zine. Joyce called out, "You'll be sorry! Took 'em six months
to send mine, and then all the letters rubbed off!" Lainie shushed her, and
Eleanor continued. "Three more prizes to go, and our next lucky winner is
ticket 2354. 2-3-5-4?"

This time Lainie's ticket paid off, and her prize was a $25 gift certificate
to the InFatuation Boutique. As Lainie returned to the table, Joyce leaned toward Jenny and snidely commented, "That might buy one pair of socks. On
sale. Connie's so generous, especially when it's tax-deductible."

The next winner was drawn, and now Jenny's number was chosen. She
self-consciously walked to the table to the enthusiastic applause of her friends
and picked up an unmarked envelope that held Lissa's donation, a manicure
and facial at the spa they'd enjoyed today.

"Well, ladies and gents," Dexter declared, "there's one lonely little prize
left. Eleanor, let's find one last lucky person to take it home."

Jenny noticed the matron peer up at the teddy-bear with what approached
adoration before she dipped her hand into the container one last time. "2369.

Our final lucky winner is 2-3-6-9!"

From across the room Jenny's boss let out a hearty whoop. Lissa glided up to the front, graciously accepting the crowd's acclaim as her just due. "Just what I need," she laughed when she read the envelope's contents. "A year's membership to this dis-organization! I'm already paid up into the next millennium, so I'll offer this instead to my favorite paralegal, Ms. Jenny Taylor."

That gesture drew the loudest huzzah of the evening, and Jenny wanted to crawl under the table as everyone around her offered their congratulations. She was extremely relieved when Dexter drew the audience's attention back to the front.

"Well, this just shows what a great group we have here. Thank you all for coming. There's still plenty of time left before they kick us out of here, so continue to enjoy yourselves. Next month is the business meeting at my house, so mark your calendars. Be looking for the newsletter before then. Eleanor will have the agenda in it, as well as her usual sprightly journalism. Once again, special thanks to all our prize contributors, and to all of you for making tonight's Sweetheart Dance our very best ever."

BECAUSE HE KNEW SO FEW OF THE PLAYERS, Paul found it difficult to get into the drawing. His distraction was understandable considering the way that Connie kept touching him underneath the table, but he was alert enough to watch Dillman's blonde receive her prize. Beaming broadly as she opened her gift cert, she looked as cool and lovely as a model in a plus-size catalog. Wren Douglas, say.

He got to the table with a drink for Connie and himself just as the first set of numbers was called. Delia had saved two chairs close to the action, but from the looks she kept flashing him, it was clear she wasn't too thrilled by his presence. She looked like a dieter who'd just been told carrot sticks upped your cholesterol level.

He was less successful reading Connie. She kept her face impassive throughout the drawing, though when her offering came up, she came close to tearing his pantleg with her nails.

"Everybody's Jewish mother," Delia couldn't resist sniping as Lainie Somebody-Or-Other, the recipient of InFatuation's prize, made her way back to her seat. "Definitely could use a fashion makeover."

"I recognize the man at the table," he asked Connie. "But who's the lady with him? His wife?"

"She wishes," Connie snorted. "That's Eleanor Bollen. Chapter vice-president."

"For six more months, anyhow," Delia added, pulling a package of Virginia Slims out of her handbag. She put one between her thin lips without lighting up. A few minutes of this, and you half expected her to unwrap the cigarette and pull a strip of pink gum out. "Dexter and his smoke-free zones," she muttered once Paul sent a questioning glance her way.

He would have said something but for Connie's fingertips.

"Wish you could've won something," she said once the final number was called. "But maybe we can make up for it later." Her face dimpled suggestively, and Paul felt his redden.

Mr. Sophisticate, he thought. Over the juke a fat black singer was walking to New Orleans. On the dance floor Logan was gracefully leading his fellow officer through a slow dance.

"Damn, I missed it!" Paul suddenly heard Dillman barging through the doorway. "Paul! Who won my boombox?"

Paul pointed in the direction of the winner. Greg squinted toward her table, made a face, then shrugged.

"What's the matter, Greg?" Connie asked from behind her club soda, visibly annoyed by Dillman's intrusion. "Miss your chance to be the mighty philanthropist?"

"You know me, Connie," Dillman answered. "I'm not looking for credit—I'm a giving kinda guy."

"I've heard that, Greg," she said sweetly. "S'why they invented penicillin, isn't it?"

"What'd I tell you about this 'un, Paulie?" the insurance man said, pulling back in mock dismay. "The woman's ferocious. Should've seen her when she was president. You wanna talk about throwing your weight around—"

"Fine talk from a man who nearly got his ass banned from this group for life," Connie said, picking out a clump of ice and popping it into her mouth. Beneath the table, she'd stopped paying attention to Paul's leg.

"Is it true what they say about women who chew ice?" Dillman asked, swiveling and heading off in the direction of his prize winner.

"Not this woman," Connie said, her round face clouding. "Baby boombox, my sizable ass. S'not the only small unit that Greg's given away." She tipped the dregs of her drink out of her glass, then turned her attention back toward Paul. "Getting a bit stuffy in here, don't you think? Let's head outside."

The night was hot and exhaust-ridden, not much of an improvement over the inside of the SkyAire. Still, it was a relief after the crowded lounge. They grabbed a concrete bench and let the semis roll by.

"So you know Dillman pretty well?" Paul couldn't keep from asking, now that they were away from the crowd.

"Not the way you're asking," she said. "I was chapter president when Greg got caught taking pictures at a pool party. Did it without members' permission, a big no-no in RADFAm. If I had my way, he'd have been booted from all public functions. But bleeding hearts prevailed."

"So you were a mover and a shaker," Paul said, lacing his fingers with hers.

"Of course," she grinned. "Every time I move, I shake."

"And very attractively, too."

"If I were an ingénue, I'd probably be blushing right now," she said.

She rose, then pulled him up against her abundant forefront. Their clothes whispered as they came together. Paul stretched his arms around her, heedless of the night heat. They kissed for the first time, and it was like every adolescent fantasy he ever had—magnified to the nth degree.

"I'm ready to leave," she said. "How about you?"

EPISODE SEVEN

"**WHAT A WONDERFUL BOSS!**" Lainie greeted Lissa as she came over to the table with Jenny's certificate of membership.

"Yep, I'm a peach," Lissa replied as she flopped into a chair.

Lainie reached over and pinched Lissa's cheek. "Come on, you know what bosses are usually like. They treat us like slaves, if they bother to hire *us* at all."

"Yeah, this peach knows it can be the pits," Lissa punned as everyone groaned. "But I also know talent comes in all sizes, and Jenny was the best job applicant. It's just a nice bonus that, as a sister-in-size, I can bring her to stuff like this." She turned to Jenny and smiled. "Have you been having fun, sis?"

"I've had a great time. And you really shouldn't have given me your prize," Jenny scolded.

"Well, as you'll learn, I do lots of shouldn'ts. However, it may have been a miscalculation on my part after all," she confided. "There are certain people who, due to envy or meanness, may misread my actions and treat you weirdly. So don't you pay them any mind. Our relationship is none of their business—"

Jenny replied with some force, "Damned right! You're my boss, but more importantly, you're my friend. And I'm doubly blessed to have both those people rolled into someone like you."

"Pshaw! Enough of this mutual admiration society crap." Lissa glanced around the lounge speculatively. "Just weighing the damages. Who's scored, who's scorned. Speaking of which, watch your purses, ladies. Here comes Dillman."

Greg oozed up to their table, snagged a chair, which he straddled backwards, and drawled, "Now here's a bouquet of American Beauties if I ever saw one. Gee, Jenny, I didn't see you come back from the john. Couldn't find your contact lens, huh?"

"No, I'm sorry to say," she answered coolly. "Guess I'll just have to be Ms. Four-Eyes until I can get a replacement."

"Pity." He now turned his attention to Patsy. "But unless I miss my guess, your vision's 20/20, just like you're a vision to me."

Patsy blushed deeply at the compliment while the rest of the women guffawed.

Greg continued, "I was gonna get some coffee at the Denny's next door. Anyone want to join me?"

Each of the old-time RADFAm members quickly declined his offer, so he peered speculatively at Jenny and Patsy.

"Well, lovely ladies. It's just a cup of coffee. And, of course, the pleasure of my company."

Jenny glanced at Lissa and caught a barely noticeable frown. "Thanks for the offer, Greg," Jenny replied. "But I rode with Lissa and it's quite a long drive home."

Narrowing his eyes, he considered the two workmates, then turned in dismissal back to Patsy and purred, "Well, doll? Coffee and maybe a piece of pie—my treat."

"Your treat?" Joyce cackled harshly. "That'll be a first."

Taking this as something of a challenge, Patsy's resolve wavered and she accepted. "It would be a pleasure, Greg. But could I have just one more dance?"

"Only if it's a slow one," he chuckled as he took her hand and pulled her to her feet. "I want to hold you close so no one else can steal you away." As they walked onto the dance floor, Greg turned back and sneered. *Nyah, nyah, nyah.*

Lainie shook her head sadly. "I hope she has enough sense to watch out for his tricks."

Lissa suppressed a sudden yawn. "Well, I don't know about y'all, but it's way past my bedtime and I need my beauty sleep—"

"You sure do," Valerie cut in. Lissa stuck out her tongue, and Valerie blurted, "I wouldn't want that dirty thing in my mouth, either."

"In your dreams, strumpet. In your dreams." Lissa yawned again. "Are you about ready to go, Jenny? I hate to be a party-poop—"

Jenny smiled at her boss. "Any time you are. Bed is sounding pretty good right now."

Valerie and Joyce exchanged a knowing glance, but said nothing. Lainie rose and hugged Jenny, then Lissa. "It was such a pleasure to meet you, Jenny. And Liss, thanks for bringing her, and especially for making her a member of our happy clan."

With that, the two women wound their way through the lounge, nodding and waving to friends and acquaintances as they went. The lounge had noticeably emptied, but a few diehards still lined the bar or danced languorously. Jenny noted that Greg and Patsy were intertwined on the dance floor—he pressed inexorably into her body, she evidently enjoying every moment of it.

"There but for the grace of God…" she murmured. And then they passed through the door, leaving her first Sweetheart Dance behind.

CONNIE LIVED IN A RANCH DUPLEX in the northwest suburbs, only twenty minutes away from the airport. Paul followed her in his Metro, self-made tape blasting out the windows, Louis Jordan rhapsodizing about his love of fat women: *"She's reet with me because you see I like 'em fat like that."*

"Amen, brother," Paul said, parking his car in a visitor's space close to Connie's building. He locked his car and dashed over to the supersized beauty waiting for him by the entrance.

"Points for promptness," she said, lightly kissing him. She unlocked the front door and bid him enter, gently stroking his back as he passed before her.

The living room was spacious and dimly lit, but from the look of things it was pricily furnished. First thing Connie did on entering the room was to grab a butane candle lighter and start a pair of candle lamps. "Give me a minute to freshen up," she told him, aiming a remote toward her home entertainment center, then stepping out of sight.

Light jazz washed over the room as Paul found a seat for himself on the mission oak couch.

When she returned she was in a red silk tricot lounger, carrying two wine glasses of carbonated grape juice. "I noticed you weren't drinking," she said as she offered a glass to Paul. She sat beside him, and though there was plenty room on the couch her hip pushed against his. "I like that in a man. Gives him better stamina."

"Didn't like the person I became when I was drinking," Paul told her, sipping his Welch's. "It's okay when you're in college and don't care much what people think of you, but as I got older, I got less and less comfortable with myself that way."

A slight smile appeared on the corner of her lips. "Don't tell me you were a jerk under the influence. You're so sweet, I hardly believe it."

"Believe it, I was the King of the Jerks. But what about you? Got any deep, dark secrets you want to let out now?"

"I've got plenty of secrets," she said with a throaty laugh. "None that I want to broadcast, though." She swigged her drink, then moved in closer toward Paul. Candlelight flickered across her full-cheeked face. Her eyes once more threatened to overwhelm him.

"You always bring guys home on the first date?" he asked.

"Only the real cute ones," she purred. "And this was no date. It was a pickup."

She'd freshened her perfume, he noticed as she planted her lips firmly on his. Her hands caressed his sides, and he started to return the favor.

She was only wearing a chiffon chemise beneath her covering, he soon discovered. Between the light layers of night clothing, her body was easily explored. Soft, spreading excitingly against his hands, it was wonderful in its womanly sumptuousness.

They stayed on the couch without talking through a half hour of lounge ballads. By the time they both rose to take things elsewhere, Paul's shirt was unbuttoned and Connie's tricot on the floor. Her chemise showed both her cleavage and her dimpled upper arms to maximum advantage. He'd already spent some time on them all.

"Let me show you the rest of my place," she said, leading him through a dining area and a kitchen. "This is the bathroom," she said, "in case you need to find it later." He looked inside, noted both bidet and wide sunken tub, and whistled.

"Had a little extra work done," Connie told him.

"Very nice."

"It can be," she said.

Then she took him through the rest of her place.

EPISODE EIGHT

CONTRARY TO WHAT JENNY HAD TOLD GREG, the ride from the SkyAire Lodge to her apartment only took thirty-five minutes. But she was glad for the opportunity to hash out the evening with Lissa. "You know," Jenny commented after she'd given a thumbnail sketch of her experiences and interactions, "You were right about weird vibes. Sometimes I felt like a piece of meat, sometimes like I was trespassing. And sometimes I was made to feel like I wasn't fat enough to be there."

Lissa snorted. "The old 'I'm-so-fat-nobody-else-can-understand-the-hell-I've-endured' syndrome. Don't let size-elitism scare you off. You have as much right as anyone to be a member." She paused to negotiate through an area of road work. "As for the other vibes, some guys will always see women as meat, regardless of size, just as some women will always see other women as a threat."

"Well anyway, thanks again for taking me, Liss. I had such a good time, and I got to meet some really wonderful people."

"I'm so glad. And now that you're a member, you'll get to know them all a lot better," Lissa added as she pulled into the parking lot at Jenny's apartment complex. "Now go inside, curl up in your nice comfy bed and dream about handsome young FAs who dance like Fred Astaire and own stock in Fannie Mae chocolates."

Jenny gave Lissa a quick hug and said, "You too. See you at work."

She let herself into her building and waved as Lissa backed out and drove away. Once in her apartment, she kicked off the sandals that had begun to strangle her feet and sprawled on the couch. The red light on her answering machine was flashing frenetically—surely a call from her mother. She pressed the play button and waited for the message to rewind.

"Hello, Jennifer—This is your mother." *Duh!* "Are you there? —Guess not. Call me when you get home, no matter how late it is." *Click. Beep.* "Jennifer? —This is your mother again. It's almost 11 o'clock—I hope everything's all right—be sure to call—I'll wait up." *Click. Beep.* "Jennifer? Aren't you home yet? —I'm so worried—if I don't hear from you by 1:00, I'm calling the police—" *Click.*

Jenny winced as the tone of her mom's voice got shriller and ever more nasal. Part of her wanted to just wait until morning to return the call, but she knew that police intervention was not an idle threat. She punched in the appropriate speed dial number and winced again as her mother answered with a shriek.

"Where the hell have you been, Missy? I've been absolutely frantic."

"I'm fine, Mother. Tonight was the RADFAm dance. Remember, I told you about it."

"Dance? What dance? And what's RADFAm? Sounds awful suspicious. What sort of mess have you gotten yourself into this time?"

Jenny sighed, then gave her mother a quick explanation of the who/what/where/when/why of her evening.

"Still sounds unsavory to me," Mrs. Taylor sniffed. "Men who like to date fat girls. Must be con men or perverts. I don't want you to associate with those weirdos."

"Well, Mom, since I won a membership to the local chapter, I plan to get to know them a lot better. Now I'm feeling pretty tired and I'm heading to bed. I'll call you tomorrow. Have a good night's sleep, and I love you."

With that Jenny placed the handset back on the receiver, carefully removed her lovely new clothes, and crawled into her nice comfy bed to dream of handsome FAs.

THERE WAS NO SMOOTH WAY to get around it. The moment when both potential partners disclosed their recent sexual histories had come. They were sitting on the edge of Connie's king-sized four-poster, coffee-scented tea lights revealing just enough of each other's eyes to make dialogue possible, so Paul decided to get his part over quickly.

"It's been four years," he said, "since I've—uh—been involved with anyone."

"Poor baby," Connie said, kissing him on the lips. "I assume you were careful."

'Careful,' Paul thought, was not the word. 'Frustrated' was more like it.

Back then he still thought his attraction to fat women was chimerical, a fantasy that had nothing to do with the way he was supposed to live his life. In this state of mind he carried on a futile five-year relationship with a dark-eyed school counselor named Lucy. Lucy was willowy and academic, the kind of woman who agonized more about her eyeglass frames than the rest of her wardrobe. The only plump bits on her had been her thighs and upper arms—which she fanatically exercised to get toned.

As their time together lengthened, though, Paul found himself mentally focusing on those very despised areas. He daydreamed of a Lucy large enough to fit her dimpled thighs, her rounded arms, then wondered what she'd look like even bigger. From such thoughts grow weight gain fantasies, visions of the woman in your arms becoming large enough to keep her sexual allure.

Inevitably it all fell apart. Though he repeatedly chastised himself for being shallow, such chastisements could not overcome the fact that he was growing apart from her. The real-life Lucy just couldn't hold him like the images from his fantasies. By the time Paul and Lucy finally called it quits they hadn't been intimate in months. They'd turned into friends, not lovers. Lucy took a job out of state, a training position for a national counseling association, and he hadn't seen her since.

"I've been very careful," he replied, kissing Connie back. "You?"

In answer, Connie leaned to the left, opened an end table drawer and pulled out a packet. The candle flame beneath her massage oil warmer wavered, weakened, then redoubled its size. "Some fat women act like looking HIV-free is the same as being HIV-free. I'm not one of them." Tossing the condom by her pillow, she stood and began to slowly remove her chemise. "I believe in being careful," she purred.

Paul sat back and enjoyed the view. Back in the living room, middle-period Sinatra was wrapping his cords around a Cole Porter standard.

Connie slid Paul's shirt off his shoulders. As she did, a breast brushed against him. Her prominent belly hung against his knees adamantly, pushing away all thoughts of Lucy. When her cool skin met his, Paul felt an excitement grow that was barely containable.

"I can't believe I'm here with you," he said. "You look and feel so wonderful."

"Remember this feeling," she said, "so you'll never feel badly of me."

Finally they were both in bed with nothing between them. Silken sheets pristinely stretched beneath them, they eyed each other appreciatively.

"Let me put this on," Connie finally said, retrieving the condom packet. She traced the side of Paul's torso with her fingertips, then bit off the corner of the package with her teeth. Her smile was an intensely erotic promise.

"Ready?" she asked, and she popped the condom between her ripe lips.

He was.

EPISODE NINE

JENNY WOKE SUNDAY MORNING to sunshine streaming through her bedroom curtains and her cockatiel Clouseau screaming through her door. In her distraction the night before, Jenny had forgotten to cover his cage, so the early morning light triggered his early-bird response. She stumbled out of bed to check his food and water—anything to shut up this raucousness. Foot over foot, the handsome Lutino bird climbed his cage bars to greet his mistress. "I'm a dirty bird! Gimme kiss?" he shrilled.

"Good morning, dirty bird. Gimme kiss." Reaching into the cage for him to hop onto her finger, she pulled him out and let him nuzzle her cheek. "Now, can you please tone it down until I'm more awake?"

"Gimme kiss! I lovvve yooou!" he cooed.

Jenny placed him on his jungle-gym atop the cage, where he proceeded to do ecstatic loop-the-loops on the bar. "You are so silly, bird."

She made her way to the bathroom and grimaced at her image in the mirror. "I knew I should have washed up and brushed my teeth last night," she declared as she closely inspected the ravages of melted mascara and ran her tongue around a fuzzy-tasting mouth. In her fatigue she had not even put on her usual nightshirt, sleeping instead in the nude. But to her delight, she spied a small blue dot stuck to the cleavage-side of her left breast, and delicately peeled the contact lens off her skin. *Maybe I can salvage this,* she thought as she slipped it into saline solution.

Turning the shower on to deliciously warm, Jenny stepped into the stall and adjusted the handheld massage head to pulsate. She concentrated on her calves (more dancing than usual), buttocks (less-than-comfortable bar chairs) and neck (the late-night inquisition by Mom), then switched to an invigorating pinpoint spray to complete the waking process and wash the inevitable lounge smells from body and hair.

Clouseau was flirting with his mirror image as Jenny came out of the bathroom. She wandered into the kitchen and fished from the refrigerator a Cherry Coke, her caffeine of choice, then opened the front door to find the fat bundle that was the *Trib*'s Sunday edition.

Now was her favorite time of day, though she wished it hadn't come quite so early as this. After tuning in soft jazz on her favorite public radio station, she curled up on the overstuffed couch and sorted out sheaves of coupons to peruse later. Clouseau chattered happily, bobbing and swaying, as Jenny studied each section of the newspaper. Just as she reached the classifieds the phone rang. Not quite ready to talk to her mother yet, she let the machine answer.

"Hey, girlfriend! You awake yet?" It was Lissa, cheerful as a Boston bar.

Jenny swooped to pick up the phone. "Hey yourself! Up awfully early for a lawyer, aren't we?"

"You know, the early bird and all that."

"Yeah, that's what woke me up, too."

"That damn bird of yours. What a waste of birdseed."

"Well, since I can't have a more traditional cat or dog here, and I tend to kill everything else lower on the food chain—besides, I like him. You've just never forgiven him for nipping your earlobe."

"You've got that right. Anyway, how are you this morning?" Lissa, in mother-hen mode.

"I feel great. Last night was simply wonderful. I found my contact lens this morning." Jenny paused, then added, nonchalantly, "Mom called while I was gone."

"Oops! What did the old battle-ax want?"

"Now, is that any way to talk about my mother?" Jenny insisted. "She's not that old." Jenny then filled her in on the conversation.

"Weirdos, con men and perverts," Lissa mused. "Yeah, she's just about got us pegged. But I'm very proud of you, standing up to her like you did. By the way, I've already called Ian, our membership secretary, and gave him your address and phone so you'll receive the upcoming newsletter. Hope you don't mind."

"Not at all. I wasn't sure who to give the info to last night."

"Well, he wasn't there anyway, but now you're official, at least as far as the chapter goes. To be able to vote and have full membership status, though, you'll have to join the national organization. I'll get you an application."

"Thanks! Does this mean that I now join the ranks of weirdos, cons and perverts?"

"I sincerely hope so!"

PAUL WOKE IN AN UNFAMILIAR POSITION, momentarily disoriented until he started to slowly stretch awake. A sudden tightening in his right calf, and—damn!—he had a charley horse. Curling into a ball, he started to rapidly massage his lower leg, unmindful of his foreign setting or the woman still sleeping next to him. All he knew was the stabbing pain in his leg. An auspicious way to start the day.

When he finally calmed his calf down to a dull ache, Paul took stock of his surroundings. It was, he saw, 7:45 A.M.; the room was dully lit with the promise of sunshine outside. It felt like waking in a chain motel room, at once both familiar and distancing.

Connie's bedroom was spacious, with a sliding door closet that probably took up more space than his whole bedroom. At the head of the bed was a framed photo of Connie walking down the runway at a plus-size fashion show—something from a RADFAm convention, Paul guessed. She looked regally sexy in a way that more traditional models could only approximate.

He rolled out of bed, careful not to disturb his hostess, then limped into the bathroom. It looked just as impressive in the dull morning as it had the night before. He wasn't sure how to do the bidet thing, but fortunately he didn't have to. Squeezing a line of Crest onto a convenient finger, Paul freshened up his mouth, then splashed water in his face. Didn't look too much the worst for wear, he thought.

He was less sure of his next step. Return to bed? Take a shower? Check the kitchen for caffeine? Hit the living room and watch some cartoons? (No, he wasn't that dorky.) *Go with your first instinct,* he decided, so he eased back into his space on the bed and let his mind wander.

Now that he had a chance to catch his breath, Paul considered all that had happened last night. It'd been a night of firsts, alright. He'd never done anything like this before—his relationship with Lucy had been a slow, deliberate thing.

He should be feeling more awkward, but maybe that would change once Connie woke. She was lying uncovered on her side of the bed, her body a landscape of morning shadows, her face lovely and untroubled. As he watched her, he felt himself start to forget his leg muscles.

By the time she slowly roused, he was ready for her again.

"Well," she noted, as he both pressed and prodded against her. "What have we here?"

Paul rose on his knees and began to massage her lush upper arm. "Morning," he said.

"Looks like the sun's definitely risen," Connie said, and she rolled happily on her back.

It was late A.M. when they finally were ready to get out of bed. Sipping Jamaican Mountain coffee together, they sat alongside the kitchen island and fed each other Sara Lee croissants. Connie was in a lace caftan with feather cuffs. She looked like the supersized heroine of a thirties drawing room comedy, elegant and sexy.

"You know," Paul said at one point. "After last night, I think I'd like to join your group."

"Sure you want to do that so soon?" she asked, stirring two percent milk into her second cup of coffee.

Her statement surprised him, and he showed it. "Why do you say that?"

She smiled, and for a moment, her face looked almost rueful. "Thought it was obvious," she said lightly. "I'm trying to keep you to myself. Keep you away from the barracudas."

"Barracudas?"

Connie raised her mug to her mouth, masking her expression. Then she reached across the corner of the island and grabbed his hands. "You do what you want," she finally said. "The group could use some new blood."

They finished off the rest of their breakfast in silence, and then it was time to leave.

"Sure you don't want to stay the afternoon?" Connie asked as she buttoned up his shirt. "There's room in the tub for two."

A tempting—if not entirely believable—offer, but he had to say no. "I'd love to, but I don't think Molly would forgive me," he said. From the dark look that shot across Connie's face, a quick explanation was in order. "Molly's my golden retriever."

Her face softened immediately. "Poor thing," Connie said. "She been shut up all night?"

No, he reassured her; he'd phoned his neighbor when they'd left the dance.

"Knew from the first that you were a thoughtful man," she said, kissing him in the doorway. Paul grinned, kissed her hand, then headed for his Geo Metro. Behind him, Connie languidly leaned against the door frame for maximum compositional effect.

"Think of me tonight," she said, and Paul knew that to do otherwise would be impossible.

EPISODE TEN

Ring…Ring…Ring…Click. "Blessings! You've reached 555-2772. Please leave your message for Misty Shores after the tone. Thank you."

Joe Rivera hastily pressed the disconnect button.

The contralto voice reawakened memories of Saturday's dance. After uncertain hours hovering around Misty's table like a corn moth round one of her rainbow candles, Joe had finally mustered his courage as the bar thinned to approach the enchantress and introduce himself.

There'd been little time for more than an exchange of pleasantries as the bartender and waitress pointedly clinked and clattered about, preparing to shut down for the night. Joe watched as Misty tenderly packed her cabalistic table-dressings in a wicker picnic basket, which he then offered to carry to her van. "That would be a big help," she'd smiled, and Joe helped hoist her from the seat. "I know better than to sit that long without stretching my legs."

It was his first full glimpse of a standing Misty. She was an apple-shaped supersize, even rounder than he'd hoped.

Together they'd walked to the parking lot, where Joe knew it was now-or-never. "Are you hungry?" he ventured. "We could stop at Denny's for a quick bite of something."

Misty smiled into his earnest face. "No, thank you—"

"Well, how about coming over to my place? I could whip up an omelet really quick."

"Joe," she gently answered, "I'm nothing but tired right now, and all I want to do is go home and crawl into bed."

Trying to hide his disappointment, Joe had nodded and said, "I understand. After a long day at the restaurant, I know exactly how you feel. But," he stammered, "I'd really like to talk sometime."

"I'd like that, too," Misty replied, and handed him her business card, a confection of calligraphy and celestial symbols. Then she'd driven away, leaving him standing alone beneath starry skies obliterated by the orange glare of sodium vapor street lamps.

Now, two days later, he'd finally worked up the guts to call the number on the card, and what did he get? A frigging machine.

"COME ON IN, SUGAR," Misty heard as she knocked on her neighbor's door. Carefully clutching the bowl of fresh melon balls and jar of gooseberry jam to her breast, she turned the knob, entered Kirk's fabulous apartment, and marveled anew at what a difference this talented young man had created from formerly tenement-ish digs.

When Misty's father died three years ago he'd left her a rundown apartment building with storefront in a marginally scary section of town. For a while she'd questioned whether it was a blessing or a burden. But then urban renewal moved into the neighborhood in a big way, and her old brownstone became very valuable property. Now she was the proud proprietor of six spacious, airy apartments with 12-foot ceilings, oak floors, huge windows and affluent tenants. The ground-level store became her own Isle of View Emporium.

Misty had chosen one of the two first floor spaces, and then had carefully screened hopeful applicants for the perfect nextdoor neighbor. When Kirk Young walked in, she knew she'd found the one—40ish, tall, meticulously handsome, gracious, funny. Even before he told her, she knew he was gay, but to her that was a plus. Gay men had always been there when straight men couldn't be bothered, and now she enjoyed returning the favor.

Sunday breakfast with Kirk had become a weekly ritual after he'd appeared at her door early one morning with croissants and cappuccino shortly after moving in. She'd commiserated with him over the loss of a recent lover, pored over remodeling plans for his apartment, shared remembrances and the *Trib*, and they'd become fast friends. Now, Sundays were spent with his "favorite slumlord," unless he found romance on Saturday night (and sometimes even when he did).

"You were out late last night, young lady!" he called from the kitchen. "You shouldn't worry your old mother like that." Kirk strode into the living room carrying a tray laden with schnecken and fresh-squeezed OJ. "Hope you had fun," he added, winking.

Misty couldn't help but blush, and hid her embarrassment behind a sip of juice. "I had a really nice time," she replied demurely.

"Hold it right there, toots! I saw that, and I want the straight-skinny, if you don't mind."

Giggling at his phraseology, Misty filled him in on the events of the evening, including Joe's apparent interest in her. "Dark, swarthy, and a chef, too!" he wailed. "Are you sure he's not just using you to get to me?"

"No, you grand poofter! He doesn't even know you exist."

"Cut me to the quick, strumpet!" Kirk reached over and hugged her. "All right, have your fun, but be sure that you bring me the leftovers. Food, I mean, of course."

Misty pondered this before answering, "I got the impression that if Joe has his way, there won't be much food left over. He asked several different ways if I wanted to get something to eat last night and seemed very disappointed when I said I wasn't hungry." She paused to take a bite of schnecken and delicately wiped cinnamon glaze from her chin. "Shoot, I gave five Tarot readings, ate tons of munchies and just wanted to come home to bed."

"Alone? Silly girl," Kirk chided. "Must I teach you everything about *amore?* Oh well, my pet, he's welcome anytime at our Sunday koffee klatsch, especially if he brings samples."

But as Sunday and Monday passed and Joe didn't call, Misty decided she must have misunderstood his interest. She found her attention wandering and had to discipline herself to concentrate on her custom-designed natal charts and horoscopes, which were the bread-and-butter of her business.

Naturally, Joe wound up calling minutes after she stepped out of her apartment. Returning from the store, she didn't even notice the flashing light. First time she glanced over at her machine, in fact, she had the distinct impression that there was no message. That happened sometimes—almost as if her eyes were blinking in sync with her Southern Bell answerphone—and it was always a jolt to look a second time and see that there were indeed two messages waiting for her.

Make that one hang-up followed by a for-real message. Though she'd been anticipating his call, she almost didn't recognize Joe's voice off her machine. It sounded higher pitched—was the little tapette rolling too fast?—than she remembered. Still, just the fact of his disembodied invitation was enough to send a frisson through her. Wasn't as if she was used to getting a lot of these calls.

She played the tape three times. (How pathetic was that?) What was she listening for? Some measure of his character? Psychic vibes? Back-masked messages? This was all too new for her to judge properly. Though she knew women who read for themselves, she'd never been able to do her own cards. Too much self doubt in the way.

"I hate these machines—hello, Misty? This is Joe Rivera. From the dance—remember? Uhh—we talked about going out sometime, so I'm calling to set something up. If you haven't changed your mind, uh, you can call me at—" And so on.

A simple-enough message. Should she respond to it? Dropping into her comfy chair, she watched Schmendrick, her Abyssinian, as he concentrated on invisible bugs. Rainbows danced on his ears every time he darted within reach of the window crystals.

Finally she picked up the answerphone and prepared to punch up Joe's number. It loudly rang in her lap, so startling her that she practically knocked the phone to the floor. Regaining her composure, Misty picked up the receiver, butting in ahead of the answering machine.

"Hello?"

"What?" the voice on the other end said. "This really you? This is Joe. I was calling back because I forgot to tell you I'd be in all evening."

"No need to leave the message, Joe. Looks like we're both in."

"Great! Shit! I can't believe this. Look, can we go out? I mean—would you like to go out with me? Sometime? Like later this week?"

Schmendrick was looking at her curiously. "I'd like that, Joe," she said. "Got any place in mind?"

"I was thinking of maybe a movie or something?"

Goddess help her. This was like passing notes in junior high school. "I don't know if you noticed, Joe," she slowly said, "but I don't easily do movie theater seating."

"Oh. Right. Well, how about some place nice for dinner?"

"Very doable," Misty decided, and with that, she was finally, officially, making a date. "It's the week after next. But I know the place to meet."

"ALRIGHT!" JOE SHOUTED to a VHS image of Caprial Pence (kinda cute—if only she was hippier) as he slammed the receiver into its cradle. He'd vanquished the mighty answering machine and hooked up with Misty! A date with Misty!

Thinking back on it, he'd probably been too eager the night of the dance, too ready to bring up food. He didn't blame her for being skittish; there were a lot of stories floating through the movement about guys like him. Best approach was to let her get to know him first.

Pulling out a Trapper Keeper, Joe went to work on redesigning his ideal dinner. He'd been doing this for years, working up meals for a girlfriend that up to now had been imaginary. The girls he'd dated all had been self-conscious about eating, worried about gaining weight. They couldn't accept what he had to offer. Misty just had to be different. A girl her age didn't get to be the size she was without occasionally giving in to the call of the meal.

So what would she like to eat? Something exotic, perhaps? Middle Eastern, maybe? Hard to tell. He'd have to sound her out at the restaurant. Subtly.

Best to put the notebook away for now. Once he got to know her better, he could work up something irresistible.

He turned his attention back to *Cooking with Caprial*, fast-forwarding through the usual boring commercials. He wondered if Caprial's husband—a chef like her—got the same charge out of feeding his wife. Probably. Was there anything sexier than preparing something for a loved one? Something that would remain with them the rest of their life?

If there was, he didn't know about it.

EPISODE ELEVEN

POURING WATER INTO A LARGE SUN TEA JAR, Dr. Dexter Logan listened to his wife hum as she chopped vegetables. The tune was irritatingly familiar; something '70s—a decade with zero nostalgic appeal for him.

He'd still been working at the hospital back then, too unsure of himself (and the way patients would take him at his size) to take the plunge into private practice. For him, the '70s were a decade of stasis. An exhausting work schedule. Hospital politics. A host of distractions that kept him from paying proper attention to his first wife or to the way he'd been letting his view of himself as a fat man hold him back. "I was so much older then," Dex said out loud. A '60s music quote—Dylan by way of Roger McGuinn.

Stepping away from their water cooler, he set the jar on a shelf by the kitchen window, then ambled over and hugged Neeko. She gave him that combination smile/"What-you-want-now?" look she did every time he got unexpectedly affectionate with her. Dex always felt the need to be a bit more demonstrative before chapter happenings; Neeko tended to get a little tense among all those fullsized women.

They'd met in the '80s—a much more promising decade—at a conference in Japan. She was a professional translator, temporarily hired by a pharmaceutical company; he was on an education/vacation trip. First time he saw her she was translating a seminar on weight-loss surgery, but they didn't officially meet until the following night.

She took several conferees, American and British GPs, to a demonstration of sumo wrestling. As usual he was the largest guy in the group, but when he saw the wrestlers in the ring Dex no longer felt unique. Here was a whole stadium of adult men and women watching men fully as fat as him—and they were cheering them! Not just cheering—idolizing them!

He saw the same look in Neeko's eyes. This slim, nearly frail Japanese woman was avidly watching two supersized guys try to push each other out of a circle, and she was getting excited by it. The sight was so astounding that he did something that he'd never expected—he asked her out the next night.

For two years theirs was primarily a paper courtship. But in 1986, the same year he joined RADFAm, Dex took his sixth trip to Tokyo and returned with Neeko. They married two months later.

It was the second time for both of them. Dex's Lindy had died in 1983—not really the '70s, but for some reason he slotted it as such—from complications following weight-loss surgery. The fact that he, the medical man, had been unable to dissuade his wife from a procedure he knew was risky still haunted him. She'd gained a phenomenal amount of weight both during and after her pregnancy; it'd depressed the hell out of her. At the time he didn't have it in him to talk her out of it.

Rachel entered the kitchen, grabbed a carrot from the cutting board and bit into it. "Stir-fry," she said. "Looks to me like another potluck."

Dex smiled at his daughter. Short and plumply bottom-heavy, in jeans and an Aeon Flux T-shirt, she was a 15-year-old echo of the young Lindy.

"You saying we're in a rut, young lady?"

"Heck, no," she answered, rolling her eyes with adolescent irony. "I love your stir-fry. But Kelly and I'll make do with burgers and a movie instead." Kelly was the daughter of another chapter member; whenever they had get-togethers, the two girls hooked up and entertained themselves.

"What are you two seeing?" Dex asked.

"*The Nutty Professor*," Rachel said. "And don't give me any lectures on how it's demeaning to fat people. The movie's supposed to be funny."

"Wouldn't dream of lecturing," Dex said, when, of course, he had. "I'd like to hear your take on it tomorrow."

"Will do, doc," she said, jouncing out of the kitchen.

"Tell your brother we need him in the kitchen, why don't you?" Dex called out.

Neeko sighed, sliding the last of her chopped victims into a bowl. "Movies making fun of fat men," she said. "Some parts of Western culture are too screwed up for me."

"Welcome to the club," Dex said, leaning over and kissing her on the lips.

KIRK BRANDISHED THE PALM-SIZED CAT FIGURE in front of Misty and grinned. "Isn't this a delightful thing to be carrying around in your pocket? Sculpted shit."

"Just because it's called a Pocket PooPet doesn't mean it belongs there. You always believe everything you read?"

"Always," Kirk said. "I'm like Marian in *The Music Man,* ready to believe everything Harold tells her."

They moved from the garden area of The Gifters shop to the grown-up toys. Kirk was looking for the perfect present for a nephew in Iowa. "He knows I'm gay, though his parents would *plotz* if they found out."

"Nothing worse than *plotz*ing Iowans," Misty said, holding up a brightly colored kaleidoscope and peering at her friend through it.

"Tell me about it," Kirk replied. "Better yet—tell me what's up with Antonio Banderas. What's the word on our Latin sous chef? He still calling nightly?"

"As constant as the blinking light on my VCR," Misty said. She adjusted her top, then lowered herself on a plus-sized-customer-friendly bench. "Have I thanked you for setting that for me, by the way? I can record anything I want as long as it comes on at noon or midnight."

"Changing the subject, are we?"

"No," Misty protested. "It's just that I continue to get these odd vibes from him. He asks about how my day went, but the part that always seems to get the most attention is the meals I've eaten."

"He is a chef, after all," Kirk said, picking up a 3-D jigsaw of the Millennium Falcon. "Jesus, look at the price of this! —So what do you expect him to talk about? City politics?"

"You know what I'm getting at," Misty said. "I'm just wondering if Joe's—"

"A feeder? An encourager? Mist, this is your first date in ages! You trying to talk yourself out of it already?"

"Maybe I am," she admitted. "My self-esteem's still recovering from my time with Dwayne."

"Dwayne wasn't a feeder. He was just an abusive asshole."

"But what does that say about my ability to pick men?"

With that, Kirk moved away from the toy counter and sat on the edge of Misty's bench. "I swear, you straight gals are the best when it comes to taking on everybody else's hangups. Just because you had a bad fling doesn't mean it's your fault. Everybody has at least one good horror story. Remember Dodd?"

"Looked like a young Burl Ives—"

"—acted like Ivan The Terrible," Kirk finished. "The pickings are slim everywhere you look. Don't write this boy off yet. How else will I get my vicarious thrills?"

"Yeah, right," Misty snorted. "The Great Bear Hunter looking to someone else's love life for excitement."

"Maybe it's like that theory where whenever someone loses weight, someone else gains it. Maybe you and I can't have boyfriends simultaneously. It's like some unwritten law of the cosmos."

"Wouldn't that be depressing?"

"Tell me about it," Kirk said. Then he dashed across the aisle and pulled out a large figure. "What do you think?" he asked. It was a lifesize standup photo of Anna Nicole Smith. "Won't his parents have a conniption?"

"They'll *plotz,*" Misty agreed, wondering about the night ahead.

Like most women in the movement, she'd heard horror stories of FA who were heavily into weight gain—so much so that no matter how big their partners were, it never was enough. Misty had spent years growing comfortable with her present form; she'd be damned if she'd ever let another testosterone factory start shaming her into something different. As far as she could tell, feederism was just the flipside of diet fascism, and she'd experienced too much of that from Dwayne, whose physical attentions were constantly undercut by his snipes about her weight.

Kirk was right, though. She couldn't judge Joe on the basis of a few short phone calls. So many FAs were socially awkward—like most fat adults they'd had little experience in the proving grounds of adolescent dating. She'd just have to see how the evening went.

But if he asked one question about her vital statistics, that was the end of it.

EPISODE TWELVE

CANDLELIGHT FLICKERING WITH THE WHIR of the air conditioner, Paul gazed across the dining table at Connie. Behind them repackaged lounge music was playing on the stereo. At times, Paul would catch a snatch of it and be reminded of childhood visits with the NYC contingent of his family. Those old Jackie Gleason platters had formed the soundtrack for the Good Life.

He took a sip of white grape juice, then smiled at his hostess. Over the last four weekends he'd gotten to know Connie's place pretty well, though he still hadn't gotten to the stage of packing a toothbrush. She was easily the sexiest woman he had ever dreamed of knowing.

"Got my national membership in the mail today," he said, though he'd half decided not to say anything about it to her. In the past, whenever he'd talked about joining the local RADFAm chapter Connie had gotten an odd expression on her face. A part of him was annoyed at this—as if she assumed he was so flighty that just being around other fullsized women would be too much for him—but another part understood. The number of uncloseted FAs was so limited that a woman might want to hold onto what she had.

He hoped his joining national would be a good compromise—a statement of commitment to the ideals of size acceptance without the local social temptations. His mouth masked behind the rim of his glass, he waited for her response.

She took her time contemplating, concentrating instead on her salad. Finally, round face betraying nothing, she softly replied, "Why, that's sweet, Paul. But you didn't need to join up only to please me. Just being yourself is all I need."

"I can't just do that anymore," Paul told her. "I never used to be this way, but every time I see something offensive on TV—or anywhere else—I get pissed off. It's like they're all being obnoxious to you. I want to feel like I'm being supportive."

"Most of the time I don't even see that stuff anymore," Connie said. "You want to survive as a fat lady, you learn to ignore a lot."

"I can't," Paul insisted.

"You've just had your eyes opened. You may have known about fat-bashing before, but it wasn't real to you until someone personalized it. After a while, the freshness of the revelation will wane."

"Do I want it to?" Paul wondered. He couldn't tell if Connie was being matter-of-fact or just cynical.

"Stay as sweet as you are," Connie joked, rising to retrieve their main course.

He watched her marvelous hips as she turned toward the oven. He was struck by the irony of this onetime chapter officer discouraging his involvement in the size acceptance community, but perhaps that would change once they were together longer than a month.

He was thinking of her more at work. Once while running a video he'd been so caught by the memory of her that he had to wait a few seconds before he could turn the lights back on in the classroom. It was like something out of adolescence, and he was simultaneously embarrassed and thrilled by it. Walking out into the world he actually looked at fat women, something he never would have let himself do in the past. He wanted to take Connie out into this brave new world, to show her off and explore parts of the city he thought she'd enjoy.

To date, Connie had resisted invitations away from her place. They spent much of their time in bed, though. To be fair, there were occasions when Paul himself had discouraged going anywhere else.

"I turned the oven down to warm," she said, returning empty handed. She'd shed her blazer, now showing off her abundant arms and shoulders. The candlelight made her pale skin glow, like a haze-shrouded starlet in some black-and-white movie. Paul rose and put his hands on both upper arms, then planted a long and lingering kiss on her lips.

"You saying you're not hungry yet?" he asked.

"Not for food," she answered, and she pulled him hard against her exquisitely overstuffed body.

"So THIS OUTFIT is appropriate?"

"For the third time, yes," Lissa smiled, steering her Lincoln around a Trailways bus. Friday night tollway traffic was typically crazy—they were still ten minutes from the turn-off to Dexter Logan's house. "It's a meeting, not a dance. You look wonderful. Sexy, casual yet confident."

"Right!" Jenny snorted. "I just don't want any food stuck in my teeth."

"Always a risk at potlucks," Lissa agreed. "If I notice anything, I'll flash you a signal."

"Thanks, boss lady." She inspected herself in the passenger side visor mirror and saw that her face was still intact.

In a way, it'd been tougher figuring out what to wear to her first RAD-FAm meeting than getting ready for the dance. She'd ultimately settled for a floral pattern blouse with some wine-colored slacks—more out of exhaustion than definitive decisionmaking. Now that she was committed to it, of course, Jenny was rethinking her choice.

"Stop it!" Lissa commanded, eyeing her from the other bucket seat. "Am I going to have to kick your ass every time we go to one of these gigs? You look great; your outfit's smashing, blah blah blah. You've only seen the way these women dress for a big to-do. You've got nothing to worry about."

She zipped around a rust-colored pickup, then shot toward the tollway exit. Minutes later they were at the Logan residence, and, from the look of things, one of the first arrivals.

"Lissa! And this is our newest member, right?" Dexter Logan was waiting for them in the doorway as they came up the sidewalk. "Jenny, isn't it? We've got to hook you up with our membership secretary tonight." He turned and caught the attention of a slightly balding man in a Northwestern polo shirt.

"Ian," he called.

Ian raised a quizzical eyebrow, then caught a glimpse of Jenny. Smiling, he made his way over. "Always a pleasure to see a new face," he said, stepping forward to shake Jenny's hand.

His fingernails, Jenny noted, were unevenly bitten to the quick. His whole manner seemed slightly overcaffeinated. He had a way of looking at her, though, that was innocently appraising—cute once you got past his nervousness.

"You a friend of Lissa?" he asked, leading her into the dining room. Both Lissa and Dexter had moved out of sight.

"More like a student/mentor relationship," Jenny joked. "She's been shoving me back into the dating pool again."

"Really?" He picked up a small paper plate and started piling cauliflower from a nearby veggie plate into it.

"I'd been pretty discouraged," she admitted. "Didn't really know that FAs existed until Lissa started talking about the RADFAm dances. Nice to know you guys are around." She paused, then backtracked. "Or am I making an assumption when I say 'you guys'?"

"You are, but it's a correct one," Ian answered. "So I take you're between—umm—guyfriends?"

"That's one way of putting it," Jenny said. "And you?"

"No guyfriends—or girlfriends, either," Ian said as he spooned a dollop of dip onto his plate. For an instant Jenny thought of asking if it was fatfree, then thought better of it. She grabbed her own appetizer plate and started to fill it.

"Grab a seat," Ian offered. "If you don't mind, I'd like to take your membership profile."

Jenny didn't mind.

EPISODE THIRTEEN

JOE WAITED NERVOUSLY BY HIS VINTAGE IMPALA, parked several houses down from the Logans'. A quieter neighborhood than he was accustomed to, a small suburban enclave just a couple quick turns from the Northwest Highway. Down the street he could see two kids desultorily playing in the driveway. On the second floor of the Logans' bi-level, a small silhouette spied on him. He waved, and the figure ducked out of sight.

About ten folks had already made their way into the Logan home. Joe recognized half of them from dances, but not a one of them had been Misty.

The longer he stood, the more he felt his carefully curbed composure start to unravel. He resisted the urge to check himself for the umpteenth time in the windshield reflection. Instead, he looked down at his lightweight khakis and saw some grunge from the car on his pant leg.

Damn! He couldn't let Misty see him like this. Reaching down, he rubbed the offending spot, only to see it smear beneath his fingertips. Frantic, he reached into the back seat of his car, grabbed the soft-sided cooler, and headed for the house. A slender Oriental woman answered the door. She cased him up and down, then smiled. "Come on in," she said. "My name's Neeko. I'm Dex's wife."

"Joe Rivera," he muttered. "I hate to be rude, but could I see your restroom first?" She nodded, then directed him to a small room just off the foyer. Joe dashed inside, took a quick once-over in the mirror, then used a dab of liquid soap on the offending grease spot. It helped, a little.

He found Neeko and her husband both waiting for him outside the bathroom. "Another familiar face," Logan boomed. "This is your first chapter meeting, isn't it?"

"Misty invited me," Joe said. "I guess I beat her here."

"Guess you did," Logan chuckled, taking Joe's cooler and leading him into the living room where the group of RADFAm chapter members were sitting. A few looked at him curiously, but the majority carried on their respective conversations.

There were several sturdy trays with basic potluck appetizers on them, Joe noticed. To his left a midsized brunette in a jumper and cotton T was dipping a Triscuit into cheddar cheese spread. A little small for him, but maybe if she'd keep hitting the cheese spread—

The music on the stereo sounded old, like something his big brother would have listened to. The furniture could be described as culturally eclectic. The entire house was brighter than he expected. In a way, the light made the women look even bigger, but for once that fact didn't comfort him. There was no dark bar space for him to retreat to.

"Make yourself t'home," Logan said. "Is there anything we need to do with your offering?" He held up the cooler for emphasis.

Joe shook his head. "Just some dessert," he said, wondering (not the first time) whether he should have brought something so nutritionally questionable. "Some meringues."

"Something refreshing," Logan nodded. "Probably belongs in the fridge at least, for now."

Joe cast his eyes around the room for a vacant seat, found some space on a piano bench and claimed it. He was sitting next to a professionally dressed black woman, who smiled as he sat, then turned back to the woman she was talking to. Joe caught some snippets of their conversation. They seemed to be talking about insurance or something. Wasn't that Greg guy into insurance?

He switched to the conversation on the other side—a recent airing of *Jenny Jones*.

"It's not like it was a couple of years ago," the speaker, a middle-aged woman in neat but outdated polyester, was saying, "when a fat-positive guest could make an appearance without getting beat up. These days they go out of their way to humiliate their guests."

"Never thought those shows were a good forum for us, anyway," her companion said. "Even when they'd broadcast something fat positive, they'd follow it with a Rader Institute commercial."

"I look at commercials like that," Joe put in, "and all I can think when I see them is, 'Man, you looked so much better before!'"

The two women looked at him like he'd just spoken gibberish in church, then the older of the two smiled and answered, "But, of course, you'd think that—you're an FA."

At that point—thankfully—Misty made her appearance. Joe rose from his place on the bench, dashed across the living room and offered to take her picnic basket. The look on her face was enough to banish every sense of nervousness and uncertainty he had. He hadn't really noticed how angelic her face was.

"Sir Walter," she said, daintily handing the basket to him. She was wearing a flowing batik tunic, her face lightly made up. From the basket Joe could catch a whiff of shrimp spring rolls. "I hope I didn't keep you waiting long."

"You didn't," he said, beaming back at her.

WHILE THE GENERAL COTERIE enjoyed leftover hors d'oeuvres and chit-chat elsewhere, the officers' business meeting had quickly gone downhill. They hadn't even gotten out of Old Business when Delia Cotton brought up the T-shirt situation again.

"Thought we resolved this last meeting," Lainie muttered loud enough for Misty to hear. Dexter, as usual, rushed in to smooth the waters.

"We appreciate Connie's efforts on the chapter's behalf," he began, adopting a speaking voice loud enough to echo through the rec room. By his side Eleanor was arduously taking notes that would ultimately be encapsulated into a three-sentence newsletter report. "But the fact is, she commissioned the shirts without chapter approval. As nice as they are, they don't fit our budget."

"I thought since she wasn't here tonight, we might reconsider," Delia pushed. "Connie's done a lot for this chapter. And the shirts are worth the money." She indicated her own 4X T-shirt, light pink with the chapter's heart logo in the middle, for emphasis.

"No one's denying that," Dexter said. "But nobody, no matter how much they've done, can just order five hundred shirts without getting chapter approval. We simply don't have the money."

"How much did we make from the dance?" Delia persisted.

"You know the profits from the dance have been going to national," Lissa said from the sidelines. "They need all the support they can get."

"Seems like we might've saved some money on a deejay last time," Delia said.

"Dan practically does that for us gratis," Dexter explained to the group at large. "It won't cover what Connie's been asking for the T-shirts."

"I hear she's been selling them at twice the price at her boutique," Lainie whispered.

"I wonder if the woman who designed the logo is getting any commission," Misty thought out loud.

"Maddie? She resigned from the chapter during Connie's reign."

Misty looked over at Joe, who'd dutifully followed her downstairs. He looked a little bewildered—or maybe his thoughts were just elsewhere—but he quickly noticed her looking at him and smiled. He had a sweet smile, she realized, like an innocent from a Maxfield Parrish daydream.

"Sorry I brought you into this," she mouthed. She hated these kinds of chapter debates—Delia couldn't take no for an answer and was incapable of hearing opposing viewpoints. At times she could get downright snotty, but tonight she appeared to be on her best behavior.

"Look, Doctor," Delia was saying. "All I'm asking is for us to do the right thing—pay Connie for the work she's done promoting our chapter."

Dexter sighed, then threw it open to the room. "What do the rest of you think?"

Lissa was the first to offer her opinion. "This has come up the last three meetings," she said. "I'm tired of hearing about it. Connie jumped the gun and has boxes of T-shirts in her storeroom. Maybe she can donate them as a charitable deduction and bump the price up even more in the process."

Delia glared at the lady lawyer and probably would have said something impolitic but for Neeko's sudden appearance at the doorway. She was carrying a tray with a large Krup coffee pot and some mugs, looking unsure about whether to enter the room.

"Who wants coffee?" Dexter asked, seizing on the distraction.

Eleanor put her notepad down, raised her hand, then seemingly thought the better of it. Neeko crossed the room, jostling the tray as she reached the coffeetable holding Eleanor's purse and papers.

"Damn!" she said as the pot sloshed onto the open notepad. "I'm sorry, Eleanor. I hope I didn't get any on you."

Sponging her paper with a wad of napkins, Eleanor nervously shook her head and muttered "it's okay" as she frantically tried to rescue the minutes.

"Can we return to what we were talking about?" Delia sneered.

"Wait! Hold on! I've got to get some paper!"

"Christ, Eleanor!" Delia finally exploded, all vestige of goodwill gone. "You never put any of this in the newsletter anyway!"

That was more than enough for Misty. "Looks like we need some paper towels," she said. "I'll go get some."

When she got to the kitchen, she discovered Joe was behind her. "Sorry you had to endure this," she said. "The meetings can get to be like family Thanksgiving sometimes."

"S'okay," Joe reassured her. "It's been interesting."

"Which is polite talk for boring," Misty finished. "Tell you what—let me bring the paper towels back in, then we'll sneak out for some coffee elsewhere. I know a great little coffeehouse not too far from here."

"Sounds good to me," Joe agreed. "I'll buy you a biscotti."

"Tiramisu or nothing," Misty countered with a grin.

EPISODE FOURTEEN

THE GATHERING DOWNSTAIRS WAS GETTING LOUDER, but Jackie barely noticed. Seated in front of his Compaq, scrolling down the newsgroup table, he was totally focused on his monitor. Looked like Mr. Natural was re-posting some pics that he'd missed. Clicking on the first, he watched the photo download—a moody black-and-white picture of a supersized blonde reclining on a divan. Her only covering was a plate of pastries on her ample tummy.

"Gross," Jackie whispered, pulling out a 3.5 diskette. How could anybody be turned on by this? It was almost as inconceivable as the thought of his parents having sex.

He downloaded the image, then moved on to Mr. Natural's next offering. Same woman, different position, no plate. *Probably ate it all,* he thought, skipping down several entries to see if anyone different had been posted. He found a jpg photo of a woman he remembered seeing on one of those joke calendars at Spenser's.

"Okay," he said, and clicked his cursor one more time on "save." This time, however, the screen told him he didn't have the space. Rotating in his chair to get a fresh diskette, Jackie found himself facing his father. He was standing in the doorway, a stunned expression transfixing his round face.

"How'd you get on this?" Dex demanded. "We had the newsgroups blocked out!"

Jackie felt his face redden. *Stop it!* he tried to tell himself, but it was no use. The only thing to do was be honest, an approach that didn't always help with his father. "I knew your password," he explained, minimizing the monitor image to placate Dex. Then, to keep things from being totally truthful, he fabricated some details. "Saw you punch it in one night, and I was able to get a close enough approximation to figure it out."

Actually Jackie had found the password on a slip of paper in Dad's desk. But why tell him that when he might put the new one in a similar place?

"You're too young for this, Jackie," Dexter said, and he gestured him out of the chair. "I thought we had an understanding about this."

Dad and his understandings—if he only understood half of what he claimed, then Jackie would be in a total shitload of trouble.

"I was just checking it out," he said. "Some friends at school were talking about the newsgroups, and I was curious. It was my first time, honest."

Fortunately for Jackie, Dex didn't click on the subscription list. Instead he scrolled down the postings, clucking his tongue at some of the headlines. "This is pretty raw stuff," he said, backing out of the newsgroup. "I'm not even sure I'm old enough to look at some of this."

"It's pretty bad," Jackie agreed. "Don't really see why they're so popular."

"All kinds of people in the world," Dex said, as he took the Compaq back into Safe Territory. Then he turned to his son, chair squeaking heavily, and said: "No more on the computer tonight. Not until I can put in a new password."

Looked like that was going to be it. Still, Jackie felt the need to put up some kind of protest. "When will that be?" he asked. "What am I supposed to do tonight?"

"Watch some TV," Dex told him. "Or here's one. Why not read a book?" He rose and gave Jackie's room the once-over, as if to say that all this kid stuff should be enough to keep his son entertained, then headed back downstairs.

Jackie sat on the edge of his bed, looking at the now-blank monitor. It'd probably take a few days to get Dad's password, he thought. Fortunately, he'd saved a month's worth of postings.

"HOPE YOU DON'T THINK ALL OUR MEETINGS are like this," Ian whispered to Jenny. As he leaned close to her, his knee brushed against her hip—he had the kind of nervous energy that frequently resulted in unexpected contacts, she suspected.

Said meeting had regressed to a general state of chaos, Dexter having momentarily left the room. Members were chatting among themselves as Neeko apologetically mopped up the spilt coffee. Every time she wiped the table she managed to sprinkle Eleanor with a few drops of French Columbian.

"Not to worry," Jenny said, straightening her slacks. "I work as a paralegal—I know about the gamut of human emotion."

"We've got some members capable of reaching the stratosphere," Ian said. "I sometimes think it's because—shoot, I'm about to put my foot in it."

"You were?" Jenny asked, stifling the urge to grin. "How so?"

"Never mind. You barely know me, and I'd hate to blurt out something that'll type me as a jerk forever."

"I promise not to jump to any conclusions," she said, crossing her blouse with her finger.

"Okay," Ian sighed. He had, Jenny thought, much younger eyes than you first realized. "It just seems that the tenor of RADFAm politics is set by the fact that the majority of members are women."

"Is this a sexist observation or one of those Men-Mars/Women-Venus things?"

"Both, probably," Ian admitted, an answer that Jenny liked. As a paralegal, she'd seen enough domestic arguments to have an open mind when it came to male/female communication.

Dex had returned and was once more calling the meeting to order. "If you'd like," he said to Delia by way of turning the conversation to more productive realms, "I can talk to Connie myself about this T-shirt business."

"I'd like to call for a vote," Delia pushed. "See how the rest of the room feels."

Dexter nodded, shrugging his massive shoulders at the same time. "We've got a motion to vote on paying Connie for the T-shirts. Any seconds?"

The room was suddenly deathly silent. Jenny felt like a visitor at an auction, afraid to move or even clear her throat lest either be mistaken as a statement. She glanced across at Lissa, who was surveying the room with the casual yet thorough scrutiny she used on jurors. When she caught Jenny's eye, she winked at her.

"Okay," Delia finally demurred, when it became obvious she had no backup.

"Times like this, I'm thankful for Roberts' Rules," Ian whispered, brushing up against her again.

"Maybe we should move onto other business," Dexter said. "Next month's our annual pool party. This is your baby, isn't it, Ian?"

"Got the pool reserved through my condo association," the membership secretary said as all eyes in the room turned toward him—and Jenny. "It's fat-friendly, with steps and a railing at the shallow end. Got an idea for spicing it up even more, too. This year's bash will be a Celebrity Beach Party! Everyone's encouraged to attend as their favorite celebrity. We can give out prizes for costume and presentation." With that he opened up his notebook and pulled out a paper mask of Gerald McRaney, holding it up to his face. "I'm thinking of going as Mr. Delta Burke," he told the group.

"Only you could come up with this," Dex chuckled.

"Actually," Ian admitted, "it was Misty's idea."

Dex unsuccessfully scanned the room for Misty, then threw the topic open to the rest of the room. "Comments? Input?"

"Well, it's something different—" someone from behind Jenny began.

"Umm—think I should come as Mae West?" she whispered as Ian retook his seat.

"Think you'd be perfect for the part," he said before turning back to the meeting. He patted her on the hand—an intentional contact, this time. "Can't see you as anybody else."

Yeah. She was definitely going to like Ian Johnson.

EPISODE FIFTEEN

DEX SHOVED THE REST OF THE MEETING'S paper plates and cups into a second heavy-duty Hefty bag; the sign of a good turnout. A few years back, he reflected while toting the detritus down the deck steps, we would've been lucky to stretch the seams of a single sack. Whenever he found he was getting too agitated at chapter politics, he reminded himself that theirs was a healthy chapter. A lot of RADFAm chapters had been struggling over the past few years. A few had folded for lack of interest, or perhaps frustration.

He dropped the sacks in his mini-dumpster, then turned back toward the house. The sky was clear, dotted with stars and a jet's distant running lights. The evening felt deliciously cool. Looked like they'd sleep with the windows open tonight.

Inside, Neeko was straightening up the kitchen. Dex wished she would stop treating Eleanor as a rival. There was a point where jealousy became insulting, the green-eyed spouse basically implying that the partner had no willpower. As a fat man, as well as a doctor, he was ultrasensitive to any assumptions about his capacity for self-control.

But what was he going to say to Neeko? Dex was at a loss. So when he got back into the kitchen, he decided to skirt the subject. "Know what I caught our son doing?"

The conjugal possessive was Neeko's cue that something was remiss. Jackie as the model son was hers. When he became a problem child Dex added himself to the mix. Neeko knew her husband was trying to be supportive of her, but she suspected Jackie saw it differently—the only way he was going to get any attention from his dad was to screw up.

"What's the matter, Dexter?" she asked, scrutinizing the already immaculate kitchen to make sure she hadn't missed anything. Behind her, two white metal speakers were playing Chess blues—Howlin' Wolf bragging about both his size and sexual prowess.

"Caught him upstairs downloading cyberporn."

"Cyberporn?" she echoed, cut short in her inspection.

"Off one of the newsgroups," Dex said, reaching into the fridge for a Fruitopia that had been left behind. "One devoted to fat models."

"Fat?" Neeko said, puzzled. "But he's always so insulting to his sister."

"Seems that's just sibling rivalry," Dex answered. He took a swig of Kiwi Kiss and lowered his voice. "What bothers me is the fact that he was even able to get into the newsgroup. I thought we had him locked out of the adult areas."

"Jackie's always been resourceful," Neeko said, winding an arm around her husband's broad back. "He's like his dad that way."

"God, I hope not. I remember what I was like as a horny adolescent."

"I've seen your yearbook picture," she mused. "Not as hairy but pretty darn attractive." She ran her hand across his torso and twined a slender finger through the aforementioned chest hair. Her palm felt cool against his breast.

"You trying to distract me, brazen woman?"

"Maybe," Neeko admitted as she kneaded her husband's shoulder. "It's been a long evening. What did you do with the boy?"

"Banned him from the computer for the rest of the night," Dex said.

"And he didn't just turn around and log back on once you left the room?"

"He knows better. Besides I stole the plug to the modem."

"Plug! You're so techno-savvy," Neeko grinned. "And Rachel's at the movies. That gives us some time to ourselves, doesn't it?"

She moved in front of him and planted a kiss on his lips. Dex grinned at his wife. "It sure does," he said.

"So whatcha think?"

"Are you asking me as a professional?" Joe countered, sampling a spoon of Misty's tiramisu. Dramatically rolling the morsel around his tongue as if taking a mental inventory of his tastebuds, he finally pronounced, "Pretty good—for the competition."

"I shouldn't have ordered it," Misty confessed. "I had plenty to eat at the potluck." She cut into the crust of cocoa-powdered decoration and took a bite, making a small moan of pleasure as she savored the creamy delicacy.

What are you doing? she chastised herself. Carrying on like this—was she so desperate for approval that she was willing to act like a food slut?

"Some things," Joe told her with a smile, "aren't meant to be denied."

"You should know when it comes to food, right?"

He didn't answer immediately, just slowly surveyed the coffeehouse. Kuppa Joe'a/Eatz 'n' Java had pirated its name, as well as its island decor, from a classically cheesy volcanic disaster film. Ceiling fans stirred gentle breezes, wafting ridiculously fake palm fronds that framed a lurid mural of violent geological upheaval. Drawn by whatever meager correlation it held to the traditional South Seas proclivity for adipose adoration, the shop had become a favorite spot for many local RADFAm members. Of course they were no more idolized there than anywhere else in our weight-conscious nation, but the chairs were adequate, the coffee high-octane, and the desserts divine.

The place was mildly busy with couples of all orientations, though Misty couldn't help noticing that she was the largest woman in the room. Staff was typically fat-neutral here, though when Joe had gone up for their order, the waifish counter girl had scrutinized her with that superior expression only the very thin can manage. Joe had noticed, and she could see him getting irritated by it and was mollified by his reaction.

"I guess I do," Joe admitted. "Good food's important to me."

"Spoken like a true chef," she said, sipping at her decaf iced mocha.

"As opposed to a sous chef?"

"Everybody has to start somewhere," she retorted, taking another generous bite of dessert, then slowly sliding the spoon out of her mouth. Goddess, but she was shameless! The look in Joe's eyes when she put her spoon down was enough to rein her in, though. It was like discovering someone at the window when you've been dancing by yourself. Misty felt herself begin to blush.

"Joe," she finally asked, "what exactly do you want from this relationship?"

Talk about your loaded questions. If the guy didn't bolt and run from the room right now, she'd be amazed.

To his credit, Joe took less time answering this than he had her earlier query. "That's a hard one," he said. "I've watched you at the dances, and you've always seemed so nice. I just thought it was time to stop watching and get to know you."

"Fair enough," Misty replied. "What do you want to know about me?"

"I don't know. How about—everything?"

"That'd take a while," she chuckled. "There are things about me that I probably shouldn't spill on the first date."

"It's settled then," Joe responded. "We'll have to make more dates." He raised his glass of Italian soda, chagrined yet pleased by his bluntness, and took a dramatic chug. "Glad that's out of the way."

"Me, too," Misty admitted, and amazingly she felt herself start to relax for the first time that evening. "Anything you'd like to ask me that is good first-date fodder?"

Joe smiled at this foodish allusion, then offered, "You never told me how you got involved with RADFAm."

"A Unitarian Church workshop, if you can believe such a thing," Misty said. "About five years ago I went to a women's spiritual retreat up north and sat in on a session about body image. The presenter, a lovely midsized woman who walked with an owlhead cane, had a bunch of brochures from the organization. Turned out she was also into Tarot. Afterward, we spent half the weekend comparing life experiences. I grabbed an entry form and sent it out that very week. Haven't seen the woman since."

"Sort of like the Lone Ranger," Joe said.

"Yeah, sort of." As Misty smiled at the memory she glanced over Joe's shoulder toward the front door. "Oh no," she groaned. "Ian Johnson just walked in. And we bailed out of Dex's early!"

Holding the door, the chapter membership secretary was leading in the attractive blonde from the meeting. (What Misty wouldn't do for a pair of legs like that!) He smiled in their direction and steered the mid-sized Jenny—that was her name, Jenny—toward their table. "Misty!" he called, drawing unwanted attention to all concerned.

"Mind if we join you?" he asked once they were close enough for the question to be unavoidable. "Thought I might catch you here. Figured you'd want to hear how your idea went."

"Idea?" Misty repeated, distracted from her continuing mental self-comparison with the stunning Jenny. Last time she'd weighed so little she'd still been in high school—convinced, of course, that she already was the fattest thing on Earth. Were those limpid blue eyes from contact lenses?

"The celebrity luau," Ian persisted, pulling out a chair for Jenny. She sat without spilling over the seat, Misty noticed.

Misty turned to Joe, who politely sat back observing, and mentally slapped herself. "Probably helped that I didn't introduce the concept," she countered. "All my theme parties have been bombs."

"I thought the birthday party for Venus of Willendorf was fun," Ian said. "I could have done without those yonic place settings, though."

Jenny burst out laughing. "Too Judy Chicago?" she giggled.

Misty grinned at her and shook her head. Across the table, Joe looked bemused.

"Fair warning," Misty advised. "Don't believe every third sentence to come out of this man's mouth."

"One out of three?" Jenny teased. "That's not bad, for a guy!" She glanced at the counter menu, then turned back to Misty's empty plate. "What's the most sinful thing they've got in this place?" she asked.

And with that, Misty ceased all jealous thoughts about RADFAm's newest chapter member.

EPISODE SIXTEEN

JENNY'S CAUTION METER wasn't yet fully functional or she would have let the machine do its job as the jangling phone intruded on her morning. She really had only herself to blame. If she hadn't stayed out so late she wouldn't have slept so late; if she hadn't slept so late, she wouldn't have imagined that Ian just could be calling. In her experience, men weren't usually that romantic.

Since crawling blearily out of bed to the cockatiel-brand reveille of Clouseau's "bring me breakfast" shrieks, Jenny had lounged back in the recliner, nursing a cup of Cafe Vienna and reliving her evening with Ian. Why shouldn't he be calling? She lifted the handset and—soundly kicked herself.

"Miz Taylor? Greg Dillman here. I hope you got my letter the other day?"

Jenny certainly had—a tacky form letter with his portrait business card paperclipped to the top left corner. She'd shown it to Lissa, who had showed open disgust in return.

"Greg's been warned about this," she informed Jenny after scanning the letter's contents. "Soliciting members is a major chapter no-no, but in real life it's just this side of legal, so I'm not surprised he's still doing it."

"What Greg does is offer health insurance to RADFAm members who've previously had difficulty being approved. His policies are shockingly substandard and the rates unconscionable, but many fat adults are so desperate for insurance they don't thoroughly examine the contract. Anyway, I can assure you, you'll always get better bennies here than from Gregory Oliver Dillman, Esquire."

"Yes, I received your letter, Greg," Jenny resumed. "But I'm not interested in health insurance at this time. I've got sufficient coverage from work, thank you."

"I surely would love to come over and review that policy for you," Dillman wheedled in honeyed tones. "I bet I could give you perfect coverage."

Jesus, Jenny groaned, *this actuarial lounge-lizard makes the simplest statement smutty.* She wasn't sure whether the emotion rising through her innards was upchuck or uproar. Across the room Clouseau perched, kissing and cooing to his mirrored pretty boy. This shared male preening turned it comical, she decided.

"Perhaps," Jenny replied, firmly, "but I'm really quite satisfied as is."

"10-4. I know when a lady means no," Dillman backpedaled. "I, uh, did have another concept I'd like to float by you. A few of the younger members have just started a small spinoff group, more strictly social and less in-your-face. Politically, you know. Don't have a name for it yet, but we'll be scheduling dances and other events on those months that RADFAm isn't doing anything really important.

"We're also working on a newsletter—personal ads, photo shoots. You'd be a truly inspired premiere pictorial."

"You're kidding, right?" Jenny blurted. As soon as she said it the reasoning part of her brain berated, *why are you even wasting time on this jerk? Just hang up!*

"Me thinks you protest too much, ma'am," Greg said jovially. "You're very attractive, you know. Would make for a lovely and artistic pictorial. No, don't decide now. Please just give it your consideration. Catch ya later."

PAUL GOT HOME ON SCHEDULE that Sunday (his weekends had taken on a certain routine), dog-tired as usual. But, he wryly reminded himself, it was a good tired. He was sitting crosslegged with an O'Doul's and a lesson plan on his lap tray when Ian called to tell him about the celebrity luau.

"Sounds like fun," Paul considered, muting his stereo with the universal remote. "You say it was set up at Friday's meeting?" Over the receiver Paul could hear Ian's computer singing cyber-ditties from its tinny computer speaker.

"The details were nailed down then," Ian told him. "But it's been on the calendar for months. The chapter traditionally has a pool party in August to say goodbye to summer. Why do you ask?"

"No reason," Paul replied.

He thought back to Saturday morning. He'd just come out of the shower to find Connie on a long, covert phone tete-a-tete with her friend Delia, and from the snippets he could glean through her whispers it was obvious that they were discussing the meeting. She hadn't mentioned word one about the luau, though.

This was starting to take on a creepy edge.

"Think you can come?" Ian asked.

"What did you say the date was again?" Paul replied, reaching for his calendar and wishing the O'Doul's wasn't nonalcoholic. *You don't want to go there,* Paul told himself as he jotted down the details, but of course a part of him needed to.

MISTY HAD BEEN THINKING about her costume for a week now, but it always came back to her first choice: Mama Cass Elliot.

"You're a neo-hippie," Kirk teased one night. They were watching *Victor/Victoria* for the umpteenth time on the tube, chatting through Julie Andrews' (interminable) version of the Shady Lady and her matador. "Too young to live the Summer of Love, you've been scattering incense fumes (and others) across the landscape ever since. *This is the dawning of the—*"

"Oh, please," Misty cried. "Anything but *Hair!*"

"Come on, it's a play that demands exhumation," Kirk shot back. "A richer palette of songs than, say, *Grease,* and far campier for fancying itself ART. Plus multiple-gender nudity! Imagine the throng of schlongs making their *Hair*-y debuts over the years. A very yummy image.

"Speaking of oral gratification—how's it going with the Master Chef?" Kirk grabbed a handful of Light Orville Reddenbacher and threw her one of his patented dish-me-the-dirt-sugah looks.

"He's been very—chivalrous, so far," Misty answered coyly. "Invited me to the movies this weekend."

"Didn't think you did the cinema scene in for-real theaters."

"This one's supposed to have friendly seating. So there," Misty drawled, dragging the bowl of popcorn off his lap. "Now hush. There goes King Marchand into the closet."

"Drat!"

IT TOOK JACKIE TEN DAYS to get the new password. Instead of leaving it in his credenza, Dex had it jotted on the inner cover of *Internet for Dummies*. This ordinarily was secure, since he knew his son had graduated from such baby-tech stuff years ago. But Jackie was on a mission, and if at first—yadda yadda.

Access restored, Jackie curtailed his serious net surfing when his father was around, which was generally predictable. That still left him plenty of opportunities. His mom always knocked before entering his room, and he was quick to hide his tracks.

Another week's worth of nude photo downloads on diskette. A school-chum treasury, but Jackie had become heartily bored with all those acres of fat. However, he had found something even cooler to do. Just uplink with a newsgroup like "alt.support.radfam," then dis and piss all over those freaks.

Right now he was inserting himself into the middle of a discussion about dress sizes. "Tents are for circuses! Nobody wants to see your blubber butts, anyway!"

He kept changing IDs so no one would learn to bypass his trolling. With each fresh assault he pictured someone from Dad's group reading it and blowing a gasket. Much more satisfying than collecting a bunch of gross photos.

Scrolling down the news list, he saw that one of his earlier postings had snagged a reply. Choice! Sniggering, Jackie double-clicked the message to retrieve the response.

PROOFING MISTY'S HOROSCOPE COLUMN as it glowed on her well-used Smith-Corona word processor screen, Eleanor Bollen massaged her forehead with soothing fingertips and sighed deeply.

Each time she laid out another issue of the newsletter she promised herself this would be her last year as VP. It really took a lot out of her. The only way she kept up with it was by doing dribs and drabs throughout the month. Last time she tried to put together an entire issue in a single weekend, it was utter chaos. She'd goofed up the time for the business meeting and had to phone everyone with the correction. Most embarrassing! A roseate flush came over her at the memory of Connie's extended harangue.

But no one could accuse her of not learning from experience. With the pool party only two days off, she had most of the rest of the current newsletter on diskette, saving half a page of writeup for the luau. She'd be able to get the RADFAm RoundUp out on schedule. And, hopefully, a repeat of Neeko's "mishap" all over the meeting minutes would not delay her again.

Eleanor couldn't comprehend how Dex's wife could be so hateful and cold. Dex was a saint for taking it. Every time Neeko walked into a meeting, the room turned icy. All she knew was that the looks Neeko shot her held far more poison than anything Connie Donovan could inveigh.

Well, it was highly unlikely that Neeko would show up for the pool party anyway. And though Eleanor's reflections did seem rather un-Christian, her private heart yearned for time with Dex.

She moved away from the kitchen table and opened the fridge, taking out a pitcher of Brita. It was getting near time to shell out for a new filter again. Ever since reading that *Newsweek* article stating that using an old filter was no better than running water through a used sponge, she'd gotten religious about regular changes. She couldn't not use the pitcher—her son had given it to her as a Christmas present—but she made a point of following the accompanying instructions diligently.

It was the only way to get through life, Eleanor firmly believed: Follow instructions.

"Sure you can't come in tomorrow? I really need you!"

"I'm sure," Joe answered, and he could see the disappointment in Caspar's ruddy face. "Got a date."

"Last of the Latin Hot Lovers," Caspar said scornfully, rubbing a hand through his thinning hair in exasperation. Before his sous chef started seeing Misty, Joe could be counted on as an easy last-minute sub. Now that he'd gained a social life, Joe wasn't so predictable.

Joe could tell it irritated Caspar, but he had no intention of backing down. He'd be the first one to tell his boss that, if anything, Misty's inspiration seasoned and spiced his every culinary creation.

Perhaps if Caspar could just see a picture of Misty, he would lighten up. Joe had briefly met his boss's wife at the restaurant's Christmas party, and she was decidedly womanly. Though fifteen years younger than her husband, she was at least sixty pounds heavier. And Caspar was certainly not slender. Made you wonder—

"You need to bring this girl of yours in some night," Caspar said, softening. "I'd like to meet the woman who's been distracting my protégé."

"Sure thing," Joe agreed, smiling at his boss. One great thing about working for Caspar—he knew nothing of grudges.

As Caspar turned in search of another suitable victim, Joe continued to set up preparations for the night, all the while thinking ahead to the chapter luau. He just kept imagining Misty in a grass skirt and lei, hula dancing to those island rhythms.

EPISODE SEVENTEEN

IAN'S CONDO SEEMED TOO SPACIOUS for its furnishings—too much exposed, scuffed monotonous eggshell ceiling-to-floor and too little decor camouflage. The first thing Jenny noticed in the living room was the computer table; the second, an eclectically ensembled home entertainment center. A typical guy space, she decided, fingering a teetering pile of 3.5 diskettes that threatened to escape their shoe box confines—11D. The only atypical touch: a framed black-and-white Ned Sonntag print signed by the artist.

"Decs ahoy!" Ian shouted, leaning over the railing at the top of the stairs and dangling two Walmart shopping bags.

"Dex? When did he arrive?" Jenny caught the bags one at a time, giggling as a flock of cardboard flamingoes spilled, wafting gently to the floor.

"Got to have pink flamingoes," Misty said, wandering in with a pair of pickup tongs in hand. She lifted the pink placards from the floor and deposited them in the Walmart sack. "Always wanted one of these things, Ian," she said. "Where'd you get it?"

"Mail order," he called from somewhere overhead. "Was going to be a present, but things happen."

"'Things?'" Jenny repeated, loud enough to reach upstairs. She sent a questioning look toward Misty, who smiled ruefully and whispered, "If Ian doesn't tell you, I'll give you the scoop later. Wouldn't want you to get ambushed."

"Ian was seeing someone in the chapter?"

"Psychic intuition or just a great guess?" Misty winked, snapping at the air with her tongs. She took a bag from Jenny, then headed for the door, pausing to let Dex Logan in.

Unlike the rest of them, Dex was already in costume: faux coonskin cap, tropical bathing suit and fringe vest over a white v-neck T.

"Davy Crockett?" Jenny ventured as he stepped into the room.

"Grizzly Adams," Dex replied with a toothy grin. Cap tail flopping, he turned to Ian as he reached the bottom of the stairs. "Neeko has all the episodes on tape."

"She should compare notes with my neighbor," Misty said in parting. Ian snorted, but Dex only looked puzzled.

"Before I forget this," Ian said, reaching unerringly into the shoebox and turning to hand Dex two rubber-banded diskettes, "here's the program you asked for. Webstodian—the best parent shield on the market." He tossed the diskettes to Dex, who put them in the flap of his gym bag.

"Hate to even be using something like this," he responded. "What will it say to Jackie? That we don't trust him?"

"Do you trust him?" Ian asked.

"After the last month, no."

"Then shouldn't you be honest about that with him?"

"Only someone without children could be so sure about what to do," Dex sighed. "No matter how I approach Jackie these days, it seems like the wrong thing to do."

"The eternal joys of parenthood," Ian said. He put a hand on Jenny's shoulder. "Can I talk with you a minute?" Jenny nodded, so he dashed into the kitchen, returned with a bag of groceries and led her out the patio door.

The pool was a block-and-a-half away, so neither of them loaded up with too much. The afternoon sun was bright and hot; like most midwestern Septembers, it hadn't given up on the idea of summer yet. Jenny and Ian ambled along the street to the clubhouse, site of the upcoming celebrity luau.

"I suppose I should have brought this up sooner," he said. "But she wasn't at the last meeting, so it didn't really come up."

"If you don't want to talk about it yet—" Jenny began.

"No, I should. Because she might be here tonight. Val prefers the social events, and in fact, I kind of avoided the last few chapter social outings for that very reason."

Ahead of them, Misty and Eleanor were stretching and reaching to attach colored fishnet to the fence around the pool, then weaving plastic lobsters within the netting. A nearby patio table held a pile of cheap sunglasses and a boombox blasting the overture to *South Pacific*.

"You really don't need to—" Jenny started again, all the while trying to pull up Valerie's face from the Sweetheart Dance. All she could remember was a striking streak of white in her hair.

"Ian!" a voice boomed from a cruising yellow pickup. A tan, pudgy face leaned through the passenger window. "Can I borrow a kitchen knife? Got a bunch of veggies that need discipline."

"Just don't cut yourself, Carl," Ian countered, chuckling. "My homeowners' won't cover it."

They walked the rest of the way to the pool, but the interruption had obviously dislodged Ian. Finally Jenny grabbed his hand and let him off the hook. "I met Val at the Sweetheart's Dance," she said. "I can see how you were attracted to her."

"It ended last spring," Ian replied. "Nobody's fault. It just ended. But if she shows, it will be the first time we've seen each other in months. Could be awkward."

"I'm a big girl," Jenny said.

"Thankfully," Ian said with a grin, leaning over and nervously bussing her on the cheek.

THE LUAU WAS IN FULL FEST when Joe arrived. About ten chapter members were in costume; the music was blaring. Seated at the ticket table was Misty in her Mama Cass costume—long straight wig and flowery muumuu. If she hadn't told him beforehand who she was going to be, Joe might not have gotten it. He wasn't real familiar with music from that era.

"Like it?" she asked. "It's a replica of the same dress she wore on the cover of *If You Can Believe Your Eyes and Ears*. Took me forever to find a comparable fabric."

"You look great," he said, elevator-eyeing her as he plunked down his two bucks. "Where can I change?"

"There's a bathhouse behind me, but if you're modest, you can use Carl's condo over there."

"That's okay," he said. The last time he'd undressed before a group of guys had been for P.E. at St. Viator's, but he wasn't bothered by it. Blowing Misty a kiss, he headed for the men's shower.

The only one inside was the guy he'd met at the last dance. Joe couldn't remember his name, but he thought he'd left the dance with that Connie Donovan. Joe had been watching her throughout ten months of dances. The woman had a gorgeous body, but she never seemed to stay with any one guy too long.

"Joe, right?" Connie's newest asked. He was dressed in a tuxedo jacket with black swim trunks. As he leaned down to buckle his sandals, a water pistol and holster poked out of his jacket. "Don't know if you remember me, but I'm Paul." He held out a hand.

"I remember," Joe said, dropping his chef's outfit onto a nearby bench. "That was your first dance, wasn't it? So you decided to come back for more."

"Ian got my name from a list National sends to chapters," Paul explained, straightening his jacket. He kind of looked like James Bond. "Sounded like a good time."

"You here with Connie?" Joe asked, envisioning the bottom-heavy brunette in a swimsuit.

An unreadable look passed over Paul's face. "Yup," he finally said. "Took some doing to get her out of the apartment, but here we are."

"Who's she coming as?"

"Mae West," Paul said, brandishing his pistol, "while I get to be Cary

Grant. And you?"

"Chef Boyardee," Joe announced, affixing a large gray mustache to his lips. "A boyhood idol."

"I bet," Paul said with a weak smile, and something in the tone of his voice rubbed Joe the wrong way—like he knew all he needed to know about Joe and didn't care to know anymore. "See you outside."

When Joe was fully costumed, he rejoined Misty at the table. "Did Mae West and Cary Grant ever make a movie together?" he asked.

"Just one," she told him. "*She Done Him Wrong*. Why do you ask?"

"No reason," Joe said, glancing over toward the pool. Whatever Connie did to this guy Paul, the guy probably deserved it.

EPISODE EIGHTEEN

DECKED OUT IN BRUNETTE WIG and Southern finery, Jenny was pleasantly startled every time she caught her reflection in the bathhouse mirror. Her cheeks weren't as full as Delta Burke's, but for the most part she made a passable Designing Woman.

"Suzanne Sugarbaker, Ah do declare!" Ian shouted as she hit the pool area. Standing by the goodies table, he doffed his cowboy hat in a flamboyant salute, then sidled toward her with his thumbs in his trunks. A big goofy smile accentuated his fake mustache. No way could he be mistaken for Gerald McRaney, but he looked pretty cool in his boots and buckaroo swim trunks.

"Why, it's Major Dad," she drawled back, kicking a beach ball back into play. "Still keeping the world safe from democracy?"

"Uh-oh, Lib Alert!" Ian accused once he got within speaking distance. "You ain't one of them opinionated modern gals, are you?"

Jenny batted her eyes. "Not if y'all don't want me to be," she said in her best belle voice.

"You do that so well it's scary," Ian replied, leading her to Dex and Eleanor's table.

Once seated, Jenny took a quick look around to see who she recognized. Boss lady Lissa wasn't going to show, she knew; she'd begged off with some family commitment. Joyce and Patsy splashed in the pool, playing volleyball with some unfamiliar folks. Joe was standing by the boom box, watching the pool action with a smile on his face. Several tables over, Connie was dressed like—who? Lillian Russell?—with a scowl on her face. When she caught Jenny looking her way, she shot a look so venomous it almost dislodged Jenny's wig. She'd come with the handsome young man from the Sweetheart Dance, but did not seem at all happy about it. Delia, though, was nowhere to be seen. Maybe she wasn't the costume type.

The crowd was even bigger than the dance, which worked since they had more room. For an instant Jenny flashed on the image of the pool shrunk to the size of the SkyAire's dance floor, and it got her giggling.

"Love to see a pretty lady enjoying herself," a voice said behind her, and the moment turned suddenly arctic.

Greg Dillman had arrived on the scene, clad in trunks and retro terrycloth jacket and looking for all the world like a faux Hef—or at least like something out of a real bad 1968 spy flick. He was carrying a camera with a big old flash on it.

"Who are you supposed to be?" Ian asked.

"Be?" Greg repeated with a smirk. "Why would I want to be anything but myself?" He snapped a photo of Dex and Eleanor close in conversation, which turned the chapter president's attention his way.

"Greg?" Dex asked mildly. "You taking pictures?"

"Looking for subjects for my social club newsletter," Greg explained. "I'm sure you've heard about it—"

"I don't remember you getting permission to do this," Dex persisted. "You know the chapter rules: You need to get consent before taking chapter members' photos."

"No problem," Greg answered. "I'll have the folks sign a release later."

"Give me the film, Greg. You've been warned about this in the past. Permission first; pictures second."

"But I've already taken a full roll."

Dex held his hand out and said nothing further.

Dillman sighed, then popped his camera open and tossed Dex a roll.

"And we'll hold the camera until afterward," Dex concluded. The insurance man complied, then stomped away looking totally pissed.

"A couple years ago some unflattering rear shots from a RADFAm convention were published in one of the supermarket tabloids," Ian told Jenny. "A lot of members are sensitive about getting their pictures taken."

Jenny could understand that. Her high school yearbook picture still gave her the willies (who was that tragic looking fat girl?). Yet tonight, she didn't think she'd mind being captured on film. There was freedom in disguise.

"I wouldn't be," she told the table. "I'd kind of like to see the photo Greg took of me, in fact."

"I bet you're a real star, Miz Suzanne," Ian said, sending a blush across Jenny's carefully madeup face.

THE BOOMBOX WAS BLASTING SOMETHING by the Beach Boys as Paul eyed the veggie tray. "Carnie Wilson's dad," he told Joe, nodding toward the music source. "One strong argument in favor of genetic predisposition."

Joe merely grunted, then made a point of turning toward Misty and the ticket table.

What's with him? Paul wondered, spooning a dollop of Marie's Garden Vegetable dip onto Connie's plate. He grabbed his own platter and muttered a "catch ya later" to the chef.

"Didn't know the chapter was this healthy," Paul said once he rejoined his Mae West. He indicated the pool, which was crowded with at least twice the number of the Sweetheart Dance.

"About half the group's from neighboring states," Connie told him, selecting a buffalo wing from Paul's plate. "They always come, sponging off our chapter events. Used to charge out-of-staters more, but Logan nixed that idea. 'They're part of the RADFAmily, too,'" she said, mocking Dex's deep resonance. "Just once, I'd like to see another nearby chapter do a big event so successfully."

Whenever Connie talked about chapter business, her face hardened unflatteringly, making it look older than her professed age. Paul quickly changed the subject. "Where's Delia tonight?" he asked. "I was looking forward to getting to know her better."

"Don't think she'd be interested in you!" Connie snapped. "The woman's practically asexual."

"That's not what I meant," Paul said quickly. "I know that Delia's a major part of InFatuation; you two seem to go back a long way."

"What's that supposed to mean?" she demanded, eyeing him suspiciously.

First Joe, now Connie; he seemed to have the knack for putting people on edge tonight. "Nothing," he said, offering a fresh buffalo wing as a peace offering. He steered the conversation into safer waters. "Have I told you yet how gorgeous you look in that dress?"

"You have, but it's worth saying again." She paused, taking time to dip her buffalo wing into blue cheese sauce, then asked. "Am I the prettiest woman here?"

"No competition," Paul said, looking into her eyes. "You're the fairest of them all."

She smiled, and in that one moment, the statement was more than just a line. "Always thought that Queen got a bad rap," Connie said. "She certainly had far more sense of style than that simpy Snow White.

"The Black Queen was a woman; Snow White was just a girl."

"Nice distinction," Connie said. She smiled and stripped the meat off her chicken wing with the slow, deliberate use of her wide lips.

Watching this act, Paul could understand the full appeal of Joe's fantasies. He'd once read an article stating authoritatively that within every FA there was a potential feeder. He didn't believe that, but he couldn't deny how sexy Connie looked when she used her mouth like this.

The volleyball game had progressed into a free-for-all, an inevitability since no one seemed to be keeping score anyway. Two happy FAs were standing in the midst of the chaos and soaking it all in, watching women of all shapes of fat bobble in the water around them. No wonder this was such a big draw.

"For someone who claims to only have eyes for me, yours are doing a lot of wandering," Connie noted.

"Just making sure I was telling the truth," Paul said with a grin. He took a look behind him and saw Dex's table. Seated with Dex and a guy who had to be Ian based on his nervous manner was a lovely midsized woman dressed like some modern-day Scarlett O'Hara. She was laughing at something Ian was saying, not noticing the sudden change in the membership secretary's expression. Walking up behind her, also dressed in Southern antebellum garb, was a tall brunette with a streak of white in her hair.

"Well," Connie said, following Paul's gaze. A catlike look crossed her face. "How interesting."

EPISODE NINETEEN

VALERIE!" Ian blurted. "You've lost weight!"

"Eighty pounds," the second Suzanne Sugarbaker informed all in earshot. Both Dex and Eleanor had seen her on enough occasions to already note her weight loss. To Jenny's eye, she didn't look that much smaller than at the Sweetheart Dance, but that had been in lounge light.

Back then Ian and Valerie were still in that avoidance phase, which in part explained his startled reaction. But even if his surprise was justified, did he have to sound so—whole-hearted about it?

"Better living through chemistry, I always say," Valerie added, turning to briefly wave to Patsy and Joyce in the pool, then swiveling back to Ian. Fanning herself with a lacy handkerchief, she gave him a smile that bragged of shared history. It was meant to shut Jenny out, and it damn near succeeded.

"A new prescription drug?" Ian asked, thankfully keeping the conversation in check. Beneath the table he grabbed Jenny's hand and squeezed it companionably. Over the boombox, a reggae singer was boasting about the beauty of his chubby girlfriend.

"Delia, of all people, turned me onto it," Valerie told them, gesturing like a game show girl showing off a prize—only this prize was her own voluptuous body. "Never thought I'd be thanking her for anything, but then you never can tell who your real friends will be."

There was something disorienting about weight-loss talk at a RADFAm event, particularly when it came from the lips of Ian's former girlfriend. Try as she might to talk herself out of it, Jenny felt like those missing eighty pounds had insinuated themselves onto her body. Looking up at the statuesque Valerie, she felt squat and graceless by comparison.

"What are you taking?" Dexter asked from across the table, but Valerie was too focused on Ian to answer.

Skirt rustling loudly, she wiggled up closer to the membership secretary and smiled. "You look good with a mustache, Ian," she purred, lightly touching the accoutrement with a lacquered sculptured nail. "Maybe you should grow a more permanent one—you know I like my men all natural."

"Never could," he answered, glancing up from his seat into her impressive bodice. "It grows too sparsely. Like the rest of my hair." He took off his cowboy hat for emphasis. His thin hair had been flattened by the costume, making him look more like a little kid in cowboy drag than an adult.

"Just shows the testosterone is flowing someplace more important," Valerie replied with a smirk. She gave him a lascivious wink, then shifted toward Jenny. In the turn of a head, all goodwill vanished from her face.

"Well," she noted, "the new kid on the block. Love your costume—makes me feel like I'm looking at a funhouse mirror." She moved close to Jenny's face, the scent of something minty, alcoholic on her breath. "How do you like our little group so far?" she asked. "Membership secretary doing his job, helping you into the fold?"

Jenny felt her face grow warm. Damn it, she told herself, this wasn't right! Why was she suddenly feeling so defensive? She had a right to be there.

Looking past Val's wig, she saw Connie and her date observing the confrontation. The supersized Mae West had a look of anticipation that reminded Jenny of her one experience watching Chippendale dancers, but her companion at least had the grace to look uncomfortable. The sight was enough to rout all sense of defensiveness. Looking Valerie straight in the eye, she said simply, "Ian's been wonderful. He's done a lot to make me feel welcome."

"I bet," Valerie snorted. "Your first FA, right? You've still got that 'I Can't Believe There Are Men Like This' look about you. Well, don't worry your li'l old head about it. They're still just men."

Tired of Miss Mint Julep already, Jenny rose from her seat. Valerie backed up, nearly forcing a doublesized Anna Nicole Smith in a pair of homemade Why Guess cutoffs and bikini top to drop her plate of Sun Chips into the pool. By her tottering posturing, it was obvious that Val had partaken of more drink than Jenny had first thought. That didn't make her any less easy to deal with. If anything, it made her even more irritating.

"And the point of all this?" Jenny demanded tightly.

"I don't appreciate some fresh-faced sharkette honing in on Ian," Valerie announced. She looked over at the man in question, who had appeared by Jenny's side, and in that moment Jenny saw a look of longing so intensely naked that it almost made her want to hand him over to her.

"I didn't think you two were an item anymore," Jenny said, trying to smooth the waters. "I thought the relationship was over."

"A mistake," Valerie muttered.

"Could be," Jenny rebutted, "but it seems to me that Ian might have something to say about it, too."

"Definitely," Ian came to the rescue. "You were the one who wanted to see other people, Val. You can't just barge in and change it all back."

He put an arm around Jenny, and she felt like the heroine on a paperback romance cover. If she was blushing now, she didn't care.

"I should have known the first time I saw you," Val accused Jenny. "I should have seen what kind of woman you are!" She looked to the rest of the pool area for support, but only their table and Connie's seemed to be paying any attention. "I should have known!" she shouted above the music and splash of pool games.

"Look," Jenny began, "if you want to talk about this, can't we go somewhere else? Like back to Ian's condo?"

"I want to talk here in front of God and everybody," Val decided. "Let the rest of the chapter know what's going on! You going to try and stop me?"

"LOOKS LIKE IT'S DOWN to a few stragglers," Misty said from behind the ticket table. "Perhaps we can get Ian or Eleanor to keep an eye on things so we can hit the pool before it gets too chilly. I want to see you in wet speedos."

"Haven't seen your swimsuit yet," Joe stated, so she lifted the hem of her psychedelic dress to show an old-fashioned swimsuit underneath. Joe whistled appreciatively. The first full glimpse he'd gotten of her legs. Her knees were nicely dimpled, her thighs as full and exciting as he'd imagined they would be.

"You really do like my legs," she marveled, watching him smile as she rose and lifted off her dress.

Joe knew what to say. "Like the rest of you, too," he added as she reached to lift a piece of potato chip off his Boyardee mustache.

"Ooh, two points for that one," Misty approved. She straightened her dress once more. "When I was younger I used to dream about being crippled like the Little Mermaid. Sitting in a wheelchair with my dainty little legs just showing under my blanket. Instead, I wound up being built like the sea witch in the Disneyfied version of the story."

"Ursula," Joe recalled. His nieces and nephews had the cartoon on tape, and he'd watched it with them one weekend. The sight of the supersized villainess undulating underwater had been pretty sexy.

"Yeah, Ursula," Misty said as she locked the cash box and placed it in a cloth bag. "A humanoid octopus. Can you imagine eight of these legs? No thanks. I'd never be able to get my hips through the door."

Was she trying to flirt with him, saying stuff like that? Joe still didn't know how open he should be about his fantasies with Misty. "I'm pretty handy with a toolbox," he finally offered with a grin. "If you want, I could widen all the doors of your apartment."

"Good with tools and he can cook," Misty marveled, kissing him through his mustache. "Tell me you hate sports, and I think I'm yours for good!"

"I hate sports."

"What about water sports?" Misty said, grabbing his arm and pressing against him. "Let me talk to Eleanor, and you can get a glimpse of this fabulous bod in H2O. We fat girls are world class floaters, you know."

"So I've heard." They paused at the door prize table, and an inspiration hit him. "Think I could offer a gourmet dinner as a door prize sometime?" he asked. "I once did it for a school raffle, and it was a lot of fun."

"Only if I get to be your assistant," Misty decided.

"My own sous chef," Joe said. "I'd like that." The image of Misty squeezed tightly in a bistro apron and sampling his wares throughout a well-laden kitchen danced deliciously through his mind. It was so delightful, in fact, he almost didn't see Valerie hit the water.

EPISODE TWENTY

"YOU PUSHED ME!" Valerie shrieked, thrusting a dripping, accusatory finger at Jenny. As if rooted waist deep in the shallow water, Val reached out with palpable, quivering wrath. Her dress clung to her salaciously; her makeup runneled grotesquely down her face. In the lambent glow of dusk the silver stripe in her hair gleamed like a shaft of neon light. Ian was already kneeling by the side of the pool. Dex lumbered over to help.

"I never—" Jenny started, feeling far too many eyes on her. Across the pool Greg Dillman had turned away from a table of unfamiliar BBWs to watch the show. Nothing sexier to some guys than a good old-fashioned cat-fight, Jenny thought with a sigh. How had she gotten into this, anyway? She'd come to RADFAm to feel good about herself. "You slipped and fell of your own accord," she told the streaming, steaming Valerie.

"Yeah, right," Val shot back, turning and cleaving through the water to the nearest pool exit. From her speed it was clear the wet dress slowed her down. "That big nudge I felt right between my tits was just a gust of wind!"

"I didn't touch you!" Jenny protested loudly. The music had stopped and so had the games. Could this be any more embarrassing?

Connie brushed past her and thundered toward the steps. "Poor dear," she was cooing to Val as she held out her fleshy hand. "Some people just don't know how to act in public."

Once Val reached the top, she took Connie's offering.

"We've got some extra towels if you need one," Connie suggested, careful to keep Val from dripping too much on her. "I wasn't planning on swimming anyway."

"Neither was I," Valerie declared.

The whole moment was so absurdly theatrical that Jenny had to bite back the impulse to laugh. This was like something out of a nighttime soap, she thought. "You fell!" Jenny shouted. How could a day go bad so fast? "By yourself!"

"Whatever you say," Valerie answered, grabbing a towel from "Cary Grant" and using it to wipe her face and shoulders. "You're right—I'm all wet!"

Connie commiserating by her side, Valerie took a seat at the supersized brunette's table. Connie's date offered a second towel for her hair. Whatever sympathy Jenny thought she'd seen on his face before had certainly disappeared.

Somebody added a fresh tape to the boombox, and with Leslie Gore crying about her own party the pool area once more began to fractionalize into groups. One small cluster had moved over toward Connie's table, Jenny noticed. Still standing by the pool, fuming, she considered going home.

"Come with me," Ian leaned close, whispering. "Let's get away from here for a while."

Jenny nodded gratefully.

"YOU REALLY HAVE LOST WEIGHT," Connie said appraisingly. "I've got some outfits in the shop that would suit you to a T." Paul had never seen her quite so publicly maternal—an aspect of Connie he hadn't expected.

"Been meaning to come in," Valerie answered, wringing one last strand of hair onto the concrete. "How awful do I really look?" she asked Paul.

"Not that bad," Paul said gallantly. "Ever see that poster of Sophia Loren rising from the surf?"

"Bet she didn't have runny mascara."

"No," Paul admitted, "but the general effect is close." He handed her some napkins to daub her eyes. With makeup removed, the effect was a lot less disastrous.

"You saw her push me, didn't you?"

"Well—" Paul began. Suddenly he realized that a good half-dozen chapter members had positioned themselves within easy earshot.

"Of course we did," Connie interjected. "It's the innocent-looking ones you've got to watch out for."

"Well, I've got to change out of this," Val decided. "I feel like a flooded basement." She stood and passed through a clump of RADFAmites, all of them offering condolences over her spill, then disappeared into the bath-house.

"I didn't see that girl push her," Paul protested. "She wasn't close enough to do it."

"You weren't seeing it from the same angle as I was," Connie told him, and before he could discuss it any further she shushed him. Dex and Eleanor had moved over to the prize table to announce the evening's raffle winners.

"I BELIEVE YOU," Ian stated. "No matter what, I just want you know I believe you."

"Didn't you see?" Jenny begged. "You were right beside me."

Ian shook his head.

"It all happened so fast." He gently took her by the hands and looked her in the eyes. "Don't worry about it. If you let this get to you, then Val's succeeded in ruining your evening. And I don't want that to happen," he smiled.

As soon as they'd returned to the condo he'd yanked off his mustache and tossed it in the trash. He definitely looked much nicer without it, Jenny decided.

"You never said what you thought of my place," Ian said, moving back to let her appreciate the surroundings. "Hired Merry Maids to sandblast it yesterday, just for you."

"I appreciate the effort. And envy all the space you've got."

"It's really meant for two," Ian admitted. "Perhaps some day it will be put to its best use." With that he moved in and kissed her, first lightly, then—when it became clear she had no intention of going anywhere—less tentatively.

His arms were around her, holding her, sheltering her. Who would have thought that so slight a body could feel so firm and strong against hers? The room grew dim and everything else faded compared with the touch of this wonderful man.

Finally, when it became inevitable that they either stop right now or let the moment progress to another level, she broke away gently, wiping away a single tear. "I'm sorry," she said, noticing the look of alarm on Ian's face. "Don't worry about this. It's been an up-and-down kind of day."

"Well, I hope this is one of the up parts."

"It is," Jenny reassured him, touching her lips to his. "It very definitely is."

"I'M GLAD YOU TALKED me into coming tonight," Connie said as they drove out of Ian's subdivision. "This must have been the most exciting RAD-FAm event since—" She paused, then grabbed Paul's knee. "Since I met you," she finished.

"I feel kind of sorry for the girl with Ian," Paul said. "I bet she wasn't expecting her night to go like this."

"Ian's helping her feel better," Connie sniffed. "Notice they never returned to the luau. Makes it pretty damn inconvenient for the rest of the chapter, leaving us with all that work."

"The decorations were all disposable," Paul replied. "Wasn't that much left to clean up."

"Still, as a chapter officer, and since he lives there, he should have been around to help. Not let himself get distracted by some childish blonde bimbo."

Paul said nothing, preferring to concentrate on finding the tollway exit.

"Noticed at least one other new couple," Connie continued. "Misty and that Hispanic boy. It seems to have really been a busy summer for this chapter." She gazed out the car window at the passing forest preserve, autumn's touch painting its landscape.

"Well, I sure can't complain about the summer," Paul said, spotting a highway sign. Smiling, Connie stroked his right thigh. Whenever he had the slightest doubt about their relationship, all she had to do was touch him and it vanished.

"You'd better not," Connie leered, half-joking.

EPISODE TWENTY-ONE

"**P**UT A SOCK IN IT, Clouseau!"

The cockatiel was simply not in the mood to be mollified. Fresh food, clean water, new paper on the bottom of the cage—and still he was bitching. If Jenny weren't in such a good mood from her previous evening with Ian, she might have taken it personally. But she was strong; she was invincible; she was Happy Fat Woman! Nothing could get to her today.

The phone rang, punctuating Clouseau's plaints. "You there, Jen?" she heard Lissa ask her machine, so she quickly snatched the receiver.

"Sure am," Jenny chirped, settling into her comfy chair with breakfast banana and Cherry Coke in hand. "How's your fam?"

"Never mind that, Miss Manners," Lissa shot back. "What's this I hear about Delta Burke running amok at the luau?"

"You got the wrong Suzanne Sugarbaker, boss lady. It was Valerie who made a Southern spectacle of herself, not me."

"You didn't push Val into the pool? Sweetie, you may be in need of some serious spin control, because word is out already about your alleged misdeed."

"She slipped and fell without a bit of help from me," Jenny protested. "She was drunk, dammit! Do I have to hire my own boss to defend me?"

"Whoa, Jen," Lissa backpedaled. "Valerie can have a mouth on her. I wouldn't be surprised to hear she gets pushed into pools on a daily basis. To tell the truth, when I first heard it I thought it was funny."

"Funny or not, I didn't push her," Jenny persisted. "Where'd you hear this, anyway?"

"Connie Donovan's phone tree. One of the first women she phoned was Delia."

"Delia? How did you hear this from Delia?"

The pause on the other end seemed to last longer than it actually did. "Um-m-m, you remember when I said I was spending the weekend with family? I may have prevaricated just a bit. Actually, I spent it with Delia. To be more precise, I'm at her house right now."

"Delia?" Jenny dumbly repeated. "How did this happen?"

"It's a long story, and I'd rather not get into it over the phone." Lissa hurried on, "What about you and Ian? Second part of the story has you two doing a Houdini just before the door prizes. Or is this more yellow journalism?"

"No," Jenny admitted. "That part is true. Ian was really sweet, trying to take my mind off the—mishap."

"Haven't ever heard anything really bad about him, though he's a skosh too skinny for me," Lissa considered. "Whatever you do, I hope you're careful."

"Lis! I'm no babe in the woods. Besides, we didn't do anything."

As if in rebuttal, Clouseau started making kissing sounds.

"Well, just remember my advice when you're ready to be a bit less innocent."

"Thanks, mom."

"Hey, if your mother was capable of talking like this without getting all high strikey, I wouldn't have to be doing it."

"Ain't that the truth?" Jenny sighed.

THE CADRE OF CLASSMATES on the TV screen attentively watched as their instructor hustled them through a busy Florence market. In the midst of this group was Joe's favorite, a midsized twenty-something whose demeanor promised something special once she graduated cooking school and took over her own kitchen. Encased in a lightweight floral frock, she was small compared to Misty, but clearly had plenty of potential. You could tell by the passion in her eyes.

When the phone rang he turned down the volume but continued to keep his eyes on the TV. He'd watched this videotape, *Cook's Tour: Italy*, a dozen times and anticipated every moment the lovely student appeared, a serious expression on her dimpled face. Once he realized the call was from Misty, he muted the tape completely.

"Talked to Dex about your gourmet dinner," Misty told him. "It's going to be the big ticket item in our charity raffle. Think you can do a dinner over the holidays?"

"I'd need to set things up as soon as possible," Joe mused. "Already I've been getting some grief at the restaurant for taking so much weekend night time off."

"Not a problem, is it?" Misty asked. "I wouldn't want you to get into any trouble at work."

"I won't. But I'll probably have to beg off the next dance."

"You won't be able to make it to the Harvest Moon Hoedown?" Misty groaned in mock dismay. "The chapter's first country-western dance! I was dying to see you in leather. Chaps, that is," she chuckled. "How's your line dancing?"

"No idea. My culture's south of the border—I can do the Macarena."

On the screen his Italian beauty was examining a cart of fresh scallops. Her fleshy arms were crossed; her eyes sparkled hungrily. Though he knew this moment by heart, Joe momentarily forgot where he was in the conversation. For an instant Misty's face superimposed itself over the cooking student's.

"That's nothing to brag about," she teased, unaware of his mental mix 'n' match game. The video was eight years old; he bet the young girl had caught up to Misty by now—maybe even surpassed her. But wait—he was in the middle of a conversation here! Joe turned back to the phone.

"I think I've just been insulted," he accused, cued by the sound of Misty's chuckling.

"No," she answered. "I just think of you as the close-dance type. At least, I like to think of you that way."

Joe stopped the tape, no longer willing to be distracted by a VCR fantasy.

EPISODE TWENTY-TWO

IT ONLY TOOK JACKIE A WEEK to crack Webstodian.

The program's Achilles' heel was its password. Using software he'd downloaded off a hacker site several months before, the twelve-year-old cyberpunk was able to retrieve it from a hidden cache in his dad's computer. The trickiest part had been finding the right moment to sneak unobserved into Dex's study.

Saturday morning he saw his chance and seized it—Dad out getting some coffeehouse pastry, Mom in the shower, his lazy-ass sister still in bed. He had more than enough time to get in and out. Like he was a spy or something, he gloated as he jotted Dex's password onto a Post-it note. It'd only taken five minutes, so he killed some time rummaging through Dex's desk for anything of interest. He found a packet of photos in a drawer, and as soon as he checked out the first one he knew he'd hit paydirt. Swimsuit shots from the chapter pool party! His hands shook with excitement as he flipped through the pack, waiting for Dex's snapshot scanner to warm.

Midway into the pile of pix he uncovered the Mother Lode: a head shot of his father beard-to-cheek with that lady Eleanor. From the way the two were posed it looked like he was getting ready to nibble on her ear. Forget swimsuits! This was way cooler.

Hastily Jackie slid the photo face down into the scanner, transferring the image onto diskette. After quickly returning the pile of photos to the drawer he raced upstairs to play with his prize.

"COME ON, BOSS LADY! It's been more than a week, and you still haven't given me the scoop on Delia."

"Can't hear you," Lissa shouted, turning on the Green Machine and applying it to a puddle in the break room. They'd arrived at work after the weekend to discover that the water cooler had sprung one of those pernicious pinprick leaks that only manifest themselves once the bottle is opened and upended. The carpet was a soggy mess, the office swampy smelling.

Jenny pulled a wastecan out of Lissa's path and placed it on a counter, then waited for her boss to shut off the motor. Raelette, the office receptionist, poked her head into the room, then wisely ducked out of sight. When Lissa finally rose there were great wet spots on the knees of her Big Mama hose.

"You shouldn't have to do this," Jenny tsked. "You're the one who needs to look best-dressed in this joint."

"I live here just as much as everyone else," Lissa answered, wrapping up the cord. "Anyway, what were you about to ask?"

"What's the delia with—I mean, the deal with Delia?"

Lissa made a come-hither gesture with her free hand, then carried the machine into the library. Shutting the door behind her, she began. "Delia phoned two me weeks after we had our little—disagreement at the business meeting," Lissa explained. "She wanted to discuss her legal options. For the last eight months, before all the news stories started coming out, she'd been taking that diet drug. Fen-phen."

"Good Lord, is she okay?"

"We still don't know. She hasn't gotten all the test results back yet from the pulmonary specialist. But she's been having trouble breathing." Lissa paused as she swung the carpet cleaner into its cabinet. "It could be simple anxiety, though.

"I don't know which aspect of Delia has given her more distress—her size or her orientation. But I never thought she'd be dumb enough to take that drug. There were warnings about it in the size acceptance community from the day it was introduced."

"A magic pill," Jenny sighed. "What's she been doing since the FDA removed the drug? Not trying that herbal crap, I hope."

"No," Lissa shook her head. "She's wised up that much, at least. Though from what Delia says, at least one other chapter member had been seeing the same doctor."

"Valerie!" Jenny realized.

"Now you know why I've been putting off telling you about all this," Lissa confirmed. "Val's refusing to believe the bad press the drug's gotten, so I don't know what she's doing now."

"You going to take the case?"

"Don't think it'd be ethical," Lissa answered, "now that we've renewed our relationship. I'm just hoping the test results will make a lawsuit unnecessary. You've never seen a relaxed Delia. Away from Connie, she's a much nicer person."

"In that case," Jenny said, "I'd like to get the chance to get to know her."

JOE DROVE STRAIGHT TO THE DANCE from work, so he was still wrapped in the delicious aroma of dinner. Misty was waiting for him outside the lounge. She was dressed like a gypsy from a traveling show, and was sitting alone at the ticket table. Only a few lonely stragglers were visible in the bar.

"So how was the Hoedown?" he asked, after savoring a long and very enjoyable hug.

"A real Hoedowner," she replied. "Guess we don't have a lot of Urban Cowtypes in this chapter." She grabbed her basket from under the table. "Offered to read cards for Halloween, but only got a couple of takers."

"You know, you've never offered to read my cards," Joe realized, offering to carry her basket.

"I can't read the cards of someone I'm too close to," Misty explained. "Need a clear head for a clear reading. You smell yummy, incidentally."

"Good enough to eat?" Joe asked.

"That's not something you ought to ask a gypsy on Halloween night," Misty joked, heading for the parking lot. "She might take you up on it, literally!"

A breeze from the street rose and sent chills through them both. Misty grabbed Joe's free arm and gave it a squeeze. "In pagan lore, tonight marks the beginning of winter," she noted. "A time when folks hunker down in their relationships. When the weather's cold, you want a warm body to snuggle."

"Snuggling's good," Joe declared offhandedly. He gave her a kiss before they got into their separate cars, and they both headed for the coffee shop.

Misty, he discovered, was a much faster driver than he. By the time he got there she was waiting outside Kuppa Joe'a's with a copy of the chapter newsletter rolled in her hand.

"Wanted to show you this," she said, handing him the latest issue of *RAD-FAm Round-up* as they walked inside. On the back half-page was an ad for the Charity Raffle. According to the blurb he was an "up-and-coming gourmet chef for a well-known downtown restaurant."

"Might be able to do New Year's Eve," he told Misty while they waited for their decaf. "I bet the boss gives us all the night off, since some old CIA cronies of his will be visiting. Traditionally they break into the wine cellar and then have a chef showdown."

"I didn't know CIA agents were gourmet cooks."

"Culinary Institute of America, silly. Meringues and canapés, not machine guns and karate chops."

"Dueling pastry bags! Much better." Misty picked at the streusel on her coffeecake muffin. "New Year's Eve," she mused, "a time of endings and beginnings."

KD LANG WAS SWOONING on the car stereo over a "Big Boned Gal" when Paul arrived at Connie's. Snapping off the tape, he smiled at the thought of Connie at the Sweetheart Dance, sashaying toward him with a sexy glint in her eyes. He wondered what she would have looked like in cowgirl denim, but Connie had begged off the Hoedown, claiming it just wasn't her style.

Sighing, Paul walked up her sidewalk. She'd given him her key the week before, but had passed when he'd offered her a copy of his. She'd only visited his apartment once in six months. Paul suspected that the golden retriever made her nervous. If they took this relationship to the next step, though, the Molly Issue would definitely have to be resolved. He couldn't leave his dog with the neighbors every day.

When he entered the duplex he found Connie in the kitchen on the phone, a computer paper list under her elbow. He bussed the back of her neck and she looked up to blow a kiss his way before continuing her conversation. Paul headed to the fridge for an O'Doul's.

"I really think this type of behavior needs to be firmly dealt with," Connie was telling her phone audience. "This girl's a new member, and I don't want her making these antics a regular part of our chapter activities."

The voice on the other end murmured what sounded like agreement.

"Well, it pretty much ruined the pool party for Paul and me," Connie continued. "I don't know who she thinks she is—" She trailed off to let the listener provide her own punchline. When they did, she barked her amusement. It was not, Paul decided, a pleasant sound. "Well, I have to wonder if the girl even has a place in our chapter," she finally said. The voice on the other end obviously had a few thoughts about that, too.

"Well, Paul just got here," she eventually said, as if seeing him for the first time. "We'll talk about this more later." Hanging up, she turned to Paul and cooed, "Got two more phone calls to make. Could you be a dear and give me a few more minutes?"

Sulking, Paul took his fake beer into living room. More than a month since the luau and Connie was still obsessing on it. Every time she replayed the Valerie Incident, she seemed to get more indignant. This was definitely a side of her that he didn't like.

"THE ONLY FA SITE YOU'LL EVER NEED" had been updated for the first time in months, but the additions turned out to be a collection of photos swiped from some of the paying sites. Ian was of two minds about this practice. As a longtime nethead he supported the idea that everything should be free on the Web; as an FA, he knew that fat modeling was not a very profitable proposition.

He was about to hit his default home page ("Where Big Is Beautiful") when the phone line rang. Though Ian had half been expecting this call, he still felt a start when he heard her voice.

"Ian?" Val began. "It took me six weeks, but I finally got the nerve to call and apologize."

"No need to apologize to me," he said. "I'm not the one you were rude to."

"I know," she agreed, chastened. "You want to know the truth? I kind of surprised myself. It was okay as long as you weren't seeing anybody. I had no idea I'd get so weird with the first woman you started dating. But once I heard about you and her, it was all I could think about. I'm okay now, though, and would like to make it up to both of you sometime."

"I'll pass that on to Jenny," Ian replied, "but perhaps you should talk to her, too, personally."

"I intend to," Val assured him. "By the way, I assume you and her have plans for Thanksgiving?"

"Actually, we do. Why do you ask?"

"No reason," Val answered. She paused, and Ian could hear The Carpenters playing in the background. Val always played Karen and brother Richard when she was feeling low. For an instant he almost considered telling her that he really didn't having anything going on for Thanksgiving. But that impulse passed quickly.

EPISODE TWENTY-THREE

SOME KID CLEARLY OFF HIS RITALIN shot in front of Jenny, stepping painfully on her new blue flats in the process. Nothing like a day in a crowded mall at Xmastime to make you feel more graceless and bulky than usual. Add Mom to the mix, and you've got the extreme way to start off the season.

Tradition, Jenny sighed. Tradition sucked—and had since she'd first been towed in her mother's wake through the post-Turkey-Day shopping tsunami. "Christmas holiday doesn't start until St. Nick drives down the street at the end of the Macy's Parade," her mother invariably pronounced, and to literalize this belief she held off gift shopping until the stores were at their most frenzied. Though Jenny did most of her own gift shopping by mail, alas, she still felt obliged to go along with Alice. Let's hear it for Holiday Guilt.

"This is a darling little shop," her mother noted with a wave of her Virginia Slim, indicating a boutique with offerings Jenny wouldn't have worn even when she was young enough to match its demographic. "Too bad they only go up to a size sixteen."

Two quick counts to ten; deep cleansing breaths. "That's okay, Mom," Jenny finally said. "My wardrobe's in pretty good shape now. You don't need to get me anything."

Alice scrutinized her daughter—in stirrup pants and Venezia top—as if to say the evidence before her wasn't all that convincing. Alice was by no means a petite woman (one more argument in favor of genetics), but she'd never admitted that her size was anything more than a temporary inconvenience. A temporary inconvenience that she'd battled, bullied (and perhaps even bulimia-ed) for three decades. When Jenny had announced her intention to give up dieting last New Year, Alice had responded with her patented combination of histrionics and insult. "Giving up on yourself again?" she'd pronounced. "I shouldn't be surprised."

Yet Alice had traditionally been the one pushing food at Jenny every chance she got. Thanksgiving was a prime example. Though Dad had been out of the picture for fifteen years, she still cooked enough turkey breast, stuffing, mashed potatoes and broccoli casserole to feed a small platoon. Throughout dinner she'd incessantly offered seconds, as if dealing with a stubborn five-year-old reluctant to eat her vegetables.

"Whatever you say, dear," Alice demurred, barging forth once more through the mall, holding out her lit cigarette as if brandishing a cattle prod. "Just thought you might want to wear something more—flattering to your figure. A girl needs to be conscious of those figure flaws."

"Ian seems to like my figure okay," Jenny muttered, and though her mother was known for not hearing what Jenny wanted to hear, Alice stopped abruptly and turned to her daughter.

"Ian? Who's Ian?"

"Just this guy I've been dating from the chapter, Mom."

"The chapter!" Alice spat this last with the same tone of distaste she usually reserved for her ex. "So when was I going to hear about this young man? Before or after the wedding?" She collapsed against a concrete bench, unmindful of the other occupant's packages, then began to fan herself with her cigarette hand. The bench's co-inhabitant began to cough pointedly, but Alice ignored it.

"Mom!" Jenny cried in exasperation. "It's not that serious. Ian's just a nice man I met through RADFAm. Don't try to make it more than it is."

"You've got to watch out for men like that," Alice advised sagely. "Most of them will think you're easy just because you're a big gal. Don't sell yourself short."

"I'm not, Mom," Jenny assured her, though she suspected Alice didn't believe her. "Ian is a gentleman."

"He's not gay, is he?" her mother demanded above the din.

Jenny slowly shook her head, which was throbbing to the rhythms of the holiday Muzak.

"THANKS FOR HAVING ME OVER," Paul said as he stood in the doorway.

"You kidding?" Ian responded. "It's not often I get to gab with another FA. One of the reasons I like being membership secretary." He led Paul into his condo, then offered a can of Cherry 7UP from the shelf of his fridge. "So what did you want to know about the chapter?" he asked.

"This and that," Paul said vaguely, lowering himself onto a living room futon. He had phoned Ian earlier in the week with the intent of passing on a warning to his girlfriend. But now that he'd arrived, he wasn't sure how to proceed.

"I assume Connie's given you some chapter history already," Ian ventured.

"Actually, no," Paul told him. "She doesn't talk about RADFAm much with me. I'm not sure why." Particularly, he mentally added, when she seemed ready to discuss chapter politics with everyone else and their cousin.

"Well," Ian began. "We're one of the longest running chapters in the organization. New York's the oldest, of course, since that's where the group's founders all originated…"

After fifteen minutes of history, Paul was eager to return to the present. His eyes kept drifting to the screensaver on Ian's computer, a Terry Gilliam cartoon of a tiny man bouncing on the belly of a massive grinning beauty. "From what I've seen," he interrupted, "we've got a pretty active chapter."

Ian took the interruption in stride. "Active on the social level," he agreed, "but at times I think we fall down on activism." He indicated his computer terminal and added, "It's not just our chapter. Look at the Internet and you'll see a ton of social clubs, chat rooms and so on. But not much in terms of political action."

"Perhaps FAs and fat adults need to get used to themselves as social animals first," Paul suggested. "It's a radical step to say, 'Hey, I'm okay as I am.'"

"Maybe—but some of us have been saying that for years now." He shook his head, then slid over to the computer table. "You don't want to hear me rant," he said. "You familiar with the FA websites?"

"Not really," Paul admitted, moving to get a better glimpse of the screen while Ian logged onto his server.

"There are a lot of cool sites for the discerning FA," Ian explained as his default window started to pop up. Paul watched, fascinated, as Ian gave him a quickie cyber tour of the size acceptance world, until finally they hit the newsgroups.

"Let's look at one of the moderated groups," Ian decided. "The unmoderated ones are full of unsolicited ads," he explained as he honed in on a grouping entitled "alt.sex.no-feeders." A list of postings started to roll up on the screen. "This is a good one," Ian explained. "The moderator is a bit cranky—given to RADFAm bashing at times—but the debates are lively."

He started to scroll down the list until they both saw an intriguing tagline: "RADFAm leadership in action." Ian clicked on the item, and to their amazement a face shot of Dex and Eleanor opened onto the screen. The two looked embarrassingly close. Added to the image was a cartoon word balloon with the legend "Hmm! Your ear wax tastes just like chicken!"

"This," Ian observed, "is not good."

EPISODE TWENTY-FOUR

THE CALL FROM RADFAm NATIONAL came the day after Dex heard about the photo from Ian. He'd been half hoping all this hype about instant communication was hooey—that the posting would time-out before anyone outside of a few computer nerds had seen it. He'd forgotten this basic truth: Nothing travels as quickly or efficiently as embarrassing news.

"We received a complaint today about it," Dex was told. "She wouldn't identify herself, but she certainly was vocally indignant." A typical Connie ploy, Dex thought with a sinking feeling. He hated this political crap.

He eyed Jackie's Compaq, disconnected and lying forlornly in a corner of his study. It'd be a cold day in Hades when the boy got it back, he decided. Maybe he could donate it to the school system. Or sell it and buy manacles.

"I only just heard about it," he told the sweet-voiced woman on the other end of the line. "I suppose the first step is to contact the newsgroup's moderator and see if they'll remove the picture."

"Perhaps," he was told, "though the picture by itself is pretty innocuous. Best thing might be just to ignore it. The more fuss you make about something like this, the longer a shelf life it has."

Dex fingered his beard irritably, then took a deep breath. This was what he deserved for letting a piece of software do his parenting for him. In the future, they'd be keeping Jackie's computer downstairs in plain sight.

When he finally hung up, he found Neeko watching him from the study doorway.

"Something wrong?" she asked, so Dex gave her the full story. "You told me yesterday," she said when he'd finished, "that our son was being grounded for getting back on adult sites—not for posting some photo."

"A half-truth," Dex admitted, feeling his face flush beneath his beard. "I didn't want you to get upset."

"Well, let's see it," Neeko decided, her voice dead calm, making it clear she would not accept anything but "okay" for an answer.

"Okay," Dex acquiesced. He swiveled his chair to start the computer. Though Ian had upgraded the Acer for him less than a month ago, the machine seemed to crawl. It growled ominously as Dex double-clicked to the newsgroup.

When the offending photo finally appeared on the monitor, Neeko took one look, hissed, and disappeared from the study.

Hefting himself from his chair, Dex tried to follow. But she was much too fast, and he'd never been built for speed. Grabbing her coat from the foyer closet, Neeko dashed out of the house and into their Plymouth Voyager. She was backing out of the driveway when he got to the front door.

She hadn't uttered a single word, a sure sign she was really angry.

Trudging back to his study, Dex glared at the photo on his monitor. A few years back he remembered seeing a sci-fi movie about a town whose citizens had lost control of all their violent impulses. Good thing he wasn't in that movie now, or he'd have taken Jackie's Louisville slugger to the computerized image.

"This too will pass," he told himself. One advantage of middle age was the realization that most indignities are transient. He wished he could have spared Neeko this humiliation, though—and Eleanor, too, for that matter.

He still hadn't called Eleanor to tell her about the picture. Dex wasn't relishing the task, but if he didn't do it she was sure to get blindsided at the chapter Christmas party, which Eleanor was hosting.

The phone rang as he was pulling her number from the cardfile. "What now?" Dex huffed as he lifted the receiver. The voice on the other end was nearly enough to wipe out his composure for the remainder of this too-long-day.

"Logan? This is Greg Dillman. I understand you're circulating one of my photos without my permission."

"SO WHAT ARE YOU GIVING OUR CHEF for Candlemas?" Kirk teased, holding up a Caprial cooking video. "Twenty-five extra pounds in a formfitting dress, *peut-etre?*"

Misty grimaced, then pulled a rental tape off the rack. "We haven't seen this one yet," she offered.

Kirk eyed the title and guffawed. It was a copy of *Big Night*. "Oh, I get it," he said, "handsome cooks and a food orgy on film! Getting in the mood for a date with Chef Encourager? Is he as good in any room beside the kitchen?"

"Keep it up, smartass, and I won't invite you to help out with our 'big night,' the New Year's charity dinner," Misty threatened, heading for the musicals section.

"Big deal," Kirk shot back. "Some of us have better plans for the holidays, anyhoo. Yours truly is going on a cruise."

"Since when aren't you cruising?"

"Oh, ye of the ragged fag jokes," Kirk pronounced, waving a copy of *Follow the Fleet* from its slot. "This is my idea of travel—a 'teddy-bear' cruise to the Caymans for bulky boys and the guys who lust for 'em. If all goes according to schedule, you won't be the only one getting lucky on New Year's Eve."

"What makes you think I intend to do anything on New Year's?" she bristled.

"Mist," Kirk clucked, grabbing her free hand. "It's time to get serious. It's obvious that our culinary suitor hasn't made the moves yet. I know the Seven Warning Signs of Celibacy—and lady, you're flashing eight of 'em."

"Pshaw," Misty answered, "you're projecting."

"Am I? Then riddle me this, girlfriend: How come you haven't missed a weekend breakfast with your handsome gay neighbor yet? Keeping Joe locked in the bathroom? You know I'd love to watch him whip up something."

"I was expecting Joe to be a little more assertive," she confessed.

"Maybe he's just being a good Catholic boy. But remember, he's also a fledgling chubby chaser," Kirk said. He held up a copy of *Holiday Inn* and Misty nodded in agreement.

"No *White Christmas*?" she couldn't resist asking, knowing Kirk's views on that holiday flick.

"Must be out of stock," he mock pouted, pointedly hiding its box. "This is by far the superior film—why do you persist in asking for that drivel?"

"*Holiday Inn* doesn't have Danny Kaye," Misty answered. "Guess I've been a fag hag from birth and beyond."

"No comment," Kirk replied, piling a copy of *Gypsy* on top of the Crosby/Astaire tape. "Let's return to the subject at hand. You've got to make the first move with Joe. He's probably afraid that the first time he does anything, you'll bolt and run."

"Bolt and run? Me? Hardly likely."

"In relationships, it's easy to flee without even moving," Kirk said, leading her back to the cashier's counter. "He may be a novice, but it's clear he's no fool. I think this guy's showing a lot of sensitivity."

"Yeah," Misty admitted, "but sometimes sensitivity can be a totally frustrating pain in the ass."

EPISODE TWENTY–FIVE

DURING THEIR DRIVE TO ELEANOR'S, Jenny pumped Ian on chapter member histories. He had a different perspective than Lissa, in some ways more objective. The information was so fascinating that she barely noticed where they were going. Once she did, however, she was startled by how upscale the neighborhood looked.

"I didn't know Eleanor lived out here," Jenny marveled as they passed a snow-covered country club course. To the right, tastefully overdecorated homes glistened in the night like something out of a John Hughes movie.

"Her husband was a wheel in local real estate," Ian explained as he turned into a long circular driveway. "Made a killing in the mall boom. He died about ten years ago. It wasn't until his death that Eleanor found the size acceptance movement. I guess George Bollin wasn't the most progressive of guys."

Eleanor's house was an elegant split-level with plenty of tall window work. From the driveway Jenny could see a RADFAm-sized silhouette through the translucent draperies. A few cars were parked in the circle; on the front porch a concrete goose roosted, dressed in Santa garb.

Bedecked in a glittering red top and black silk pants, Jenny stepped from Ian's four-wheel Geo into the brisk night. It was warm enough to do without a coat from the car to the house, and since her winter parka definitely clashed with the rest of her Jenny left it on the car seat.

Eleanor answered the door looking like old money. She smiled graciously at Ian and Jenny. "So good that you could come," she greeted the couple nervously, stepping back to let them enter. They followed her up two steps into the living room, which was warmly lit and sparsely populated. On an old-fashioned ivory console stereo Fred Waring and his Pennsylvanians were dashing through the snow.

"You have such a lovely place," Jenny told their hostess as they passed a fullsized Christmas tree crammed with fragile glass decorations.

"It's a bit too big for me," Eleanor admitted, "but I can't imagine living anywhere else. I spend most of my time downstairs in the study, though. It's where I do the newsletter and watch my soaps."

"I didn't know you were an addict," Jenny said. "I used to be a soap fiend when I was an undergrad. Never used to like watching the Christmas episodes, though. Everything slows down—they all stand around, being nice to each other in the name of the season. That's not what you watch soaps for."

"I always like the Christmas episodes," Eleanor responded. "After all the characters go through in a year, they deserve a day of relaxation."

"More likely the writers deserve a day of lazy writing," Ian said with a grin.

"Maybe," Eleanor admitted, "but when you're really involved in a story, you don't remember there are writers involved." The doorbell rang and she turned to answer it. "Enjoy yourselves, you two," she smiled as she walked off to the foyer to greet her newest guests.

Though they'd arrived a half hour after its starting time, the party was still pretty sedate. Dex stood off by himself, lost in thought, looking uncomfortable in a tux. At the hors d'oeuvre table Lainie and Joyce waved welcomingly. Another trio of vaguely familiar faces looked their way with less enthusiasm. From an offstage kitchen Jenny could hear Lissa's voice, among others.

"Thought we'd see more people," she ventured to Ian, who was doing his best dressup in a Norman Rockwell Santa tie, blue shirt and Dockers.

"Greg Dillman's new social group, Full-Figured Friends, is having its first dance tonight," Ian explained, honing in on the appetizers (like many single men his age, he ate like a teenager and still managed to stay skinny). "I think we're mainly going to get the old guard here tonight."

So perhaps Valerie would be at the dance, Jenny hoped. Ian had told her about Val's phone apology, although to date she hadn't received anything from the woman herself. The thought of running into Valerie had almost kept her from coming tonight.

"Happy holidays," Lainie told them from behind the punch bowl. "Whatever you do, don't skip the stuffed mushrooms."

Jenny eyed the expensive-looking spread of appetizers, trying to gauge which would do the least damage on her blouse. "You surviving the holidays?" she asked.

"It's not hard," the older woman told her with a grin. "I just double my daily dose of Vitamin B and stay out of shopping malls. The key to a successful holiday—that, plus keeping your kids a couple thousand miles away."

"That sounds like a dream," Dex said, joining the conversation. The rest of the group chuckled awkwardly. From the stereo Liberace was reciting Clement Moore's Christmas poem over syrupy orchestration. In another home it would have sounded ironic; in Eleanor's, it somehow fit.

"I miss my grandkids," Lainie said, "but not at Chanukah. I'd rather catch 'em on my own terms in limited dosages. This *bubbe* doesn't do group family gatherings if she can help it."

According to Ian, Lainie was married to the owner of a small machine parts company in the Northwest suburbs. He rarely showed at chapter events, but was supportive of his wife's involvement in RADFAm. Probably knew better than to stand in Lainie's way.

"Stay away from stores," Jenny sighed, spreading crab and cream cheese on a Town House cracker. "Wish I could convince my mom to do that. Less than a week from Christmas and she's still calling up, complaining about how she can't find everything she wants."

"Some people thrive on holiday chaos," Lainie said.

As if on cue, Connie Donovan entered the room. "Well," she opened, zeroing in on Jenny. "What have you got planned for tonight's entertainment? Pushing the tree over on someone?"

PAUL WAS NO NOSTRADAMUS. But once Connie realized who was in the living room, even he could see disaster was inevitable. Shrugging her coat into his hands without so much as a backward glance, she'd thundered up the stairs and headed for the appetizer table, leaving Paul and Eleanor in her wake.

"Where's the closet?" he blurted, all but dropping Connie's fur to the floor in his haste to hang it up quickly. When he got to the table Connie was asking Dex if he intended to do anything about "this situation."

"Which situation?" Logan asked—calmly, but with an edge to his voice that would have warned off anybody but Connie.

"This girl," she answered, black beaded dress swirling dramatically as she focused on Jenny, "assaulted another member of our chapter! That's inexcusable behavior."

"Now wait a minute," Dex began, "from what I gather, it was an accident."

"Accident my ass!" Connie spat. "You forget I was there as a witness."

The room suddenly grew crowded as people from the kitchen spilled in to watch the show. Delia, Paul noticed, kept herself back from the scene, though her companion, a striking mid-sized black woman in a sharply cut tuxedo of her own, was pushing her way to the table.

"This isn't a formal meeting, Connie," the chapter president said. "It's no place for chapter business. This is a Christmas party."

"That may be," Connie shot back, "but I want to have it publicly known that I can't approve of the way this chapter's going. If we don't want RAD-FAm to become a public laughing stock, we've got to police ourselves."

"I don't disagree with your sentiments," Dex began, "but this is hardly the place—"

And I'm not the only one who feels this way either," Connie interrupted, looking to the rest of the room for support. Several heads nodded vigorously.

"But I didn't push her in the pool!" Jenny suddenly cried out, stepping forward and reinserting herself in the spotlight. "And if Valerie were here, she could tell you that herself!"

The look of disdain that Connie put on her face was broad enough to play to a Broadway theater. It was also enough to prod Paul into action.

"She's right," he said, stepping from behind Connie. "I also saw what happened. Valerie fell by herself. This young lady didn't come close enough to push her."

"Paul—" Connie began, putting an arm across his back as if to rope him in.

"Let him finish," Lissa put in, while an unseen voice murmured her agreement.

"Really, dear," he told her and the rest of the room, "I know what it may have looked like from your chair, but I had a good, clear view. I'm sorry you didn't ask me about it earlier, but I can see how you could have made the mistake." He gave her an affectionate squeeze back, but from her frozen posture he could tell it wasn't being appreciated.

"Was there anything else you wanted to bring up?" Dex asked, but Connie shook her head. "Well," Dex boomed jovially, sounding like some kindly figure from Dickens, "it was all just a misunderstanding, then." He looked around the room, saw the crowd starting to relax and announced, "Our chef hasn't arrived yet, but since most of us all seem to be here, why don't we hold the drawing for our Charity Dinner?"

It was at least an hour before Jenny could get to Paul alone in the kitchen. While he'd pretty well blended into the background at the luau, he'd clearly piqued everyone's interest tonight. Sensing a crack in his connection to Connie, more than one distaff chapter member made a point of introducing herself. Joyce had been brazenly flirtatious with him, but Jenny noticed that she'd only done it out of Connie's view.

"I wanted to thank you," she began as he intently perused a row of soda cans on the counter. "That can't have been an easy thing to do."

He turned to face her and smiled wryly, his face looking even craggier than normal. She wasn't much into the cowboy look—the men who attracted her typically looked nerdy like Ian—but she could see how a woman might fall for this guy. His eyes had a sensitive, boyish quality that alleviated any severity his face might have possessed.

"Wish I'd had the opportunity to correct this earlier," he said, pouring himself a plastic wine glass of raspberry club soda. "I know how these kinds of stories can spread."

"You did what you could," Jenny reassured him. "Ian told me about your visit a couple of weeks ago. You obviously were trying to head things off. But Connie's not the kind of person you can head off."

"She is a force of nature," Paul said, taking a long swig from his glass as if it was something more potent. "Nice to see your boss win the New Year's dinner," he continued. "From what Ian tells me, she gives a lot to the chapter."

"Things going to be okay with you and Connie?" Jenny persisted.

"Probably not," he replied, "but I think things were heading in that direction anyway."

Impulsively she grabbed his hand and was shocked by a surge of static electricity, but held on. "Well, again," she said, "thanks." She squeezed his hand, then turned to get back to Ian.

"Merry Christmas," Paul replied, raising his wine glass in a toast.

THOUGH THE TRIP BACK TO CONNIE'S was tensely silent, Paul still wasn't sure how it would end.

They'd pointedly stayed away from each other throughout the rest of the party, Connie holding court by the fireplace, Paul hanging out in the kitchen. It was not like he was being exiled—plenty of partygoers seemed eager to introduce themselves. At one point Joe, who'd arrived at the party late with Misty, came up to him and gave him one of those companionable guy punches on the shoulder. "I heard what you did earlier," he said. "I think I had the wrong idea about you." He walked off without further elaboration.

Still, it felt like some sort of invisible iron curtain had fallen over the party. In correcting Connie, he'd somehow managed to irrevocably define himself in ways that weren't yet clear to him.

It was lightly snowing when they arrived at her place, one of those light sugar donut powderings that had no staying power. The streetlights were gar-landed with flameproof faux evergreens, the row of townhouses uniformly decorated with blinking lights. It had gotten at least fifteen degrees colder since they'd left for the party.

Paul got out, holding his unzipped coat together with a single gloved hand, and hurried to open the passenger door. It was one of those gestures she usually appreciated, but tonight she'd have none of it.

Still seated, Connie crossed her arms over her ample front and said accus-ingly, "You didn't support me, Paul." In the parking lot light all softness had left her face. Her voice was as clipped as a British newscaster's.

"Yes," Paul slowly answered. "I know it may seem that way—"

"Bullshit," Connie snapped, swinging her legs toward the pavement. "It *is* that way." She grabbed the edge of the door, ignoring the hand outstretched to help her, and hefted herself out of the car. "'I can see how you could have made the mistake,'" she sneered. "Who did you think you were pacifying with that crock?"

She slammed the door with her hip, then turned away from him. "Good-bye, Paul," she said.

He watched her hustle up the sidewalk dismissively, limned by the blink-ing lights, and a sick feeling washed over him.

EPISODE TWENTY–SIX

LISSA'S KITCHEN WASN'T EXPANSIVE, but it was nicely equipped and roomy enough for both Misty and Joe. They'd been given the run of her lakeshore apartment and had worked on preparation most of the evening. Every once in a while Lissa or Delia popped her head in, but Joe politely shooed them off.

Misty was still blown away by the new Delia. "Ever since I've been in the chapter," she whispered to Joe at one point, "she and Lissa acted like mortal enemies. Who'd have thunk they had a history? Or that they'd be able to keep it from the rest of the chapter?"

"Nice to know some secrets are still possible," Joe observed from the cut-ting board. In his pressed white chef's uniform he looked more urbane than Misty could ever remember seeing. Obviously she was a sucker for a man in a uniform. "I sure don't want the chapter yammering about my life. It's nuts—just look at how ballistic some folks got over that stupid photo."

"I know," Misty sighed. Perched on a sturdy white oak stool, she was plucking plump purple grapes and placing them by the dozen into tiny silver baskets. "Chapter politics can be a pain, particularly when you consider some of the personalities in our little group. I wouldn't be surprised if either Dex or Eleanor decided to call it quits. You can just bet Connie would love to step back in." She shuddered, then took an orphan grape and flicked it into her mouth for comfort.

"Got to be hard for Delia," Joe considered, "still working at Connie's boutique—what's it called? InFatuation? Wonder how she manages it."

"Can't be easy," Misty agreed. "But then I've always been my own boss. I don't know how anybody works under someone else without ultimately going postal."

Joe thought for a minute about Caspar, who'd been nothing but good to him, and shrugged. "Must be the way you're built," he decided, running a colander of shrimp under cold water.

"What's my body got to do with this?" Misty asked flirtatiously. She vogued like a model in a plus-size pantyhose commercial, her tie-dye dress framing her substantial but still insufficient apron.

"Not a thing," Joe grinned. "And you'll get no complaints from me for showing it off."

GOLDEN MOLLY WAS STILL EYEING PAUL suspiciously, as if to ask "who's this stranger staying up so late with me?" Paul didn't blame her; he deserved her doggy chastisement for abandoning her over so many weekends. Still, the silky retriever didn't hold a grudge for long. Once he pulled out a large beef-basted Chew-eez she was all wags and bounces.

Too bad Connie wasn't as easily won over. She'd rebuffed his phone calls all week. At one point when he tried to get her at the boutique, she'd informed the shop assistant who'd answered the call— in a voice loud enough to carry over Paul's receiver—that she had nothing to say to him. She was using her answering machine to screen out his calls at home, too.

It should have been frustrating, but it oddly wasn't. Paul remembered his first big breakup in college—how he'd made a real pest of himself, moping around, wallowing in self-pity. Night after night he'd spent hanging outside his ex-'s dorm window, hoping she'd spy him and guiltily call him back into her life. These days that kind of behavior could get you arrested for stalking. Back then it'd seemed like the Byronic thing to do.

Of course he'd been drinking quite a bit in college. His repertoire of healthy coping behaviors had been pretty spare.

This was different, though. For some reason the thought of breaking up with Connie wasn't as distressing as he thought it would be. It was just that with all these empty days off from school, the unresolved tension nettled him like a deeply embedded splinter.

On the tube Dick Clark was getting ready to rev up for another rockin' New Year's Eve. Rising from the floor, Paul headed to the kitchen for a can of O'Doul's. Molly happily followed with the leather chew chip in her mouth.

He couldn't help but wonder what Connie was doing at that moment.

As Jenny expected, Lissa had not been able to countenance Joe and Misty's absence from the festivities. It made things a little close—even with the leaf added, four RADFAm women and two average-sized adult men took up the entire perimeter of the oak table. "It stimulates togetherness," Lissa nonchalantly observed. "Just think of it as cozy."

Joe's main course, *chorizo con huevos,* had been a success. ("A symbol of new things," Misty had noted at one point. This was the sort of evening you could get away with that kind of talk.)

The television was visible from the dining area. With the sound off and Bessie Smith on the stereo, the Times Square ball was waiting its moment in the limelight. All over the country people would be focusing on this tacky symbol of fresh beginnings. Looking over at Ian, Jenny wondered what the New Year would bring.

At least the old one was going out on a good note—Delia had come through her medical tests with flying colors.

"The problem I was having breathing," she explained to the table as Misty passed out the mysterious baskets of grapes, "turned out to be anxiety-related, after all. Got a clean bill of health." She paused, took a sip of pink champagne, then smiled at Lissa. The look transformed her plain face into something almost angelic. "Of course my personal physician still thinks I need to lose weight."

"This from the ass who prescribed fen/phen in the first place," Lissa snorted. "I think you need to change GPs."

Delia leaned over and patted Lissa's hand. "No argument there," she agreed, and the look of irritation passed from the face of Jenny's boss. Delia kissed Lissa on the cheek.

Next to Jenny, Ian was fidgeting. A bit of homophobia, perhaps? No, that wasn't it—Jenny turned to see Ian pull a vibrating pager from the inner pocket of his sports jacket. *Don't let him be called out,* she mentally prayed to the god of technical support staff.

"Call from work?" she asked, holding her breath.

Ian squinted at the pager number in the candlelight, then decisively shoved the device back into his jacket. "Nothing that needs to be handled now," he told the table, and Jenny exhaled audibly. "Anybody making any resolutions for the New Year?" he asked the table.

"Outside of signing up for Jenny Craig, you mean?" Lissa joked.

"Holiday guilt and television," Jenny joined in. "Best way I know to ruin your New Year is with a futile diet."

"Almost midnight," Joe announced, bringing in a large box from the kitchen. Clearing some space on the buffet, he pulled out a large, encased Westminster clock.

"I was wondering what that was," Lissa said. "Isn't Times Square sufficient?"

"The ball isn't always accurate—it was two seconds late in '97. Besides, Times Square doesn't chime," Joe explained. "This is an old New Year's tradition from my family. See those baskets of grapes? When the clock chimes, you take a grape and eat it. Do this through all twelve chimes and you'll have a great year."

"Are those seedless?" Ian asked. "I'd hate to choke to death on a pit."

"Wouldn't that put a damper on your New Year?" Jenny chuckled as she picked up her basket.

"I hate when that happens," Lissa laughed.

"Get ready," Joe directed. So the couples turned their seats to face each other and waited for the first chime. When it came, they each popped a grape into their own mouths. By the sixth grape they all were feeding grapes to each other.

"Looks like we'll be making it a good year together," Ian whispered to Jenny when the final stroke of midnight had passed.

"THANKS FOR THE LOAN OF THE CLOCK," Joe said to Misty as they finished packing up his cooking supplies. Beyond the kitchen door he could hear Ian and Jenny leaving. Misty folded her apron and gently placed it atop his cooking gear. In the bright kitchen light she looked more beautiful than even Joe would have expected—more substantial, more provocative, more womanly.

"Glad to do it," she replied, and before Joe could say anything she moved up to him. He felt her press against him, her soft arms surrounding him, and the two kissed slowly. It was nearly overwhelming, but Joe held on and relished the sensation.

"I'm being a brazen hussy," Misty said when they finally separated. "Hope you don't mind."

"Mind?" Joe croaked, and he stepped back in for an even longer replay. Halfway into this second kiss Delia stepped into—then quietly backed out of—the kitchen. "Not a bit," he said when they uncoupled a second time.

"This really is going to be a New Year," Misty stated, fanning her face happily with a plump hand. At the top of her dress neckline Joe could see the start of a revealing blush. "What would you say to making this a long night? Together?"

EPISODE TWENTY–SEVEN

"**D**RAT," MISTY KVETCHED as she unlocked Kirk's front door. It would have been so easy to blow off checking on Howland, his seriously dysfunctional dachshund. But while fetching OJ and champagne for wakeup mimosas she caught sight of his postcard on the fridge—a vivid montage of hibiscus, tropical scenery and semi-nude sun worshippers. The note was equally exuberant:

> Ahoy! Hoist up the John B. sails! Plenty of Captains Courageous here on board to offer a paddle if I'm upstream without! Huggles and kisses to my favorite goddess and the mighty mutt. 'See you next Wednesday.' (Actually Sunday!)
>
> Love, Kirk

After beating off the shrieking whirlwind that was Howlie lonely, Misty made a cursory exam of the apartment. Kirk still had his holiday decorations up. This wasn't at all unusual; he always left them up past Martin Luther King Day. Poised on the TV an impressive United Design mountain man Kris Kringle, clad in buckskin and leather, strode up his resin summit surrounded by woodland critters, one hand caressing a grizzly bear and the other grasping a rugged staff. Misty admired this handsome vignette (the perfect symbol of her friend's bear-loving propensities, and what about that phallic walking stick?) as she aimed the watering can at a pot of parched poinsettias. Last of the plants—she'd already tended to the hound's culinary requirements and stuffed the soiled sani-pad provided for his privy into a garbage pail for future disposal. (Doggie diapers—what would you expect from an agoraphobic wiener dog?) With luck, she'd still find Joe warmly snuggled under the covers back at her place.

The scent of melted butter told her that she'd dallied too long next door. In the kitchen she saw Joe making crepe batter, a bowl of blueberries and container of sour cream waiting to be stuffed. He smiled as she came into view, and that glance banished any misgivings she might have had about his presumptuousness. Last night had been one stroke short of mythic.

"Happy 1997," Joe announced, backing away from the stove to kiss her hand. "Hope you're hungry."

She was, but she also had to get a niggling notion off her mind first. "Joe," she began, "could you please turn the heat down for a sec? We need to talk."

With a puzzled look he complied, then turned her way. "Something the matter?" he asked.

"Not yet," she replied carefully. "But I feel we share a common destiny, and New Year's morning is the perfect time to make sure we're on the same path."

"Go on."

"Joe, I really love being with you in every way, and last night was beyond wonderful! But I think we need to be clear about what kind of relationship we have. I like food, and I like an occasional dash of food play. But I also don't want to grow much bigger than I already am. So I hope you're not expecting anything like that from me."

Joe nodded slowly. "Is that what this is about?" he asked, a hint of dismay in his voice. "I shouldn't have made breakfast. Not without asking."

"Oh, no. It's sweet that you want to make me breakfast," Misty demurred, "and if that's all there is to it, I feel flattered. But please accept the fact that I'm not interested in just being some feeder's fondest fantasy."

She paused, clenching her hands on her wide hips, and hoped she wasn't being brutally blunt. Schmendrick, who had the catly knack of appearing in the middle of emotionally tense scenes, slipped under her caftan and started rubbing around her generous calves. For an eternally long minute the only sounds in the kitchen were his booming purr, the rhythmic tick of the cuckoo clock, the crackle of browning butter. Then Joe answered.

"I'd be lying if I said I didn't have my own FA fantasies," he replied, "but I also know the difference between fantasy and reality. Getting to know you has been the best thing to happen to me in years. I'd be a real idiot to ruin that."

Misty gratefully pulled Joe against her, and they twirled within a floury cloud. He dropped his spatula on the kitchen island and covered her face with blueberry kisses.

"I would love breakfast," Misty panted, "but do you think we could put it on the back burner just for the moment?"

Joe grinned and they rushed from the kitchen, abandoning the sour cream to an all-too-eager Schmendrick.

THE FIRST GOOD SNOW of the New Year had totally transformed the court behind Ian's condo. It made for good packing, so he and Jenny had taken advantage of it to fashion their own snowfolk. Jenny was still working on the face of hers when Ian asked for her critical scrutiny.

"What do you think?" He indicated the primitive snow goddess by his side.

"A new chapter recruit," Jenny chortled. "She's shaped like me—who'd have guessed I'd have so much in common with Frosty of Willendorf here?"

"Our bodies are mostly water," Ian answered. "So are theirs. You've never heard a snowman worry about his weight, though."

"Of course not, it's all water weight! But you might get a different response from a snow-fem. "

Ian peered around Jenny to get a closer look at her creation. "You should talk," he decided. "I've never seen one shaped like Lillian Russell before."

"Can I help it if you've lived a limited life?" Jenny shot back, grabbing a hand of snow and rubbing it into the open neck of his jacket.

Ian backed off quickly, grinning devilishly, then grabbed some snow of his own. "Shouldn't start something you're not prepared to finish," he mock snarled. In a matter of moments, they were both sopping wet.

"Truce!" Jenny finally called. Ian nodded in agreement, dislodging clumps of snow from his coat collar and hood.

After microwaving two cups of instant mochaccino they retired to the living room. On Ian's PC screen Jenny saw a series of floating purple Gaias—it was clear where Ian had gotten his inspiration.

"I'm so glad you could come over today," Ian said. "Did your mother call on New Year's after all?"

"Of course she did," Jenny told him, warming her palms around her mug. "Right in the middle of the Rose Parade. She'd have freaked if I weren't home to answer the phone."

"There will likely come a time," Ian pointed out, "when she can't get you. When you've been out, say, dancing all night with Fred Astaire. Or even me." He smiled nervously, as if worried that the last might seem pushy.

"I know that," Jenny said. "But I wouldn't want to sic my mother on anybody before they've had sufficient prep time."

"I'm not worried," Ian reassured her, then inched closer and slid his arm around her shoulder. She turned, and their lips met. It was, Jenny thought, so much more warming than her coffee had been.

Shutting her eyes, she gave in to the pleasant sensation of floating while rooted to the couch—until the sound of the phone brought her crashing back to reality.

"Ian," Valerie's voice cried over the answering machine. "I need you! I may be dying!"

EPISODE TWENTY-EIGHT

WHEN THE KUPPA WAITER brought her plate of tiramisu to the table Misty felt a slight guilt-twinge. She'd thought she had cast aside calorie-counting countless years past, but ever since talking with Joe two weeks ago she once more found herself perversely tabulating the dietary data. If she didn't watch out she'd be pulling her dusty old bathroom scale from the storeroom.

To make it even more confusing, she couldn't be sure a hidden agenda wasn't lurking behind all these calculations. Was she merely trying to be healthfully cautious? Or was some deep part of her actually considering acting out Joe's feeding fantasies? Perhaps ordering any food was a psychic gamble.

"Looks good," Dex told her, oblivious to her comestible conundrum. He still wore his winter parka, which of course cemented his mountain-man air in spite of the decidedly contemporary coffee mug in his hand.

"It is," Misty decided, casting aside her momentary doubt and grinning at the chapter president. "So good it makes one wonder if the food-pietists don't make a valid point when they insist scrumptious equals sinful."

Dex laughed as he dunked a biscotti into his mug of Jamaican Roast. "Let he who is without sin cast the first scone," he declared, brandishing his snack.

Misty smiled back. Though she generally favored smaller men than he, she'd had more than a few fantasies about Dex in the past. The man had the kind of generous spirit that she'd always found darned attractive.

"I don't remember any food fights in the New Testament," Misty commented.

"You've got to read between the lines," Dex assured her. Then, turning distractedly toward the door of the coffeehouse, he nodded and returned his gaze to Misty. "I need to discuss something important with you before the others get here."

"I figured as much when you asked me to come early," Misty replied, carefully slicing into her dessert.

"I'm not running for president in the spring election," Dex informed her. "I'd originally planned for one more year, but it's simply not something I can do right now."

"It has been a pretty stressful year for you," Misty affirmed.

"Politically and personally," Dex said. "So I've promised Neeko that I'll get out of chapter politics for a while. I need to spend more time with her and our son."

"You're a thoughtful father," Misty said. Her own father had been on the road so often that she could almost count the times spent with him on one hand.

"If I was, Jackie wouldn't be acting up just to get my attention," Dex responded. "You don't know how easy it is to lose track of your kids. The older you get, the quicker time goes. Yet for them, time is still crawling. It's that difference that makes it easy for you to become—disconnected."

"I've never been the parenting type," Misty told him. "I prefer to just borrow kids for a couple hours. They're easier to manage with the leverage of cutting your time short if they misbehave." She took another bite of tiramisu. "I don't need to be psychic to guess why you asked me here early for the officers' meeting," she continued. "But why me?"

"I think you'd make a good president," Dex answered simply. "You're experienced in the chapter, yet not aligned with any one group."

"That's me—Little Ms. Noncommittal."

You know what I mean. There are a lot of strong personalities in our group, and it takes a well-centered person to keep abreast of them all."

"I do have a good center of gravity," Misty said, patting her hips. "And am more abreast than most." Through the coffeeshop window she could see Ian heading for the entrance.

"Best way to get out of this job alive is to have a good sense of humor," Dex replied. "Don't give an answer now. Just think about it and get back to me."

"I will," she reassured him.

AFTER THE WATERCOOLER DEBACLE the kitchenette had retained a swampy smell, especially on humid days—Lissa threatened more than once to pull the carpet up herself, since the landlord had been slow to act—but with the microwave emitting the aroma of Progresso lentil soup, Jenny could just about ignore it. Pulling a resealable bag of low-fat mozzarella from the mini-fridge, she waited for the ding that signaled lunch was ready.

"Any word on Val yet?" Lissa inquired, dropping a bag of KFC (without the C) across the table from Jenny. She'd been asking the question daily, as if by doing this she could bring the answer out more quickly.

"Talked to Ian last night," Jenny said, "and Valerie still hasn't gone to the doctor yet. She keeps finding excuses not to go."

"It sounds to me like she's milking it," Lissa decided as she thumbed open her mashed potato container and started to pour chicken gravy on it. This was as close to vegetarian as Lissa got. "When Delia started worrying about the side effects from her fen/phen use, she had sense enough to get herself checked pretty quickly. What's Val waiting for?"

"I don't know," Jenny sighed. "It's really getting to Ian, though. She calls him at least once a day now, and he doesn't feel like he can hang up on her."

"How are you doing with this?" Lissa probed. "Looked to me like you and Ian were on the verge of something serious. Where are things now?"

"Still dangling on that verge," Jenny admitted. She lifted her soup spoon, twirling strands of mozzarella around it, then shrugged. "I can't compete with an afflicted former flame, now can I?" she said. "Nor would I want to."

"That's assuming she's not doing a Sarah Bernhardt," Lissa pointed out.

"You damn lawyers," Jenny grinned. "Always ready to believe the worst in people."

"Only the people I know personally," Lissa countered. "The rest could all be angels. I must note that Val has a tendency to get melodramatic, particularly when she drinks."

"I had noticed," Jenny said dryly.

"So you have." Lissa glanced up as the receptionist appeared in the doorway, looking grim.

"Delia's on the phone. I think you'd better talk to her."

Lissa rose, and Jenny eyed the receptionist questioningly. She knew better than to ask. Raelette shook her head slowly and returned to her desk. Jenny ate her soup and waited. From the outer area she could hear Tori Amos asking God if he needed a woman to look after him.

Finally her boss reappeared in the kitchenette.

"Delia's lost her job at the boutique," she announced. "Connie laid her off."

° EPISODE TWENTY-NINE

FRIENDS LOVE THE PERSON YOU WERE and the person you've become.' Sounds suitably Valentiney," Lissa commented, holding up the candy wrapper to read its message in the dim bar light.

"Not entirely true," Delia admitted, "but a nice thought."

"And you say you don't know who sent it to you?"

"Thought it was from you," Delia answered with a flirt, closely scrutinizing the lady lawyer as if trying to delve an answer from her bemused mocha face.

"Nope," Lissa parried, handing back the wrapper. Delia rubbed the foil wrinkles out against the table top, then carefully placed it in her right blouse pocket.

"So we've got a mystery," Delia concluded. "Message in a Dove bar nugget—comes in a kiddy valentine—no name or return address, just a city postmark. I assumed you sent it."

Lissa shook her head. "I know your propensity for milk, not dark, chocolate. Besides, much as I'd like to take credit, babe, my own wrapper says 'You work too hard—promise yourself a reward.'" Then, frowning slightly, she added, "The sentiment's sweet—or at least semi. But the lawyer part of me knows better than to accept unsolicited rewards, so I chucked the chocolate."

"One thing's for sure—Connie didn't send it." Delia lifted her glass of white Zinfandel, considering the liquid's texture for a second. "She's made it clear she has no use for the woman I've become."

"The woman you always were," Lissa amended. "Plus she has no use for altruism unless it's in her own self interest."

Delia nodded. She looked around the Figs 'n' Dates Lounge, which had a whole different tone when it wasn't hosting a RADFAm dance, and took note of the couples represented. No single orientation held sway—which she preferred, actually—but she couldn't help noticing they were the amplest couple in the room. On the jukebox a Eurodisco group was taking on Barbie.

"What are you thinking?" Lissa asked.

"I've been trying to get mad at Connie," Delia answered. "We've been friends for so long that every time I start to get upset, a part of me wants to rationalize her behavior. But then I become the culprit, and I haven't gotten so brain-washed as to buy into that."

"You need to get pissed at her," Lissa advised. "A dose of righteous indignation is definitely called for."

"Indignation is your strong suit. I'm better at surly," Delia mused. "I could use a good Indignity Coach. Connie always did it for me. Want the job?"

Lissa shook her head adamantly, Afro-dangles clashing with each swing. "I refuse to become anything remotely Connie," she hissed. "It's high time you got POed on your own two feet."

"Like you're not going to give me your 'objective' take on things anyway," Delia giggled, stroking Lissa's shoulder. "But don't worry—Connie can't do a single thing you don't do infinitely better." She sipped her wine thoughtfully. "That doesn't change the awful fact that I had a massive crush on her," she finally admitted. "Once, a long time ago."

"You and half the bruised FAs in the city," Lissa consoled. "But—and I've said this all along—the woman just doesn't know a good thing when it's face-to-face." She reached across the bar and brushed a strand of hair from

Delia's cheek.

"'**PUSH YOURSELF TO NOTICE** the extraordinary in the ordinary,'" Misty recited. "I may just embroider that on a sampler."

Joe inspected the silver and red foil message. "They've changed the layout of the wrapper," he noted. "It used to be you had to unwrap the whole candy to get to your Promise. Now you only have to unwrap one edge."

"It's all a marketing ploy. Makes it easier to match the fortune to the person you've sent the candy," Misty deduced. "Wonder who's been mailing these cards. According to Lissa, all the women in the chapter got one."

"Some anonymous feeder?" Joe offered. He turned toward the kitchen counter to refill his coffee mug. "How was the chocolate?"

"Must have run afoul of disgruntled postal workers, 'cause it arrived a tad smooshed in the envelope," Misty admitted. "So I tossed it. Besides," she indicated the gold-wrapped box of Rubens Belgian chocolates that currently tantalized Schmendrick, making him sneeze, "I knew you'd be getting me something ritzier for Valentine's."

"You have no idea how long I took just trying to figure out the right size box," Joe confessed. "If I went too big, you might think I was up to something; too small and I'd look chintzy."

"You did just fine," Misty assured him, sidling off her kitchen stool to give him a kiss. "Candy's always acceptable on Valentine's Day."

Joe grinned and was about to pursue her gratitude when Kirk materialized in the doorway. Though it was close to noon, he still was in his velour robe and slippers. "No, don't stop on my account," he gestured. "Just dropping off a few photos."

"Vacation pics?" Misty asked. "Took you long enough to get them developed. Got any shots of the Cayman Islands?"

"Ha, ha. As if they'd let me close enough to see men. Ahem, I mean, see them." He slid the pack of photos across the counter. Poking from the folder was a picture of a large-bellied hirsute man in his late forties, posing with an open Hawaiian shirt and leaning on a cane.

"And who, pray tell, is this?" Misty demanded. As she fanned through the photos, the figure popped up frequently.

"Him?" Kirk demurred, feigning nonchalance. "That's just Brian. He's this city planner I met on the cruise. Lives transcontinental, unfortunately."

"Sir, I am truly impressed. You haven't said boo about this hunk since you got back, and now you choose to spring him on me like this. That is so very un-Kirk."

"Turning coy in my dotage, girlfriend," he smirked, turning to take in

Joe's reaction. "I simply adore flabbergasting Miz All-Knowing/All-Seeing. It was worth playing him close to my chest just for the look on her face.

"We've been dating via email ever since the cruise," he continued. "So maybe you and I can both have relationships at the same time after all. Long as they're not in the same state." He twirled on his Betty Boop slippers to head back down the hall. "Well, I'll let you two kids get back to what you were doing. Try not to drool on my photos too much, Mist. It ruins the finish."

"Silly boy. I'm not into teddy bears. Besides, pics ain't got nothin' on a man in the flesh." Kirk popped back into the doorway, tongue childishly wagging, but as he left they heard him whimper once, pitifully.

Try as he might, Joe mused, he still couldn't get over the discomfort he felt when Misty's fave friend-and-tenant was in the room—a sense of being judged by standards that weren't even clear to Joe. He smiled at Misty, who surreptitiously continued examining Kirk's photos with an amused expression on her delighted, dimpled face.

EPISODE THIRTY

"EVERY DAY IS VALENTINE'S DAY," the balloon-festooned banner boldly proclaimed. Suspended precariously from the ceiling by fishing line near a heat vent, it flickered and twitched like a failing computer monitor, its filigreed welcome occasionally indistinct. Someone had put a lot of effort into that banner, Paul thought; too bad it worked against the message.

The Full-Figured Friends *Après*-V.D. Dance was in full swing by the time he'd arrived. He wasn't familiar with downtown, and it had taken forever to find safe, reasonable parking near the upscale hotel. But he had to admit he'd also dithered half the evening away waffling whether to answer the invite from Greg Dillman's new social group. Why waffle? It was highly unlikely Connie would attend anything sponsored by that guy; more than likely he'd be meeting a whole new group of people tonight.

Resolutely adjusting his bolo tie, Paul marched up to the ticket table, staffed by a vaguely familiar black man in a three-piece suit. "Welcome to Full-Figured Friends," the man—identified by his name tag as "'Jefferson"—beamed broadly. "Are you looking to become a member?"

"I came for the dance," Paul answered. "Do you need to be a member to get in?"

"Not really," Jefferson replied. "But it's a better deal in the long run. Members pay only half price." He gestured to a plainly lettered placard—no filigree here, thank you—denoting the admission fees. Even FFF members' attendance cost twice what he'd paid for the previous RADFAm dance. Rental space must be steeper downtown, he supposed.

"Just here for the dance," he decided, pulling a twenty from his wallet.

"You change your mind, you can sign up when you leave," Jefferson confided. "I'll make you a deal."

"Fair enough," Paul agreed, stepping into the ballroom.

The festively decorated room was palatial compared to the chapter dance's. It made the event seem less populated, though a cursory head count put the numbers about even. Red and white streamers swooped from the ceiling, punctuated by dangling Mylar balloons and a hideous Cupid-shaped piñata waiting, Paul guessed, for some later game. By the dance floor a portly deejay in a retro suit was spinning something techno, while nearby two plumpers clad in black leather bustiers and spandex were dancing, lost in their own independent rhythms, amid a smattering of heart-shaped red and white balloons. Around the dimly lit portable bar several tables with folding chairs were occupied by revealingly dressed singles and couples. And lounging against that bar, talking to a reporter, was Greg Dillman.

"Of course RADFAm has its place," he was intoning condescendingly, "but some people just aren't interested in politics. F3 is about fun, pure and simple—a place where plus-sized beauties and their fans can get together socially without a lot of hassle."

"Ooh! A fresh face," one of the leather twins purred as she slid onto the barstool beside Paul. She was zaftig in a turn-of-the-century kind of way, though her fashion was was pure 1990s—spiked shiny black hair and enough ear studs to make a metal detector go tilt. "You a dancer, Tex? Or is Garth Brooks more your speed?"

Paul gave her a half grin. "I can white-guy dance with the best of them," he said, "which means I can do fine as long as there aren't any actual steps involved."

"Then you're a step ahead of this group," she answered brightly, pulling Paul out onto the floor. The deejay had replaced the electronica number with a slower, bluesy tune in praise of women "just a little bit fat." The leather-bound brunette began to sinuously move to the rhythm.

"My name's Paul," he volunteered. She smiled but didn't reciprocate, as if waiting for a fuller critique of his dance moves before divulging her own name. She seemed about ten years his junior, incongruously cute-faced within her street punk garb, which cast a tawdry edge to her youth. She danced with the ease of someone who'd practiced for years with music videos. About halfway into the number her "twin" joined them. Paul introduced himself, and she, too, nodded agreeably.

Three songs later and Paul was parched. The dance floor was scattered with couples lost in each other's embraces. His first dance partner had finally revealed her name as Sonya; her companion, Kathi. Sonya, he learned, was going to be a model in Greg's next newsletter.

"I'd love to be one of those plus-size fashion models," she told him. "You know, like Emme. I'm a perfect size 16, so I'm hoping this'll lead to something better. I'm tired of working for a living." Work, he learned, was behind the counter of a mall-based Phone Mart. Kathi, it turned out, was a commercial art grad student.

"What do you do when you're not at F3 dances?" Kathi asked.

"Mold young minds," he smiled, swizzling the lime spear through his seltzer. "I'm a school teacher." Sonya made a disagreeable face, as if she'd rather suck a lime than think of school. "Special Ed," he added, and she visibly softened.

"That must take a lot of patience," she told him, sipping her Bahama Mama coquettishly.

"No more than most jobs," he replied modestly.

"If I'd had a teacher as good looking as you, I might've paid more attention in class," Sonya said in a low voice. She looked at him expectantly, awaiting his suitably flirtatious reply.

"And how are my two favorite ladies?" Greg Dillman had suddenly appeared at their table, forestalling Paul's response. "And you, you cowpoke!" Greg turned his attention to the teacher. "So you like to double your pleasure? Always been one of my favorite fantasies. 'Course," he whispered conspiratorially, "after that old nag you've been straddling, these two fillies gotta make your spurs jingle! Yee-hah!" And with that, the F3 sponsor oozed toward a neighboring table.

Paul grinned sheepishly at the two young Full-Figured beauties. For an instant he saw them both through Dillman's eyes—as empty, beautiful vessels to use and discard—and he knew that for him the night had come to an end.

THE THEATER SEATS WERE "FAT FRIENDLY," at least as far as Jenny was concerned, though she had difficulty imagining how some of the chapter's supersized members would fit. While the armrests were suitably well-spaced, the leg and forefront area were still pretty tight. She said as much to Ian once they'd gotten themselves situated.

"You're right," he agreed, "though the handicapped seats against the back wall are roomier." He pulled a bag of Tootsie Roll Midgees from his coat pocket and offered it to Jenny.

"Not a Dove bar, but it'll do," she accepted.

"I heard about all those Valentine's Day Promises," he commented. "What was your Promise?"

"'Time flies; spend it with people who mean the most to you,'" she quoted. "I thought at first that you'd sent it, but I hear from Lissa that all the women in the chapter got one. Unless that's one of the responsibilities of the membership secretary?" she smiled.

"Nope," he shook his head. "And were you okay after eating the chocolate?"

"I didn't eat it. Why do you ask?"

"Word is that Patsy got ill after eating hers. Not violently sick, but sick enough to spark the rumor that some of the chocolate was tampered with."

"Who on earth would do that?" Jenny asked in disbelief.

"Good question," Ian sighed.

Someone bumped against the back of Jenny's seat, nearly making her drop the bag of candy. A quartet of teenagers, two boys and their dates, were jostling their way down the row behind them. As soon as they sat down they started murmuring and giggling.

Teenagers in a pack—no other sight could bring out the panic and defensiveness in Jenny so quickly and completely.

"Maybe we should move," she murmured to Ian. He gave her a puzzled look, then one of the boys behind them stage-whispered to his friend, "Good thing this theatre has a wide screen. Or we'd miss all the action."

"I hear that," his cohort guffawed. "That's a lotta back blocking our view of Dante's Peak!"

Their dates giggled appreciatively as the boys high-fived, but before they could continue Ian twisted around and glared at them.

"You two have a problem?" he asked, his voice registering an anger that was a new sound to Jenny.

The first kid, middling build with a short and very unsuccessful mustache, laughed nervously and said, "What?"

"I asked you if you had a problem," Ian repeated as he stood up to face the group.

"No, man," he answered.

"Good," Ian told him, "because I'd hate to have paid good money only to have our movie-going experience ruined by a bunch of teenage fuckheads." He grabbed the back of his seat and leaned menacingly over the first boy. Through her chair Jenny could feel his quivering rage.

"It was just a joke!" the teen's date whined in an aggrieved tone, as if they were the ones with the right to be offended.

"A joke?" Ian answered, his voice rising derisively. "Well, shit, why didn't you tell me? I love a good joke!" Jenny could feel the eyes of everyone in the area on them, and she wished she could sink into the floor. "But I came to see this movie, not to listen to your dipshit boyfriend jerk off." The boy's date was near tears, but off to the side his buddy was snickering.

"Asshole," the kid muttered, but he didn't say anything more.

As Ian turned back to Jenny the crackle signaling the beginning movie chattered over the theater sound system. Still embarrassed, yet also empowered by his defense, Jenny grabbed Ian's hand and squeezed it gratefully throughout the Coming Attractions.

EPISODE THIRTY-ONE

"A BUFFET," Joe grimaced, scanning the crowded Chinese restaurant. "I'm not much of a buffet fan."

"Odd thing for a man with feeder fantasies to say," Misty teased, scouting ahead for the private meeting room.

"I am also a professional chef," he reminded her tartly. "Buffet food tends to be overcooked, soggy and tasteless. All those crisp vegetables turn to mush." They made their way across the room to the chapter's meeting site, Misty openly scoping out the serving tables as they passed.

"These pea pods don't look too limp," she decided. "Though I know they're not as crisp as anything you'd come up with." Misty gave a Mae West wink and patted her hair coquettishly. She was wearing a long, royal blue mega-sized tunic festooned with a beaded-and-sequined zodiac sign on the front. It fell to just above her shapely knees over her metallic silver leggings. The effect, for Joe, was heavenly.

"For a woman not into feeder fantasies, you know exactly the right words to say," he grinned.

Funny thing about those fantasies—though they'd been frequent and familiar for years, they'd recently become fewer and farther between. Whenever he was around Misty, her vast and bounteous beauty was enough to make such daydreams inadequate. And when they were apart, the memory of her flesh-and-form reality (enhanced a bit, perhaps, but not all that much) easily replaced any illusion. Was he outgrowing his fantasies, or was he simply taking a vacation from them? Joe didn't know for sure, but the way things were going he didn't plan to worry about it.

The conference room was set up for the meeting with three 8-foot-long tables arranged in a U—room enough for about twelve to fifteen RADFAmites, though, according to Misty, business get-togethers were seldom a hot ticket. Besides the officers there was a smattering of attendees. The only face he could put a name to was that Jenny girl.

Misty grabbed a place by Dexter, Ian and Eleanor, who were seated mid-bottom of the U, while Joe was able to snag a seat right beside her on the corner. Dex and Ian were winding up a conversation that sounded personal, not political.

"His computer's in the dining room now," Dex was telling the membership secretary. "Looks like hell, and Neeko claims it wreaks havoc with the spatial flow. But now we can always see what he's up to. At least while we're awake. And I refuse to sleep on the couch with one eye open."

Ian shook his head sadly, squeezing a packet of duck sauce over his spring roll. Then the membership secretary noticed Joe's presence. "Our newest member," he announced to the room at large, and Dexter nodded in welcome. Beyond Ian Eleanor was interviewing Jenny, jotting down notes with studious seriousness. "Eleanor will want to spotlight you in an upcoming newsletter, if you're willing."

"I'm not very exciting," Joe demurred self-consciously.

"That's a matter of opinion," Misty smiled, kneading his shoulder affectionately. Joe grinned back and rose to get some appetizers. "Spear me a couple of potstickers," Misty requested, and he nodded in agreement.

On his way to the steam tables he passed a determined-looking Connie Donovan. Although everyone else was dressed casually, she had decked herself out as if for a formal cocktail party. Grabbing a seat at the open end of the U, seemingly as far from Dex and the other officers as she could maneuver, she pointedly smiled at the rest of the room. A couple of unfamiliar visitors waved at her cordially.

By the time he got back into the room, the discussion had turned to the upcoming election.

"Okay, we've got a candidate for every position but one," Dexter was saying. "Since Misty's running for president, her old position will need to be filled."

"Only one candidate for president?" Connie asked, dramatically placing a heavily be-ringed hand across her prominently displayed cleavage. "Why, that hardly sounds like an election at all."

"No one else has declared their candidacy," Dex answered with a shrug.

A smirk spread across Connie's wide face. "I'd be willing to," she announced, "if only to keep things exciting."

Beside him Joe felt Misty stiffen in her chair. For reassurance he squeezed her hand under the table and she glanced at him, smiling gratefully.

"I'd have thought," Dex said slowly, "that things were exciting enough last year." He took a sip of green tea, the dainty cup engulfed in his massive fist.

"Then you don't know what true excitement is, Dexter," Connie purred. "The more I consider it, the more interested I am in running for office again. You wouldn't want to withdraw your nomination now, would you, Misty?"

"No, thank you," Misty replied sweetly, though the way she continued to apply pressure to Joe's hand belied her tone.

"Fine," Connie concurred. "Who's up for the other positions?"

"Ian is running for vice-president, and Eleanor has graciously agreed to be membership secretary as well as staying on as newsletter editor," Dex tallied. "They're both unopposed, unless someone else is thinking of going for either position." He paused, then continued. "That leaves chapter treasurer. Anyone interested?"

The room grew deadly silent, as only a roomful of folks eagerly avoiding an administrative fate-worse-than-death can get. From her end of the table Connie eyed the members imperiously, as if by her very presence she could coerce someone into it. Delia and Lissa, Joe noted, were both conspicuously absent from tonight's meeting.

A soft voice finally broke the tableau. "I'd like to try." Connie frowned at these words, and her visage grew even darker as she identified the volunteer. Sitting with her hand raised, a shy smile on her youthful, attractively madeup plump face, was Jenny.

"Why that's marvelous," Connie finally murmured archly. "I'm sure we could work together just fine."

"'JUST FINE,'" Lissa snorted, with such vehemence it practically frayed the phone line. "Can you believe that woman?"

"Just being the seasoned campaigner," Jenny responded. She hadn't always been this casual about it, since it had taken two cups of Tension Tamer tea to soothe her once she'd gotten home from the meeting. "Just four months ago Connie was actively lobbying to get me drummed out of the chapter; now she wants to work with me. Politics does make strange bedfellows."

"Not an image I'd want to reflect on," Lissa sniffed. "I'm still pissed at that bitch for the way she treated Delia."

"How is the job search going, by the way?" Jenny inquired. On the muted television screen a tribute to a recently demised fat comic was being broadcast.

"Delia starts as assistant manager at Plustique next week," Lissa replied proudly.

"Really? Which mall?" Jenny knew the Plustique chain, having purchased much of her everyday wardrobe at one of their stores. Lissa named a shopping center in the southwest burbs.

"They don't even carry her size in the store," she added, "though their mail order goes up to 6X. I'm just happy to see her working again." Over the phone Lissa's relief was almost palpable.

"Amen!" Delia shouted in the background.

"Perhaps she can encourage them to expand their stock," Jenny mused. "We convince enough chapter members to become satisfied customers, and it would be worth their while."

"Wouldn't that just fry Connie's ample ass?" Lissa guffawed. "No, I guess that wouldn't be fair—even to her." Delia's voice murmured in the background. "Oops," Lissa amended, "my roommate is giving me grief for that fat-bashing remark."

"Roommate?"

"Yup," Lissa gloated. "She's moving out of her overpriced roach trap at the end of the month."

"Hey! Congratulations, to both of you."

"And what about your love life, little girl?" Lissa pursued.

"Nothing to write home about, one way or the other," Jenny admitted. "Even if I did write home. Ian's been pretty busy at work."

"He says."

"He says," Jenny echoed. "The chapter meeting was our first time together since the movie —and there he was all business. Before the group even broke up he was paged on a work call and was gone the rest of the night."

"You'd better figure out where you stand with that boy if you're going to serve as chapter officer with him," Lissa cautioned. "It could be damned awkward, otherwise."

"If Connie wins over Misty, it will be damn awkward, anyway," Jenny sighed. "That'll teach me to raise my hand in class."

EPISODE THIRTY-TWO

THE ARBORETUM BENCH WAS COLDER than Ian expected, but then botanical settings were not his usual stomping grounds. The closest thing to arboreal in his home was a dusty plastic palm, so what did he know? The setting for this rendezvous was her idea.

He glanced around the building, which was empty except for an anorectic woman dressed in groundskeeper green. Not entirely surprising for a week-day morning; Ian had also gotten there early to give himself some thinking time before she arrived. Swigging one last gulp of Surge, he dropped and crumpled the can beneath his sneakers. As he tossed it into a recycle bin he saw Valerie.

He waved at his former paramour as she followed the path through a forest of potted Easter lilies, ducking once to avoid a drip from the roof. She was dressed in a windbreaker and long skirt, a look that brought back memories of college days. Her face was flushed and serious.

"Sorry I'm late," she puffed. "It took forever to get in to see the doctor."

"What did he have to say?"

Val didn't answer, but instead took a slip of paper out of her purse and handed it to him. Ian read it, puzzled. It appeared to be a leaflet offering chapter discounts at InFatuation; in the bottom right hand corner was a pho-to of Connie Donovan asking the recipient to "Redeem this coupon and vote for me!"

"What in the world?"

"Shades of Student Council, eh? Thought I'd show it to you first," she said dryly. "We both could probably use a good laugh."

The tone of her voice told him everything he wanted to know, but Ian asked again anyway. "And the word from the doctor?"

"Not good," Valerie replied.

SITTING AT HER CRAFTING TABLE arranging quilt blocks, Eleanor Bollen was trying not to think about the chapter. But it was like an old trick her late husband would play on their nephews—he'd hold out a dollar bill and tell them "I'll give this dollar to you if you can go the next five minutes without thinking about it." He always gave them the money anyway, but Eleanor still thought it was a pretty mean trick. "What's the point of having family," George would answer, "if you can't torment them occasionally?" When he talked like that, she found herself feeling grateful they'd never had children.

She didn't know how Dexter managed it, balancing his duties as a doctor and a father plus remaining involved in the chapter. No wonder he'd backed out of the political arena. If she had any sense she'd be getting out herself.

But she owed the chapter a lot. When her husband died she'd been rud-derless—RADFAm was her first step into a world outside their marriage. She couldn't give up on it, even if it seemed the easy way out.

But did she want to be an officer with Connie? The woman could be so hateful. Eleanor heard she was actively campaigning, and there were enough new chapter members who didn't remember her previous presidency to sway the election. While Eleanor found some of Mystique's interests odd (to say the least), it was clear that she was the better candidate. But did she have the gumption to overcome Connie's campaigning?

She shook her head and turned her concentration back to her quilt top. The Upstate Quilting Society was sponsoring its spring competition in a week, and she was a long way from finishing her entry. Between quilting, church and the size acceptance chapter, she was always racing to meet some kind of deadline. No one could accuse her of having idle hands, she thought, rising to pin together the final arrangement of panels spread out before her.

THE STORE WAS FILLED WITH SLIGHTLY DINGY computer cabinets, keyboards and monitors, shelves of battered software boxes and all the supportive detritus of computer life. Dex felt the same vague discomfort he always experienced in used car lots, a sense of how tenuous his own adulthood was. Perhaps he should have brought Ian along for some much-envied tech support.

Jackie was rifling through a large cardboard box of remaindered CD-ROM games, seated on the floor with his legs crossed, an eager look on his face. It'd been a long time since he'd looked so kid-like, Dex mused; their trip to the pre-owned computer shop had been a good idea. When Jackie had suggested it he'd balked at first—it seemed too much like setting them both up for further troubles down the road—but his son had been good all month, and Dex wanted to spend some time with him on somewhat familiar turf. It was either this or the roller rink, which could have been really disastrous.

He watched his son check out the sale items, was relieved when he discarded a package with the less-than-edifying title of *Freak Show*, and saw him finally select one of the martial arts games. "Can we get this?" Jackie asked.

The cover showed two overly muscled types, one male and one female, in kung fu stance against a towering ogre. The content, the box assured him, was not excessively graphic but filled with good, clean, ass-kicking action. Dex smiled and handed the box back to his son. "You a fan of this martial arts stuff?"

"Who isn't?" Jackie shrugged, rising from the floor with an ease Dex had never possessed.

"That's how your mom and I met, you know," Dex said as they took the box to the unshaven college student behind the counter.

"Sumo isn't martial arts, Dad," Jackie explained patiently. "It's a whole different thing."

"Perhaps," Dex replied, and they headed for the parking lot. "How about getting some lessons in the real stuff some time, then?"

Jackie stopped mid-stride, then called to his father. "Really? Rad, Dad!"

"We'll look into it," Dex concluded. From the grin on Jackie's face, he knew he'd finally done something right.

"DAMN, WOMAN, WHATCHA GOT in here? Bowling balls?" Lissa dropped a large box on the already crowded Scandinavian daybed, then took a deep swig of raspberry Snapple. Behind her Jenny was carrying in the box's near twin, setting it gently on the floor.

"Last box," she told Delia, who was opening each one to make sure the contents matched their inventory.

"Great," Lissa exclaimed. "Too much more shit and there won't be any room in the joint for two old fat ladies."

"Who you calling old? Besides, I'm just trying to get you closer to me, babe," Delia cheerfully replied. She rummaged through the upper layer of Lissa's box and dropped a pile of clothing on the floor. "No wonder it's so heavy," she revealed. "It's my sewing machine."

"A skill I never developed," Lissa admitted, "though God knows my Mama tried to teach me."

"At my largest I had to do a lot of altering and construction," Delia explained. "Too much torso and not enough leg."

Lissa put an arm around her waist. "I don't know," she said, "you seem just right to me."

"Where do you want these?" Jenny asked, indicating an open box of kitchen supplies.

"Just put them on the counter by the sink," Delia decided. "Don't know if we need anything from that box or not, but judging from Lissa's cooking, we probably do!"

"Never said I was the domestic type," Lissa sniffed. "It's why I hitched up with you."

"You got a bad deal, then," Delia answered. "I know three good meals, and they're all boring down-home food."

"Midwest farm-fare," Jenny nodded. "Beef, pork and chicken, and every potato recipe ever invented. It was all my Dad would ever eat. The first time I tried Chinese was the day my folks divorced." Carrying the box into the kitchen, she returned with a can of Swiss Cream soda and a bar stool.

"Now there's a touching memory," Lissa commented, shoving boxes aside to make enough space to sit on the daybed.

"Only kind I have when it comes to my mother," Jenny joked.

"How is the old battle ax, anyway?"

"Same old same old," Jenny replied, perching on the stool. "She calls once a week to twist the guilt-screws for 'abandoning' her."

"Hopefully it's not working," Lissa teased. "If that's all it takes to get to you, then watch out, Exalted Chapter Treasurer! Connie will eat you alive."

Jenny made a face behind her can of pop.

"Don't you let her get away with that," Delia shouted. "Why don't you ask Lissa about her stint as chapter VP?"

Lissa made a show of ducking the questioning look Jenny shot her way. "It was a whole different chapter then," she asserted. "I'll tell you about it someday."

"Count on it," Jenny answered with a laugh. "And if Connie does win, I'm counting on you two old pros for pointers on dealing with her. Blackmail, anyone?"

THE PHONE WAS RINGING when Paul got back to his apartment after walking Molly. Not enough rings to start the answering machine, he heard, so he led the dog into his apartment and answered it.

"Paulie," Dillman's voice opened, "just doing a little QA around the F3 dance. Got a few minutes?"

"Sure, I guess," Paul sighed, kneeling down to unleash the golden retriever. "What do you want to know?"

"Just trying to provide a place that meets the needs of both FA and admiree," Dillman said, vaguely enough. "Any comments on the facilities or the music?"

"Looked okay to me," Paul told him. "Of course I'm not always familiar with the needs of supersized members."

"That's not what I heard," Dillman snickered. "But if that's your story, then stick with it. Planning on voting for your ex, incidentally?"

"I haven't really thought about it," Paul answered. Molly wagged her tail expectantly; typically their walks were followed by a handful of Snausages.

"The advantage of starting your own social club," Dillman preened. "You don't have to bother with elections and all that political nonsense."

"A benevolent dictatorship, eh?" Paul noted.

"Just a business," Dillman corrected. "A fat-friendly one, of course."

"Of course."

"Any other constructive criticism you want to offer?"

"Not that I can think of."

"Suggestions, then?"

"If I think of any, I'll give you a call." Paul let a note of exasperation creep into his reply.

"Well, our next big bash will be an Easter weekend Spring Fling. Rumor has it Sonya will be showing up in Bunny garb. That is, if I can get her to wear it."

Paul chuckled softly, then shook his head at Molly. Greg Dillman: would-be Hefner. Why was he not surprised?

EPISODE THIRTY-THREE

"ANOTHER GRAY HAIR, MY LOVE," Neeko noted as she wrapped the curly chest hair around a long fingernail, then watched it spring back against her husband's broad pectorals. She looked like a gardener checking the ground for fresh shoots.

"That's been there for weeks," Dex told her with a grin. "You've just lost track because they've become so plentiful." He rubbed his hand through his salt-and-pepper beard for emphasis.

"Am I responsible?" she asked with mock meekness, propping her elbow against the Sobakawa pillow. Dex shook his head. In the armoire TV across the room a late-night comedian was making tasteless presidential fat jokes.

"Being your husband is a joy," he answered truthfully. "Being a father is what ages you."

"You're a good liar," Neeko softly replied. "I know I've been a bitch recently, giving you grief about that photo. I also know what it meant for you to drop out of chapter politics, and appreciate and love that you thought to do it for us."

Dex leaned forward and kissed his wife slowly, stroking her back beneath the loose nightshirt. "I've still got to deejay the sock hop on election night. But after that I'm free and clear." He paused to let Neeko return his kiss. "I called the Y today," he said after awhile, "and they've got a good deal on Tae Kwon Do classes. We've still got a family membership from the time I was taking water-walking."

"You mean we've been paying them all these months and not using the facilities?"

"No comment." Out of the corner of his eye he could see a commercial for a citywide chain of health clubs. "But maybe I can sign up for another water aerobics class at the same time he's learning his martial arts moves."

"That would be a good thing," Neeko decided. The phone rang, and as she went back to examining his chest Rachel hollered up the hallway.

"Dad!" Rachel bellowed. "Phone for you!"

"She almost sounds surprised that anyone but she would get a call at this hour." Dex reached across his wife and picked up the receiver as Neeko continued her hirsute explorations.

"Dex?" Lissa opened. "Hope I didn't call too late."

"You know better than that," Dex assured her. Ever since his residency he'd remained a short-shift sleeper. "What can I do for you?"

"Remember the Dove bar mystery last Valentine's Day?" Lissa began. "Well, there's been another anonymous candy delivery. Today all the chapter women received little Easter presents: tiny baskets filled with Jelly Bellies."

"Jelly Bellies? Is that meant to be a bad joke?"

"Hard to say," Lissa replied. "Delia and I had two baskets left outside our door last night. Remembering Patsy's bout of queasiness, shall we say, from the last time, we didn't touch the candy, and have been calling all the other women to warn them, too."

"You think the candy was tampered with?"

"Delia suggested we have you check it out," Lissa answered. "Figure you must have some laboratory connections that could do it expeditiously, and without going legal at this point."

"You figure right," he responded gravely. Neeko, catching the tone in his voice, had stopped and was watching him questioningly. "But if it is, we have to contact the cops."

"No argument there. I'll bring the candy over tomorrow, though most labs probably aren't open on Good Friday."

"Hospitals, and hospital labs, are always open," Dexter averred. "Plan to bring it by in the morning." He hung up the phone and then gave the gist of the call to Neeko.

"So," she commented, "'free and clear!' Out of politics, but not out of chapter business."

"How can I be? Someone could get hurt with this. Would you really want me to be?"

"No," she admitted, smiling lovingly. "I would not for all the world have you become someone you aren't." Then she snuggled against him provocatively, effectively ending further discussion of RADFAm for the night.

CASPAR'S WAS BUSY, BUT NOT TOO BUSY to find room for Joe and Misty. The maitre d' smiled as he led the couple to a primo table in the center of the room. Misty felt simultaneously flattered and much too conspicuous.

Since meeting the boss seemed so important, she'd ventured to Plustique and gone all-out on her Battenburg-lace-trimmed rayon ensemble of dolman-sleeved top and matching godet skirt (shorter than she'd worn in years!) in Easter pastels. She'd even squeezed herself into pantyhose and real shoes, not her usual Birkenstocks. Joe was amazed at the transformation, and couldn't seem to stop complimenting her.

"You look so wonderful tonight," Joe declared for the umpteenth time. "Don't worry about a thing." Misty smiled to show her appreciation, but the truth was she hadn't felt this nervous on their first date. Maybe it was just realizing that Joe was beginning to introduce her to his life outside of RAD-FAm—keeping it all inside their own little world was so much easier.

"Can't stay away, even on your night off," the head waiter, Samuel, was joking as Joe pulled out a seat for Misty. "Caspar has been most eager to meet you, Miss. I'll tell him you've arrived." He raced to the kitchen with an impetus that left some of the regulars eyeing them curiously.

"So," a voice suddenly boomed behind her, "this is the woman who's been stealing my sous chef from me on weekends! His words didn't do you justice, Mystique. You're even lovelier than he's described. And," the voice stage-whispered in her ear, "he hasn't stopped describing you."

Caspar's roundly paternal figure adequately filled the meager space between the neighboring table and theirs. Red-cheeked and smiling, with a belly that almost rivaled hers, he held out both arms and gave Misty a welcoming embrace. All of her anxiety melted. The man fit his namesake restaurant—gourmand and gourmet.

"Joe speaks highly of you as a wonderful boss," she smiled, "but if he's imposed on your kindness by asking for too many days off—I'd really hate to see him get in trouble."

"Not a bit," Caspar chuckled, stepping back carefully to take them both in. "I used to tease him when he wasn't dating. Can't have it both ways, can I?" He patted Joe on the shoulder then told them both, "Tonight's on me. You must have the duck *l'orange*."

"Sounds scrumptious," Misty replied, and Caspar beamed at her.

"If it isn't, there will be floggings all around," he declared broadly. "Besides, I want you to come back—keeps Joe here if you become a regular." He winked, turned and left to give the remainder of their order to the head waiter.

"Are all chefs feeders?" Misty wondered aloud, fanning herself after they'd finished the sumptuous, and stupendous, feast.

Joe shrugged his shoulders. "It's not 'feeding,'" he opined. "When you do something well, you want to share it with your friends." Changing the subject, he added, "Caspar likes you. I could see it in his eyes."

"I could feel it in his hug," Misty countered. "I'd hate to have him mad at me with arms like those."

"Comes from kneading all that dough and cutting all those veggies. Now, the next step," Joe said, filling her glass from a carafe of water, "is meeting the family."

"One meal at a time, please," Misty groaned, leaning back and melodramatically daubing her forehead with a moistened napkin.

"Change the subject, you say? Then how's your campaign going?"

"I'm simply not a writer," Misty confessed. "I keep trying to find a way to distinguish myself from Connie without resorting to personalities—and failing miserably. What am I supposed to say? 'Vote for me! I'm not a bitch'?"

"That would get my vote," Joe answered.

"You can't vote; you're a 'friend' of the chapter, not a member."

"I am a member," he said, pulling his wallet from his sports jacket. "When I joined the chapter three weeks ago, they told me I needed to be a member of National to have voting status, so I paid those dues as well." He proudly brandished his RADFAm membership card, grinning. "And it was worth every penny!"

On his salary, Misty knew that forking out for both memberships in the same month was no small feat. She felt like the heroine in that O. Henry story with the watch fob and hair combs. "You didn't need to do that!"

"Sure I did," Joe assured her. He reached across the table and kissed her hand. Misty felt herself blush, and knew he could see the rosy glow through her lace bodice.

"You'll come up with the right strategy," Joe reassured her. "Just write from your heart. You just don't have it in your nature to be mean or cruel."

"Yes, I do," Misty answered, "but I'm flattered to hear that you believe otherwise." She lifted her wineglass and took a meditative sip. Though she seldom used the Tarot for her own advantage, this might be one of those rare occasions. Time to seek the wisdom and guidance of the Vision.

But that was for later. For now, she basked in the warmth of Joe's loving smile.

EPISODE THIRTY-FOUR

RECENT STORMY WEATHER HAD PIRATED AWAY one letter from the fieldstone welcome sign in front of the SkyAire Lodge. The remaining message, "RADFAm Sock Ho," read more like a gathering of rappers than the innocent dance it was meant to be. Remembering his first, tentative steps in embracing size acceptance—and the way embraces can subtly turn comfortable—Paul took a deep breath and headed for the meeting room housing the Sock Hop. He could hear folks chattering excitedly.

Election night: Connie was sure to be there.

Dressed and coiffed as Our Miss Brooks and looking like every high-school prom chaperone, Eleanor sat wedged behind an unsteady card table, staffing the ticket booth just inside the door. She smiled at Paul rather nervously as he bought a member's ticket, then indicated a poster with the officer candidates' names on it. Connie's contest, it appeared, held the only competition. "If you want a ballot, Dexter's playing election judge near the podium," Eleanor informed Paul, who nodded agreeably.

The meeting room was much more crowded than Paul had ever seen at a RADFAm get-together—peopled with anachronistically dressed women and men, clustered in cliques or going up to Dex to ask for ballots. There had to be at least eighty people in the room. The walls vibrated with old album covers and repro Elvis movie posters. Pink and blue streamers hung strategically from the ceiling, interspersed with old varsity banners.

An agenda flier lying on a table strewn with empty glasses said officer selection was the first order of business, to be followed by the dance. Paul scanned the room for the candidates. Connie was nowhere to be seen, but Misty was at a table with Joe. Pleasantly packed into a black sheath skirt, checked blouse, neckscarf and beret, she looked like a well-fed French café singer. Joe's stovepipe chef's hat and white jacket reinforced that notion.

As for Dexter Logan, the soon-to-be-former chapter honcho had opted for pre-Beatles rebel rags: leather jacket, jeans and white T-shirt. At his side a slim Oriental woman stood, decked out in poodle skirt and bobby socks, her long hair slicked back into a scarf-tied ponytail. She wore a 3XL high school letter jacket that belled out from her slender shoulders and nearly reached the top of her white anklets. Dex's, without a shred of doubt.

"Great outfit," Paul greeted the couple as he approached their table. In addition to a ballot box and ballots, the table held two towers of 45s and a vintage record player reminiscent of old Coke dances.

"I was trying for Brando in *The Wild Ones*," Dex said with a chuckle, "but I'm afraid the best I could do was Marlon circa 1990." He pulled a chained leather notebook from his hip pocket, flipped through to the appropriate page, checked Paul's name off, and slid the book back in, letting the heavy silver chain dangle ominously.

Neeko gazed up at her Marlon, rubbing his vast tummy. "Well, some women found him very sexy in *Don Juan DeMarco*," she smiled. Dex bent down and kissed his bobby-soxer on the nose.

Coughing self-consciously, Paul noted, "Looks like a pretty good-sized turnout."

"There's been a major membership surge in the last month," Dex explained. "Unusual for this time of year."

"Not when you factor in all the F3 members who've joined in the last few weeks," Ian offered, joining them. He'd dressed as the quintessential science student in the standard Bill Nye uniform that hadn't gone out of fashion in four decades. His usual companion, the zaftig blonde from the infamous pool party, was nowhere to be seen. "I've talked to a few, and it seems that Greg's been encouraging them to sign up."

"An act of benevolent community spirit," Paul pronounced in his best W.C. Fields. "How unlike Greg."

"You can say that. You don't have to be politely politic," Ian responded, as an unfamiliar couple approached the table.

"You've got to admit, it's pretty uncharacteristic," Paul pressed. "Last time I saw Greg he was slamming RADFAm to the media."

"Take a gander over there," Dex announced once he'd finished checking in the two newcomers. "That might explain a lot." He arched his head toward the entrance. Entering arm in arm were a dazzlingly bedecked Connie Donovan and a tuxedoed Dillman. Paul couldn't remember ever seeing her so regal.

"Now that Connie's here, maybe we can make our final statements," Misty suggested, joining them at the ballot table. "Then we can wrap this up and get on to the dance floor."

Ian dashed across the room to retrieve Connie, so Paul took advantage of the opportunity to sidle over to a portable bar. Dexter turned on the podium mike. After he offered a brief intro, Connie launched into her spiel.

"Most of you know me already," she told the room. "I've been with this chapter through quite a lot, and I'm not giving away any secrets when I say that it's been a rough year for our organization. It's hard work running a chapter, and I certainly don't blame the current officers for any of the problems.

"But something has got to change, and I believe it's the leadership. We need a chapter leader who's responsible—with a firm grasp of the realities of leading. This is serious business, not the Psychic Friends Network. This year we forfeited our annual Winter Dance due to missed opportunities, and the last pool party was an utter disaster.

"We need to improve our image in the community as a fun place for fat women and men to be! We need to make sure everyone in the chapter is a worthy representative of RADFAm and size acceptance. Not an embarrassment." Her eyes sparkled dramatically as they raked the room, and for a moment Paul thought she was going to single somebody out. Then she continued.

"It's not too late to change. I've been talking to several other social groups in the area with the proposal to pool our resources. The brass ring is within our grasp. I believe that working together we have the power to make this the brightest year yet!"

Connie smiled confidently around the room, and it seemed she smiled at each person individually. Paul took a long drag on his bottle of O'Doul's as several attendees applauded. If she could just bottle that charisma, he imagined, Coco Chanel would crawl out her grave to market it.

Connie gestured magnanimously to Misty and handed her the spotlight. Misty stepped forward, looking over at Joe first before she started.

"Like Connie, I'm going to keep my speech short," she began. "I wanted to say how much this chapter has meant to me. It isn't just the dances or the parties, though I've had plenty of fun at them. It's something much bigger than that. It's being in the same room with so many beautiful fat women and men. It's being in a place where I'm not the Fat Girl. Here, I'm one of many. Being in this group has given me such encouragement to feel okay about myself.

"I became an officer because I wanted to give something back to this group. I haven't been in the chapter as long as Connie—but every year I've been here has had its high points and low points. If I try to change anything, it will be to make us more welcoming as a chapter, as well as more supportive to the members who are already here."

At that point, Paul saw the blonde from the pool party enter the room with two other women. Jenny Something—the candidate for treasurer. She was dressed in a pink cashmere sweater and form-hugging white jeans. She looked as innocently sexy as the heroine in an Archie comic—a hell of a comparison for a schoolteacher to be making, come to think of it.

"I'd work to make us visible by having the chapter promote the positive," Misty was concluding. "Something that shows the outside world there's more to RADFAm than just a bunch of fat people whining about sizeism. We have the potential to benefit the larger community as well. Thank you."

She stepped back alongside Connie. Paul hadn't realized how physically close the two women were until now. Both supersized and beautiful, they could have been sisters separated by about ten years. And a lot of attitude.

Cupping his hands around his mouth, Dex bellowed like an auctioneer, "Last call for ballots! The voting's about to begin!"

"LOOKS LIKE WE JUST MADE IT," Lissa said to Dex as she received her ballot.

Connie sent a frosty smile in Delia's direction as she passed with her own ballot in hand, then scowled at Jenny. "Shouldn't you have been here early with the rest of the candidates?" she asked. "The people would like to see who they're voting for."

"We were gapers-blocked on the expressway," Delia explained to everyone within earshot. A few heads nodded understandingly. Connie snorted, then deposited herself alongside Greg Dillman.

It took only a few seconds for Jenny to fill out her ballot and deposit it in the box. Looking around the room, she spied Ian beside the record player. Happily waving, she made her way over to him.

"Nervous?" he asked as she came up and grabbed his hand.

"A little," she admitted. "I wasn't expecting so many people."

"Once the election brouhaha dies down, we'll probably drop down to the usual suspects," Ian suggested, "though we may get a few new long-term members from the F3 group."

The last of the voters had dropped their ballots into the box and Dex was tallying the results, Dillman hovering officiously in the background—the unofficial election monitor, Jenny supposed. The votes were tallied twice. Dex showed his results to Dillman, then pulled out the leather notebook listing all the chapter members. The two rifled through the list, then Greg shrugged and stepped back. Dex stepped up to the podium to announce the winners.

"It was an extremely close election," he said. "But the number of votes matches the number of eligible members, and we've recounted. Here are the results. For president: Connie Donovan, 36 votes; Misty Shores, 37. For vice-president: Ian Johnson, 68 votes. Membership secretary: Eleanor Bollen, 70 votes. Treasurer: Jenny Taylor, 66 votes. New officers, please stand up and be recognized!"

A generous smattering of applause greeted the newly elected slate as an excited group of well-wishers rushed up to congratulate Misty. Dex took this opportunity to slip back over to the record player and New Orleans piano started tinkling over the speaker, followed by a voice Jenny dimly recognized as Fats Domino. He was, she quickly realized, bragging about being a fat man. Dex pulled his wife onto the dance floor, and several other couples followed.

"Care to dance with the new chapter treasurer?" Jenny asked Ian, holding out her hand. Though neither one of them knew what, if any, moves the dance called for, they entered into an impromptu boogie-woogie. Halfway into the number they took one look at each other and paused, giggling. "Let's wait for a slow number," Ian suggested.

"Misty did it," Jenny exulted as they left the dance floor. Near the phonograph the new chapter president was being hugged by her beau Joe. "Despite Connie's politicking, she managed to win."

"Guess enough old members remember Ms. Donovan's reign as a previous chapter president."

"You'll have to fill me in on it sometime," Jenny cajoled, grabbing a vacant seat and indicating its twin. "Whatcha doing the rest of this weekend?"

Ian did not sit down. "Um-m-m," he began, cracking his knuckles distractedly. "I'm not really free this weekend."

Dex had shifted to a slower song, Brenda Lee crooning "I'm Sorry." But they didn't head back to the dance floor.

"Other commitments," Jenny mouthed, an awful feeling suddenly coming over her. She looked up at Ian's face closely, but he wouldn't maintain eye contact. "Valerie?" she asked.

"She's got it," Ian said, looking down at his scuffed gray Hush Puppies. "Pulmonary hypertension. She's really scared."

"I bet. You too."

"Yeah. Val needs some support right now, and I have to be there for her."

"I'm sorry, so sorry, I'm sorry, so sorry—" Dex's 45 had stuck in an offending groove. "I'm sorry, so sorry—" Suddenly Brenda Lee was cut off mid-apology, to be replaced with something more uptempo.

Jenny felt as if her sweater was crawling over her flesh. "You two have a shared past together," she finally answered. "I understand."

"I knew you would," Ian said, relief written all over his face. "Um-m, would you like something to drink?"

"Sure," Jenny replied, so Ian gratefully shot off toward the bar.

Why was she being so sweet and calm about this? She'd just been dumped, for goodness sake!

As she turned, she caught sight of Connie walking by the bar. For a moment she envied the older woman's steely grace in defeat. She looked totally unfazed by the night's events. A bland expression impressed her round face; her back was unbowed.

Perched on a stool, Jenny's gallant rescuer from the Christmas Party was saying something to Connie in passing. Suddenly Connie swiveled toward him, sequined dress swirling dramatically, and raising an elegantly manicured hand she swiftly slapped him across the face. Then she turned and stormed from the room.

"This from the woman concerned with appropriate behavior," Lissa noted wryly to Delia as they came up to congratulate the new chapter treasurer.

EPISODE THIRTY-FIVE

"**S**HE'S VERY CATHOLIC," Joe said for the second time that night, eyes on a snaking beatup Camaro in a lane abreast of them.

Misty fought to keep from snapping back, "You've said that already!" *You're nervous, girl,* she chided herself. *Don't take it out on Joe just because he's acting paranoid that your pagan-ass self won't be sensitive to a Very Catholic mother.*

"I know," she finally sighed. They were traveling through an area of the northern burbs that was virgin territory to her. Nothing really upscale, but certainly more middle class than she'd initially expected. "Anything else she's into? Or more to the point, not?"

"Don't laugh," Joe cautioned, turning off the business highway into a quiet neighborhood full of trim brick ranch homes. "She's gotten into Beanie Babies. Big time. Hundreds of 'em. Claims they're an investment. My old bedroom's crammed with them. When Jimmy moves out, they'll probably invade his room, too."

Misty reached over to Joe and patted his near knee. "I promise to keep any overt snobbery under control." She then pulled down the visor to nervously examine herself in the mirror. Maybe she should have used a little blush or lipstick or something. "Tell me again how I look—" she asked.

He didn't say a word until the car was parked in the driveway. "Just like a festival, all by yourself," he told her. As he leaned forward to kiss her, Misty let her anxiety melt.

"Here goes," she said once their lips parted. "Time to meet the fam!" Joe reached across the back of the seat for a small picnic basket, then they both got out.

The house was plain brick with a minimum of trim, its one concession to suburban kitsch a gaily costumed goose statue on the front step. According to Joe it was a third generation concrete bird—the previous two had been fowl-ly goosenapped in the night. As they approached the porch a motion-sensor light strobed on.

The matronly lady of the house—and object of Misty's concern—greeted them from inside the entrance, her brightly festive dress showing through the screen door.

Joe had given Misty a thumbnail sketch of his family to prepare her for this first, important visit. Petra Silvera had immigrated to the city as a teenager and found a job sorting skillet and iron handles at a small suburban parts factory contracted to a major appliance company. She'd met Joe's father,

Darryl Rivera, on the floor of the factory where he was, at the time, day-shift supervisor. A quiet, stocky midwestern urbanite, he'd fallen hard for this slight, shy teen.

Petra was the type of woman who might draw out the protective instincts of some men and the abusive ones in others. Luckily Joe's dad had fallen into the first category, and they'd lived devotedly ever after. That is, until his death from cancer five years before, shortly before Joe's graduation from the Culinary Institute. Rather than finding a job in any of the dozens of lucrative cuisine capitals (or cruise ships) around the globe, the young chef had come back to the Midwest for his mother.

Now the family home sheltered Petra, Joe's older brother Jimmy, and a coterie of cuddly stuffed critters. And a lifetime of memories.

"Happy Cinco de Mayo!" Petra cried. Joe grinned at Misty knowingly.

"May 5th was always a big day in my house," Joe had explained on the way over. "The rest of the year we didn't talk about our Hispanic heritage. But the Cinco de Mayo celebration was mandatory."

"No mixed messages there," Misty had mused. "But that's what holidays are all about—channeling the forbidden."

"There you go again," Joe smiled, "getting heavy on me."

"I thought you liked me heavy!"

"You know what I mean—"

Which had led to that reference to Petra's religious affiliation. The first reference.

"You must be Misty," Petra announced as they mounted the porch steps. Her voice was lilting, and accent free. "You're just as lovely as I expected. What beautiful hair!" She held the screen open in welcome, releasing a burst of Tex-Mex polka from the console stereo.

Despite the musical atmosphere the home interior was firmly midwestern. Sturdy no-nonsense furniture, family photos in a framed montage, and strategically placed basket-urns filled with pampas grass were much in evidence. On the living room shag a slightly older and slighter version of Joe was watching a Seinfeld rerun. He barely acknowledged the two of them as they entered the room.

Petra turned to Joe, examining him critically. What was she looking for? Misty wondered. Whatever it was, it didn't appear serious, as his mother shrugged and reached for his basket.

"Fresh avocados," she smiled with satisfaction. "I can always count on you, Joe." She led them into the kitchen and lifted the lid from a large bubbling kettle, revealing a savory soup glistening with the rainbow hues of beaded fat.

"Menudo," Joe explained. "It's a traditional Cinco de Mayo soup made with tripe, hominy and chili."

"The main course is *pollo en molle*," Petra told them, rummaging through a drawer for a paring knife.

"Chicken breast in chocolate-flavored gravy," Joe translated, pulling a stool over for Misty.

"Chocolate gravy? Why haven't I heard about that one before?"

"We're being bad today," Petra simpered as she deftly pitted and sliced the avocados into mashable size. Overhead, a Beanie Bat looked down on them. "But it's just for the holiday, right? We can go back on our diets tomorrow."

"Not tomorrow," Misty answered with a chuckle. "That's International No-Diet Day!"

From the look Petra shot her, it was as if Misty had suddenly begun speaking in tongues. She laid down the paring knife deliberately, then turned to fully face the two of them. "How's that again?" Petra asked.

Uh-oh, Misty thought—looked like she'd inadvertently stepped into it, taboo-wise. She'd assumed that Joe's mom knew all about his preferences, and possibly even approved of them since Hispanic women were so often prone to ampleness. *That's what you get when you assume, girl—*

"It's got to do with the group Misty and I belong to, Mom," Joe interceded. "You know, the size acceptance organization."

"This 'No-Diet Day' is a holiday?" Petra considered. It was almost as if she were concerned that her beloved Cinco do Mayo was somehow diminished by its temporal proximity. From the living room the sound of a sitcom laugh track suddenly rose in volume.

Clearly, there were worse things than just being a pagan.

JENNY'S MOM WAS IN THE KITCHEN when her daughter arrived to pick her up for the Mother's Day brunch. Seated at the metal and Formica table that had been there since Jenny's childhood, Alice Taylor was breathing through a face mask connected to an unfamiliar machine. She waved Jenny onto a plastic-padded metal chair, then quietly continued inhaling for another few minutes. By the time she switched off the machine, Jenny was beside herself with worry.

"Mom! What's this? How long have you been on this thing?"

Alice paused long enough to pull a pack of Virginia Slims out of her purse, then apparently thought better of lighting up immediately. "If you were around more often, you'd have known," she snapped, rising to grab a Bic lighter off a shelf by the stove.

Jenny held off until she could get her voice under control, then pressed the issue. "No, really, when did you have to start doing breathing treatments on a—what's it called?"

"A nebulizer. About a month and a half ago," she replied. "I woke up one night, couldn't catch my breath. Got up to open a window—or I tried to get up but couldn't even walk across the room. Phoned Missus Frizzell next door, and she took me to the emergency room."

Alice got up to leave the kitchen and, pulling a vinyl windbreaker from the closet, stuffed both cigarettes and lighter into a pocket. "I'm not going to bring my purse, if that's okay."

"What? Fine." Jenny looked more closely at her mother than she had in years. When had Alice gotten so pale? So old?

"I was expecting you to bring that boyfriend of yours. What's his name again?"

"Ian. But he's hardly my boyfriend."

Alice eyed Jenny cannily. "I had a feeling he wouldn't stick around. He didn't sound all that stable to me."

"Mom, the only thing you knew about Ian was that he was attracted to me. Is that a sign of instability?"

"Well, you've got to admit that there haven't been very many suitable romantic prospects in your life." She paused, then turned back toward the kitchen. "Maybe I should bring my purse after all. Where are we going to eat?"

"Caspar's downtown," Jenny answered. "And Mom, the only reason Ian and I aren't going together right now is he's involved with caring for a sick former girlfriend."

"Caspar's? That's too far to drive. I'd just as soon eat at the Steak 'n' Shake." She pulled open the front door and stepped out into the afternoon sunshine.

Jenny bridled. "You always do this! I make more than enough money to take my mom out to someplace nice for Mother's Day." Following Alice out onto the front lawn, she saw her already lighting up. "You'd better finish that before you get in the car. I can't believe you're still smoking after all that's happened to you."

"Every time I've tried to give them up, I gained weight," Alice pouted. "If I hadn't gone back to smoking, I'd be as big as you." She glared at her daughter as if daring her to respond to this damning accusation.

She's your mother—don't scream, Jenny inwardly chanted. She held the passenger door open, waiting for Alice to stub out her half-finished cigarette. Reflected in the May sunlight, a streak of white gleamed in her mother's always-Claroled hair. A streak not unlike Valerie's.

EPISODE THIRTY-SIX

WHEN KIRK SAUNTERED INTO Mystique's Isle of View Emporium, setting the door chimes to tinkling, the proprietess was perched on a stool behind the crystal-laden display case, perusing a new Red Rose Collection catalog and wreathed with fragrant wisps of incense. Naturally, the first thing he did was give her grief about her choice of music.

"Enya," he sniffed, standing in the doorway with a smirk on his face. "Thinking of moving to the mall? Surely you could come up with something a little less—VH-1."

"Such as?" Misty growled.

"In deference to this establishment, something spiritual." Kirk paused for effect, then chirped, "*Golddiggers of 1933!* Ginger Rogers singing 'We're In the Money' in Pig Latin. It doesn't get any more transcendent than that!"

"Kirk," Misty shot back, skewering her neighbor with a jaundiced glance. "You are so full of it-shay. Why aren't you at work, you malingering flit?" She lay down the catalog and took a long appraising look at her friend.

"Had a Steinway to tune in the neighborhood, so just thought I'd drop in to see my favorite landlady," Kirk answered coyly. "Also to grab a bite upstairs and check my email. Seems that a certain burly city planner from the Pacific Northwest will be visiting our fair city next month."

"Brian? Really? What's the occasion?"

"Business. Some sort of a conference. Lots of other municipal government types," Kirk said airily. Misty huffed at his vagueness. "Hey, I can't be expected to get all the details straight."

"Or anything else, for that matter," Misty replied archly. She walked over to the store's complimentary hot tea jug and pumped two cups of Celestial Seasonings. "So when do I get to meet your mystery hunk?"

"Soon," Kirk promised, stirring two packets of sugar into his Tension Tamer. "The conference is set for mid-June, but Brian is also taking some time off to—um—followup on our correspondence."

"You're so cute when you're euphemistic," Misty grinned between sips.

"Yeah. Well, we may have finally beaten our mutual curse of Dual Relationships," Kirk mused. "And how did dinner go with The Catholic Mama? Have I detected a note of—peevishness, hmm?"

"Petra hates me," Misty replied with feigned nonchalance, tipping the plastic honey bear into her "Wild Women Don't Get the Blues" mug.

"Then she's a stone fool."

"Maybe—or maybe she just wants the best for her boy. I sure got exhausted, though, trying to read her. She made this elaborate traditional Cinco de Mayo meal, then she couldn't decide whether she wanted me to eat it or not! Every course she served, she'd say, 'You won't offend me if you don't take any.' And she'd smile when I took some, then frown when I bit into it.

"But the capper came when she pulled out dessert—fried ice cream or a really nice assortment of fresh fruit. Felt just like being plopped in the middle of that lady-or-tiger story we read in junior high."

"Mom's a wee bit fat-phobic, could we say?"

"If so, she wouldn't admit it out loud. But I made a faux pas early on. I pooh-poohed the D-word. Seems it's okay to be my size so long as you're miserable about it."

"And the answer to the dessert puzzle?"

"Thought I'd figured it out," Misty continued. "The correct response was to have neither."

"So that's what you did?"

"Actually I had a bowl of fried ice cream," Misty grinned. "I was getting pretty pissed off by then. She certainly wasn't pulling that crap on Joe or his brother."

"Brother? I had no idea. What's he like? Another stud-boy like Joe?"

"Chill, chum! Remember Brian," Misty laughed. "I couldn't tell you. The guy didn't open his mouth the entire dinner. Except, of course, to shovel in whatever Petra dished up."

"Healthy appetite, eh? Bigger than Joe?"

"Wrong-o! Jimmy seems to be one of those people who burns off calories pressing the channel changer on the remote."

Kirk snapped his fingers in mock disappointment. "So how did the rest of the evening go?"

"The rest of the evening? Dinner *was* the evening."

"Sounds like Joe's picked up something from his ma," Kirk considered.

"Ha ha. Once we got done with dessert she showed off her Beanie Battalion. I've never felt so many beady little glass eyes staring at me."

"Sounds creepy."

"You're not kidding," Misty agreed. She waved to the UPS man as he came in with a pair of packages. "Speak of El Diablo," she said, scanning the smaller of the two. "Looks like Petra sent me something."

"Open it carefully! Better yet, let me see myself out—" Kirk edged dramatically away from the counter.

Grabbing a pair of scissors, Misty slit the packing tape and pulled up the flaps to find a stuffed unicorn in a freezer bag. She recognized the figure from her night at Petra's. Nestled beside it within the plastic peanuts was a small envelope addressed to her in flowing calligraphy.

"It's Mystic the Unicorn," she said, showing off the tag. "There seem to be three different versions of this beanie." She indicated its iridescent horn. "This is the most recent one. The most common."

"Too bad she didn't send you a big-money Mystic," Kirk remarked as he finished off his tea. "It'd certainly be more indicative of her high esteem, wouldn't you agree?"

HER EYES ON THE PRIZE, Molly gallumphed after the bright yellow tennis ball as it arced over her head. Ever since he was a kid Paul had wanted a dog who could play fetch. With Molly he'd finally gotten one. For her, an afternoon of catch and return was the closest thing she knew to doggie nirvana.

Of course she occasionally stumbled. Fourth throw of the afternoon she wound up tripping over her forepaws and losing sight of the ball. Paul watched it roll and sputter to a halt at the edge of a picnic shelter. There a ubiquitous sign of the season, a family reunion, held sway, the sound of polka music sparkling in the air.

One of the kids present dislodged himself from a table and looked for the ball's source. He spotted Molly first, still dazedly trying to right herself. When he caught sight of Paul, he lobbed the ball toward him.

Paul moved in to make the kid's throw less humiliating. As he did he got a better view of the shaded reunion-goers. Seated behind the boy was a female figure whose silhouette was teasingly familiar. It was the same supersized frame as Connie's, though Paul doubted she would ever put herself in so unflattering a sundress. It was the kind of tentish outfit fat women had been sold for years to hide themselves, but which, of course, only drew unflattering attention to them. Say what you would about Connie, she knew how to package herself properly.

This thought was enough to send him back to the RADFAm election, a moment he'd re-lived frequently over the past few weeks. It was one of those moments so striking—literally— that he could still see it with utmost clarity. She'd come close to knocking him off his stool.

In retrospect he probably shouldn't have said anything to her. But seeing her after the election, he'd felt the need to say something comforting, offer his condolences. This he'd done, stumblingly, as she passed him. A simple "Sorry about your loss; you ran a good campaign"—and then she hauled off and slapped him.

"Save the sympathy for one of your feeb students," she'd sneered, glaring at him as if he'd just insulted her and her ancestry. "I don't need it!" Before he could think of a proper response she was out of the room.

All he could do was finish his O'Doul's and hold off leaving until he felt less conspicuous. He passed a smirking Dillman by the exit, caught a Valentine's Dance attendee muttering something derogatory as he left.

Next day, Dex had phoned to ask if he was all right. One of the regulars, an older woman named Lainie whom he'd barely noticed, had apparently overheard the entire interaction and passed the info on to the retiring chapter president. Paul appreciated the gesture.

Picking up the ball, he found Molly panting eagerly in his face. "Know something, girl?" he told the ball-happy hound. "You're a much nicer woman to be with."

EPISODE THIRTY–SEVEN

STILL DRESSED IN WORK CLOTHES, Jenny raced to make it to the chapter meeting on time.

It had been one hellacious day at the office—when it came to no-fault divorces, at least, June was busting out all over. So although Lissa repeatedly urged her to leave and arrive promptly for her first RADFAm officers' meeting, it simply wasn't in Jenny's nature to leave work unfinished over the weekend. Skipping dinner, she'd finally whittled through her paperwork, leaving less than half an hour to brave Friday night burb traffic to reach Kuppa Joe'a's. She was cutting time awfully thin, though—and the expressway was anything but.

She had, however, borrowed a cell phone from the office, and thus was able to warn them at the coffeehouse of her impending tardiness. Fifteen minutes after start-time she hit the entrance. The rest of the group had graciously waited for her, or at least had found far more important chit-chat to attend to than organizational politics.

From the way the conversation hushed as she came within earshot, Jenny suspected she was being discussed. But Ian's guilty glance clinched the topic: Valerie.

As Lissa's paralegal, Jenny had conducted research on primary pulmonary hypertension back when it seemed Delia was one of its unlucky numbers, so she recognized the treatment being discussed. Sounded like Valerie might be considering Flolan. The jury was still out on that particular regimen's efficacy.

"Here comes our new treasurer," Misty welcomed, smiling. "Now we can get started!" Perched over a large, frothy cappuccino granita, the newest president held court robed in a tie-dyed copen-to-amethyst T set, gracing a goddess-thewn moon tossing stars and comets from her capacious skirt. Around the old oak table from her Ian and Eleanor studiously shuffled their notebooks, for all the world looking like two kids caught mid-indiscretion by their teacher.

Jenny pulled up a chair into the larger of two gaps on Misty's left—furthest from her erstwhile beau. She turned to gesture at the waitress, ordering a vanilla Italian soda plus a cucumber-cream-cheese sandwich for dinner. "Lissa told me about the candy today," she opened as she settled in. "According to Dex, it tested clean."

"That's a big relief," Ian commented. "I would like to know who's been sending these 'goodies,' though."

"Probably some shy FA," Misty posited. "As much as we love you guys, there are a handful of fat admirers who are, shall we say, näif in the niceties of girl-boy relationships."

Ian sighed loudly, then slugged a chug of espresso. Jenny noticed dark lines, magnified by myopic lenses, etching patterns around his eyes. She didn't know whether to sympathize or gloat.

"I can accept that," he finally responded. "But for now it's a mystery, unsolved until we have more data. Shall we get down to business?"

"Well, first," Misty began, "I want you to know I've been thinking about my new responsibilities as president." She chuckled with self-deprecation. "And, as some of you know, a little 'Misty thinking' can be dangerous.

"I want us to head in fresh directions, as allies, a team. Therefore, please take your neighbors' hands around the table—" and she gestured to Jenny and Eleanor beside her. A trio of rather shocked looks greeted this pronouncement, followed by tentative compliance. Misty just smiled serenely. "Oh come on, officers don't bite each other. Though I have heard of the occasional nibble." She grinned at some remembered tryst.

As the hand-circle closed, Misty loosened her fingers long enough to light a bundle of twigs. A pleasant fragrance bathed the table, wafting toward the open coffeeshop door. "As it may have become apparent during the campaign, my esteemed opponent made several rather pointed references to my personal spirituality. Well, it's all true. It's my business, and it's my life.

"I sincerely hope this doesn't make you uncomfortable. But celebrations of any faith inspire, and spontaneity can spice up nearly any occasion. Plus our chapter needs all the help it can get!"

Her voice husked to a deeper contralto, her foot tapping a slow beat. "Let us close our eyes, looking inward, and begin to sway, gently, to the heartbeat of the Mother. Ground us and give us roots. Refresh us in the breath of cosmic breeze. Test us in the pyre of truth—" This brought a nervous cough from Eleanor's direction. "Quench us in Gaia's cauldron. And witness our pledge that in all things we seek justice for the embattled."

For one timeless moment the circle held, then hesitantly dissolved, each officer self-consciously retrieving hands. "Now, if you want to take me to the Supreme Court over Freedom of Religion ethics, be my guest—I admit I abused your rights," Misty chuckled. "But right now our chapter needs a healthy dose of divine guidance. And no, silly guy," she waggled her finger at Ian, "not John Waters' favorite cross-dresser."

"Now, down to 'bwass tacks.' Dex has bequeathed all his files to me," Misty said. "And honestly, I've only gone through about half of 'em. Some of the stuff's worse than Greek. Add to that the fact that I didn't get a chance to talk it over with him. He scooped up the fam at noon for a week-long north-woods vacation in a cabin four hundred miles from nowhere."

"Moose County, perhaps?" Ian joked, and Jenny hid a small smile. He knew she was a big fan of the detective novels about Qwill and his Siamese sleuth-cat.

"Anyway, Jen, I do have a few of my own materials to pass your way," Misty continued, pulling a knapsack off the floor and opening it on the table. Inside were two ledgers and a checkbook—plus something wrapped in tissue paper. Jenny pulled the latter out, revealing a resin-crystal brooch sculpted in the form of the Venus of Willendorf.

Jenny smiled hesitantly, stroking its artistry.

"Didn't have an official placard to welcome you to the ranks of chapter officerhood, so I thought some jewelry just might suffice. Blessings, sister-in-size."

Jenny held her gift up to the light, which flashed rainbow brilliance, and felt improbably touched. "For the first time I do feel blessed to be one," she answered shyly, pinning it onto her blouse.

Misty beamed, then brought the meeting back to business. "So far we have one really important short-term commitment—the district convention in early winter. It's beyond time to be setting this thing in motion, and in fact it may be too late as it is to hold it before the end of this year. Eleanor, what has been done so far?"

The newsletter secretary ducked her head nervously. "Well, you know Dexter has had an awful lot on his mind recently—"

"Ellie, I'm certainly not placing blame on anyone. But as incoming officers we do need to know what's happened so far, so we don't waste time retracing old steps. So please organize any notes you took on everything that's been done so far and mail them out to us ASAP." Misty smiled at Eleanor, who nodded awkwardly.

"That's more than enough for the short-term," Misty continued. "I've also been considering something longer term, something meaningful for the chapter to do for the community at large. We all know how hard it is find quality used plus-sized clothes, especially when funds are limited. And to be successful in finding a new job, attire certainly does make a difference. Therefore I'd like to see the chapter set up a clothing pantry for women returning to the workplace—somewhere they can get appropriate professional wear at good prices. For the time being there's enough space in my storeroom to start out. And I've already talked to several agencies that work with these clients. They all agree a service like this would make a big difference."

Ian interjected, "Hate to be a wet blanket, Misty, but we've got enough trouble bringing out bodies for something as popular as chapter dances. And with the convention looming and Dex backing out—do you really think we have the people-power?"

"Bringing me to my third item. I've been talking with Greg Dillman—"

Moans rose from all around the table.

"No, please hear me out. He's approached me about our two groups co-sponsoring a dance. If that works out we could do it regularly, combining resources and freeing up bodies for other projects."

"Dillman? Are you joking?" Ian collapsed skeptically, as if boggled by the mere mention of the insurance hustler.

"It really is possible," Jenny rose in defense. "We'd need to make arrangements beforehand, nail things down, do an informal contract. No, thinking about it," she reconsidered, "let's do make it formal."

"Spoken like a true paralegal," Ian sniped. *Where did that come from?* Jenny wondered. "You willing to work on drafting this historic document?"

"With Misty's help," Jenny told the table. "And Lissa's. The main thing is to make sure every duty and responsibility is clearly, evenly delineated. Yes, I think it's doable."

"What's your opinion, Eleanor?" Misty asked, turning back to the secretary.

"Well. I don't know—" Eleanor waffled, looking up from her notebook timidly, still stung by Misty's earlier inquiry.

"Let's not commit ourselves either way," Jenny compromised. "We'll draft up something and bring it to next month's meeting."

"You do realize we'll have to meet with Greg beforehand," Misty noted, a half tone of warning in her voice.

"Hey, I've been sitting in on divorce settlements all week. Dillman will be a breeze."

THOUGH SHE'D TALKED AROUND IT for weeks, Joe knew his mother would get to it eventually—Petra was both deliberate and tenacious. So when she finally phoned to offer her view of Misty, the young chef had had plenty of time to rehearse his response.

"Joe baby," she began. "It's been hard getting ahold of you. Spending all your time away with that woman, I suppose."

"I do have a job, Mom—" leaving the "unlike my brother" part of the sentence unspoken. "Caspar's down one chef, so I've been filling in a lot. I haven't even had much time for Misty." *A small lie,* he thought, smiling across the room at his supersized love. She blew a kiss his way, then continued fingering through the *Gourmet* magazine in her lap. "Could mean a promotion."

"Well, it's about time that man started to appreciate you," Petra sniffed. "Have I told you lately how proud I am of you?"

"Not lately."

"Well, I am. And your father would be just as proud. Did I tell you Misty sent me a thank-you note?"

"No again, Mom. But I'm not surprised. She really liked your gift. In fact, she's got it displayed behind the counter of her shop."

"She's not trying to sell it, is she?" Aghast.

"Of course not," Joe reassured her.

"Well, there's something about her that's got me concerned," she continued. "Your brother wasn't too impressed with her."

"Mom, I stopped listening to Jimmy when he got kicked off the police force. When was the last time he brought home any woman worth talking about?"

"But you're my baby; I just don't want to see you ruining your life. Like your brother has."

"He's thirty-two—his life's hardly over!"

"Maybe," she allowed, then switched topics once more. "By the way, did you hear that Luba Hernandez is getting married? A good June wedding in a Catholic church. You know, I used to imagine you two getting together."

"She's built like a boy. We were never an item."

"Didn't you two go to a dance together?"

"It was a seventh grade parochial school dance. And we didn't go together, we just danced a couple times while we were there." He took a deep breath, then brought the conversation back where it belonged. "Mom, you'd better get used to seeing Misty because she's the woman for me!" Misty beamed at him happily, then rose to kiss him on the cheek.

"Well, you know I just want the best for my baby," they both could hear through the receiver.

"Believe me, Mom, I've got it, and you should be happy for me."

"Well, I am, as long as you're happy—"

She's still leaving herself an out, Joe realized, but he knew it was probably the best he could hope for tonight. Reassuring Petra that he was indeed happy, Joe hung up the phone and turned to Misty. "Ears burning?" he asked, standing and reaching down to kiss her plump lips.

"Just don't touch my earrings," she joked. "You might blister your fingers."

"I'll be careful," Joe said, as he cupped her face within his palms and moved in closer.

EPISODE THIRTY-EIGHT

THE HOSPITAL CORRIDOR STRETCHED FOREVER, cramped and bustling, unfriendly even to a midsized woman like Jenny. It was almost a relief when she finally made it to her mother's room. At least there was a place to sit down, she thought gratefully, stepping around the nylon curtain separating her mother from an empty bed nearer the door. She found Alice half asleep, dressed in one of her thin cotton nighties, a nasal cannula leading from her nostrils, IV drip trailing along her left arm. Tinges of blue-gray still suffused her lips and cheeks.

Her mother had been transported to the hospital around three in the morning. "Difficulty breathing," explained the head nurse, a matronly size twenty with a rhinestone flag pin on her ample right breast. "What we call paroxysmal nocturnal dyspnea. Which is just a fancy way of saying she woke up and found she couldn't inhale."

The nurse backed out of view, leaving Jenny with her mother. Alice's eyes fluttered, then focused on her daughter. "Mom," Jenny started. "How you doing?"

"You off work today?" her mother asked weakly.

"No, I got a call at work," Jenny replied. "I've got both Friday and Monday off for the Fourth. But that's not important now. How are you feeling?"

"Like an octopus—has been sitting on my chest," Alice described, and Jenny spent a few seconds pondering the source of that simile.

"Why didn't you call me?" she finally posed, as gently as her concern allowed. "I could have brought you to the hospital. You didn't ask your neighbor again, did you?"

"Ambulance," Alice said simply. "Didn't want to bother you." She paused to gather strength for her next sentence. "Wish I had a cigarette—I know it'd help me breathe." Leaning back into the pillow, she coughed once and closed her eyes.

Sighing, Jenny took the chair and silently watched her mother pretend to sleep. On the mounted Panasonic a muted soap couple were in serious conversation.

"Jenny! Good to see you again!" a deep voice came from the doorway, and she looked up to see her mother's doctor. Dr. Paul had been her physician, too, during girlhood. To this day Jenny associated him with a vast parade of speed-laced prescriptions designed to make her lose weight. He strode into the room, grabbing the clipboard at the foot of the bed, then adjusted his trifocals to read the scribble.

"Your mother had a PND last night; it's her second in as many months," he intoned. "Congestive heart failure. She really needs to change her lifestyle."

"Mom's heart problems," Jenny began, "could they be from using fen/phen?"

"I never prescribed fen/phen to your mother," Dr. Paul answered. "She asked me for a scrip, but based on her history I couldn't in all conscience write one up for her."

That didn't stop you from prescribing every other drug under the sun, Jenny screamed inwardly. But she held her tongue.

From the bed, Alice had opened her eyes and was beaming at the physician. "Dr. Paul," she said, giving him a smile that bordered on flirt, if not for the plastic tubing draping over it. "I hope my daughter—isn't giving you a hard time."

"Not at all, Mother," he answered, jovially moving to the side of the bed. "I was just telling her about your pulmonary edema. It's most likely you had a small heart attack last night."

Linus Paul was thin and gray-haired, a few years past traditional retirement, and in Alice's eyes could do no wrong. When Jenny switched to a more fat-friendly woman GP her mother had reacted like she'd just been told Jenny was involved with a married man. "What kind of woman wants to be a doctor, anyhow?" she'd snorted derisively at her daughter.

"Same sort of woman who wants to be a lawyer," Jenny had answered. "I just feel more comfortable with her than I do Dr. Paul."

Still, Dr. Paul clearly had the proper bedside manner with Alice. Patting her hand in that too-bright hospital room, he spoke with the benign seriousness of the master of a children's puppet show. "I'm going to be honest with you both—" as if his every other utterance had not been. "This level of CHF calls for an aggressive response—anticoagulants to thin your blood, maybe some beta blockers. This is way beyond the 'cut down on salts' stage."

Jenny rose, grabbing her mother's free hand. For once, Alice had nothing to say.

THE DAY WAS SO HUMID that Paul was looking forward to a delicious blast of movie theater air conditioning. His own little window unit was struggling bravely, but in desperation. As he rang Ian's bell he peered through the door window into the entryway. There were, he saw, quite a few boxes piled precariously against the wall. Must be Valerie's stuff, he supposed.

"Paul!" Ian exclaimed as he opened the door, a what-the-hell-are-you-doing-here? look on his face.

"'The truth is out there!' Sort of," Paul announced portentously, stepping into a burst of central air. His hand grazed an unopened box with a bright red "As Seen on TV" logo. It looked like some sort of exercise contraption.

"We were going to check out *Men in Black!*" Ian remembered. "God, I'm sorry, Paul—I haven't had it together at all lately." Ian led him into the living room, which was, Paul noted, also crammed with boxes and well-stuffed lawn bags. The only free seat was in front of the computer. Scoping out the room as if seeing it afresh, Ian quickly swooped to sweep a corner of the couch clean, then gestured Paul into the space.

"Haven't had a chance to straighten up yet," Ian muttered apologetically.

"S'alright. Looks like you've been pretty busy," Paul ventured.

"Things are starting to ease up," Ian told him. "Val's decided not to go with the Flolan at this time; it's a pretty intense treatment with a breathing tube or something. The doctor's got her on some other medication that seems to be helping. She's breathing better, anyway."

"I had no idea it was that serious," Paul said.

"Oh, we have good days and bad days." Suddenly Ian's head jerked up, cocking like Molly's when she heard something beyond Paul's auditory abilities. "Be back in a minute," he said, dashing upstairs. A second later, Paul heard it: a plaintive voice calling Ian's name. Was this her second call, or had Ian just gotten good at anticipating it?

Paul sat back, picking a "Rose Is Rose" collection from the arm of the couch and scanning it for fat-friendly strips. Finally Ian re-emerged carrying an empty Big Sip glass.

"Sorry, Paul. Don't think I can make the movie today," he informed him ruefully.

"Need any help?"

"Naw. I've had to bring a lot of work home lately, and I need to catch up on it." He indicated his workstation, which for once was the least disheveled location in the room.

"Okay." Paul rose and watched Ian rush into the kitchenette to pull a Brita container from the refrigerator. "I'll let you get back to work then."

"Let me know if the movie's any good."

"I'll Gene and Roger it for you." Paul headed for the door, pausing to say something but not sure what it was. "Happy Fourth," he settled for as he left Ian and Valerie's condo.

EPISODE THIRTY-NINE

WE REALLY NEED NEW SHEETS, Ian decided, lifting the corner of his queen-size mattress to free the fitted percale bottom. Neither he nor Valerie owned any bed linen less than four years old; the fabric's dinginess only added to the whole depressive atmosphere. On the clock radio an old Stealers Wheel song was jauntily thumbing its nose at Ian—stuck in the middle, all right.

Valerie had shut herself into the bathroom, doing some heavy duty shower-massaging from the sound of it. Since moving in Valerie had developed uncharacteristic modesty. Ian blamed it on the fact that she seemed to be regaining all the weight she'd lost. Val claimed it was a side effect of her medication. But Ian was familiar enough with the dynamics of yo-yo dieting to believe otherwise.

Sighing, he pulled the sheets off the bed and began to bunch them into a wad. As he turned to deposit it in the laundry chute he heard a rattle at the side of the bed. A loose corner had knocked Valerie's medications to the floor.

He stooped to pick up her pill bottles. Worse luck—one of the "child-proof" caps had been incompletely fastened, spilling a mélange of multicolored pills onto the carpet.

Odd, Ian thought as he scooped up a handful of caplets. Not only were they different colors, they were also variably shaped. Examining the prescription label, he found the medication's name was covered by a yellow sticker that advised the patient to "take hour before meals."

Ian carefully slid the pills back into their bottle. Once he'd resealed it he squinted at the label, then began to peel away the yellow sticker. It came off remarkably easy. The name was still unreadable, but he knew it couldn't possibly account for the smorgasbord of pills inside. A sticky residue on the unlabeled portion of the bottle hinted that the yellow warning had originally been placed elsewhere.

Ian wasn't sure what this meant, but it was clear something wasn't right. Reopening the bottle, he took a couple samples and shoved them into his shirt pocket. In the bathroom Val had shut off the water. Ian quickly returned to making their bed. Once Val had crawled back in he'd see what he could find on the Web about this "prescription."

"IS THIS THE WIDEST SHOWER STALL you've got?" Lainie asked, stepping inside the object of her query. Dressed in an Uppity Blues Women T and jeans, she bumped her upper midsized frame against the shower door and put both hands up like some silent-film heroine struggling to keep the walls from closing in. Framed within the bathroom entrance, Eleanor was checking items on her clipboard. Between them a youngish hotel manager watched them both with concern.

"We've never had any complaints about our showers before," he replied in puzzled tones. Stepping out of the stall, Lainie turned her attention to the toilet. It was, she noted, mounted on the wall.

"We have attendees who'd have real difficulty with this bathroom," she finally explained. "For a toilet like this to work, for instance, you need to put something under it for support. Just a block of wood would do. That is, unless you want a lot of toilets coming out of the wall."

The manager glanced from Lainie to Eleanor—obviously gauging their sizes—and asked thoughtfully, "What was the name of your group again?"

"RADFAm," Eleanor answered softly. "We're a size acceptance group."

"Which means you'll be getting a hotel full of fat people," Lainie elaborated. "We need a space that's fat friendly." She led the manager from the bathroom into the center of the smokefree room, taking the clipboard from Eleanor as she passed.

"Your guest rooms," she read, "are located a long way from the conference rooms. There are no benches in the hallway for folks to rest on. Your pool needs steps and a handrail on the shallow end—narrow ladders just won't cut it. All the seats in your restaurant have armrests, as do the chairs here." She tapped a chair by the phone for emphasis. "Plus you don't get HBO."

"HBO?" The man now looked totally perplexed.

"Joke," Lainie smiled, handing the clipboard back to Eleanor, who seemed glad to have something to hold onto. "This doesn't mean you're out of the running. Just that you'll need to do some work if you want to deal with a convention in excess of 300 fat men and women."

The way the young hotel manager was eyeing Lainie, it was clear he was weighing whether he wanted to deal with said convention or not. "How—um—fat are we talking?" he finally asked.

"Never can tell," Lainie answered. "But it sure wouldn't be right for a size acceptance group to hold a three-day convention somewhere that couldn't comfortably accommodate its members' special needs. Enough hassles out there the other 362 days of the year."

The manager nodded with what he apparently imagined was a knowing look. They headed back to the reception area, Lainie all the while complimenting the hotel's decor—which went a long way toward soothing the thoroughly nonplussed manager.

"You do this so much better than me," Eleanor remarked as they walked across the parking lot to Lainie's Dodge Caravan. The afternoon was hazy, filled with the acrid smell of highway exhaust. Overhead a 747 was circling, waiting its turn at the airport.

"Come from a family of pushy broads," Lainie joked. "Earl says I'm the cream of the crop, though."

"Well, I'm glad you're with me," Eleanor admitted as she slid into the passenger seat. "If you hadn't agreed to join me, I might have put this off even longer."

"Didja tell Misty you needed some help with this?"

"Not exactly."

"'Not exactly,'" Lainie parroted. "I swear, Ellie, sometimes you can be too damn wishy-washy. Just be glad Connie didn't win that election. If she had, you'd be chewed up and spit out in little pieces by now. Misty may be a bit flaky, but she won't bite your head off if you ask for assistance."

She steered the minivan out of the lot and toward the highway. Traffic was starting to heat up as the area's industrial parks let out first shift. It was the kind of driving that Eleanor would do anything to avoid, but Lainie seemed undeterred.

"I liked how that last one asked questions," Lainie decided, snaking between lanes with a speed Eleanor was doing her best to ignore. "How many more hotels do we have?"

"Two more on the list," Eleanor informed her.

"Can we hold off 'til tomorrow then?" Lainie asked. "Earl's on the road tomorrow, and I'd like some quality time with him tonight."

"Sure," Eleanor nodded. Lainie's second husband was twenty years her junior (what could they possibly talk about? Eleanor often wondered), a consultant for the state's Department of Human Services. To Eleanor it appeared that he was out of the house more days than not, but that didn't seem to bother Lainie. She'd lived both married and single—Earl's schedule, she asserted, gave her the best of both lives.

Eleanor couldn't imagine. She'd been a widow for so long. The thought of some man sharing her home—the sound of his key in the lock, even his foot-steps, opening the refrigerator—why, it would probably scare the very wits out of her. When had she turned into such a solitary soul? She wasn't sure. But she was probably too set in her ways now.

Still, if Dexter were free, she might be willing to risk trying—again.

"So Dad, think we could do a movie? After all that backwoods action, I need a flick fix."

Dex chuckled and exchanged looks with Neeko, who was prepping beans and franks for the microwave. Clearly Jackie wasn't the only one who'd missed the conveniences of the 1990s. "Any particular 'flick' in mind?" he asked, wondering which of the season's popcorn fare had caught his son's fancy. Since he'd started martial arts class Jackie hadn't been to a movie in months.

"*Jurassic Park II!*" Jackie shouted. "I must be the only kid in the world who hasn't seen it yet."

"Big dinosaur movies—ah, so size really does matter," Dexter noted.

"That's what I've always said," Neeko put in as the microwave dinged.

"You can come, too, Mom," Jackie offered. "They bring a T. Rex back to the states in this one."

"Boy Movies," Neeko sniffed. "Will you please go and get your sister, Jackie? Tell her lunch is ready."

"So are we going to the movie?" Jackie asked again. "I don't know if I can make it all the way upstairs with all that uncertainty tying me up."

"And I thought you were learning how to rise above such petty concerns," Dex shot back. "Looks like I'm wasting all my money, kung fu boy. But, sure, okay, we'll go."

"All right!" Jackie raced out of the kitchen and disappeared from view.

"He really does seem a whole lot happier," Dex commented.

Neeko nodded, leaving the counter and putting her arms around his vast middle. She smiled up at him companionably. "He's got a good father," she said, giving him a very slow kiss.

"Do that again and to hell with the matinee."

"Try to hold that thought for later, Rex." She cocked her head and indi-cated the returning Jackie. The two of them reluctantly separated.

"Count on it," Dexter winked.

"Rachel's not hungry," Jackie announced, grabbing a plate. "Can I have hers?"

"Eat what's on your plate," Neeko answered, "then we'll see."

For one moment Dex felt a shudder of uncertainty. Ever since they'd re-turned from vacation Rachel had spent all her time sequestered in her room.

Obviously there was something on her mind.

"I'll go talk to her," Neeko said, reading his concern. "You two check out the matinee times."

Dexter sighed and watched his slender wife head for their daughter's bedroom.

"You're not trying to give me the runaround, are ya, Gorgeous?"

Misty took a deep cleansing breath, then centered on the sight of Joe, who was watching from the couch. It didn't take long for Greg Dillman to get her ire up, but she couldn't afford to be Ms. Self-Righteous today. "No," she explained, "but the chapter treasurer has had a death in her family, and she won't be available for at least a week. We are very interested in working out a mutually beneficial plan, but I don't feel comfortable meeting without her present."

"Okay, okay," Dillman sighed. "Why don't you call back when your friend can join you?" Even over the phone he could manage to make her explanation sound suspect. Misty agreed, then gratefully hung up the phone.

"I've really got mixed feelings about this whole deal," she confessed to Joe. "Every time I talk to Dillman I feel like I should take a shower afterwards."

"I've got a loofah," Joe offered helpfully.

But before she could ask to see it there was a brisk knock at her door. Joe rose to answer it, stepping back to let Kirk and Brian into the apartment. They were both wearing garb from their cruise, though Brian's was quite a few Xs larger than Kirk's.

"Well, you two have obviously been keeping yourselves busy," Misty noted. "We've hardly seen you!"

It was a familiar plaint for Misty. Whenever Kirk found a new beau, he tried to keep them both cloistered from the world as much as possible. Once, in a fit of pique, she'd accused him of hiding his lovers from her because he was afraid they might secretly be straight FAs.

"Yeah, yeah, yeah," Kirk moaned. "I told you, Brian, this girl's so egocentric she barely begrudges me a moment's pleasure."

"It's been one pretty long moment," Misty snipped. "Brian's been in town for more than two weeks, and we haven't had dinner together even once."

"What did I also tell you?" Kirk smirked, nudging his friend's ample paunch. "These two are notorious encouragers! They work in tandem and are infamous throughout the city."

"Sounds like you've been keeping something from me," Brian answered. His voice was not as deep as you'd expect coming from that thick diaphragm, but it was pleasantly professorial. Steering himself to the couch where Joe had been seated, he lowered himself onto the cushion with a sturdy wolf-handled cane, Kirk perching on the arm next to him. Joe moved to stand beside Misty's chair.

"Of course I have," Kirk told the room. "Can you blame me?" He pulled a pamphlet from his shirt pocket and handed it to Misty.

"What's this?"

"Some new 'art' at the Botanical Gardens," he explained. "Thought you two might want to tag along tomorrow and have brunch—on us. Whatcha say?"

"'Big Bugs'?" Misty read quizzically. She looked toward Joe, who shrugged and said nothing.

"Classy, eh? I just knew you'd go for it." Twirling, Kirk grabbed Brian's cane and gestured to the door. Grimacing, Brian rose and followed, silently apologizing for their too-soon departure. "See you at eight, and don't be late! Also, don't forget the Flit! Industrial size!"

In spite of herself, Misty smiled. Only Kirk would bring up some long-forgotten WWII-era pesticide just because its name was so utterly un-PC. "Considering our host," she shot back, "how could I?"

EPISODE FORTY

JENNY HAD NEVER BEEN MUCH FOR TRAVEL—too-small airplane seats, terminals that required track shoes and cattle prods, hotels with all the amenities of solitary confinement. But this was by far the worst 'vacation' of all.

It'd started with the visit from her mother's lawyer. Alice had seemed to believe that death would never affect her (or at least never wanted to reveal such weakness to her daughter). So while she had prepared a will and made arrangements with Mr. Burton for her final disposition, these plans were unknown to Jenny.

Andrew Burton, Esquire greeted Jenny at the hospital shortly after Alice's passing. As executor of the estate he had brought the documents outlining her last wishes. Even in death, her mother held a few surprises.

"She wanted to go home—to Independence, Missouri," Mr. Burton stated, reading from his notes. "There's a family plot there, with space reserved for her. She hadn't consulted with a funeral home regarding a casket, although she has earmarked a sum of $2,000 toward it and any funeral service you may desire."

Great, Jenny groaned inwardly. *A whole $2,000.*

"I know a local director who can handle the, uh, travel arrangements for Mrs. Taylor. Will you want to accompany her?"

Until that moment, Jenny hadn't really understood the scope of this undertaking.

Now, 48 HOURS LATER, she'd rather have been left blessedly innocent. Oh sure, everyone had been very kind. The folks at USA's TLC program had taken charge of her mother's remains, found Jenny space (or what jets call "space") on the same flight, and made arrangements with the Woodlawn Memorial Home and Cemetery in Independence for transfer to their facility. All Jenny had to do was sit back and "enjoy the ride," as one perky flight attendant suggested. Her mother lay in a casket in the cargo hold below.

Since there was no airport in Independence, the closest she could fly was Kansas City International, a huge hub facility that made her head spin. But as promised a representative of Woodlawn was waiting, name board in hand, as she disembarked, ushering her to a long black hearse and collecting the casket from its holding area.

Thus she found herself being ferried to Independence by Mr. Seals, the archetypical funeral director: gray-suited, gray-skinned, slim to the point of emacia, utterly serene. The rolling miles melted beneath the powerful tires of the hearse as she watched city fade to suburb to rural. Advertisements for Truman's home and library, Vaile Mansion and the Mormon Visitors Center began to spring up the closer they came. Finally after many twists and turns Mr. Seals pulled into the gate of the cemetery where Alice's final act would be played.

Jenny timidly entered the funeral home, sniffing suspiciously at the too-fresh odor of the place, poking her head into the various viewing rooms, taking in all the Victorian touches. In another setting she was sure they'd seem charming, but in her state of mind all the drapes and carpets and velvet wingback chairs were permeated by the stench of decades of death. "Just stop it," she shook herself. "You can get through this." She wished she had taken Lissa up on her offer of companionship, though.

Finally Mr. Seals returned from whatever duty had left her on her own. He sat down with her on a small tapestry settee and began, "I understand that your mother made no plans for a funeral service. Since our Memorial Home has taken care of the needs of the Hall family for many years, we've arranged a simple service by Reverend Pope from the Methodist church where her mother and father were lifelong, steadfast members.

"The service has been set for tomorrow morning at 11," he continued, "with visitation an hour before. I hope this is acceptable to you, Ms. Taylor?"

What would he say if it weren't, she wondered, then decided it wouldn't shift a muscle in that placid face. "That would be fine, Mr. Seals," she replied demurely.

"There is a lovely bed-and-breakfast two blocks from here. I told Mrs. Campbell you might want to stay tonight. May I give you a ride?"

And with that, Jenny was once again whisked somewhere she had little power to protest.

YES, THE B&B WAS LOVELY—refreshing and cool and most welcoming after the stresses of the past few days. And yes, Mrs. Campbell had gone out of her way to take care of her "poor little lamb" of a boarder. But Jenny felt that if this whole ordeal didn't end really soon, she would go stark, screaming lunatic.

The hour for the visitation came all too soon for her, however, and once again the gray little funeral director collected her—not in the hearse this time but a sleek black sedan, funeral flag flapping on its antenna. The morning sparkled after a gentle overnight shower, and Jenny almost enjoyed the short ride back to the cemetery.

Several cars were already parked in front of the memorial chapel. Since her mother hadn't visited her childhood home for decades, Jenny wondered why people who didn't know her would take time out of their days to attend her funeral. She'd personally rather have a root canal.

It was a slow day for the mortuary, it seemed. Only one funeral listed on the board in the vestibule. She walked to the indicated parlor and down the aisle to her mother's casket. Whoever had prepared her had done a beautiful job—Jenny expected Alice to sit up at any moment and demand a cigarette. But the hands remained folded, cold and stiff, face masterfully madeup to imitate the bloom of life.

Mr. Seals appeared unobtrusively beside Jenny as she stared dry-eyed at her mother. She glanced up and said, "Thank you for all you've done. I think she'd be very pleased." What else could she say?

"Thank you. When you're ready, you may either sit in the private room behind that sheer curtain, or in the front row here. There are Kleenex under the seats." Was he chastising her for not crying?

Jenny made her way to the chair farthest from the aisle on the right, sheltered against the wall. There she watched as her fellow mourners marched in to pay their respects. The usual funeral group, she supposed—bluehaired matrons, mostly, with a smattering of wizened men of incalculable age, taking notes for their own festivities.

But one woman stood out from the others. Younger than most, no more than forty. Mousy hair pulled severely back from a full face unadorned by cosmetics. Stout figure corseted into a dark brown doubleknit dress topped by a scalloped white collar. Sensible shoes. All in all like a human baked potato. And also unlike the others, she was quietly crying. Jenny wished she'd turn around, but when she finally did her face was obscured by a tissue as she took a seat near the back.

Promptly at 11 the minister walked through a side door, taking his place behind the ornately carved podium. Jenny hadn't noticed until then that soft organ music had been playing, but at a gesture from the minister the hymn stopped and the service began.

"We gather here today to say goodbye to our sister—Alice Gertrude Hall Taylor." A noticeable pause as the reverend glanced down at his notes. "The daughter of Kyle and Margaret Hall, longtime residents of Independence, she spent her childhood here until moving—out of state."

Jenny gritted her teeth as during the next twenty minutes the minister prayed, read Scriptures and Psalms, related totally unrelated anecdotes, and continued to forget Alice's name. At surreptitious signals the bespectacled organist interspersed "Rock of Ages," "Amazing Grace," and other faintly familiar hymns within his eulogy. Finally Reverend Pope announced that a private interment—no mourners, please—would take place in the cemetery, and with that he walked out the side door once more.

The audience began to file from the room, until only Jenny and the baked potato lady were left. Jenny felt that since this woman seemed even more affected than she (and did that make her a truly horrible daughter?), it was her duty to offer some condolence. So she got up and walked back to where the woman still sat, alone and bereft.

"Uh, hello," she said to the top of the seated woman's head and slid into a chair in front of her. "I'm Jenny. Did you, um, know my mother?"

The woman glanced up, and Jenny was shocked to see an older self mirrored back at her. "No," she said quietly. "I never knew her. But she's my mother, too."

EPISODE FORTY-ONE

"I ALWAYS KNEW I WAS ADOPTED," Cassandra Stewart began as Jenny scrutinized her new-found sister's face across the diner table. "Every night Mama and I would kneel beside my bed and say our prayers. And Mama would always thank God for the grace of Alice Hall, who gave her the most precious gift of all—me."

Jenny quelled a guilty feeling of discomfort (or was it envy?) at this earnest remembrance. Breaking eye contact, she leaned back in her chair and took in her surroundings.

The Koffee Kup Diner would not have been her first choice as the scene for such revelations. But after the funeral the two women decided that a heart-to-heart was in order, and the homey family restaurant was convenient. Besides, Jenny was famished after the ordeal of the morning.

The clientele was just as homey—leathery, salt-of-the-earth types in jeans and Ts, sporting John Deere and Funk Seed caps, hunched over bottomless cups of coffee and discussing the weather. Dolores, their harried waitress, was paper-thin and wafted an aromatic blend of sweat and nicotine every time she hove by.

"Whatcha have, ladies?" she asked, after slapping two menus onto the still-damp table and giving them scant seconds to decide.

"I'd like the Skinny-Minny plate, please," Cassandra replied, "and a Fresca."

"BLT with fries sounds great," Jenny countered. "And how 'bout a Cherry Coke?"

Dolores peered down, scrutinizing the young blonde, and pointedly said, "I'm sorry, we don't have diet Cherry Coke. And is that fat-free mayo or regular?"

Jenny smiled up at her sweetly. "No, regular mayo will be fine, and I hate the taste of NutraSweet." The waitress turned on her heel, swirling reproach and cigarette fumes in her wake.

Cassandra smiled nervously. "To tell the truth, I miss the old diet soda, too. That new stuff leaves a nasty aftertaste."

"I wouldn't know about that. Never drank the stuff. Too many lab rats died testing it."

Her sister squirmed.

"Never mind," Jenny grinned sheepishly. "Please go on with your story, Casssandra."

"Oh, just call me Cassie. Cassandra was my Gram's name. Daddy's mother." A stray wisp of brown hair had fallen across her cheek and the older woman smoothed it back, relaxing as much as her girdle would allow. "Mama told me all about your mother. Alice was only seventeen when she had me over the summer between her junior and senior years."

"What a scandal that must have been!"

"Not as much as it might," Cassie replied. "The timing couldn't have been better. Your mother was a good-sized girl and was able to hide her condition under loose dresses." A sad note crept into her voice as she continued. "Heaven knows my 'father' didn't want anything to do with me. For him Alice was just a conquest—'not bad for a fat chick.' He joined the Army to avoid the responsibility.

"Mama, of course, knew about the pregnancy. The Halls were longtime family friends, had known them at church, even watched Alice as a little girl. At the time Daddy and Mama had been married for ten years, and they wanted children so much. But whenever she got pregnant she'd miscarry, and finally her doctor told her that she simply had to stop trying or it would kill her.

"And so when your mother got into trouble, the two families decided it was in everyone's best interest if she went away for the summer to a distant aunt's home to give birth, come back and finish school. I was born on August 1, 1961, during a thunderstorm." As she finished this extended narrative, Cassie took a deep breath and glanced at Jenny for her reaction.

The tableau was interrupted by the arrival of Dolores with their lunches. "Anything else right now?" The question came across semi-sneer.

"No thanks. This looks really yummy." With that Jenny popped a fry in her mouth and grinned at the scandalized waitress. As Delores stalked off, Jenny turned back to her sister. "All I can say is I wish I'd known about you sooner. I've never even sent you a birthday card."

A mixture of relief and pure joy spread over Cassie's face, and her eyes began to well up. Jenny handed her a napkin. "I'm just being silly, I know," Cassie sobbed. "But I was so afraid you'd hate me!"

"Why, for heaven's sake? I've always wanted a sister! I could just shoot my mother. Did she even stay in touch?"

"Sure. For the first few years she sent me remembrances, little toys and gifts and notes from 'your secret friend.' I knew they were from her. Then, after she got married and you were born, the notes came less often. But she always sent me a Christmas card with a $5 bill and the message to buy myself something pretty. Through your grandmother I started to send her letters and cards as a young adult, and once, when she came alone to visit her parents, we met in Kansas City for dinner. She loved to talk about you and all your accomplishments. She was so proud of you."

"Why couldn't she tell me she was proud? I can't ever remember her saying one single positive thing about me."

Cassie took Jenny's hand and gave it a squeeze. "Alice felt she'd ruined everyone's lives with one youthful 'accident.' I can't speak for her, but I'll bet she simply wanted to keep you from making the same errors in judgment." Cassie looked deeply into eyes that so mirrored hers. Jenny felt her own eyes start to moisten. "Don't doubt her love for you. She'd just learned early that loving too much meant losing.

"Now," she continued briskly, picking up her fork and poking at the cold hamburger patty. "Where do we go from here, little sister?"

"Well," Jenny answered, wiping her eyes, "Do you have a spare bedroom?"

"**THINK I COULD BE JAMES WHITMORE?**" Kirk was asking, striking a manly pose in front of the 700-pound wooden ant. Brian stepped back with his Canon before answering and snapped a picture of the gesticulating Kirk. Brian sure got around pretty good for a guy with a cane, Joe thought.

He hadn't expected to be having such a good time with Misty's neighbor. But he was realizing that FAs had plenty in common, no matter what their orientation. Also, Kirk had a history with Misty that Joe envied.

"You don't have the movie hero look, Kirk—more like a movie critic. Michael Medved, maybe," Brian scoffed, snapping his camera case shut.

Perhaps it helped that Brian did not fit any of the stereotypes that Joe still carried. In a safari shirt and greying hair he looked like your average weekending suburban businessman.

"If you're gonna be nasty," Kirk parried, unabashed, still in movie geek mode. "You've got to admit that *Them* is the pinnacle when it comes to giant bug flicks. I remember it gave me nightmares when I was a kid." He smacked the ant on the snout as if to chasten it for those childhood terrors. Yards away two equally colossal ants trudged across the manicured lawn, poised to disrupt someone's picnic. A camera-laden couple circled them, trying to find the best angle to capture all three ants in the bright summer light.

"The movie does have a great opening," Brian admitted. "It's effective until they actually show the monster ants. But—I'm sorry—giant insects simply don't compute biologically. At this size," indicating the towering vine-constructed statue, "gravity would make Them collapse."

"He's even more of a killjoy when it comes to encourager fiction," Kirk confided loudly to Joe. "'Nobody can gain weight that quickly—or get around so effortlessly at that size.' Another argument against gravity of any kind, I say."

Joe glanced toward Misty, who was resting on a shaded bench near a faux alpine waterfall. Tilting her head back and dabbing a handkerchief of Evian water on her face and cleavage, she examined an impossibly delicate damselfly. He saw that the supersized beauty was flushed and disheveled, her batik top and crushed silk skirt sticking to her sweat-slick body, looking for all the world like she'd just barely survived a Saharan trek. Perhaps, he suddenly realized, this trip to the Botanical Gardens hadn't been such a great idea.

"I get all my science from Bill Nye," Joe said as he turned back to the duo. "And he hasn't done a show on weight gain fantasies yet. I did see one on giant insects, and Bill would side with Brian." He smiled, then dashed over to Misty's side.

"You okay?" he asked, easing himself into the small slice of wrought iron bench still available. Despite the shade the bench had absorbed the late morning's upper eighty degree heat. Misty snorted derisively.

"'Okay'?" she echoed. "I've been huffing after all three of you since we got here! I'm pooped. And more than a little PO'd, too." She took a swig of bottled water, then continued. "I expect it from Kirk—he's too besotted to notice anybody but Brian. But I was hoping for a little more consideration from you.

"I'm no speed demon. I've got a lot of woman here to maneuver. This is our first time on an adventure like this, so we can chalk some of it up to inexperience. But if you really hope to have a relationship with a supersized woman, you're going to figure size and ability into the equation."

His face flushed with embarrassment. "I know," Joe said meekly. "The truth is, I wasn't thinking."

She softened at the sight of his fidgeting discomfort. "Hold my hand when we're out like this," she suggested. "That will keep us closer together." Joe nodded agreeably. At that moment Kirk and Brian were moving toward the shady oasis. "Like the song says, 'I'm built for comfort, not for speed.'"

"I know that one," Kirk chimed in. "It's by—some old blues guy! How you doing, Mist?"

"Fine now," she told the couple, reaching over to pat Joe's knee. "Enjoying the gardens, Brian?"

"Quite lovely," he told them, "though all this walking is hard on my knees." He gestured toward an island with his cane. "You two up to checking out the Japanese garden, then calling it quits?"

Joe looked to Misty. Smiling, she nodded and intertwined her fingers with his.

"Sure," Joe replied. "Go on ahead, though. We'll catch up."

EPISODE FORTY-TWO

RING...RING...CLICK! "Greetings! You have reached the law office of Lissa Jones. I'm sorry I am unable to take your call at this time, but if you'll leave your name, telephone number and a brief description of the nature of your call, I will return it as soon as possible. Thank you."

Jenny fidgeted through the message, which seemed longer than she'd remembered. You noticed every second when you were phoning long distance. But it was important that she leave word for her boss about her soon-to-be-extended leave of absence.

Beep! "Lissa, it's Jenny. I wanted to tell you this personally, but I can't for the life of me remember your home phone number. With all that's happened, it's a wonder I could remember this one. And of course I didn't bring my address book to Missouri.

"I'm sorry, but I need to have a few more days off. Don't worry, I'm fine. But something has come up, a really wonderful something.

"If you need to reach me, leave a message at 816-555-8397. Wish I could tell you more right now, but I'm still sorting it all out. Please call Misty for me and tell her when I'll be back. I'll see you next Monday and fill you in then. Thank you! Bye!"

"You have no clue what's keeping her down there?"

"No—and it's taking every ounce of willpower to keep from calling and grilling her," Lissa snorted. In the background Misty could hear Delia shouting that Lissa had her permission to call Jenny back.

"From what you've said, Jenny's life is in major flux," Misty considered. Across the room on the television Leonard Nimoy was mouthing faux mystery-history on the ancient Aztecs; the show pre-dated captioning, so she had to make up her own words along the way. "It's best to let her find her own way."

"I knew if I called you'd reel me in," Lissa conceded. "If she needs anything, she'll call. But perhaps I should leave my home phone number? Just in case she really needs to suddenly reach me."

"Come on now, Lissa. Jenny just lost one mother; she doesn't need a surrogate."

"Damn, I'm really doing it, aren't I? It's just that she's so much younger than—" Her words trailed off. As if on cue, someone knocked at Misty's front door. Only her tenants had such damnable timing.

"Be right with you!" Misty called, quickly buttoning the cotton big-shirt that was serving as her only morning wear. "Got someone at the door, Lissa. You want, we can talk about this later. I'll reach Greg and set a meeting up for her return."

"It's just me," Kirk said through the door. "Brian's gone, I'm utterly bereft and even Howlie's lookin' mopey—but take your time."

"I'll let ya know if I hear anything else," Lissa promised before hanging up.

Misty rose to let in Kirk, back from taking his hunky beau to the airport.

"**Hold still**," Paul warned Molly as she twisted, whining piteously in his grasp. "Just one more cocklebur left." Along with nail trims and flea baths, bur removal ranked high on the golden retriever's list of Things Best Avoided. This morning for a change of scenery they'd visited a new park, but on the basis of this maddening mess Paul didn't think they'd be going back anytime soon.

Lifting her chin, he carefully searched the hairy terrain of her vulnerable throat with scissors for the final offending patch of weed and hair. Just as he honed in on the culprit the phone rang, startling Molly and causing Paul to quickly drop his scissors.

"Daily, you there?" Dillman demanded through the answering machine. "If so, pick up!"

"What do you want, Greg?" Paul sighed, as Molly gratefully scooted behind the couch. Tying the previously trimmed fur in a plastic grocery bag, he neatly tossed the prickly parcel into a nearby wastecan.

"I'm calling with an opportunity, Paulie," Dillman got right to the point as Paul answered. "I've been talking with Misty Shores—the Good Witch of the Midwest—about teaming up with RADFAm for some social events. Thought you might want to be in the action."

"Why me?"

"Well, you know both groups, yet you don't have a lot of ties to either one," Dillman explained. "I don't wanna be outnumbered by the Estrogen Squad. You'd make for a good referee."

"Are you sure about that?" Paul asked. "Last size acceptance gathering I attended turned out to be a bit intense."

"Oh hell, we've all been slapped by Connie one way or the other," Dillman responded lightly. "It's practically a badge of honor."

"So who's going to be at the meeting?"

"Me. You. Misty. And that blonde chick who pushed Ian's girlfriend into the pool last year."

Paul let that remark pass. What was Greg really up to? he wondered. He knew better than to take this man's words at face value, but he couldn't see why he was angling to bring Paul into this venture. "And the agenda for this meeting is—?"

"We're gonna be pooling resources; we need to establish what these resources are. RADFAm's got geezers with moola (present company excepted, of course), and we've got youth and vitality."

"Sure hope you didn't use that, uh, distinction on Misty."

"Give me a little credit! I've been soothing and smoothing big beautiful broads for years. Well, you in or not?"

Paul visualized the blonde—yeah, Jenny—as he'd last seen her, election night. At the time he'd thought she was Ian's girlfriend, but that hadn't seemed to last. Now the thing he most remembered were her eyes. A man could drown in their sapphire depths.

"So when and where is this meeting?" he finally asked the eager Dillman.

EPISODE FORTY-THREE

THE CD JUKEBOX was in the process of randomly pulling a disc from its cache. Ian watched as it finally started spinning something old and harmonic. Doo-wop—the song was at least ten years too old for him, though his older brothers had played it when he was a small fry. Behind him, Dex was descending the stairs, two glasses of ginseng ice tea in his meaty hands.

"My newest grownup toy," Dex explained apologetically. "Rest of the family doesn't want to hear these moldy oldies, so I keep 'em down here." He handed Ian a glass, then lowered himself into a Dex-wide recliner. The former chapter president was wearing Saturday casual—Bears jersey and jeans, sandals with white socks—and looked more relaxed than Ian had ever remembered seeing him.

"Pretty nice," Ian understated, pulling up a barstool and straddling it with his long legs. On the juke young Frankie Lymon was asking the world why fools fell in love. Good question. "So how's things with Jackie?" Ian opened, as a means of delaying the most pressing question.

"Jack's been doing great," Dex answered. "He's really been getting into his martial arts classes. Now it's Rachel I'm worried about. She's been acting overly secretive lately, and I'm not sure what it's all about."

"If she told you, it wouldn't be a secret."

Dex smiled weakly. "I suppose, though it'd sure be nice to have a breather between kid worries." He swizzled the ice in his tea, then took a sip. The basement ceiling creaked from someone moving around in the kitchen above. "The joys of parenting—think I saw her for a whole fifteen minutes over our entire family vacation." He tapped the chair's armrest, then looked over toward Ian. "Maybe it's nothing," he concluded. "So you're here to ask about Val's pills."

"Did you find out anything?"

"Between you and the chapter, I'm beginning to feel like Quincy," Dex joked. "First it's that anonymously delivered candy; now this. I don't know what it means, but the tablets you gave me were nothing more than vitamins and diuretics. The vitamins weren't even listed in the PDR." He looked at Ian seriously. "You say Valerie's been taking them regularly?"

Ian nodded glumly, putting his glass down without even touching his tea.

"Well, the vitamins won't hurt her, but if she's taking too many of those caffeine pills, she'd better be careful. Particularly if she's still drinking."

"She claimed they were for PPH," Ian moaned. Yet Dexter's words were only confirming a suspicion he'd refused to examine seriously ever since Val had gotten back into his life.

"Primary regimen for pulmonary hypertension is prostacyclin," Dex told him. "Flolan. It's a pretty severe treatment, not just a handful of pills. If she were doing Flolan breathing treatments, you'd know it."

"I never even watched her take her meds," Ian said. "What an idiot I am!"

"We aren't handed guidelines on the correct way to live with a sick loved one," Dex told him. "From what I've seen, you've been doing your best."

"Not enough," Ian responded glumly. He lifted his glass, saw he'd left a ring on the counter, and quickly started wiping it up with his T-shirt sleeve.

"The best you can do is the most you can do," Dex said softly. He tossed a box of Kleenex to Ian and smiled wryly. On the juke The Platters were keening their way through "The Great Pretender."

Ian sipped his tea pensively. Now that his worst suspicion had been confirmed, what was he supposed to do about it?

WITH BETTER ATTENDANCE, we can hire the Grand Ballroom." Greg gestured broadly, his voice echoing around the empty hall.

Jenny spun slowly to take it all in. Even empty the room had art deco elegance—a far cry from the SkyAire. A hint of stale cigarette smoke spoiled the full effect, however.

"And maybe even charge a bit more. In the best interest of both chapters, of course," he hurried to add.

"Well, right now RADFAm has eighty-five paying members," Misty calculated, "though only fifteen to twenty are what I'd call 'active.' The dances have typically brought ten to fifteen non-members."

"Small beans," Dillman snorted amiably. "With the right publicity we can pack this ballroom!" He threw wide his arms in emphasis.

Jenny and Misty exchanged amused looks behind his back. "Now there's a straight line simply begging for a fat joke," Misty noted in a low voice. Jenny waggled her finger disapprovingly, then guiltily dropped it when Dillman turned back to them.

"So what do you think, ladies?" he asked. Dressed in a checked shirt with plain blue tie, navy blue Dockers and a pair of deck shoes, the insurance salesman was obviously working hard to keep things lowkey. It was so different from his usual Studboy-on-the-Prowl image that Jenny had to keep reminding herself what the real Greg Dillman was like.

"We could do a lot with this room," Misty agreed, eyeing her reflection in a mirrored column. With her hair pulled back she looked a lot more matronly than Jenny had ever remembered seeing her. The chapter president was almost as unflatteringly dressed as Jenny's sister; perhaps she thought it made her look more businesslike. "It will take a lot of commitment from your group, though. Most of us are going to be tied up with plans for the upcoming convention."

"Understood," Dillman agreed. "The main support we're looking for at the moment is fiscal. Full-Figured Friends has been running pretty close to the bone, so to speak. There's plenty of eager fresh faces in the group, though. And of course some overlapping memberships."

As if waiting outside all this time for his cue, a figure appeared in the ballroom's doorway and called Greg's name.

"I found out at the desk that you three were in here," Paul said as he approached the group. He was wearing jeans and a polo shirt with an embroidered school logo on the pocket, a pair of well-scraped walking shoes covering impossibly long feet. As a grin crossed his well-etched face Jenny felt an unexplained sense of disappointment. What was he doing here? she wondered. Paul seemed like a really nice guy—so why was he aligning himself with Dillman?

"Paul!" Dillman shouted back, rushing over to lead him in by the shoulder. "I invited him to our little meeting," he explained, "to help balance out the estrogen level." Now that was the Greg they knew and loathed.

Paul smiled at all three of them, ultimately settling on Jenny. For some reason this ticked her off even more. *What you gawking at, Cowboy?* she thought with a flash of irritation. If the salesman's goal had been to throw her off guard during negotiations, he'd certainly succeeded.

EPISODE FORTY–FOUR

WHEN MISTY KNOCKED Kirk was fast-forwarding the VCR, almost shooting past his target as he got up to answer the door, but he luckily turned back just in time. Misty glanced at the frozen figure of a white-suited Cab Calloway on the screen, then collapsed in exhaustion onto Kirk's calculatedly sturdy futon.

"*Blues Brothers*, eh?" she noted, smiling wanly. "You watching the whole movie, or just doing a musical revue?"

"What do you think?" Kirk smirked, stopping the videotape and muting the set. "Tell me—do you think Minnie the Moocher was a fat girl? Brian and I've been debating this."

"Evidence?"

"Well, the song says she had a heart 'as big as a whale,' and when she eats each meal has a dozen courses. I personally visualize some salty mama in a form-hugging cocktail dress. Aretha-size, at least."

"Well, I'd better 'Think!' about this. It's a good theory," Misty conceded, "but maybe Minnie had the type of metabolism that burned off every course. And I wouldn't stake too much on the 'big-hearted' metaphor, either."

"Brian says the same thing. Minnie, we hardly knew ye!" He sighed, then rose to get a one-liter bottle of flavored seltzer, asking Misty if she wanted anything to drink. She demurred, but Kirk brought a second bottle back anyway.

"So you two are still corresponding," Misty noted. "All that time here together didn't take the bloom off the rose."

"Or nip it in the bud either. Though I may have nibbled his bud a time or two." Misty groaned, and Kirk had the good graces to look contrite. "Online romance," Kirk went on to explain. "I've had more memorable sex via email in the last three weeks than the real thing in the last three years. Other than our short face-to-face last month, of course."

"Well, it's certainly safer."

"That's debatable. We may be having our own child," he mentioned nonchalantly, then laughed as he caught Misty's startlement. "Gotcha! A furry, four-legged child, my dear! You knew we went to a cat show while he was here? No? Well, we did, and that got us thinking about finding a baby of our very own. Never mind all those scrawny, pewly purebreds. The one breed that really spoke to us was the Maine coon. Big and beefy and utterly cuddly— definitely chubby-chaser material."

"How do you think the weiner dog'll take this?" Misty asked. "He's getting pretty crotchety in his own old age."

"Howlie'll adjust," Kirk said. "He's flexible. Just like his papa." With that he finally seemed to notice Misty's decidedly unperky demeanor and gave his landlord the once-over. Her eyes, he saw, looked tired. And certainly not in that I've-been-energetic-all-night-ooh-I-feel-good way.

"Do I look that bad?" Misty asked, noting his concern.

"Oh no," Kirk hastily lied, weighing his next words carefully. "But is there, uh, something you want to talk about?"

"You know me so well," she answered affectionately. "You see, I might have made a boo-boo yesterday. Stephanie upstairs told me she'd be moving out the end of next month. So, last night at dinner, I mentioned it to Joe."

"And—?"

"I could just see those wheels turning in his head. Straight men can be so transparent."

"And this is a bad thing how?"

"I don't know," Misty moaned. "I don't know if I'm ready to have Joe moving into my building. I think we're doing okay, but—"

Kirk leaned over and patted her knee. "Is this my cue to start cluck-cluck-clucking?" he asked. "If this were Brian, I'd be rushing out to rent the U-Haul. And even putting it on my American Express!"

"Easy for you to be so brave. Your boyfriend's two thousand miles away."

"That may be," Kirk shot back. "But you knew the job was dangerous when you took it. You want my advice, or would you rather wallow in your own uncertainty?"

"Wallow," Misty picked.

Kirk pointed his remote at the VCR, bringing Cab Calloway back to movie life. "Fine with me," he pouted. She always did this to him—brought him halfway into her problems, then cut the conversation off. "Sit and watch the Hi-De-Ho Man. Maybe you'll learn something. He's got the secret to life, you know."

"So he's the one," Misty replied with a half smile. She twisted the top off her raspberry seltzer and took a deep swig. "And I hope that Minnie was huge!"

"Got a call from Paul Daily last night," Jenny said. She was picking out pieces of brown romaine lettuce from her deli salad as Lissa joined her in the kitchenette. "Why do I order from this place anyway?"

"Three words—'cheap' and 'they deliver,'" Lissa replied. She was sipping a can of Fudge Royale Ultra SlimFast, not (she insisted) to diet, but because such lunches took no effort to prepare. Dinner, on the other hand, was a whole other kettle of fish (so to speak) at Lissa and Delia's. "So what'd Paul want?"

"We're supposed to be discussing the first dance, the All Hallows Happening." Jenny told her, giving up on her salad in disgust. "I'm a little wary about meeting with him, though."

Lissa offered a can of SlimFast from the refrigerator. French Vanilla. Jenny quickly shook her head in response. The mere thought of drinking one of those things made her queasy, bringing back memories of all those diets Alice foisted on her.

"What makes you wary? He seems like a very nice guy."

"He came to the meeting at Greg's beck and call," Jenny answered. "Guilt by association."

"Delia used to hang out with Connie," Lissa rebutted, "and that turned out okay. Come to think of it, Paul used to hang around Connie, too."

"Six degrees of Connie Donovan," Jenny joked. She tapped the table top lightly, then came to a decision. "Okay. I guess I can give him the benefit of the doubt."

"That's my girl!"

"Also got a call from my sister last night," Jenny continued.

"What? Nothing good on prime time? What did Cassandra have to say?"

"I was going through Mom's stuff last week, and I found a few things I thought she might like—old photos of Mom in Missouri and such. Sent a package south, so she was phoning to thank me."

Lissa smiled at Jenny companionably. "You're really getting a kick out of this sister thing."

"Wouldn't you? All my life I thought I was an only child, and now Cassie pops up. You've got sibs—you must know what I'm talking about."

"My sisters haven't spoken to me since I came out to Mother. I'm not the best one to talk about family stuff."

"Who is?" Jenny sighed, rising to retrieve a rye bagel from a white bag on the counter and slide it into the toaster oven. "I invited Cassie to come up for the holidays," she went on. "She always does Thanksgiving with the Stewart family, but she sounded excited about coming up afterward."

"How about before, for the Halloween Dance?" Lissa suggested. "Keep her away from Greg and she should be just fine."

"I don't think she does Halloween," Jenny considered. "Cassie seems a bit, uh, too conservative for that."

"Religious?"

"As only a small-town midwesterner can be," Jenny answered.

"In that case, she simply must come to one of our chapter get-togethers," Lissa decided. "Give her some quality time with your favorite attorney, throw in Misty for good measure, and we'll cast the scales from her eyes."

Jenny chuckled and rose to answer the toaster's bell. "I do declare, Miss Lissa, you do look powerful devilish when you yammer on like that," she drawled.

"It's just the lawyer in me," Lissa drawled back.

EPISODE FORTY-FIVE

HE **DIDN'T RECOGNIZE** the girl behind the counter, but she was definitely worth noticing. Upper midsized with an hourglass shape. Denim blazer over a brocade top. Tightly curled blonde hair and limpid green eyes behind big owlish glasses. A little too much makeup. The kind of girl you knew was just getting used to dressing well, a look Greg Dillman especially liked. Upping the wattage as he slid up to the InFatuation saleslady, he asked for Connie Donovan.

"She's in the back," the zaftig beauty told him. "Anything I can do for you?"

"I'm sure there is," Greg purred, which brought a satisfying blush to the twenty-something's face. "But right now I've got to have a few words with your boss lady." Notching a finger at her playfully, he glided through the racks of winter wear and pushed aside the stockroom curtain. He found Connie seated at her desk, making entries in a ledger book. Behind her a CD boombox was playing Sinatra.

"Like the new help," he said without preamble. "She at all interested in modeling?"

"For you?" Connie snorted, sliding off her reading glasses and letting them dangle by their chain. "I doubt it. Lisa was raised an Apostolic Christian."

"Not a big concern," Greg blithely reassured her. He pulled a stool over to the front of her desk and leaned forward companionably. "Why, Miss Donovan," he gasped in mock surprise. "With your glasses off, you're beautiful!" As expected, she didn't react to this bit of playacting.

"So how goes the Mighty Alliance?" she asked, her glasses nesting in the cleavage of her lowcut white silk blouse.

"The Halloween Dance is a go," Greg answered. "Just dropped a press release off at the *Trib*. We should have a good turnout."

"And Paul?"

"Got him working with that blonde girl, Jenny. You should've seen 'em together at that first meeting. *Très* chilly."

"Wonderful," Connie said, thoughtfully.

"I was a little unsure when you suggested him in the first place," Greg continued. "But he brings something to the table."

"Paul gives your group that aura of Midwestern niceness," Connie filled in. "Something that's alien to either one of us, though Lisa out front would probably connect to it."

"Niceness has its uses," Greg agreed, reaching into his sports jacket for a

164

tin of Altoids. As he popped a pair into his mouth, he contemplated Connie in the dim office light. She was still undeniably gorgeous. There were days when he wondered why he spent so much time pursuing women that his buddies from high school would have ridiculed. At times he even found himself pissed off at these women for their hold over him. Yet all he had to do was gaze upon a classy package like Connie and those nagging questions were answered.

Until the gal opened her mouth, at least.

"—," Connie said, once more breaking the spell.

"What was that?" he asked, forcing his eyes back up to her face.

"Paul gives your group something; you give something to Paul," she repeated.

"And that is?"

"A reputation for the kind of behavior that draws out special prosecutors," she laughed, her generous front jiggling in emphasis.

"I should probably be insulted."

"I could never insult you," Connie cooed. "That's the basis of our partnership."

"Maybe," Greg grinned, "but I don't feel like I'm being treated all that lovingly. Maybe I should turn to Lisa for some comfort."

"Her fiancé is AC, too," Connie told him.

"Oh well," Greg shrugged. "Plenty of other Full-Figured Friendships to be made."

WHEN RACHEL CAME HOME FROM SCHOOL she found her stepmom in the dining room, fingering through a coffeetable history of rock 'n' roll. Not the sort of thing you usually associated with Neeko, so Rachel couldn't resist asking what was up. In answer her stepmom held the book open to a photo of a shaggy haired male and his Oriental companion standing together on some dirty urban street.

"John and Yoko," she explained. "Our costumes for the RADFAm Halloween party. I wanted Dex to go as Akebono Taro, so I could be his off-again/on-again girlfriend, Christine. But your father's way too modest." She half smiled at the thought, an expression Rachel found infuriating, and looked to her stepdaughter for a response.

Hard to know which was more distressing—the thought of her dad in a sumo outfit or the realization that he was still involved with the chapter. He was supposed to be cutting back on those activities once he dropped out of the presidency, but Dex seemed to be as active as ever. Worse yet, now Neeko was just as involved. Didn't the woman have any backbone? Didn't she know how ridiculous the two of them looked?

It took an effort, but Rachel kept her face noncommittal. "Dad's too big to be John Lennon," she finally said, scrutinizing the photo. Neeko just smiled enigmatically and shook her head.

"Too big?" a voice challenged from behind her. "Well, I refuse to be typed!" Her dad appeared in the foyer, tie and shirt collar loosened, his jacket draped over his shoulder. "Anyone can do a Fat Elvis; it takes talent to pull off John Lennon. He was the Walrus, you know." Dex moved around the table to kiss Neeko on the mouth, squeezing Rachel on the shoulder in passing. This contact only served to heighten her irritation.

"Old codger humor," she snorted, turning to take her bookbag up to her room. "I've got to do my homework," she mumbled as she stalked out.

"Everybody's a critic," she heard her father moan with mock dismay just before she kicked her bedroom door shut.

Collapsing across her bed, Rachel flung her knapsack in the direction of the closet. She just couldn't understand why Neeko let her dad get away with things. If she were as thin and beautiful as her stepmom she'd hold a tighter rein on her husband.

Fat chance of that ever happening, though—not with her parents' genes. Rachel had a body her mother had called "peasant stock," which sounded like something you kept locked up in a pen. "Round up the Peasant Stock!"

Examining herself from the bed in the dressing table mirror, she viciously poked an exposed gap of flesh between her jeans and T-shirt. As usual, the sight depressed her. God, she was such a pudge. No wonder nobody was interested in her.

One thing was certain, though—she was damned if she'd let herself get so desperate that the only place left for her was a Fat Dance!

Sighing loudly, Rachel rolled on her stomach and reached beneath her bed for a bag of Halloween candy. She knew she was being unfair to her father. But ever since that photo had gotten posted on the web—and plastered all over her locker in school—his involvement in RADFAm had grown steadily more mortifying. Tearing open the sack, she pulled out a dark chocolate Milky Way and examined it thoughtfully.

EPISODE FORTY–SIX

MEETING NIGHTS were the hardest.

Most days Ian could keep his own counsel. But with the latest RADFAm meeting looming, the burden of his knowledge was intolerable. He'd look at Valerie sitting up in bed and he'd want to start shouting all he knew about her deceptions.

Driving home from work (damn the DOT for springing roadwork in late autumn), Ian tapped the steering wheel nervously and took advantage of the evening's stalled traffic to berate himself. "All Things Considered" was muttering on the radio, but he'd stopped listening to it several stories ago. All he heard was the echo of Val's coughing.

He'd endured her charade in silence for weeks now. What kept him from bringing it up? In his worst moments Ian suspected it was cowardice. Not very compatible with his role as a valiant size acceptance crusader.

Val spent most of her evenings and weekends in bed, claiming to be too out-of-breath to get around. She hadn't taken an assignment from the temp agency in weeks. Yet he knew she was moving through the townhouse during the day—years of single living attuned him to the changes in even the messiest corner of their living space. He hadn't caught her at it, though.

A minivan dodged in front of him without warning. Cursing, Ian nudged the brakes to keep from kissing fenders. Behind him some clown in a nouveau Volkswagen honked in annoyance.

"Sorry—you Yuppie asshole," Ian mouthed.

He didn't doubt that Val had really been taking fen/phen. From what he'd read, her rapid reclamation of the weight she'd lost was a typical response to its cessation. But watching her daily, it was quickly obvious that she wasn't experiencing the debilitating symptoms of pulmonary hypertension.

One good thing about her little drama—it kept Valerie away from alcohol. With all the medication she was supposed to be taking, there was no way Ian would accept her continuing to drink. Perhaps that was a factor in his reluctance to break the illusion; it really was paying off, healthwise.

Still, there was no getting around it. He was going to have to confront her. Turning off the business highway, Ian headed for the deadend street that was his neighborhood. Another week and it'd be getting dark early, he thought.

As soon as he walked through the door he could hear the television upstairs. Female voice yelling at another female voice with crowd jeers in the background—it was too early for professional wrestling, so it had to be a talk show. Setting his softsided satchel on the bench beside the door, Ian sighed and climbed the stairs, loosening his knit tie as he did.

"Sweetie," she gasped, muting the set as he entered the bedroom. "I need to get my prescriptions refilled this evening. Could you drive me to the drugstore?" She looked up at him, neatly combed hair and makeup face announcing her desire to leave the house if only for this bogus trip to the pharmacy.

"About your medication—" Ian began.

"**ALIEN EGG**," Paul read off the package, a bug-eyed ET smiling beneath the legend. He pulled the item off its display peg and examined it more closely. Might make a good Halloween gift for his students, he thought.

"Fox Mulder, I presume?" a voice asked from the end of the aisle. He looked over to see Jenny, still dressed in legal eagle clothes, hands resting on her well-shaped hips.

"That'd make you Dana Scully?" he answered. School shopping was for another day; today's task was to purchase decs for the All Hallows Happening.

"I've never been here before," Jenny said, taking in her surroundings. "This place is great."

"They tend to go all out for Halloween," Paul explained as he led her past a lifesized gorilla holding a mannequin wearing a Monica Lewinski mask. A tad too skinny to be La Monica, Paul thought, but that was to be expected.

MasqueRitz was a store wholly devoted to the frivolous—costumes, magic paraphernalia, novelty gifts and party favors were its very *raison d'être*. Two weeks before Halloween the joint was jumpin'. More than once Paul felt Jenny get jostled into him by some hyperactive kid. Fortunately, the party decoration area was the least crowded.

"How did you learn about this place?" Jenny asked, seemingly unfazed by the cramped quarters.

"Fellow Special Ed teacher," Paul explained. "You need a lot of gimmicks to keep the kids' attention."

"I knew you were a teacher, but I didn't realize it was Special Education."

"Behavior Disordered," Paul told her. The look on her face told him she was familiar with the distinction.

"I wouldn't have the patience to work with kids like that," Jenny said. "I admire anyone who does." She flashed her wonderful smile, cheeks dimpling as she did.

He really liked that smile.

After the meeting with Greg and the two RADFAm women, he'd been dreading further contact with the blonde chapter treasurer—the vibes she'd sent that night were downright frosty. A brief meeting at her workplace hadn't done much to change the situation either way. They both had taken care to keep things neutral and businesslike, short and to the point. Here at MasqueRitz, though, she definitely seemed more relaxed. Perhaps it was the party tone of the place.

"You learn to ignore a lot," Paul said, "and keep the group on task. An occasional sleight of hand helps." To demonstrate, he pulled a quarter from his pocket and made it walk across his knuckles.

"I like a man who's good with his hands." She paused, then reddened slightly. "Did I just say that?"

"I don't think I could do what you do either," Paul rescued. A beat, then a little grin. "What is it you do again?"

Jenny laughed.

"Beaucoup paperwork," she declared. "All in the name of truth and justice." She indicated a package of accordianed paper skeletons. "What you think?"

"A good start," Paul agreed. "We don't want gruesome, but we don't want overly cutesy either."

"Ditto. We've got a free hand: the only instruction I had from Misty was 'No hag witches.'"

"Easily done," Paul said, holding out a honeycombed tissue pumpkin centerpiece.

"We need a basket," Jenny decided, looking for the nearest register. She retrieved one and Paul tossed a half dozen pumpkins into it.

"So what are you going as?" he asked.

"Not sure I'm staying for the party itself," she confessed. "My last costume party didn't go so well."

"I remember, but there aren't any pools in the ballroom. The room seems fairly safe. I'm going, and my last RADFAm dance had its bumpy moment, too."

"So maybe we should go and protect each other, eh?" She considered, putting several rolls of black and orange crepe in the basket. "What'll you be going as?"

"Fox Mulder, of course. How about you?"

"Maybe a hag witch."

"Impossible," Paul replied before he could second-guess himself. "There's not enough makeup in this place for that."

"You haven't seen me without caffeine," Jenny assured him.

"Maybe. But I'm still skeptical." He held up a plastic tablecloth festooned with fall leaves and naked branches. "Go with the pumpkins?" he asked.

Jenny nodded, then started reaching for some companion napkins.

"Would you like to do a Starbucks after this?" he slipped in. "There's one a couple blocks from here."

She froze in midreach and cocked her head toward him, considering his unexpected invitation for one of those eternal moments. An entire troupe of sugar-crazed kindergartners could have walked between them and neither would have noticed it. "I've got a chapter business meeting at seven," she finally announced. "If you like, you can come along to that, too."

EPISODE FORTY–SEVEN

"**L**OOKS LIKE I GOT HERE A LITTLE EARLY," Patsy said as Ian dragged the ticket table to the side of the door. Inside the ballroom other RADFAm regulars (plus some Full-Figured Friends) were putting the finishing touches on the dance decorations. Aretha Franklin was cruising down the Freeway of Love thanks to a boombox brought in by one of Dex's kids. The deejays hadn't arrived, but there was still another hour before the dance. Patsy really had arrived early.

Ian hadn't paid much attention to her in the past—there was always something sad about Patsy—but he felt grateful for the distraction today. Standing before him in a cowgirl outfit, she looked a whole lot cuter than he remembered. A supersized Dale Evans. It was a look Val never could have pulled off.

Hold it. He was trying not to think about Valerie, not to worry about her whereabouts. She'd left the night he confronted her about her phony meds. When he told her what he knew, she'd just looked at him from her bed, nightshirt slipping off her right shoulder, and shrugged.

"I guess we don't need to drive to Walgreens after all," she'd said quietly. Not the response he expected—no denials or attempt to defend herself, no histrionics of any sort.

Her response was so blasé that it infuriated him. Angered beyond the capacity to articulate it, he'd turned and left the bedroom. "We need to talk this out," he'd said between clenched teeth, "when I get back."

Only Val hadn't been there when he returned from the RADFAm officers' meeting. Her half of the closet was stripped; most of the boxes downstairs remained. He supposed she'd have to get back in touch eventually to retrieve the rest of her stuff, but that didn't stop him from worrying now. Two weeks since she'd left. Where the hell was she?

Damn! He was doing it again. Pinching his nails into his hands, Ian smiled back at the concerned looking cowgirl, then held out a stinging palm. From the ballroom he could hear one of Dex's kids whining over the music. Patsy returned his smile nervously. He supposed he looked a bit manic.

"Wanna help with tickets?" Ian asked.

"**T**HERE ARE SOME FOLKS HERE** that I haven't seen in ages," Misty told Joe as they headed for the dance floor. She waved toward a striking bottom-heavy brunette ("Hi, Brie!") in a French maid's costume, carefully keeping an arm on Joe to indicate they were together.

The dance was still early, so there was plenty of room on the floor. On the sound system someone she didn't recognize was crooning something about a "wonder wall;" if she didn't know the song it was still a sweet-sounding slow number. Dressed in a formal gown that looked like it could've been handsewn at the start of the century, she felt like an extra in an ultraromantic video.

"Members of Greg's group?" Joe asked as they both settled into the rhythm.

"Perhaps," Misty acknowledged, "though some of the folks are from out of state." She indicated a passing figure in motley carrying two drinks along the edge of the dance floor. "Like Cat over there."

He followed her direction, but quickly looked back. All these gorgeous fat women around—some of them bigger and much more beautiful than Misty—but still he kept his eyes on her. At times such focused attraction unnerved her.

"It is a good-sized crowd," he told her. "Best crowd I've seen yet." They danced over toward the deejays' table, which was being manned by two men in Blues Brothers suits, feeling the warmth of each other through their costumes.

As the song ended she spied Dillman entering the room. Dressed in formal evening garb, he was smiling unctuously to every woman who greeted him.

"I need to talk to Greg a minute," she told Joe. "Could you go get me a club soda?" Over the sound system a husky-voiced male was singing about walking on the sun. Sounded like the deejays had notched the volume up considerably.

"Going to ask him about the ad, are you?" Joe asked in her right ear as they moved away from a speaker. Misty nodded. Joe let go of her hand, moving around a well-dressed supersized blonde in a wheelchair to head for the bar. Misty watched him move through the crowd, his white chef's costume practically glowing in the dance hall dimness. Next year they just had to get him a different costume.

Look at her—thinking about next year already! How many different assumptions were packed in that single premise? Unaccountably she felt herself start to blush. Good thing the room was dark.

She had to make a decision about her empty upstairs apartment soon. Joe was still dropping hints about it.

Setting her sights on Greg, Misty reluctantly turned from Joe and waved her arm to catch his attention. Also within view, Jenny and Paul—both dressed in severe-looking suits and trench coats—caught her gesture. Misty led them all to the hallway outside, pulling Ian away from Patsy and Jefferson at the ticket table as they went by.

"Madame President," Dillman said once they'd gotten far enough away from the noise of the dance to talk. "You're looking particularly lovely tonight."

"Coming from anyone else I'd be flattered," Misty answered as she pulled a folded piece of newspaper from her palm-sized handbag, "but I still need to ask you something." She unfolded the newspaper ad and held it up to his face. "Where's our name?"

Greg squinted at the ad, taken from the weekend entertainment section of the *Trib*. The rest watched him curiously to see what he'd say. After several seconds Dillman finally answered. "Right here," he indicated, tapping the top of the ad.

Misty read the words aloud. "'Full-Figured Friends—in Association with A Major Size Acceptance Organization—Presents the Halloween Happening.' We, I take it, are the Major Organization?"

"You know how it goes," Greg told the threesome. "We could only purchase so much space for the ad."

"Greg, it took more space to avoid saying RADFAm than it would have simply saying it."

He took the sheet from Misty and perused it more closely, like an accountant going over the books. Then he handed it back to her, sighing loudly.

"You see the size of the group in there?" he finally asked. "Do you think we'd have gotten that big a turnout if we'd put the name RADFAm in the ad?"

"You think—"

"I think the name's a turnoff for some people," Dillman interrupted. "RADFAm's so retro—it's like something out of the late '60s. That's not gonna bring out people these days."

"Maybe," Misty responded. "But if we're going to keep this partnership going, I expect to see our name prominently displayed in the future. In the same type size as Triple F's, thank you." She turned to Ian, Jenny and Paul, who'd been nervously observing this interaction, and asked, "What do you think?"

"I'm with you," Ian said. Jenny and Paul both nodded in agreement. Those two made a cute looking couple, Misty thought, then she re-focused on the issue at hand.

"Fine," Greg acquiesced grudgingly. "We'll try it your way next time and see how many folks come out. I'd love to be wrong about this."

"I'm sure you would, Greg," Misty said sweetly. "I'd love for you to be wrong, too." She took back her paper and returned it to her tiny handbag. Down the hall, Hagar and Helga (Tom and Jody—another couple she hadn't seen since forever) were buying their tickets. "Shall we rejoin the dance?" she asked the rest.

A look of relief flashed across the other RADFAmites' faces. Confrontation over.

"I LOVE A WOMAN WHO'S NOT AFRAID to speak her mind," Dillman observed. Standing by the entrance with Paul and Jenny, he watched Misty as she jostled around the crowded tables, passing a pudgy FA in what looked to be a Gumby suit. "If she has a mind to speak, that is."

"From what I've seen, there's no shortage of smart women in this group," Paul said, automatically clasping Jenny by the hand. Dillman noted the unconsciously protective gesture and smirked.

It was probably inevitable that Connie Donovan chose that moment to show up. She was packed within a bodice-hugging dominatrix outfit, a large plastic whip in her right hand, black domino mask over her eyes, a cloak over her shoulders. Nonchalantly casting off her cloak, Connie strode toward the portable coat rack; her great soft shoulders catching the hallway light. Passing the ticket table as if it were invisible, she joined them at the doorway.

Paul could feel her eyes daggering as she caught the two of them still holding hands. Jenny must have felt it too, because she suddenly started squeezing his fingers tightly. Connie moved up to Greg, squeezed his shoulder, and pecked him lightly on the cheek, her magnificent forefront pushing into his nearest hip.

"Thought you were gonna wear a costume, Connie," Greg said jovially. She lightly tapped him with her whip and waved her hand coquettishly. Paul, who was half steeling himself for another slap, started to relax.

"What can I say? I just threw on the first thing I could pull from the closet." She gave an innocent little half-smile to Paul and Jenny. "And how are you two doing?" she asked. "Enjoying the festivities?"

"Very much," Jenny offered. "In fact," she cocked her head toward the doorway, as if hearing the music for the first time—Martha Wash was bellowing over an insistent electronic beat. "Isn't that the song you requested, Paul?"

"Um, as a matter of fact it is!" Paul said, working hard to keep his relief from showing. "Would you excuse us for the space of a dance or two?"

"Go right ahead," Dillman told them. "It's what we all came for."

Quickly Paul and Jenny made their escape to the dance floor. One of the deejays he remembered from Greg's Valentine Dance.

Got to warn you," Paul shouted above the music. "I dance like a teacher!"

"Well, you're stuck out here for now!" Jenny shouted back. "So you might as well make the best of it!" She opened her trench coat and started to shake to the discoid beat. Dana Scully never looked as hot as this, Paul thought. Eyes half closed, she quickly surrendered to the insistent dance beat.

"Thanks for rescuing me," he shouted, doing his best to keep up. He wasn't sure if she heard him or not.

THE CROWD WAS DOING THE ELECTRIC SLIDE, 48 fat women and men—plus the occasional smaller sized FA—moving back and forth along the dance floor. There were going to be a lot of bruised hips in the morning, Jenny thought as she watched the happy group clap and laugh at its regular mishaps.

"Think Carmen Miranda will be able to keep her hat on?" Paul asked as he took his seat. He indicated a colorfully festooned brunette in the front row, boot scootin' between a bearded cowboy and a midsized Wonder Woman.

"It's anybody's guess," Jenny noted, accepting a plastic glass of Chablis from Paul. "Maybe we should have a table betting pool?" She turned to the rest of the table—Lissa and Delia, dressed as devil and angel, respectively; Dex and Neeko (sans kidlets) in a John and Yoko getup they'd had to explain to Jenny; Misty and Joe.

"I'm betting the hat's well-fastened," Lissa advised, "unlike some of the costumes here tonight." She reached across the table for a large bowl of candy and started peeling open a snack-sized Snickers.

"You're probably right," Jenny agreed. She moved to the right to let a bespectacled Cleopatra grab a dark chocolate Milky Way from the bottom of the bowl and move on.

"Hey, Lorie, you don't want that one," Delia cautioned her. "Have two Dove bars instead!"

Cleo examined the bar in her hand, shrugged and tossed it Delia's way. To make up for it, Delia handed her two snack-sized bars. "I'm a sucker for dark chocolate," Delia told the table.

"An obvious double entendre, sweetie," Lissa laughed, chucking her on the chin. "Your kids did a great job, helping out before," she told Dex.

"They were both well-bribed," Dex chuckled. "Used to be Rachel would come to these just to hook up with Kelly. But they haven't been doing that much lately."

"Kids grow apart just like adults," Neeko noted. "Just because their parents have the chapter in common doesn't mean that they have anything in common."

"Yeah," Dex noddded. "Kelly seems pretty normal."

"Rachel going through some adolescent angst?" Lissa asked.

"She's going through something, alright."

Before he could elaborate Delia made a loud hacking noise. Lissa and Dex both turned toward her with concern. Redfaced, Delia grabbed the wrapper of her Milky Way and spit her candy into it. "There's something in this candy!" she said between quick pants. "Tastes like hot sauce!"

"What?!?" Everybody at the table rose as one.

Quickly Dex grabbed the bowl and found a second Milky Way bar. Ripping open the wrapper, he examined the uneaten candy in the dim light. "Looks like I get to play medical detective again," he pronounced. Delia handed her wrapper over to him.

"Whatever it is, we'd better get that candy off the tables," Misty decided. "Think we can do this without any undue fuss?"

"We can try," Jenny said.

"We'll meet at the ticket table," Misty decided.

The group began to fan out, but before Paul and Jenny could separate a zaftig figure in a Heidi outfit stepped in front of Paul.

"Care to dance, cowboy?" she asked.

What was that supposed to mean? Jenny wondered. Paul wasn't in a cowboy suit.

"In a bit, Sonya," Paul told her. "I've got a small errand first."

"Opportunity only knocks once," she said flirtatiously. "I might not be around when you get back from your 'small errand.'" She put her hands on her hips (six inches smaller than Jenny's, she couldn't help noticing) and made a little girl pout. What was Paul even doing knowing a girl like this? She looked like she could've been his kid sister!

"Duty calls," Paul apologized. He gave Jenny a "go ahead" gesture, then moved toward one of the other tables. Sonya watched them both with a petulant expression on her face.

For some strange reason Jenny found herself enjoying the girl's look of disappointment.

EPISODE FORTY-EIGHT

DEX HATED HOLDING FAMILY MEETINGS at suppertime—it ran counter to his desire to keep dining social—but it was the only way to ensure the entire family was present. The typical American family, he thought; all over the map with precious little time in common. At least they still had meals together. He held off until dessert, but it still went against the grain. Too many memories of his own father, who never declared a family meeting until it was time to announce another move.

"We got the report back on the tampered Milky Ways," he began. "Turns out there were at least six others that had been messed with. Someone injected the candy bars with a tincture of red pepper and spices—a standard hot sauce in Japanese cooking."

"Togarishi Shichimi," Neeko guessed, ladling strawberries from a large bowl.

Dex nodded grimly. "There was a small hole on the side of one of the candy bars. Somebody poked an eighteen-gauge needle through the wrapper seam and injected the sauce into the Milky Way. It was only hot sauce, most likely only a childish prank, but it could have been something much more serious.

"Do they have," Neeko asked slowly, "any idea who might have done this?"

"The guilty party must have been on the decorating crew," Dexter sadly responded. "The candy was randomly found in bowls throughout the room." He paused, then plunged into the meat of the matter. "Nobody's making any accusations yet, but it looks like it was someone in this family. We've got a jar filled with shichimi powder in the pantry. And it's family knowledge there are syringes in my office. It could have been one of us."

"So what are we supposed to do?" Rachel asked, popping open a plastic container of Cool Whip and spooning a large dollop into her bowl. You never knew what she was going to eat—one day she was pushing aside all but the most abstemious fare, the next she was making the Devil's Point with a mound of dessert topping.

"I would hope," Dex carefully answered, "that if someone in this house were responsible, they'd feel like they could talk to me about it. So far, there haven't been any severe consequences. I'd like it to end that way."

The room was silent but for the sound of Rachel's spoon clacking against her bowl. Dex looked around the dining room. Jackie, he saw, hadn't touched his dessert and was visibly reddening.

"You're blaming me, aren't you?" Jackie accused, finally rising, overturning his chair.

"I'm not saying that," Dex protested, but his son was not in the mood to hear anything else. Jackie swirled around and dashed for the stairs, slamming his bedroom door once he'd escaped inside.

Rachel shrugged and looked at his brother's empty place. "Can I have his dessert?" she asked Dex and Neeko.

FROM: JENNIFER TAYLOR
To: Cassandra Stewart
Sent: December 5, 1997, 12:30 PM
Subject: How's tricks?

Great to talk to you over the phone the other night, Cass. Your adoptive parents sound wonderful—I look forward to meeting them someday. Hope you made it safely through to the other side of Leftover Hell.

Went out and purchased an air mattress over the weekend for your upcoming visit. The hide-a-bed can be pretty gruesome by itself (one long metal support in the most uncomfortable part of your back), but it's passable with the air cushion. Can't wait to introduce you to folks up here.

One small possible(?) problem. Paul, the guy I told you about on the phone, called me at work today with two tickets to *The Nutcracker*. It's for Saturday, right in the middle of your visit, so I asked him if he could get a third ticket. He said he'd try, but it's pretty late in the game, so he may not be lucky. I'm willing to tell him "no" if he can't get a ticket for you, too. Do you have any thoughts either way?

Let me know ASAP. I'd hate to send Paul out on a possibly futile mission if it won't make any difference anyway...

Your sister (boy, I love saying that!),

Jenny

KIRK WAS ARRANGING A BOARD GAME on the dining room table, but it was no game that Misty recognized. The pieces were plastic fat men with open-mouthed smiles and large bellies. A plastic scale was set up on the corner of the game board, alongside a cardboard fridge.

"Okay," Misty opened as she grabbed a metal chair to join him at the table, "I'll bite. What are you playing?"

"Fat Chance," Kirk started.

"Well, if that's your attitude—"

"It's an old Milton Bradley game, silly. Brian sent it to me as a Christmas present." He held up a pink game piece and cooed. "Cute l'il spud, idn't he?"

"And of course you couldn't resist opening your Xmas gift two weeks early." Lifting the box top to examine it more closely, she skimmed the rules inside. "Some kind of diet game," she noted. "Says here the aim is to go around the board without eating too much junk food."

"We play the Encourager Edition—where the point is to pack on as much as possible. First to tilt the scales wins." He rose to refill his Erika Oller mug and bring one in for Misty. "Amaretto Coffee-mate?" he asked.

"We are being festive today. What's the occasion?"

"Brian and I signed the adoption papers this week," Kirk answered.

"I know this isn't what it sounds like," Misty said, shaking her head in disbelief, "so you two boys found the perfect cat."

"Two perfect cats. Maine Coons, of course. We're adopting twin brothers from Native Cats in St. Louis," he gushed. "Big, beefy looking bruisers to be—what could be more perfect?"

"You talk to your landlord about this? I don't know what she'll say about two cats in one of her apartments—"

"She's a pushover. Besides, it won't be two cats. One of 'em will be living with Bri, the other me. It's a Fievel thing. Whenever I hold little Smokey, I'll know Brian is holding his *frere*."

"You're such a sentimental softie," Misty grinned. She took a sip of her coffee, winced and added another splash of creamer.

"I try," Kirk said demurely. "And what about your paramour? He still scratching on the door, asking to be let in the building?"

Misty sighed loudly. "No," she told him. "I caved last night. Couldn't afford to keep the place free forever."

"I thought guys were supposed to be the commitment phobes."

"I'm a feminist. Fat chicks can be just as phobic."

Kirk clicked his tongue twice, then patted Misty on a fleshy caftaned knee. "Mist, I'm going to say this once, but before I do, I don't want any 'Yes, buts' out of you."

"But it's my favorite rhetorical device!"

"What did I just say?" Kirk warned.

"Okay," Misty caved. "Lay it on me, Preach."

"I've got two words, and I want you to take 'em to heart." He paused for emphasis, then gave his message: *"You're deserving!"*

Misty rose and hugged Kirk, pressing him into her forefront. Stepping back, she looked down at him and said, "Doesn't a contraction count as two words?"

Kirk lobbed the cardboard refrigerator at her.

EPISODE FORTY-NINE

BEEP!

"Work work work work work work work work! You have reached Greg Dillman's answering machine, which means that yours truly is out trying to earn an honest buck. If you are calling about affordable health insurance that doesn't involve any embarrassing physical exams, leave a message at the tone and I'll get back to you as soon as possible. If you wish to leave a message for Full-Figured Friends—or just your name and vital statistics—you know what to do."

Beep!

"Greg, this is Connie. If you're there, pick up the damn phone.

"—Okay—so you're out. Ring me up when you get in. I'm at the shop tonight. You know the number."

Beep!

"Still not in, Greg? Or are you just avoiding little ol' me? Well, I'm at home now, so you can reach me there. I'll be up until eleven, so call me back."

Beep!

"Looks like we've gotten lucky tonight, eh, stud? I'm so happy for you. I'll try to reach you tomorrow, or you can try to catch me at the shop all day. It is our busiest time of the year.

"But what's all this about Paul and that Jenny person? Word on the grapevine has the two spotted at Kuppa's—looking very couple-like. I thought you said she could barely stand speaking to him, but it didn't look that way to me at the dance—"

HEFTING THE CORRUGATED MAGAZINE STORAGE BOX, Joe carried two years' worth of plumper men's mags into the living room. *Nothing like a move to get you pruning out nonessentials,* he thought, lifting up a two-year-old copy of *BUF* magazine and scanning it for anything worth keeping. A nice pictorial with a redhead who vaguely resembled Misty if not for that damn tattoo on her left hip. (Joe couldn't help it—he was conservative that way—but tattoos and piercings remained a major turnoff for him.) Five other pictorials, only with much smaller models. A weight-gain fantasy by B. Lewis Baird (too wordy for Joe, but the guy had his fans) with a pair of sexy Delacroix line sketches (too bad the guy had stopped drawing for weight-gain fiction). Some amateur graphics sent in by the readers, including a funnel-feeding penciling that managed to both fascinate and discomfit Joe. Yeah, he supposed he would keep this issue: *BUF* had been a pretty good title until it changed owners and went reprint.

By the time he was through he'd more than halved his collection. Joe didn't know anyone else to bequeath the castoffs, so he simply carted them to the kitchen wastecan and piled them by its side. Maybe that Paul fella would be interested in the magazines? Probably not. The guy was a schoolteacher after all. What if one of his students came over to visit? Or a student's parent?

Maybe he should just toss all the mags and leave it at that. What would Misty think if she found him with all those issues of *Plumpers* and *Big Women*, anyway? True, he'd bought most of them before he'd even met her. But why was he keeping them now that they were a couple? Misty wasn't any kind of a prude, but would she see it as a form of disloyalty?

For that matter, was it a sign of disloyalty?

Joe didn't think so. When it came down to it, Misty won hands down over those two-dimensional photos. It wasn't just that she out-classed them, though that definitely was the case. Something about their transition into photo image muted any real-life power they possessed—which Misty held just entering a room. He also suspected that if he were in the same physical space with a dozen *BUF* models and Misty, he'd still be drawn to her.

That didn't stop him from visualizing her in all of Baird's weight-gain fantasies, though.

Maybe he'd bring all his magazines, after all—keep them out of sight but still hold onto them. He hadn't been fantasizing much lately, but he still liked to do it. Considering all the weird stuff Misty was into, he was entitled to his own private life.

Returning to the kitchen, Joe stooped and retrieved the discarded magazines. Good thing he hadn't tossed them in the can! Re-boxing the pile, he carted his collection over to the "okay to move" stack by the front door and carefully placed it on his box of notebooks where he could easily grab both boxes before Misty. Just because he was keeping the magazines didn't mean he had to rub her nose in it.

He sat back and considered the heap of stuff awaiting the U-Haul. He wasn't exactly burdened with possessions. His magazines. Two boxes of clothes. Some posters and a boombox set to a Spanish music station. Secondhand furniture. TV/VCR and a box of cooking show tapes. His culinary textbooks. Loads of kitchen supplies.

This last comprised the bulk of Joe's possessions. It wasn't like he had a lot of disposable income, though with this move he'd be dropping his rent by close to $250. While she could have gotten more, Misty was insisting on keeping the rate the same as for all her other tenants. At one point she'd even considered waiving his rent altogether, but Joe had insisted on paying rent, if not a deposit.

"When we move in together," he'd said, doing his best to ignore the momentary look of panic that washed across her face, "we'll share expenses. But for now you're my landlord."

"I can do that," she'd capitulated.

Maybe the time to rethink the magazine thing was when they really did move in together.

BEEP!

"Greg, you prick, it's been two days! I know you've been home, because the recording tape's short again. This coyness shit isn't getting you anywhere, Dillman! If you want any of your 3-F bimbos to model in the RADFAm fashion show, you'd better give me a call, pronto. Convention's less than two months away, and guess who's in charge of the runway?"

EPISODE FIFTY

THE CITY WIND WASN'T LIVING UP TO its blustery reputation. Light breezes, a clear sky—it was as untypical a late December night as you could imagine. Exiting the parking garage, both Paul and Jenny automatically braced themselves for a blast of cold, then relaxed when an icy assault did not take place. Their winter wear—she in a brown single-breasted long coat, he in a navy blue pea coat—was almost too much. But nights in the city had a way of dropping cold fast.

Hordes of last-minute shoppers rushing around them, they stepped out into the holiday crowd.

"The city always looks so beautiful this time of year. Haven't been downtown for the holidays since I was a kid," Jenny said. "When I was real young my dad used to take us all to see the window displays." She paused, the smile on her lips momentarily straightening, then grabbed Paul's nearest hand. "Didn't realize we were so close to Connie's place," she noticed, stepping back to make way for a determined-looking man in a gray wool coat and ear muffs. She gestured to a shop across the street.

"Are we?" Paul started. Now it was his turn to look serious. "I've never been there. Want to go the other direction?"

"Not at all," Jenny decided. InFatuation, she saw, was dark. In the window a plus-sized mannequin was posed as if preparing to girlishly throw a styrofoam snowball. Pulling Paul along, she led him down the block to a more opulent set of displays. "You've never been to Connie's store?"

"We barely left her duplex," Paul admitted.

"Trying to shield you from the rest of us RADFAm vixens, eh? Oh, that sounds bitchy, doesn't it?"

"Not far from the truth, though." He stopped to examine an oldfashioned Christmas display composed of figures that looked more anorectic than their purported period required. "Look at it from her end—I followed her without a second thought. Odds are I might have done the same with some other woman."

They sidled over to the next display, careful to avoid bumping into any of the other window gawkers, then Paul continued.

"That first dance I was blown away," he explained. "I'd never seen so many stunning women in one place at the same time before. My basic common sense took a holiday that night." He indicated the '50s-era display before them—the archetypal family clustered around a bounty-laden tree—and smiled. "Kind of like those kids with their presents—too excited to think straight."

"I was so nervous that night I don't remember most of it." Jenny laughed, then indicated the wooden nutcracker that was tilted on a far corner of the display. "There's our athletic young soldier," she giggled. "Hope he fares better tomorrow night when he takes on the Mouse King."

"It was only a one-foot skid. At least he didn't lose his balance," Paul chuckled.

"He looked like he was sliding into home plate," Jenny reminded Paul.

"Well, neither of my students made any flubs, thank God." They moved on to the next display, an old-fashioned Kris Kringle with a properly matronly Mrs. K.

"You didn't tell me this was a student performance when you first invited me," Jenny teased. "It only came up when I asked for the extra ticket."

"Uh, maybe I was afraid you'd say no if you knew. It wasn't that awful, was it?"

"Oh no, I had a wonderful time. You know, I always used to think those ballerina types had it easy when I was in high school. Watching them as an adult—concentrating so intensely on their moves and struggling to look effortless—was kind of revealing. Nobody has it easy in high school, do they?"

"Some kids might. But I don't work with them."

A nearby store speaker had just segued into Ellington's take on Tchaikovsky. They walked hand in hand along the sidewalk for a while in silence, watching the anxious shoppers, lost in their respective thoughts. Suddenly an aggressive, well-dressed woman shot in front of them, aiming for a taxi. A trail of cigarette smoke followed her.

Jenny never thought she'd miss her mother so much on the holidays. "It was nice of you to get that ticket for Cassie," she said, shaking off her musing.

"You saw the seats. We had tickets to spare," Paul grinned. "Though I've got to be honest—I'm glad she begged off coming downtown with us."

"It was a long drive up," Jenny said. "And I think she was trying to be discreet. She doesn't know this is just our first real date."

"'Just'?" Paul mugged. "'Real date'?"

"You know what I mean!" She turned her attention to a horsedrawn carriage that had stopped on the street, its passengers obscured from view by a large faux fur rug. Paul noted the expression on her face.

"Want a ride?" he asked. "I'm sure we could find a vacant one."

"Not necessary," Jenny demurred. "I'd like to some day, though. I've always thought they looked so romantic." She squeezed his hand and smiled. "It's getting late. Maybe we can save that for our second 'real date.'"

"'Second'?"

"I think so. I hope so. How about you?"

Paul reached around and pulled Jenny close to him. In that moment all the sounds of the city seemed to mute; the night's slight breeze calmed. They were, Jenny realized, almost tall enough to see eye to eye. His hands were strong and firm, even through her coat. Then Paul lowered his lips toward hers.

They kissed, first tentatively, then with greater certainty. Two young kids *eeewwe*d as they passed the couple, then were scooted along by their parents. In answer, Paul and Jenny kissed a third time.

"Shouldn't those two be home in bed?" Jenny asked, watching the family disappear from sight around a corner. She turned back to Paul. "I've got a question for you. Maybe it's an unfair one, but I'd like to ask it anyway. You said you were overwhelmed by the sight of all the stunning beauties at that first dance. What did you think when you saw me?"

"That you were one of the most stunning women there," Paul answered truthfully. "But Greg led me to believe you two had already connected."

"You're kidding!" she snorted.

"Nope."

"And to think I didn't want to have anything to do with you at first because I thought you and he were best buds." She shook her head and glanced at a nearby streetlamp clock. "I think," she finally decided, "I'd like to take that carriage ride tonight after all."

THEY HAD NO LUCK ON THE CARRIAGE—if this were a movie they'd be cuddling together on a carriage seat in the speed of a jump cut. But real life wasn't as convenient, so Paul had to make a mental note to reserve a carriage for their "second date." (Just the phrase made him feel a decade younger.)

Driving through downtown for a last look at those stores they'd missed on foot, he flashed on his first car in high school. It'd been a boat and a gas guzzler, but it would have been much more accommodating to a woman Jenny's size than his little Geo Metro.

"What first drew you to RADFAm?" he asked Jenny conversationally. She was tinkering with the car radio, pausing when she found an '80s rock station right in the middle of the Band Aid charity single.

"My boss pushed me into it," Jenny admitted. "At least I like to tell her that. I'd also like to say it was because I had a deep abiding commitment to size acceptance. But the big reason was to meet Cute Guys!"

"Me, too," Paul said. "Not guys, of course, but you get the picture." Traffic slowed down as they reached a tunnel, breaking up the fading single. "Probably what brings most newcomers into a group like RADFAm—the hope of meeting someone."

"You might be right. But what does that say about people?"

"What do you think?"

"That we all want to be with somebody," Jenny said. "That loneliness is debilitating. And that the best way to get the energy to fight the good fights is with someone by your side."

They drove out of the tunnel and headed for the freeway. On the radio Ray Davies was pretending to be Father Christmas.

"A cynical person might have just said we all were selfish," Paul responded. "But I like the way you express it."

"I'm not being glib. I really believe it," Jenny realized. "It doesn't have to be a lover. All through the holidays I've been missing my mother. She drove me crazy, but now that she's gone—having Cassie come up, being here with you, I feel brighter than I have in months."

"It suits you," Paul told her. "I don't think I've seen you look as lovely as you do tonight."

"A nice lie, but I'll take it."

Paul harrumphed. "You know when the size acceptance movement will no longer be necessary? When your everyday fat woman is able to take a compliment without devaluing it."

"I'm afraid you could be right," Jenny apologized. "That came out before I could stop it. And it was rude."

Paul looked over toward the passenger seat. "That's okay. We'll try it again. You know, I don't think I've seen you look as lovely as you do tonight."

"Well, thank you, Kind Sir. If I wasn't sitting here, I'd curtsey. And though you probably can't see me in the light, I'm blushing all over."

"Blushing prettily, I bet."

"Is there any other way for a romantic heroine to blush?"

Their freeway exit was coming up, so he didn't say a word until they turned off. He took advantage of the red light at the top of the ramp to lean over and kiss her cheek. "Just trying to get a closer look," he explained.

Jenny may not have been blushing before, but she definitely was now.

TWO

ANOTHER YEAR

EPISODE FIFTY-ONE

ONCE HE SAW THE NEW TOM CLANCY HARDBACK, Dex decided to hit the paperbacks instead. Too damn thick to hold in bed; he needed something he could read onehanded. Another sign of growing older, he thought. With reading glasses, he couldn't lie back anymore—his eyes got tired quicker and he barely made it through a chapter before he was ready to call it quits.

He'd been given a Borders gift certificate, an annual tradition (they no longer did Christmas per se, but Neeko was fine with a generic holiday gift exchange), and it was sort of expected that he'd spend it on a Clancy novel. Three years back his kids had gotten the idea that he liked the man's books, and while Dex thought they were okay, they were no match for the straightforward Ian Flemings of his youth. Perhaps he'd buy one of those brand-name paperback series, *Tom Clancy's* Something-or-other Center, and read that instead. It might be less ponderous.

"Dex Logan!"

He looked down the Romance aisle to see Jenny Taylor and a serious-looking woman by her side. The chapter treasurer muttered a few words to her companion, then joined Dex.

"Have a good holiday?" she asked. She was holding a *Dilbert* desk calendar. The year had barely begun, and already they were discounting them.

"Fair to partly cloudy," Dex answered. "You?"

"Playing hostess to my sister," she indicated with a nod. "It's been fun taking her to the clothing stores."

Dex took stock of Jenny's sister. Though he wasn't one to pay much attention to women's fashion, even he was capable of recognizing how schoolmarmishly she dressed.

"I've been trying to get her to loosen up a little bit," Jenny murmured, noticing his glance.

"She into size acceptance?"

"Not quite. But I'm in there plugging away." She stopped as if considering what next to say, then added, "Cassie was even surprised I was dating someone. I think I'm going to have to build slowly when it comes to RADFAm events."

"She might surprise you."

"Possibly," Jenny admitted. "If she's still here next week I might even take her to the business meeting. It'd be a nice neutral way to introduce her to folks."

"Our business meetings? Neutral? Things have changed since Misty took my place."

Jenny chuckled softly. "I bet you don't miss it," she said.

"Part of me does," Dex admitted. "But it was time."

Jenny nodded, then turned to rejoin her sister. Neither of them had mentioned the candy incident. Or Dex's suspicion that one of his kids was behind it.

"I think it was Rachel," Neeko had guessed the night after his abortive family dinner talk. He'd been in bed, unable to get young Jackie's behavior out of his head, certain that his son had been the culprit, when his wife sprung this new revelation. "Found a couple of Dark Milky Ways under her bed today." She'd leaned across the bed, a worried look on her face, and patted his side. "It's all circumstantial, but don't you think she's been acting like something's going on?"

"Maybe," Dex had replied, his heart sinking. It'd been relatively easy to think the problem was Jackie—he had history, and Dex understood that history—but to add Rachel to the mix was almost more than he could stand. "You think we'll be able to get her to admit it?"

"Doubtful," Neeko had answered. "You saw her poker face at dinner when Jackie stomped off. If she's guilty, she's not going to give anything away."

If only, Dex sighed as he entered the Thrillers section, real-life mysteries could be solved as precisely as they were in books.

"OKAY. SO PATSY GETS TO STAY in the Hospitality Suite. We'll still need some relief shifts."

Outside Misty's window a drift of snow had formed on the ledge. Paper spread on her kitchen table, Misty was carrying on chapter business by phone. 1998's first big snow storm—the worst to hit the Midwest in over 30 years—had forced them to cancel last night's business meeting.

"I'll take some shifts," Ian told her from his end of the line. "And get a signup sheet passed around."

"Make sure Lainie gets a copy," Misty reminded him.

"Will do."

"I'm sorry if I keep repeating the obvious," she apologized. "It's just the convention is coming up so quickly, and we've still got too much to nail down."

"I know," Ian reassured her.

Misty had been sliding into panic mode ever since the year began. What had seemed so far away was now less than two months off, and they couldn't even get together to work out the logistics. She had a legal pad list of things to get done that was more than four pages long. So many people to call: Lainie on the hotel arrangements; Connie and Delia on the fashion show. She'd already talked to Paul and Jenny about the Valentine's Dance, the con's centerpiece, and that at least seemed under control. Who'd have imagined—Misty Shores, Queen of Control? Clearly she had to be paying off some weird kind of karmic debt.

Joe entered the kitchen and headed for the tea kettle. The edge of his pant legs were soaked, dripping onto his bootless feet. He'd been working to get his car unburied all morning, going out in fifteen minute shifts, then returning to get warmed and rested. His hair was still plastered down from his ski cap.

"I was going over the printed schedule," Misty told Ian, "and I think it holds together very well. But I'd assume that Lewis Baird would prefer to be billed by his pseudonym and not his real name. It'd be a bigger draw for the FAs."

"I'll double-check with Mr. Baird," Ian replied. The chapter VP was in charge of workshops—two different ones on self-esteem, an FA workshop, the inevitable safe sex discussion—and had put together a solid package. If they weren't snowed in, they'd be fine; if they were, Misty would have to extend her Tarot workshop indefinitely.

Joe moved around the table and began to rub Misty's shoulders, leaning over to kiss her on the cheek.

"Your lips are still cold," she muttered with her hand over the phone. He grinned roguishly, then backed off to warm them with a cup of Constant Comment.

"You say something?" Ian was asking over the phone.

"Just taking a moment to flirt with my new neighbor," Misty answered, returning to her list.

"That's allowed," Ian said. He was sounding a lot more chipper these days, Misty noted. Perhaps those rumors about Ian and Patsy had some merit to them after all.

EPISODE FIFTY-TWO

PUSHING THE DOOR OPEN WITH A JEANS-CLAD HIP, Paul gingerly carried his tray of Dixie Cups into the tiny room that was going to be the convention checkpoint. Inside, Jenny, Misty and Joe were scrambling to ready Sign-in Central. The RADFAm con wasn't set to officially begin for another half hour, but attendees already were impatiently milling outside. Misty and Joe frantically stuffed plastic sacks with schedules, flyers and convention goodies as Jenny arranged badges alphabetically on top of the counter.

"Did you know that diet guy, Jordan Lewis, is holding a workshop here this weekend too?" Paul asked the group as he set down the tray.

"No Laughing Matter Jordan Lewis?" Jenny took a cup of coffee and a container of real cream, then smiled with the sort of nostalgic expression usually reserved for high school high jinks. "I used to have his book. It was my first voluntary diet program."

"You always remember your first," Misty smiled roguishly as she grabbed a handful of fans to slip into her sacks. "Mine was Good Ol' Doc Atkins."

"Did him, too. But he wasn't as much fun to read as Jordan Lewis."

"Saw Lewis in a movie once," Paul recalled, handing hot tea to Joe. "Back when he was still a fulltime comedian."

"You mean back when he was full-bodied?" Jenny grinned.

"Fat and miserable, to hear him tell it," Misty added.

"The guy was pretty funny in an Angry Young Man sort of way. It was all the fashion when he first started out."

"He showed up on *Winnie Harper* a couple months back," Joe put in. "Not very funny, but still pretty angry."

"You were watching *Winnie Harper*?" Misty caught.

A murmur from Joe: "I was flipping past it."

"Well, I just hope he stays in his little meeting room," Jenny declared. "We don't need a bunch of Jordanites harassing anyone at our convention."

"May want to talk to the Sycamore Creek hospitality people," Misty decided, rising from behind the counter. She straightened her flowered top, fluffed her hair and examined her lips in a mirror tile. "The hotel's large enough to keep us on opposite sides of the building. I'm gonna make sure they pay attention to this."

"Want me to come along?" Jenny and Joe asked in chorus.

Misty considered them both. "It's almost time for the doors to open. You okay with starting this alone, Paul?"

"I think so."

"No," Jenny quickly decided. "I'd better stay. You two go." She turned to Paul and smiled. "That crowd out there could get rowdy."

Misty nodded, then waved Joe to follow.

"We need to find Eleanor first," she said. "Or Lainie." As the duo closed the door behind them Paul and Jenny could see several figures crowding around them. Patsy was complaining about not being able to get into the Hospitality Suite to decorate it.

"We make it through this weekend without wanting to resign as officers and it will be something to be proud about," Jenny whispered to Paul.

"You'll do fine," he reassured, taking a seat beside her at the sign-up counter. Reaching into his corduroy sport jacket, he pulled out a small box and handed it to Jenny. "Wanted to give this to you before it got too crazy," he said.

It was, she saw, a small, elegant box of Godiva chocolates, wrapped in Valentine-theme packaging. Lifting the lid, Jenny found two truffles and something underneath—a delicate goldtone pin, a sweet chubby cherub.

"It's lovely," Jenny gasped, holding the pin up to the window light. The look of pleasure on her face was so strong it made Paul blush. Quickly she applied the pin to the right lapel of her white cotton blazer. "I've never been pinned before. Wasn't that a sign of something in high school?"

"I'm sure it was," Paul admitted. "But I wasn't much into teen-aged dating rituals back when I was a gangly adolescent."

"Bet I would've fallen for you back then," Jenny grinned. "You gangly grownup, you." She gave him a quick breath-stealing hug, then headed for the door. It was still fifteen minutes away from 9 a.m. "Shall we open early?" she asked, and Paul nodded his acquiescence.

ONE OF THE VENDORS (Leena from Totally T'd) was waiting for Ian when he came to unlock the door. Dressed in a shocking pink 5XL T-shirt sporting a Susan Mason illustration, she gave a small wave of recognition as he appeared. "Ian!" she cried. "Haven't seen you since National two years ago! How's Val doing?"

"Couldn't tell you," Ian replied in as nonchalant a tone as he could muster. "We're not together now."

"Should I be sympathetic or see this as a chance to flirt?" Leena asked. Lifting the handle of her baggage cart, she followed Ian into the Vendors Room, two trunks full of stylish T-shirts rolling behind her.

She was letting her hair grow, Ian noted. When they'd first met she'd been almost punkette; now she was going for a softer look. It suited her, he thought.

"The two aren't mutually exclusive," Ian noted, "but I'm sort of seeing someone at the moment." Looked like he needed to call up front for some more tables, he noted. There were only two in the room, and Leena had claimed the first.

"'Sort of' doesn't sound very firm."

"Yeah, but she's here this weekend and—"

"So there you are, Ian!"

They both turned to see Connie Donovan in the doorway. "You owe me a dance at the Mardi Gras party tonight," Leena whispered, and she quickly turned to begin unpacking her trunks. Ian walked over to Connie. She was wearing a flared top and broomstick-pleated skirt—much dressier than you'd expect to see this early in the day, but he knew she'd be wearing something even glitzier when it came time to host the fashion show.

"Hold on, Leena," Connie called. "That corner's been reserved for InFatuation."

"Really?" Leena mewed. "I don't see any signs." She continued to unpack, but Connie chose not to rise to the challenge. Instead, she honed in on Ian.

"I just saw that broom closet you've assigned my models as a changing room," she kvetched. "It's cramped and has zero ventilation. I'm not gonna have my girls going out and looking like they spent the night trampling through the rain forest. We need a different room."

"It's the only free space we've got available," Ian noted. "Unless you want to switch and put the vendors in it."

"What about the Hospitality Suite upstairs?"

"That's doable, I suppose, but I thought you wanted a room close to your runway."

Connie paused, considering his words, though it was obvious she still wanted to argue. Before she could come up with a further objection, though, Delia poked her head into the room.

"Connie!" she said. "Just saw the changing room, and it's perfect. We'll need some fans to cool things down once we fill up, of course, but it's a nice short walk for the models."

Delia stepped into the Vendors Room, all briskly companionable. Ian hadn't seen them together in quite some time, but he realized that Delia had benefited from her time away from Connie. Where once she'd attempted unsuccessfully to emulate her mentor, Delia had developed her own style. In a checked big shirt and stirrup jeans, hair pulled back efficiently, she looked relaxed yet clearly capable of holding her own against her old boss.

Connie eyed her former lackey suspiciously, then demanded of Ian, "Of course, you'll be getting some oscillating fans—"

"Of course," Ian promised.

"—and several clothes racks. All right, then, let's see what we can do with this sauna." She swept out of the room, and when Delia didn't immediately follow in her wake, called out, "You coming?"

"Yes, Connie."

"How much of that did you hear before you came in?" Ian asked.

"Enough," Delia told him before she stepped back out into the hall.

Ian sighed and collapsed against the door frame. Leena smiled sympathetically from her corner of the room, then returned to her table.

EPISODE FIFTY-THREE

Dear Cassie,

Just a quick picture postcard between arrivals to say hi from the convention. Isn't this an absolutely stunning resort? I'll be sure to take lotsa pics of my room. And everything else, of course!

I'm at the check-in desk with Paul (yes, PAUL!) & he surprised me with the prettiest Valentine pin. You'll love it! I sure do.

Oops, the lull's over! Better scoot for now. Wish you were here!

Love,

Jenny

DEXTER WAITED PATIENTLY as the line crept closer to the table where Paul and Jenny sat, signing in the most recent wave of convention attendees. But he couldn't help but cast an occasional concerned eye toward the lobby, where Rachel guarded their luggage cart with studied indifference.

Was this really a good idea? Neeko certainly thought so—in her quietly persuasive manner she'd made the suggestion seem perfectly feasible. In fact, by the time they fully discussed it he almost believed that he'd come up with the brainstorm. "It would be a wonderful way for you to spend a nice weekend away with your daughter," she'd smiled. "Bond."

"James Bond?" he'd chuckled.

"Silly man! But, yes, sort of. Not like some Bond girl— more like Miss Moneypenny. Be gallant, indulgent, doting. Make her feel, for those two special days, like she is the most important woman in your life."

It hadn't been as easy to convince the woman in question, however. "Yuck! You really want me to hang out with all those fatties? What if one of my friends sees me? No way!" But with sincere promises about refraining from any "pigging out" comments (as if he could ever be that insensitive) and of carte blanche shopping at the trunk show, she'd finally acquiesced and thundered right up to rummage through her closet, all the time piteously declaring she hadn't a single thing to wear.

"Hi, Dex," Jenny smiled as he finally reached the table. "All by yourself?" He glanced over his shoulder again to where Rachel lounged against a faux marble pillar. "Nope," Jenny continued as she shuffled through the name tags, "I see you've brought your pretty daughter with you. What a wonderful dad!"

The dad grinned back sheepishly. "I sure hope it turns out that way." He collected their tags and goody bags, wondering wistfully where the next sixteen hours would find him.

"CALM DOWN, ELEANOR. I mean, what's the worst possible thing Jordan Lewis can do?" Lainie reached for a packet of raw sugar and tore it open into her iced tea. Across the table, Eleanor's head swivelled as she nervously cased the dining room.

"I'm afraid to even imagine," she dithered. "But I just feel so foolish, not finding out his workshop was going on here now. It was my assignment to prevent potential scheduling disasters like this!"

"Assignment? You make it sound like you're a secret agent. C'mon, compost happens." Lainie casually swirled the ice in her glass, then continued to reassure her friend. Sometimes Eleanor could be so anal. "They most likely scheduled it long after we signed the hotel contract. Nothing sinister—Lewis does these workshops all the time, all around the country."

"Oh, I know that." She lifted a slice of English muffin, too distracted to notice when a fat glob of jelly plopped onto the plate, then took an absent nibble on the crispy fringe. "But something tells me there'll be problems. I've got this really bad feeling."

Lainie said nothing, but regarded her worriedly. At many of the nearby tables scattered knots of convention attendees chatted amiably, waiting for the events to start. Or was that a wishful assumption—were they actually waiting for Lewis's anti-acceptance workshop instead?

"We still haven't heard if that writer, whatsisname, has arrived yet." Eleanor had veered on to another concern. "What if he doesn't show?"

"Then we'll have a lot of disappointed FAs," Lainie responded reasonably. "Why wouldn't he show up? You said he sounded excited over the phone. Probably doesn't get a chance to meet and greet his fans all that often."

Glancing up, she saw Lissa Jones sauntering toward them. Dressed in a chic sarong-styled Afro-print dress and black linen jacket for her 10 am presentation, "Raising the Bar on Size Acceptance," she looked every ounce—or would "pound" be more appropriate?— the competent professional. As she joined the two older women Lissa smiled, graciously declining Lainie's offer to sit down.

"Either of you seen Ian yet?" Lissa inquired. "I've got three box fans in the back seat of my car and I don't know where to put 'em."

"Last I knew he was rearranging the banquet room, laying out a catwalk for the models," Lainie told her. She indicated a set of half-open double doors across the way; as if by magic Ian passed in and out of view, sturdy metal chairs in each hand.

"Great. So it's all coming together?"

"You know how it goes," Lainie laughed. "Always a million crises at an event like this." She looked over at Eleanor, who smiled tightly but said nothing. Since Lissa and Delia had paired up Eleanor's unease had grown, making her increasingly tongue-tied around either woman.

"Well, if I can be any help—"

"I'm sure you will be," Eleanor interrupted with a visibly awkward smile.

Shrugging, the lawyer turned toward the banquet room. "Well, just let me know," she offered once more, then headed off to corner Ian.

One of these days, Lainie decided, she'd simply have to talk to Eleanor about her noisy nonverbals.

EPISODE FIFTY–FOUR

THE HOSPITALITY SUITE WAS OPULENT in a way that never quite impressed Ian—ersatz colonial home entertainment center, dark wooden bar and companion stools, two low couches, plus a stack of black metal chairs in the corner. A pair of sliding doors led to a balcony overlooking the snow-strewn golf course. The suite's bathroom inside the double-door entrance seemed cozy for a supersized occupant, but workable. Patsy's private quarters lay to the immediate left of the vestibule.

Said mistress o' hospitality was busily putting up Mardi Gras decorations when Ian arrived, taping a cardboard reminder to "Let the Good Times Roll" across the bar facade. She was dressed in a red felt corduroy jumpsuit, her perpetually unkempt hair styled into a fetching short pixie. Watching her efficiently transform the room, Ian felt as if he was looking at an entirely different woman—someone in control, nobody's victim.

Did he like this new Patsy? After all, he'd severed his relationship with Jenny to return to Val. He just seemed to have a thing for wounded birds. Could that damsel-in-distress-ness be what had attracted him to Patsy?

"Anything I can do?" he offered.

She looked up at him and smiled. "Sure could use an extra pair of hands on the table," she answered, eyes sparkling at the sight of him.

"Your wish is my command." Tentatively grabbing the table edge, he realized there was no way he could macho this by himself (though a part of him suddenly wished he could). He'd have to wait for Patsy's help. "So how's your room?"

"Fancy," Patsy answered, taking her place on the table's opposite end. "Almost too fancy. I keep worrying—what happens if I break anything?"

Ian chuckled, then saw her expression was earnest. The two of them hefted the table off the floor and carted it over to its new location.

"I cracked the legs on a chair once," she explained. "Back when I was a little girl—a whole lot littler than I am today—I broke a chair during Easter dinner at Grandma's. Leaning back. It was family lore for years."

"Another warm and fuzzy family memory. We all have so many of 'em!"

"Yeah," Patsy said ruefully, lowering herself onto a couch and surveying her handiwork. "This'll do, I suppose," she finally decided.

"Looks great to me," Ian countered. Before he could elaborate, the room phone rang. To forestall Patsy's mad dash for it, he picked up the handset.

"Ian," Connie clipped. "We need more fans. Another hour until the show, and it's already hellish in this room."

You should know, Ian grimaced. *Two more hours and her role in all this is over,* he reminded himself, *so just let Connie be the fashion diva.* He sighed, careful not to exhale too loudly over the phone.

"Paul lives fifteen minutes from here," Ian considered out loud. "He might be able to come up with some extra fans."

"'Might' won't cut it," Connie shot back. "Unless you want your models all looking like losers in a wet T-shirt contest, you'd better get more fans here pronto." With that, she cut the connection.

"Trouble?" Patsy asked from her couch.

"Connie being Connie," Ian finally muttered, and he left to relieve Paul at the sign-in desk.

THE APARTMENT WAS MUCH NEATER than she expected for a single guy, particularly when you added a good-sized dog to the mix. The only sign of chaos was a teetering pile of CD jewel cases on the shelf beside Paul's Sony modular stereo. She recognized the Saffire disc from a visit to Lissa's place.

"No time for the grand tour," Paul panted as he followed her. "The fans are in the study. Better go in first, so I can prepare Molly." Crossing the living room, he passed through the kitchenette and opened a door on the other side. A click of claws on the floor and two loud barks—Paul's pooch had obviously been waiting for him.

"Sit, Molly!" But the command was clearly not being heeded. The golden retriever dashed out of the room through the kitchenette and toward the front door, obviously expecting to be taken outside. She stopped short when she got to Jenny, however.

This, Jenny knew, was one of those moments, those snapshots in time that couples would pull out years later (assuming, of course, that they still were a couple years later) and coo over. The Big Pet Moment. She crouched down in front of the dog and slowly extended a hand, trying her best to look non-threatening. Molly cocked her massive head—

—and reared back, frantically barking.

Jenny couldn't help it; she immediately jumped in terror. Paul raced into the room, nearly dropping all three of his box fans in the process, as Molly's barks quickly became a bark/growl combination. The dog's eyes looked wild in a way Jenny had only seen previously in horror movies.

"Molly!" Paul bellowed, and at least the dog stopped long enough to aim her Cujo eyes at him. Quickly setting the fans down, Paul grabbed the beast's collar and dragged her back into the study. She was not happy about it.

"Been some time since an unfamiliar face has showed up here," Paul apologized. "Just being a good watch dog, I suppose."

Jenny kept her subsequent thoughts to herself. Instead she smiled and picked up a fan. On the other side of the study door Molly began whining piteously. For some reason this recalled the image of Valerie from that day at the pool party.

"Her nose is out of joint," Jenny considered. "She sees me competing with her for your time."

"She's just gonna have to get used to it," Paul decided.

He lifted the remaining box fans like a pair of suitcases and led her back out of the apartment. The February sky arched uncharacteristically clear and bright overhead. They stuffed the fans in the back seat of Paul's car.

"I've just been replaying that last statement in my head," Paul began as they drove back to Sycamore Creek, "and it suddenly occurs to me that I might have been presumptuous with that 'get used to it' crack."

Leaning back in the passenger seat, Jenny tried to look as if she too hadn't been replaying his comment. Why was she being so coy? Staring at the road ahead, she decided to drop the phoniness.

"I liked your presumption," she declared. "Even if Molly doesn't."

"She'll learn to like it," Paul promised.

Jenny had her doubts. From where she sat, she'd always remember the Big Pet Moment as a bitch.

EPISODE FIFTY-FIVE

RACHEL WAS WAITING FOR DEX when he got out of Lissa's legal workshop. Standing with her friend Kelly by a vast window overlooking the snow-sloppy first tee, she acted more ebullient than she had in months. Come to think of it, they hadn't seen Kelly Gleasen, a fellow chapter-child from Oak-something, for at least that long either. At one point he remembered being aware that the two girls were feuding—over some young hunk if memory served him—but apparently that was over now, since they were chatting thick as thieves. And in Kelly's case, sorta looking like one.

The pudgy teen had spun her image a full 180. No more owlish eyeglasses and painful nerdishness. Instead she'd gone Goth—jeans, long trenchcoat and nail polish, all Stygian, sporting an "Anarchy rules!" pin on her lapel. All in all, Dex observed, she resembled any number of psych patients from his residency. When he was young the only choice for fat girls had been dark and dreary fashion. How could their daughters revert back to black after so many Dark Age decades of color-free clothing?

"Dad, I'm sorry if I bitched, you know, about coming," she began. "That workshop was pretty cool."

"Bitched?" Dex bridled before thinking better of it, then wisely steered a different tack. "So you liked Miz Reynard's presentation, eh?"

"The woman's so deep," Kelly assured him in a voice at least one tone huskier than he remembered ever hearing. She was cradling a trade paperback entitled *YourSelf Is All You Have: A Guide to Body Image*, which she flipped carefully open to the frontispiece. There said author Anne Reynard had scrawled her signature, with the additional advice: "Be True to the Beauty You Imagine."

"Good advice," Dex thought aloud.

"It seems really dumb when you just read it," Rachel said defensively, "but if you could hear her saying it, out loud—"

"I don't think it's dumb at all."

"She has a way of putting things that you've always thought, but didn't know how to, you know, say. Really deep things." She cut off her next comment as if suddenly worried that she'd given away something (though Dex was damned if he knew what that could be), and shot a "rescue me" look toward Kelly.

Dex decided to give her a break. "Are you going to the fashion luncheon, Kelly?" he turned to Gothic Grrrl. "You could sit with us if you'd like."

"Old lady fashion—got nuthin' to do with me," Kelly sniffed, then dropped her superior tone, gleefully pointing down the hall. "There she is, Dr. Logan! The lady who signed my book! Anne!!"

A middling-tall, plump woman was just coming out of the second conference room. Closely permed blond hair, a neat denim blazer and white blouse, floor-length blue bandanna skirt and navy flats, a matronly expression on her rosy face—she was the spitting image of his first wife, Lindy (or, at least, a Lindy-memory from some point in her uphill yo-yo period). The resemblance was so striking that Dex half expected her to come up and intertwine arms with him and Rachel.

"Think you can get Miz Reynard to sit with us, Dad?" Rachel urged plaintively.

"Maybe," Dex answered, though the thought of lunching with this divine doppelganger, with all its inherent dangers (salad dressing stains on his necktie, enormous lubs between his teeth!) was simply too boggling.

"I'll ask if she's going to be at the luncheon!" Kelly announced, and raced over to the approaching woman. The closer the woman got the more she looked like Lindy. Despite the unseasonable A/C blasting from hallway vents, a trickle of sweat wended down Dex's spine.

"I'd even be willing to sit through the frump-a-thon," Rachel told Dex. "She's so deep."

"So you both said," Dex mumbled, absently straightening his belt. "Does she look familiar to you, Rach?"

"What are you talking about, Dad?"

"Nothing."

Rachel gave him one of those exasperated kid looks, then went to join her friend. As the two girls started chattering at Anne Reynard, a loud commotion suddenly pulled Dex's attention in the opposite direction.

"THIS GATHERING IS A SHAM! A tissue of delusional rationalization and harmful, dangerous practices! And I'm here to tell you that it doesn't have to be this way!"

Jordan Lewis was in booming, full-preach mode. Expensively dressed in a dark three-piece suit, his gray hair coifed in a distinguished style that would have elicited Uncle Tom jokes during his Angry Young Comedian days, the diet guru was standing outside the ballroom where the RADFAm fashion luncheon would all-too-shortly start. A group of J.L. devotees stood in semicircle behind him, with a videocam crew facing him, effectively blocking the room's double-door entrance.

Off to one side Ian and a Sycamore Creek desk clerk were hopelessly trying to get through Lewis's semicircle to take charge of the situation. Within the dining room a scattering of early-bird RADFAmites craned to observe the proceedings with varied expressions of curiosity and dread.

"It is within everyone's power to lose weight! I used to be one of these self-deceiving souls myself. Much like this poor woman here," and the diet maven whisked a figure from his semicircle into the camera lights. As she stepped into the harsh glare, Ian seized the opportunity to slip forward between the ardent.

"She even used to be a member of this sad little group," the tub-thumper intoned. But as Ian saw who Lewis thrust on display, his heart lurched.

It was Valerie, once again staging the most dramatic appearance possible to further confound Ian. Dressed in a severe navy blue dress, her hair pulled back in a bun, his erstwhile flame held her hands prayerfully, like a choir soloist. Or a martyr. Her persona was so contrary to her habitual manner that he almost started snickering. Then she spoke for the cameras.

"I used to be fat and unhappy," she said. "I went through a string of very miserable relationships with nothing but abusive men. These jerks were all I believed I deserved. But now I know I'm better than that! I'm following Jordan's plan, losing this sinful fat and having nothing more to do with men who don't deserve me."

"I am so proud of you, girl," Jordan Lewis beamed to the world at large. Though Ian had ducked quickly from videocam range, he knew with certainty that it had captured the initial stunned expression on his face. Lewis circled his right arm around Val's shoulder and pulled her closer. Behind him Ian could hear a camera clicking as J.L. dramatically shot his left hand to the heavens and declaimed, "Courage to those who embrace salvation!"

"Excuse me!"

Undeterred by either camera crew or the milling crush of Jordanites, Lissa pushed her way out of the dining room. *Must be another way inside,* Ian thought as she planted herself in front of the impressively towering Jordan.

"I hate to interrupt this Jerry Springer moment. But by blocking access to this private gathering, you're in violation of local township ordinances," Lissa began. "Why don't you take your paparazzi someplace where you're less of a nuisance?"

The diet preacher took a long look at Lissa, as if trying to decide where she fit in his view of the world, then he grinned knowingly. "You could be a really stunning sister if you wouldn't give in to your appetite so much," he told her.

"And you're awfully damn presumptuous," Lissa shot back. "You don't know me or a single thing about the way I conduct my life."

"Don't I?" He looked toward the camera crew dramatically, holding his glance for several beats, then asked, "We got enough here?"

A goateed cameraman who appeared to be a Lewis program dropout nodded, then hefted the videocam off his shoulder.

"Then we're gone," Lewis told Lissa nonchalantly. He gestured Valerie back to her place in line, then focused on Ian. "Did you have something you wanted to say to me?" he asked. He gave Ian the same once-over as Lissa, but the shock of seeing Val had fortunately passed.

"If you're leaving now—no," Ian clipped.

"Then we've got work to do elsewhere," Lewis proclaimed expansively and smiled. "If any of you women in the dining room would like the opportunity to turn your lives around like Val here has, then leave this place and come with us!"

"And we've got a schedule that you're threatening," Lissa said. "If you don't want to face a misdemeanor charge and a lawsuit, then I'd advise you take your advice and leave."

"Oh, my scofflaw days are history, honey," Lewis laughed, and as he cocked his head the camera crew began to shoo his coterie from the hall. "I've got nothing to hide from the public," he added, *sotto voce,* "and I pray you can say the same. But that's very questionable."

He turned to follow his followers, but of course couldn't resist one final parting gibe. "Our girl Val has really turned her life around," he told Ian. "Sure helps when you don't have a boyfriend constantly sabotaging your dreams."

As Lewis strode imperiously away, the flustered Sycamore Creek rep moved to stand between Ian and Lissa. "I can't express how deeply sorry the resort is for this—unpleasantness. I assure you that we'll never allow that man to rent space here ever again."

"Oh I'm sure he'll get by," Lissa said, then turned to Ian. "You okay?"

"Been better," he replied. Down the hallway he could see the rest of the luncheon crowd starting to arrive. "How do you know so much about local township law?" he asked as he readied the check-in table at the entrance.

"Who said I did?" Lissa grinned.

EPISODE FIFTY-SIX

RUBBER CHICKEN, Joe thought, picking at his lemon-braised breast disconsolately. You never read of anybody eating hotel convention chicken in a Lew Baird short story. Baird's FA fantasies were filled with almost as many loving descriptions of gourmet dining as they were of gorgeous gluttons. This sorry excuse for a luncheon definitely lacked such feeder fodder.

The FA fantasist probably wouldn't make his heroine president of a RAD-FAm chapter either. Misty was so focused on the convention that she neither knew nor cared about what was being served to her. Baird's men's mag beauties never let a meal go by without appreciating it to the fullest. If the heroines in mainstream sex tales never had an unsatisfying sexual experience, the women of FA fantasies were equally enthusiastic when it came to fine dining.

Still, considering the culinary crap set before them, it was probably a good thing that Misty ignored it. The fashion show was supposed to be a big draw, Joe knew, but that didn't excuse this lukewarm fare. He took a silent poll of the rest of their table—Dex and his daughter, Ian, that Anne person, and a girl who was apparently Rachel's friend—and noticed with a certain inner satisfaction that none of them ate very enthusiastically.

It wasn't his place to grouse, though. Misty was stressed enough without him being an ass. Reaching under the table, he patted her neighboring thigh encouragingly. She turned her attention from the lunching crowd and gave him a tidy smile.

"I know what you're thinking," she cooed. "That you could serve a much better lunch than this."

"It's not that bad," he muttered, caught off guard. As if to underline his words, Joe took a bite of stringy chicken and smiled.

Misty wasn't buying it. "The bird is dry, the vegetables have had all taste steamed out of them—even the twice-baked potatoes have the consistency of kindergarten paste. As a working chef, this must be your idea of hell."

"I wouldn't wanna serve this meal to Caspar," Joe admitted. "When's the fashion show starting? Baird's workshop is at two."

"You should be fine," Misty observed. "Here comes Connie now." She pointed out the nearby podium. Connie was advancing toward it with a pile of notecards in her right hand, dark swing vest trailing over the back of Lainie's chair as she passed around it to get to the microphone. By the door Delia pressed "play" on a boombox, then turned to go back to the dressing room. RADFAm's unofficial dance theme, "It's Raining Men," thundered rhythmically.

"This is so old," Rachel declared.

"Good afternoon," Connie breathily opened as she spread her cards on top of the podium. "We've got plenty of stunning items to show you today, so get your credit cards ready! Many of these items can be had this weekend if you'll check out the vendors' room or the fliers in your goody bags."

Patsy appeared in the double doorway. In a full-length lavender dress and duster, she exuded competent sexiness as she strode into the room, moving from table to table, looking far more stunning than Joe ever remembered seeing her. On the other side of their table, Ian was openly beaming.

"This rayon challis dress with mandarin duster comes just in time for spring," Connie opened. "Our RADFAmite Patsy looks both cool and casual, whether going out on a weekend date or shopping at a trendy plus-size boutique—you girls know which shop I'm talking about. It goes up to a plus-size

XL, which will fit up to 84-inch hips. Our Patsy is wearing a medium. We carry this line at InFatuation, and it's a very popular seller."

The next model, a midsized and vaguely familiar college-age girl, entered the room in a blue skirt and tunic sweater. The outfit looked far more traditional than the model wearing it. As soon as she entered the room the girl made a beeline for the table where several chapter oldtimers—Lainie, Eleanor and Lissa—had settled with Jenny and Paul. She struck a pose in front of the table's sole male occupant, looking down at Paul with a challenging expression on her face. Even from across the room Joe could see him reddening.

"Kathi from Full-Figured Friends is wearing a wedgewood scoopneck sweater with a checked madras skirt. Simple but stylish, this machine-washable ensemble is sure to get you noticed. The sweater also comes in sage, navy, and white. Its XL size will accommodate up to 74 inch busts and hips. Kathi is in a small. We carry a full range of sizes at InFatuation, though." She looked up from her cards to note that Kathi was still at her first stop. "Don't dawdle, girl—we've got a lot of clothing to show the eager audience!"

Reluctantly moving to another table, Kathi was replaced by another midsized girl her age in a peach cashmere skirt and tunic.

"God," Rachel's friend noted, "it's Attack of the Plus-Size Preppies!" This brought a derisive snort from Rachel and an uncomfortable look to Dex's face.

"You know," Joe turned away and whispered to Misty, "you could blow all these models off the runway."

"They're just too skinny for you," she said with a grin. "But I appreciate the thought."

"It's more than that," Joe answered. "Doesn't matter what their size is—they still don't compare to you."

"You do know the right thing to say occasionally." She cocked her head quizzically. "Did I hear Connie plug her shop again?" she groaned.

WHEN MISTY SAW LEENA, the T-shirt lady, sidle across the edge of the room toward their table, she knew what was up. Midpoint into the fashion show the other vendors were sending a delegate to air their dissatisfaction with Connie's presentation. The way she described each item you'd think that InFatuation was the only purveyor of quality clothing at the convention.

"It's not me because I'm just doing T-shirts," Leena opened. "But a few of the other vendors are wondering if Connie's ever gonna mention them."

Two seats over Dex's daughter and her friend were snickering at the first lingerie model—Patsy again, this time in a taupe-and-cream silk peignoir set.

"You know, girls," Anne Reynard suddenly interjected. "It takes a lot of courage to get up and model like that." Amazingly, both girls stopped long enough to look suitably abashed. If Dex had said the same thing it probably would have been met with utter disdain. "I know I couldn't do it," she continued. "I don't have the legs for it."

"Me either," Misty chimed before turning back to Leena. "I hear what you're saying. And I'll see what I can do." The vendor nodded and headed back to the dressing room. Misty pulled a hotel pad from her "Invitation to the Dance" tote and dashed a quick note. "Joe, could you take this up to Connie without being too obvious about it?"

"Strong and silent, that's me," Joe agreed, and he quickly carried out the task, slipping the folded note on top of Connie's cards.

"Think she'll do as you ask?" he wondered once he got back to his seat.

"Who can tell with Connie?" Misty sighed.

Behind the podium Connie paused to read Misty's note. On the boombox a deep male voice was croaking about being a model on the catwalk. When she finished Connie casually crumpled the note and dropped it to the floor. She did not look Misty's way.

"Not a good sign," Joe hazarded.

"Here's another piece of after-hours magic," Connie told the room as Kathi entered wearing a black mesh teddy and laced vinyl gloves. "Especially suited for our midnight minx, this Lycra dream has removable, adjustable garters and goes up to a 52 bust and 53 hips." She paused, then a determined look came across her wide, round face. "This teddy is only available from its manufacturer, though I'm told they might have a room in the hotel."

"'Might,'" Misty muttered to Joe. "The information's down on the cards! Of course they've got a room!"

"The look is so darling, though, I wish I could sell it at my shop," Connie continued. "I may have mentioned it once or twice, but you know, I'm really proud of my little place. InFatuation—it's right downtown, just a twenty minute cab trip from here."

Aiming a defiant glance toward Misty, she added, "We're open on Sundays, too."

EPISODE FIFTY-SEVEN

THE CONFERENCE ROOM WAS SMALL, with enough chairs for maybe thirty people at the most—though from the look of things it would be nowhere near capacity for Baird's workshop. Paul recognized half the scattered attendees present. The figure seated at the front of the room could only be Lew Baird.

The FA writer looked younger than Paul expected. Baird's works were characterized by an urbane, almost pretentious writing voice that led you to expect a more worldly figure. In person the man was boyish; not young by any means, but still stamped somehow by an air of puppyish inexperience. Paul had met writers before and knew there was often a discrepancy between the way they wrote and how they looked, but it still never failed to surprise him.

"Enjoy the fashion show?" Joe asked, slipping into a seat to Paul's right.

"Huh?" For an instant the discomfort he'd been feeling over Kathi's blatant flirting in the dining room re-emerged. Joe's question appeared innocent though, so he smiled wanly. "Not my thing," Paul answered, "though it did put me in mind of my early days as an FA. Back when BBW was the only place I knew to find plus-sized images."

"First photos I remember glomming onto were Rockshots cards," Joe confided. "Not very fat positive, but the women were so much bigger than anything in BBW."

"Never could get past the jokes on the cards," Paul replied.

As a last straggler wandered in Baird rose from his seat and carried a pile of sheets to the end of the first row. "Pass it on," he told Joe, who grabbed a copy and gave the stack to Paul. It was, Paul saw, a series of graphics depicting preternaturally large women, their outfits hugging mega-sized bodies like spandex on a comic book superheroine. You didn't see any getups like these in the fashion show, Paul reflected.

"Y'know, I've tried convincing Misty to put on one of these outfits," Joe whispered, grinning, "but for some reason she just won't do it."

"Before we start this workshop," Baird was telling the group, "I want to give you some advance warning. This is not a PC subject area. We going to be talking about fantasies, and fantasies operate by their own special set of rules. So if any of you have the least difficulty with this, you may not be in the right workshop."

Silence from the rest of the room.

"Some of you know me by my work; I've been writing FA fantasies for over ten years now. Most of it has appeared in men's magazines, though I have had some small success with the FA mag *Dimensions*. All of my stories have elements—weight gain, for instance—that make many fat women in size acceptance uncomfortable."

This declaration brought knowing nods from most of the FAs in the audience.

"My main intent today is not to defend these fantasies, but to look at their common threads. And because I don't often get a chance to interact with my readers, I'm going to use all of you as a sounding board. So feel free to be honest about what you like or don't like about my work."

"Just don't get Jefferson talking about his favorite fantasies," Joe whispered to Paul. "We'll be here all day."

At that moment the door creaked open. An unfamiliar plump figure in polyester and a lacquered coif poked her head into the room, seeing only males in attendance, and froze in confusion.

"I'm guessing this isn't the Jordan Lewis Weight Loss Seminar?" she hazarded.

"Good guess," Baird replied, chuckling. "My first name's Lew, though, so you weren't that far off." The woman timidly backed out of the room. "Two sides of the same coin, though," Baird mused. "Lewis sells the fantasy of permanent weight loss; I traffic in fantasies that move in the opposite direction."

A polite response from everyone in attendance.

"Okay, first question—how many of you didn't tell your fat girlfriends you were coming to this workshop?"

LAINIE AND ELEANOR WERE STAFFING Sign-In Central, so both Misty and Jenny had some breathing space.

"The boys are at the workshop," Misty offered. "Let's go check the Hospitality Suite. Put our feet up."

"Don't you have to prepare for your Tarot reading?" Jenny asked as they headed for the elevator.

"Just need to pull on my gypsy rags," Misty answered. "The readings don't start until three." She stepped aside to let a trim couple dressed in golf togs get off the elevator, then stepped in to press the floor button. "You doing okay?"

"Had a weird moment going to Paul's to get some fans for the dressing room," Jenny confided. "Paul's dog went ballistic on me. Our first face-to-face and she acts like she wants to chew my face off!"

"In my experience, dogs are no good judge of character," Misty reassured her. "Cats are." The elevator swished open at their stop. "Think the beast is jealous of you?"

"Possibly," Jenny thought, "but if so, that puts Paul in an tough position."

"Not if he's Leader of the Pack," Misty said.

"*Look out, look out, look out, look out!*" Jenny giggled.

"What?"

As they approached the Hospitality Suite the sound of group chattering rose in volume.

"Maybe this wasn't such a good idea," Misty considered. "I forgot they were doing a pizza thing for the fashion show models."

"Too late now," Jenny noted as one of the vendors broke away from the group milling around the munchies table to zero in on Misty.

"What's with that bitch?" she opened without preamble, hands jammed into fleshy hips, "Miz Conniving Donovan?"

Jenny did a quick room review. Both Delia and Lissa were seated by the bar; Patsy was moving around the suite, picking up empty pop cans and paper plates. The girl who'd been flirting so hot and heavy with Paul was working on a piece of pizza, animatedly talking to her friend. Connie was nowhere to be seen.

In the background the muted TV was tuned to an *E!* segment on daytime television. In a clip a gorgeously dressed plus-sized redhead was chastising a hunky male figure via closed captioning. When had fat girls started showing up on soap operas? Jenny wondered.

"I'm sorry about the way Connie ran the show," Misty apologized. "Is there anything the chapter can do to make it up to you?"

"I suppose comping us our rooms is out of the question," the vendor of-fered, half jokingly.

"You suppose darned right," Misty answered, grabbing the closest avail-able love seat and slowly lowering herself onto it. "But we'll think of some-thing."

"I know you will," the vendor said. "None of us get rich coming to these cons, you know."

"Only ones getting rich off of fat people," Misty mourned, "are the diet mavens. The rest of us are just working to get by." She looked over toward Lissa and Delia, sipping store-brand colas.

"Thirsty?" Jenny noticed.

"Not unless you're planning on getting something for yourself," Misty responded.

"I could do with something decaf," Jenny decided, so she left the chapter president to sooth the disgruntled vendor.

Lissa and Delia smiled as she advanced. "Having a good time?" Lissa asked once Jenny had retrieved two cans of orange soda from behind the bar.

"Yes," Jenny realized. "It's an odd experience being in this hotel all day, seeing nothing but fat people. It's like somehow we've magically become the majority."

"According to the National Institutes of Health," Lissa pointed out, "we *are* the majority."

"Is Tara giving Misty crap about the fashion show?" Delia asked, nodding her head in Misty's direction.

"Nothing she can't handle," Jenny grinned. "Bet you two are glad to be done with your volunteering."

"I won't lie," Delia admitted; "you're right."

"You doing the dance tonight?"

"Maybe—but mostly we'll be spending some private time together," Lissa leered, patting her lover on the knee.

"There's a lot of folk here from outside the region," Delia elaborated. "I'm not in the mood to be the object of their—scrutiny."

Lissa just shrugged—from what Jenny knew of her boss, it'd be less of an issue for her—so Jenny didn't pursue the matter further.

"What about you?" Lissa teased. "You and Paul going to show the rest of the room how it's done?"

"I did buy an ultra-sexy dress in one of the vendor rooms today," Jenny confessed, "but I don't know if I've got the nerve to wear it."

Lissa sat up straight. "Sounds like a job for Boss Lady Mentor. Let's go see this dangerous getup."

"Okay," Jenny decided. "If you promise to go gentle on me if it looks ridiculous."

"Small chance of that." Lissa snorted, gesturing to the exit.

"I'm still watching my models," Delia said from her seat. "You two go on without me."

"Spoken like a true movement martyr," Lissa tweaked. Delia threw a crumpled napkin at her in reply.

Jenny handed Misty's pop to her as she left. The vendor appeared to have calmed down, so perhaps they'd worked something out. On their way out they passed a supersized woman on a motorized Rascal scooter.

"Abby! Haven't seen you in ages," Lissa greeted the unfamiliar middleaged woman, who smiled tightly and rode past, saying nothing in reply.

"Friendly type," Jenny observed *sotto voce*.

"Limited social skills," Lissa noted. "She usually doesn't want to waste the ones she has on women."

"An old chapter member?"

"She's been in and out," Lissa answered. "Connie drove her away last time." She paused suddenly, looking down the hall, and saw a troupe of people speedwalking their way. At the head of the line strode Jordan Lewis, resplendent in a freshly pressed exercise suit. Jenny had never seen a pleated one before.

"What are they doing up here?" Lissa muttered. "We've got all the big rooms on this floor."

"Exercising," Jenny decided as the group split into single file and began to march past them. "Are they walking through the whole hotel?"

"Probably not," Lissa guessed, "just the floors with plenty of RAD-FAmites."

The group by then had nearly passed them. Near the end of the line a familiar figure glared at Jenny, who fixed a friendly grin on her face and kept her eyes locked with Val's until the woman walked by.

"This time I get the cold shoulder," Jenny said.

"Don't let it bug you," Lissa advised. "She probably doesn't know Patsy is the one she should be saving the daggers for. Now let's go check out that festive frock!"

EPISODE FIFTY-EIGHT

DEX COULD HEAR THE TELEVISION BLASTING through the locked connecting door. From the cartoony voices it was either an episode of *The Simpsons* or *Daria*, the only cartoons that Rachel deigned to watch. Her occasional guffaws pierced the hotel walls. For the price of these rooms you'd think they would have made the walls thicker.

Sitting on the edge of his bed, dress slacks unbuttoned to make way for his shirt, Dex punched out his home number on the hotel phone, only to be greeted by Neeko's answering machine voice (clipped and professional—her translator voice), informing him that there was no one home.

A movie, he suddenly remembered. His wife and son were going out to-gether to see a movie—an actioner with Chow Yun-Fat in it. Something right up Jackie's alley.

"Hi, sweetie! Just wanted to check in and let you know I was thinking of you. See you tomorrow—"

Damn. He wanted to hear more than just her recording voice. Ever since Dex had seen Anne Reynard striding down that hallway he'd felt off balance, in need of grounding. Anne looked so much like his late wife—even down to her mannerisms—that it was unsettling. The more time he spent around her, the stronger his sense of loss and longing.

Rising from his bed, Dex went to examine himself in the bathroom mirror. Not his best idea. The over-bright fluorescents made him look older than his years. When had all his chest hair turned grey? When had his face grown so roseate? Good ol' Doctor Dexter: morbidly obese and middleaged. Just the man you want taking care of all your health care needs.

Stop right there. What was he doing, anyway? Gearing up for a midlife crisis? He knew better than this. Dex turned away from his reflection in disgust and returned to his bed, closing the bathroom door deliberately. One thing about hotel rooms—they had no shortage of mirrors. As soon as he sat down he saw his shirtless reflection over his open suitcase. Put on your shirt, Dex chastised himself. Nobody wants to see that!

Except maybe Neeko, a calming voice in the back of his head suddenly reminded him. Though she'd never use the phrase, it was clear his wife was a fat admirer of the highest order. At times when they were alone together, it almost felt like she got a religious charge out of his size. It could be simultaneously exciting and unnerving.

After buttoning his shirt he switched on the television in search of the cartoon Rachel was chortling over. It turned out to be the *Simpsons* episode where Homer gains a hundred pounds in a misguided attempt to get classified as disabled at work. The episode had even more fat gluttony jokes than usual; at one point, after looking for comfortable clothing, the cartoon fat man dressed himself in a muumuu.

Annoyed, Dex switched off the set. Moments like this, he could understand why Elvis shot out his television.

SCATTERING CONFETTI strategically across the tables as if sprinkling chocolate over a plate of tiramisu, Joe didn't notice Misty when she sidled up behind him. It wasn't until she pressed her side into him that he turned to her. The smile he gave her was exactly what she needed.

"How'd the readings go?" he asked as his erstwhile psychic psweetie scanned the hall.

Around the ballroom other chapter members were readying the room for the late Mardi Gras celebration. Paul and Jenny stood by the deejay table twisting streamers and taping them to the table's edge. Ian was moving extra chairs around the perimeter. None of the Full-Figured Friends were to be seen.

"Not too well; my mojo was distracted," Misty admitted, shrugging. "How was your workshop?"

"Pretty entertaining," Joe replied as he finished off the last table. He still had a handful of confetti left over, so he tossed it in the direction of the dance floor. "At least until Jefferson started monopolizing the session. I don't think

Baird was prepared to have so much of his time taken."

"I haven't met this Lew Baird yet, have I?"

"Probably not, but he's planning on attending the dance, and he seemed especially interested in the golf 'n' pool party afterwards."

"FAs all love the pool parties," Misty sighed, settling onto the first chair within reach. Joe gave her a concerned glance. "I'm just a little tired," she explained, noting his expression. "These readings always take more out of me than I expect 'em to."

A loud voice suddenly seeped through the wall from the ballroom next door—Jordan Lewis, speaking to a dinner group. She'd recognize that preach-ifying cadence anywhere. Where close to two hours of talking wore her out, Lewis was obviously pumped by the activity.

"You wanna skip the dance?" Joe asked.

"Maybe," she admitted. "We'll see how I feel after dinner."

"I'd love to spend some time alone with you in our room," he whispered, leaning over a fleshy shoulder.

"The right thing to say," Misty smiled ruefully. "So are Lewis and his Anti-Fat Army staying in the hotel tonight? I thought they were just here for the afternoon."

"Don't know," Joe answered. "Maybe they decided to stay to gain a few converts."

Misty shivered and made a face.

"You can handle this." Joe smiled, in nurturing mode. "What's the matter, Misty? You look beyond drained."

"I just ran into someone that I hadn't seen in a couple years. Abby. She used to be really active in the chapter. She's close to my age and size—and she's using a motorized scooter to get around."

"And?"

"Oh, I don't know," Misty moaned. "It unnerved me, that's all." She watched Jenny and Paul across the room. The midsized paralegal had a shape she envied, a classic full-figured hourglass. There was a time that Misty would have killed for a pair of legs like Jenny's. "I don't exercise as much as I should."

"Could I be doing anything?" Joe asked.

"Just keep looking at me the way you did when you first turned around," Misty answered. She rose and chucked his chin lightly. At the ballroom en-trance Greg Dillman and Connie Donovan were finally putting in an appear-ance. "Now, where are the rest of the decorations?"

EPISODE FIFTY-NINE

THE HOSPITALITY SUITE WAS QUIET NOW, but Patsy knew it wouldn't stay that way. The Mardi Gras dance was winding down, so it wouldn't be long before the after-hours crowd started showing. Time to unveil the finger sandwiches, she decided, reaching behind the bar for the first plastic carousel of store-made deli noshes.

"Phew!" Ian exclaimed as he burst into the room. He was dressed in an old-fashioned tux, which gave him a vaguely Groucho Marxian air. "Sometimes I think that folks want to ruin things for the chapter! Just spent the last half hour trying to talk sense to two 3F-ers who were sneaking booze into the banquet room. No matter how much I told them 'Look, we need to stay in the hotel's good graces if we want to be able to come back here,' they refused to listen to reason."

"So they'd already imbibed?" Patsy guessed, centering the sandwich platter, then turning to get a jar of Miracle Whip from the bar's mini-fridge.

"Probably pointless trying to reason with 'em, right?"

"Probably," Patsy agreed. But it was awfully sweet, she thought. She'd never had a boyfriend who tried so hard to work things out, who put so much stock on reason. Her previous, admittedly short-term relationships had been characterized by threats and bullying. Even Greg Dillman, who came across so smooth and charming those first few dates, was quite adept at turning into Mr. Hyde. At first she'd thought all males were like this—then she'd thought all males who were attracted to her—but with Ian she was starting to believe differently.

She'd been moping through so much of her life, she saw. No wonder the predators had been attracted to her—she'd practically been walking around with a "Kick Me" sign on her back. She had no intention of making that mistake again.

Smiling, she came from behind the bar and kissed Ian on the neck.

"What?" he asked.

"Nothing," Patsy grinned. "So how did it end?"

"Got the group to give up the bottle, which was only down to a couple of shots anyway. Next time we may need to post a policy on this ahead of time."

"'Next time'?" she teased, handing him two fresh cartons of Marie's veggie dip. "Let's get through tonight before we start planning the next conference."

"Got to learn from our mistakes," Ian pronounced, "so we'll be able to discover fresh new ones!" He arched his eyebrows suggestively after accepting the first of two vegetable trays from Patsy. "Think we've got time to visit your room next door before the ravenous hordes arrive?"

Patsy indicated the empty room. "Somebody's got to hold the fort," she explained.

"We can watch the room for you," a sudden voice from the doorway offered, as Dex's daughter and her friend made a beeline for the snack table.

THE HOSPITALITY SUITE was on the floor beneath his room, and Dex considered stepping off the elevator to do a quick checkup on his daughter. But the desire to change into something less uncomfortable overrode this parental impulse, so he headed straight to his room instead. The dance was winding up, and he didn't think he had the energy for any post-Mardi Gras activities. He'd switch into something casual, and then go down and see how Rachel was doing.

The dance appeared to be a glowing success—a good mix of women and men, familiar and unfamiliar faces, a varied music selection, nonstop dance floor action. Though he'd had his doubts on the wisdom of pooling resources with Dillman's group, so far it seemed to be working out well. Pretty surprising considering Greg, who Dex always considered about as ethical as a pharmaceutical salesman.

He'd done the dance floor twice, both times with Anne (who—typical for a midsized woman at one of these events—had not been asked by any of the roving FAs). It had done much toward banishing the discomfort he'd been feeling around her. Holding her in his arms, dancing to one of Elvis's slow songs, her resemblance to his late wife vanished.

Anne moved and felt like her own woman. She dressed less defensively, spoke with much more confidence. Even the touch of her fingers was different. With this, his earlier confusions had vanished.

They'd talked about Rachel, her moodiness and his suspicions about her candy pranks.

"I think you did a good thing bringing her here," Anne said, "making it a father-daughter outing. She's obviously struggling with her place in the family, with her role as the Fat Girl. Where's she now?"

"With her friend Kelly on the mini-golf range," Dex answered. "She absolutely refused to bring a swimsuit to the hotel."

"Can't say I blame her," Anne reasoned. "It took me years to get up the gumption to wear one—and then it was covered with so many distracting frills I looked like I'd been attacked by a mad ribbon curler."

"And here I thought you just came across your self-assurance naturally."

"Not at all," Anne had smiled. "Self-confidence takes a lifetime to build—and maintain."

She was right, he sighed, thinking back to his moment of self-laceration before the dance. He smiled and slipped his key card into the door.

Pushing the door open with his hip, Dex loosened his tie and stepped into his room. Hadn't he left the lights on? He couldn't remember. Fumbling for the light switch, he heard an airy giggle. Then a feminine voice commanded, "No, leave it off."

Squinting through the dark, Dex saw a woman in his bed.

ABBY WAS CLOSE TO THE HOT TUB, overflowing water occasionally coming up to her scooter wheels, two young beaus competing for the privilege of getting her a can of soda. The dress she'd worn to Mardi Gras had transformed into a one-piece swimsuit with the simple removal of its skirt. Watching from a nearby deck chair, Misty marveled at the woman's energy. Abby had been one of the busiest women on the dance floor, swirling and sweeping with motorized grace.

Misty then shifted her attention to Joe, who seemed to be focusing on the activity in the bustling pool. A trio of Full-Figured Fillies was putting the squeeze on an FA who on closer observation turned out to be Lewis Baird. The erotic writer looked both titillated and embarrassed by the attention he was receiving.

"Bet you wouldn't mind being the fixings in that particular sandwich," she joked, tweaking Joe's cheek. Baird had by now retreated to the edge of the pool, pursued by the young punkette from the fashion show.

"I wouldn't want to make a sandwich with anyone but you," Joe answered, then added after quick consideration. "Of course, it'd have to be open-face."

"I love it when you talk dinner to me," Misty shot back, but the smile slipped from her face when she saw Greg Dillman approach. Through most of the pool party, she'd noticed, he'd been trying to get women to sign his photo releases—with limited success. He passed through the poolside crowd, Nikon dangling across his open terry-cloth jacket, and hailed Misty.

"Great crowd," Dillman was crowing. "Looks like we'll all be turning a very tidy profit."

"I hope so," Misty moderated. "RADFAm had quite a substantial initial outlay on the entire convention. So of course we have to make that back first."

"Of course," Greg acknowledged. "I'm sure you already have." He nodded toward Jenny, outside the pool area on the hotel's indoor miniature golf course. "Perhaps our little paralegal will have some preliminary figures tomorrow morning?"

"I wouldn't press her," Misty cautioned softly. "An event like this can create sudden expenses up until the very last minute."

"Sure," Dillman backpedaled. But you could tell he wasn't pleased with Misty's caveat. "Maybe by mid-week." He pointedly indicated the chapter treasurer, who was gesturing triumphantly from a successful putt.

"We'll set up a time to conference," Misty promised. First time she'd ever used "conference" as a verb, she thought wryly.

"Fine," Greg clipped, and he turned around with an eye toward the pool, pulling several waivers from his jacket pocket.

"Joe," she decided as she returned her attention to the flirting Abby, "if you want to go in the pool, don't wait for me."

"I've got a better idea," Joe answered, and as he murmured to Misty, she wholeheartedly agreed.

THE MINIATURE GOLF RANGE was truly mini—only nine holes rimming the pool—but it was trickier than Paul expected. His only complaint: "Too bad they don't have a windmill. It just doesn't seem like real mini-golf unless you've got to wait for the blades to pass."

Jenny laughed, then stooped to pick her ball out of the seventh hole. "Sure you're not feeling that way because I'm beating you?" she teased, playfully tossing the ball in her hand.

"Maybe," he admitted, after blowing an easy two-foot putt.

"Should I lose to salvage your male ego?" In white shorts, sandals and a floral pattern top, Jenny looked like she should be should be flirting and sipping drinks at the Nineteenth Hole. Paul, on the other hand, looked like he should be serving them. Next time, he thought, he was definitely getting a room at the convention site.

"I'm not that neurotic," Paul reassured her. He returned to the tee to get his can of Schweppes, then followed Jenny to the penultimate hole. From a table on the sidelines Lissa and Delia were cheering their friend on.

"Mini-golf's the official sport of RADFAm, you know," Lissa declared authoritatively. After their dance no-show Jenny was surprised to see both women in the pool area, but perhaps they found it a more congenial setting. "We expect all our officers to consistently shoot par or better."

"Put the pressure on, why don't ya?" Jenny groused, concentrating on her tee shot. She had to ricochet the golf ball off two walls and go over a speed bump, but she landed within two inches of the hole. She tapped the ball in casually.

"I'm impressed," Paul said, and he proceeded to shoot a hole-in-one. From their table Lissa and Delia both whooped loudly.

"You're not hustling me, are you?"

"We'd have to be betting for me to hustle you," Paul grinned. "Besides, you're three strokes up on me—with only one hole left. It's a bit late for me to start hustling."

"Oh, I know how it goes," Jenny taunted while they waited for a foursome to finish up on the loop-de-loop hole. "'Let's play a second nine, make it a full eighteen!' Then you lower the boom."

"Wish I had the energy for another nine," Paul yawned. "But I'm starting to flag. Probably should be heading home after this game."

Jenny made a face, pouting prettily. "It has been a full day," she agreed. They watched the quartet ahead of them until Jenny suddenly turned and blurted, "If you wanted, you could stay the night in my room. No commitment—I've got an extra bed." As soon as she got the offer out, she blushed.

Startled, Paul dropped his golf ball. It bounced around them merrily while he frantically struggled to catch it in mid-air.

She was looking at him expectantly, Paul discovered once his slapstick retrieval ended. What should he say? How should he say it? This was a major moment, and he didn't want to boggle it.

"Gee," he finally temporized. "You caught me off guard there."

"I didn't mean to make you uncomfortable. Am I going too fast?"

"No, no," Paul answered. "I'm just being hyper-cautious. I rushed into my first RADFAm relationship, and I don't want to mess this one up."

"I'm not Connie," Jenny grinned, "if that's what's worrying you."

"There's no way I'd confuse the two of you," Paul assured her. "But as much as I'd like to, I think I'd better go home. The dog—"

"Molly."

"I didn't make any arrangements for her."

"Why would you have thought to?"

This was not going well. Dropping both ball and club, ignoring their clatter, he grabbed Jenny's hands and looked her deeply in the eyes. "I want to spend the night with you," he said. "But I also want our first night together to be better than my wornout self could offer tonight."

She smiled and reluctantly agreed with him. "That's a commitment?"

"It sure is," Paul declared, leaning over to kiss her slowly and deliberately. It felt so wonderful he had a hard time backing off. "On second thought—" he said once they'd separated.

"Keep your first thought," Jenny decided. "I want us to be special, too." She squeezed both his hands, then reached up to plant a second kiss on his mouth. "That's to make sure you don't take too long, though."

"You two gonna play or can we play through?" a voice called from behind them.

"Go right ahead," Paul told the trio. "I think we're done for the night."

"Not quite, teacher." Jenny smiled provocatively, and she deposited her ball on the final tee. Shrugging apologetically to the waiting threesome, Paul retrieved his ball and club so they could finish their game.

EPISODE SIXTY

"WE ARE INCREDIBLY BLESSED** to be 'Living Fat' today!"

As Anne Reynard jubilantly opened her keynote speech, the room's idle banquet chatter ceased. She smiled once she had everyone's attention with this galvanizing declaration. Planted at a table close to the podium with the rest of the officers, Jenny approvingly noted how quickly the convention's speaker had taken charge of the room. This is the way TV lawyers were so often portrayed in court, she thought, though the reality was rarely quite this electrifying.

"And we have so much to be thankful for. Well, think about it," Anne continued. "When during the past forty years or so have there been so gosh-darn many positive, visible fat role models? With magazines like *Mode*, *BBW*, *Radiance* on the newsstands. Divine divas named Saffire, Carnie, Queen Latifah. Soap hawker Thea Vidal and soap vamp Patrika Darbo. British humor-wench Dawn French and lawyer-with-*The View* Star Jones." This last brought a round of enthusiastic glass tapping from Lissa on the other side of Jenny's table. "And let's not forget HGTV and the entire guest list of Carol Duvall and TIPical Mary Ellen!

"You cook-and-cookbook fans—c'mon, you know who you are, and why!" Unseen by anyone else at the table, Misty was pinching Joe on the knee, bringing out that small shy captivating smile of his. "Aren't you glad that chefs are shaped like food lovers again? So go ahead—savor Caprial's voluptuous wares. Succumb to those 'Two Fat Ladies' and their hefty hedonism. Just hold the Olestra, and deliver us from 'heaving.'

"And where, may you ask, are all our handsome Homeric hunks? —No, not Simpson!"

"Why not?" Ian, who had just joined the officers' table, called out. Off to the side Patsy shook her head in amusement and mock dismay.

"All right then, but better than Simpson! John Goodman. Dennis Franz. Pavarotti. Gerard Depardieu. A testosterone smorgasbord! All I can say is 'yum!'

As the appreciative laughter faded, Anne's face turned from sensual to serious. She'd definitely make a good trial lawyer, Jenny thought. She carried you along with every shift in mood.

"Finally, gratefully, bless our allies. 'Angels.' Brave people willing to weigh in on the side of body diversity. Influential people like David Kelley. Championing not one but three strapping *Practice* members, yet exercising the humanity to shun fat stereotyping and portray them as real people, pimples and all.

"Sadly, this last list remains short, even as the one before swells. But by confronting this culture's perversion of beauty and reality and worth, our allies help flesh out our American human landscape." With that she knocked on the podium, prompting Jenny to reflexively sit up straight, then chuckle at her involuntary reaction. "Hello? Remember the melting pot? A vibrant kaleidoscope of shades, shapes and sizes lying somewhere between Hollywood and Wall Street. It's the way fat-real-people look and act. How we work and sacrifice. How we love and laugh and LIVE!

"Tragically, corporal bigotry prevails, threatening to crush every fragile advance we've made. Magazine polls. Q-ratings. Public opinion. Media.

"That bloated, hydra-headed, self-aggrandizing industry continues to infect the world with its corpus tunnelvision. Beautiful, unspoiled children in such farflung Edens as Fiji are already casualties of the myth that only *Baywatch* babes and *Mademoiselle* models deserve love and attention. Before TV's wide introduction in 1995, their cultures idealized robust vitality, regarding noticeable weight loss as 'going thin,' an alarming sign of illness.

"But with the advent of such shows as *Melrose Place*, seventy-four percent of Fijian girls now believe they're 'too big or fat,' sixty-two percent have dieted in the past month, and disclosures of bulimia have exploded from three percent to fifteen percent.

"And the reason? A malignant multibillion-dollar media, pimped by profit-mongers like our 'dear' Jordan Lewis. Violating our humanity, raping our self-image, perpetuating the insidious message that fat people are damaged goods.

"But," she smiled, "if you're here within the sound of my voice, you are a survivor. And no longer—or at least less often—a victim.

"Wander back through your own ' tubby timeline.' I'll bet that you've had to work exponentially harder as your body broadened. Hustling for opportunities, for acceptance, for encouragement. Often settling for less instead of nothing at all. You've become a dancing rhino—strong and flexible, yet very thick-skinned."

A hearty chuckle erupted behind Paul. He turned around in his chair to see a smiling Dex, no doubt visualizing a cartoon rhinoceros in a black leather jacket. Seated to his left, young Rachel was doing her best to look as if she didn't know this embarrassing old man.

"Anybody old enough out there to remember that song lyric 'a rose in a fisted glove'? Well, no matter your years, I bet you recall every occasion when, out of the blue, the whims and words of relatives, friends and strangers viciously whipped from rose to fist. Admit it. 'You have such a pretty' still has the force to sting and stun.

"Now if you grew up in the '50s, '60s, '70s, '80s, you probably heard, 'Yew'd better larn to sew, child, cuz yo ain't NEVER gonna find nothin' to cover ya, 'ceptin' tents and granny gowns.'

"Until my senior year at the dear alma mater, slacks were strictly verboten. So unless you wanted to be a total geek, skirts meant hosiery. You remember those strangling 'one size fits all' pantyhose, pre-queensize, that even in its wildest dream simply WOULDN'T. And then the dreaded locker room showers, where those twin thigh welts prompted fresh humiliation by our exercise-Nazi.

"Gawd, how I loathed following my mom into our hometown's sole dress shop, only to find my size limited to maybe three polyester double-knit A-line princess-seamed straitjackets. In black, brown, or navy, ma'am, and if you were REALLY lucky, a tasty burgundy or flattering forest green for the holidays. So very stylish—for sofas!

"Have you ever dreamed of going back to those halcyon days? Why, for heaven's sake? Even in your younger form, did anything ever fit? Those crappy one-piece torture-rack desks? Gym suits? Band uniforms! Theater costumes! 'Oh, my dear, you simply can't be Lucy in *Charlie Brown*, because Lucy's not fat. Be a dead woman in *Our Town* instead. Nominate you for the Homecoming court? Cool joke, huh?!'

"In that graduating class of '63 I was one of the Few, the Proud, the Obese. And somehow we four 'survived'—the girl voted 'quietest' is now a nurse. The girl who'd 'put out' just to be noticed is a poverty-level housewife today. And the 'fat boy' I really wish I knew—he was a sweet boy.

"Yet we four weren't particularly close. Never shared common abuses, skirmishes, triumphs. I guess being teens was hard enough without comparing notes, but we were nonetheless inexorably linked by the isolation of prejudice and fear.

"As for yours truly, the impact of those decades of self-torture and loathing dragged me, frequently kicking and screaming, to the other side of life—*corpus acceptis*—as the outspoken herald you see here today. This to the eternal embarrassment of my poor mother, who's always suspected I was switched at birth. 'Oh, must you be so dyke-y?' To the confusion of friends when I correct their occasional sizeist slips. To that pinnacle those Uppity Blues Women call 'being in total control of herself.'"

Until now Anne had been standing behind the elegant resort podium, but after a quick sip of Evian she crossed to a flipchart whose top page showed the RADFAm logo and slogan, stylishly sketched and tinted to match a drape of floral silk garland. A neat design touch, Misty thought.

"Well, I can envision a new, wiser, wider world. And if our courage and vigilance never falter, this organization—OUR organization—can banish those desolate fat-child yesterdays forever and lead us forward into size-positive tomorrows."

Cheers, applause and 'amens' erupted from Lissa and others in the room.

"Yes, the wheel of public opinion continues its revolution, and it may not come full circle during our lives. But a harvest of recognition will flourish, from the seeds of compassion and understanding planted by you and other size acceptance groups, and by thoughtful, open-minded allies who advance the rights of every human of size.

"But to reap well we must tear out the weeds of big-otry which threaten to strangle us, and nurture our own fate. No longer begging the World to 'accept' us—" with this she turned to the chart and swept off the top sheet, revealing a modified logo, "—but demanding that it 'Measure Worth Beyond Girth!'

"Now by its very definition, each progressive organization on occasion endures the growing pains of 'progress,' and mission statements beg reassessment. In light of several recent RADFAm events, I believe we now stand at such a crossroad. Should we continue to beg for social equality? Stay silent, waiting passively for someone who isn't us to fight for us? Hell no!"

A tumult of affirmation engulfed the dais, as Anne's smile turned weary.

"But the path is arduous, pitted with potholes. Just tune in any talk show. Fat children still commit suicide to escape vicious torment. Fat students still battle to overcome academic stereotyping. Fat parents still lose fat kids to 'well-meaning' agencies for alleged abuse, or are simply denied the right to adopt abandoned youngsters in the first place. Fat employees are 'last hired, first fired,' and pay for the privilege with drastically whittled wages and soaring insurance co-pays.

"And don't even get me started on our medical 'community!'" As often happened whenever his chosen profession got brought up in gatherings like this, Dex's ears perked up. "This *1984* sort of metropolis where every effort is taken to distill our all-too-human condition to kilograms and BMIs. Distressingly, our medicos tend to gravitate to opposite ethical poles—those who see us as perambulating dollar signs, or those too lazy to promote our health. One declares 'You're too fat—let me fix you,' while the other demands 'Leave me alone—I can't be bothered,' without regard for the needs of our community.

"Well I have a message for anyone who uses shame to shove me back in their preconceived pigeonhole. I've grown, and now it won't fit me. And I am so very proud to be joined by a burgeoning alliance of dedicated visionaries, in all shades of size, who share a dream beyond body 'tolerance.'

"We seek reverence for the miraculous vessels which house our spirits. A celebration of our flesh, where we may Sing OUR Bodies Electric!"

As she stepped back to the podium the opening arpeggios from *Fame*'s finale thundered through the sound system. In answer the visceral release bursting from close to a hundred souls reached the lobby, where Val paused during her Jordan Lewis *adieu* to snort, "Fat fucking freaks!"

Back in the banquet hall, Misty was floundering in the psychic energies assailing her. The emotional backwash threatened to drown her, yet she embraced its passion. As the climactic chord reverberated, she basked in an afterglow as profound as with any orgasm.

"Well, that's pretty much it. But, as those twisted *Airplane* guys proved, it's best to wait for the end credits. So stay put! Yes, I've sat through enough of these motivational rants to know your butts are rebelling. But as your official ranter, I've got this contract to uphold so I can earn my carrot! Besides, as a fat lady I'm entitled, 'cause as you know, it ain't over 'til the fat lady sings!'

"So brava and bravo to you who hate to leave this avoirdupois oasis, who are still soaking up enough sweet vibes to make it to the next convention. And finally, selfishly, to those who are kind enough to stick around to listen to this shameless self-promoter, I offer two rewards.

"Good things come to those who wait. So, since there's scads of tickets left from the dance, we're gonna have one more raffle. But if you're not here, you can't win. And wait—there's more! If you can show your stub-end, it's bonus time! So start frisking yourselves, or your neighbors—quietly, please!—while I offer your first prize—a moral imperative.

"Every time a fat stereotype stands or an insinuation hovers or an insult shocks without re-education from you, another link in our chain of common oppression is forged.

"For years I've acted as a teacher for the diversity-challenged, and have yet to come away feeling shortchanged. I've reminded the memory-deprived of every fat person they've ever known or loved, then asked how they'd feel to witness such invective directed against them. I've questioned why they felt compelled to spew negative energy because of my body. And if they gave a valid reason, I've honestly taken it into consideration. Thus we are equally empowered to enlighten and learn.

"From birth to end the ultimate destination of our lifetime is our own best self. And it isn't about weighing less, or taking up fewer square centimeters of landscape. For all our sakes, our robust humanity needs to be involved, active, visible!

"As members of a broadening demographic, we must take advantage of every fat-positive effort, and strive to correct the converse. Earn accolades and accept them with grace. And be willing to create laurels that have not yet existed. Heck, it worked for Alfred Nobel!

"Stop being a cipher! Start by holding your head up. High! People who look like victims generally are. Get over those self-fulfilling fat prophecies that have doomed you since chub-hood. Use your natural charisma! Nurture your charms. It's a talent, and doesn't come naturally to us all. But try it, just one day, even an hour, for your own sake. Rinse and repeat.

"No one has the right to hobble you with faulty presumptions. Not even you. Stretch! That means you, honey! Now, stretch your reach! Up, through that Emme-pierced hole in the never-too-thin ceiling. Wander the in-roads blazed by esteemed guides of diverse, heroic proportions: Kathy Bates and Catherine the Great. Brian Dennehy. Howlin' Wolf. Chef Paul."

Once again, Misty stroked Joe's knee.

"But celebrity can be so tiring, as I know only too well. Besides, celebrities can only do so much. The structural integrity of size esteem needs architects and organizers, workers and craftsfolk. Never forget your talents are vital." She whirled to gesture at a back table. "And yours! And those of every last one of us! Because 'the whole is greater than the sum of its parts.' Yeah, hey, it's a cliché, but eminently apropos."

A loud chair scrape, and Paul turned to see a couple he didn't recognize none-too-subtly taking leave of the banquet room. Anne appeared unperturbed by this rudeness, however.

"Well," she continued, "the ol' clock on the wall tells me that this room's 'rump rage' has reached rampant. So let's get back to that other reward. Find your tickets? Misty, you still have the box? Hey, let's all give it up for the hostess-with-the-mostest, Mystique Shores! Take a bow for all your cohort, as well as this magical Misty-cal weekend."

Misty rose from the table, reaching down to grab a Baskin-Robbins tub festooned with goddesses, and walked to the podium. Anne flourished the lid and stirred the contents vigorously, eliciting broad laughter at Misty's jiggling response.

"Okay, is Ken Sobinski here? Ken?" (No reply from the room.) "Tanisha

Reed? Hmm. Musta had a long drive. I'm not offended, of course. All right, this one feels lucky. Rachel—what is that? Girl, work on that penmanship! You'll always be glad you did." Misty leaned over to peek and announced in unison. "Oh, it's Rachel Logan!"

Dex pummeled his stunned daughter proudly, gently urging her to get-up-and-go. Rachel, eyes shining, crossed the front of the dais to appreciative applause as Anne hugged the teen, then turned her to face the audience, laying a friendly fleshy arm across her shoulders. In that brief moment Dex felt his heart tug; they looked so much like mother and daughter.

"So here we are," Anne grinned conspiratorially, "just the two of us! Having a nice time, Rachel? Me, too. Now I'll bet you're just dying to learn what you won. Well, as you may have heard, I have this new book out. Yes? And my publisher shouldn't miss just one copy? And if it was autographed, you promise not to sell it on eBay?" Rachel shook her head vehemently. "Okay, then, okay. Oh, and did you save your stub? "

Rachel held up her cardboard tag, and Dex could not remember ever seeing her so triumphant. Grinning, Ann grabbed the sheet torn from the flip-chart and signed the page with a flourish.

"I'm no Rubens, but this may lend you inspiration. I'll sign your book a little later, so stick around. Okay, sweetness?" She shooed Rachel shakily back to her seat.

"Well, Mist, did I earn those big bucks? I miss anything?" Misty leaned forward to mutter a response. "Eh? Oh yes, there is one small additional announcement. As we all witnessed yesterday, a runway show is a stunning way to display fashion. Oh yes, kudos to our fashion mistress and her models!

"But true fashion sense requires all our senses, right? Therefore, for your shopaholic convenience, RADFAm has arranged late checkout today for our talented and loyal vendors, those gypsies who cart vast wardrobes of wearables to provide pizzazz for our gatherings. They're here today only 'til five! We're large—so *let's go charge!*"

EPISODE SIXTY-ONE

Cassie—
The convention's nearly over, and I'm totally bushed. Got lots to tell you about the dance and after—I was a brazen hussy with Paul (lotta good that did me!), but I don't feel guilty at all. Guess it's being around so many fat confident people—brings out the vamp in me!

Just got time for one last trip to the vendors—there's a dress that's

calling my name. Write atcha later.
Love—
Jenny

SOMEONE HAD DUMPED A TRASH BAG in a handicapped parking space. Dex hoped it wasn't one of the convention attendees, but he knew enough not to be surprised if it had been. Just because an event itself was affirming didn't mean that everybody was in sync with its intent. The dumpers had probably just slid it out the door of their minivan and thoughtlessly tooled away. Sighing, he detoured away from his vehicle and toward the offending debris, stooped to retrieve it and deposited the remains in a garbage can by the hotel entrance. He smiled apologetically at the doorman, who just shrugged.

Rachel and Neeko were waiting for him by the luggage carts. All around them fat men and women were in the noisy process of checking out. Women who'd been dressed to the nines the night before were now dressed down for the drives ahead. To Dex's '60s-survivor eyes, they looked even better in more casual garb. But he could understand the need to reclaim the glamour that had been denied them in the past.

"Ready?" he asked his wife and daughter once he got within earshot. Sitting on the edge of their cart, Rachel looked up from her copy of Anne Reynard's book.

"Sure you don't have any chapter business to do?" Neeko teased as she put an arm around his broad back.

"The officers have it all under control," he replied, bussing her playfully on the cheek. Her outfit was uncharacteristically wrinkled—understandable since she hadn't brought any luggage with her last night to the hotel.

She smiled and pinched his side. "I know. I just wanted to make sure you knew it."

They headed toward the exit, passing Eleanor and Lainie on their way to checkout. Neeko gave both women a small wave and a friendly smile, but Dex could feel her arm stiffen behind his back. He wished he knew why his wife was so irrational when it came to Eleanor.

They split up in the parking lot, Neeko to pick up Jackie from his friend's house, Dex to drive Rachel home.

"Know what I heard from Kelly?" Rachel asked Dex as he rolled their luggage cart past rows of cars and minivans. "There was a break-in at the Hospitality Suite last night."

"You're kidding." Interesting, he thought, that she'd held off telling him this until her stepmother was gone.

"Nope. Mr. Johnson closed the suite about two, and around three o'clock these guys got someone from the desk to open the room back up. I hear that they did major damage to the room."

Walk away from it, Dex told himself. *Misty and Ian can handle this.* "Hear anything else?" he still couldn't keep from asking.

Obviously disappointed that she hadn't, Rachel shook her head.

"You know I was in bed by then," she said with mock indignation. "I was the one pounding on your wall, trying to get my parents to quiet down!"

"Yeah, well, I hope we didn't ruin your beauty sleep," Dex joked.

"You probably should be more concerned about the emotional scars," Rachel bandied back. "I know what you two were up to, and believe me, part of my girlish innocence died last night."

"Such talk!" Dex exclaimed in amazement, unlocking the hatch of his four-wheel drive. "Sounds like something out of a bad paperback romance. What have you been reading, young lady?"

"It was Valerie?"

"Val and several other Jordanites," Ian explained. "One of them had gotten the idea that there were free eats in the room, so they decided to liberate 'em." He indicated three cardboard boxes behind the bar filled with empty soda cans and paper plates. "Unfortunately for them, there wasn't much left."

Misty shook her head in disgust. The room was a shambles, but nothing appeared to have been broken, at least. That was all the chapter needed, a group of gate-crashers making like Bluto Blutarsky. The phone behind the bar had been pulled into the center of the room, she saw. She dreaded the resultant long distance bill. "Good thing Patsy woke up," Misty thought. "I know I was dead to the world last night."

"Um, yeah," Ian agreed, and blushed becomingly. "She—uh—called my room, and the two of us phoned the desk clerk. We got to make like bouncers. Something really satisfying about having the moral right to kick Val out."

"I bet," Joe said, popping up from beneath the table with a trio of crushed cans. He stood and eyed the floor, seeking more errant trash, but it looked like he'd gotten it all.

"We've registered a complaint with the hotel," Misty said, "and they've assured us that any extra expenses will be billed to Jordan Lewis's organization. Hopefully, that's the last we'll hear of it."

"Hear of what?" Jenny interjected, coming into the room with a plastic bagged dress over her arm and Paul at her side. She looked around the room curiously. "Is this about last night's break-in?"

Misty, Ian and Joe looked toward her questioningly.

"The vendors are buzzing about it—rumors that someone invaded the

Hospitality Suite after it was closed. Some of the stories going around are pretty wild."

"If there was an Olympic competition for rumor-mongering, RADFAm could put together a gold medal team," Ian sighed. "Well, I was one of the Convention Police, and the worst thing that group did was eat their after-midnight snacks without napkins."

"No women flashing their nakedness?" Paul chimed in. "No group sex?"

"You're thinking of the pool party," Ian corrected.

"Must've missed that part," Joe laughed.

"Good thing," Misty declared, just as Patsy emerged from the bathroom with a bottle of 409 in hand.

"Bathroom's okay now," she told the rest, then noticed Jenny and Paul. "Someone wrote 'RADFat Eats It' in lipstick on the mirror," she explained, tossing a paper towel into the closest cardboard box.

"Mildly clever," Ian acknowledged. "Probably wasn't Val."

They stood and silently considered the once-festive room for a few seconds. Then Misty clapped her hands and turned to the door. "What are we hanging around here for?" she declared. "Time to go home!"

EPISODE SIXTY–TWO

"**H**ELLO? **D**ON'T WORRY, **J**OE, **I**'VE GOT IT! —-Hello?"

"Hey, Mist! So there you are. Should've guessed you're bi-residential these days. Just ignore the obscene message I left on your machine."

"Oh hi, Kirk. Okay, though I bet Schmendrick got a kick out of it. I must say it's awfully early on Saturday for you to be awake, let alone articulate, stud-boy."

"You've forgotten? Brian and I become parents today."

"Whoops, I did forget! When's the blessed event?"

"Bri flew into St. Louis last night and is driving both kitty-boys up this morning. We're gonna spend the next week together, bonding with the furry little heathens."

"Got names for 'em yet?"

"Jake and Elwood, of course. My idea."

"Of course."

"Hey, one simply can't be a red-blooded midwestern chubby chaser without a healthy appetite for all things Belushi. Don't tell anybody, but my favorite flick is *Continental Divide*."

"That's not even a musical."

"True. But seeing John with his shirt off—woof!"

"Better than fantasies of bees and samurais, I guess."

"Yup. And speaking of fantasies, inquiring minds want to know—what's Joe's Apartment really like?"

"Nothing like that disgusting cockroach movie, thank you very much. It's a tad too guy-like for my tastes, but not offensive. No RockShots calendars, at least. I'm thinking of buying him a Botero poster—the walls are so—naked."

"Think again, my dear! Too soon in the relationship. And where is our swarthy nourisher, anyway? I expected him to answer the phone."

"In the kitchen—"

"Of course!"

"—making breakfast, while yours truly lounges on the trundle bed, waiting to be served."

"Anything I say now would be misinterpreted, so I'll respectfully remain silent."

"So unlike you. But I do deserve a little pampering after the week I've had."

"Oh?"

"Every single day since the convention, Dillman has pestered me to split the profits. Only 'split' isn't quite the right word. Greg's trying to renege on his group's original financial commitment."

"From what you've told me, that's hardly surprising."

"No, it isn't. But it still ties my undies in a knot. Then I get a call in the middle of the week from Delia. Seems some of the vendors are still pissed about Connie Donovan's behavior at the fashion show and they're threatening to call National to complain."

"And?"

"And it's up to me to defend Connie when the Board calls. What a crock! When we chose her to host the fashion show, who could predict the conflict of interest that it might cause?"

"You're the fortuneteller."

"Ouch!"

"Anyway, you know what they say about hindsight."

"Yeah. It's great if you're into big butts. Plus we still haven't heard from the hotel about the Hospitality Suite fiasco. All I can say is they'd better not try to bill us for their security screwup."

"Oooh, our sibyl's stewing in righteous rampage. May I watch?"

"Trust me. It's not that impressive."

"As usual, you're selling yourself short."

"Maybe. But since Joe's just bringing in a most luscious looking breakfast tray, I've gotta tamp down my spleen so I can enjoy it. So when can we come by and coo over the new arrivals?"

"Two-ish should do it. We'll supply the Starbucks; you bring the petit-fours."

"Great! That'll give us plenty of time to nosh and nuzzle. Ta-ta, Papa."

DURING THE ENTIRE DRIVE BACK from the vet's Paul swung between worry and self-chastisement. Hip dysplasia! Why didn't he notice it sooner? One look at the X-ray and he instantly felt like the world's most irresponsible pet owner. Molly's right hip bone wasn't even in its socket. She'd obviously been walking around for months in constant pain.

Dr. Towne had tried to ease Paul's guilt. "These things come up gradually, so you don't notice them," he explained in the same low-key tone that Paul himself often used during parent-teacher conferences. "Molly's thick coat helped mask her problem. It wasn't until she began to show obvious discomfort that we recognized there was something really wrong."

"I guess," Paul had acknowledged, though even now his guilt-meter was running at full power. He glanced at Molly in the rearview mirror. Though he knew she couldn't see his reflection, her big brown eyes seemed to return his gaze imploringly.

"When does she go in for surgery?" Jenny asked after he gave her the news at Kuppa Joe'a's.

"Monday morning," Paul replied. "It's a fairly new procedure called femoral head re-sectioning. Instead of replacing the hip they cut the ball of the joint down so it fits in the socket."

"Poor baby. Sounds gruesome."

"Well, at least this explains her recent snappiness," Paul said, and he could see Jenny wrestle with her relief at this revelation as the waitress arrived with their mocha cappuccinos. "This morning when I got her leash she was really touchy—so rather than taking her to the park we visited the animal hospital instead."

"Molly's at home now?"

"Uh-huh. Doc prescribed some Rimadyl—he said that would help ease her pain through the weekend."

"Are you sure you want to go out this afternoon? We could reschedule if you'd rather spend the day with Molly."

"She crawled in her crate as soon as we got back to the apartment," Paul said. "That's a sure sign she's not feeling good. I think it's best to let her rest quietly." He took a sip and then smiled. "You need to meet her when she's up and healthy. She really is a great dog. You two just met under the wrong circumstances."

Jenny smiled at his reassurance and stirred a little extra cream into her cappuccino. "It was a crazy weekend, but I sure enjoyed Saturday night."

"Me, too. But I think I liked our time behind the check-in counter just as much." He grinned back at Jenny. Just being with her had helped his earlier guilt dissipate. Her eyes looked particularly soft in the late morning light.

"Paul," she suddenly asked, "am I too small for you?"

The question was so unexpected, he nearly spilled his coffee. "Why do you ask that?" he finally fumbled.

"Seeing all those stunning supersized women at the convention. And Connie—she's so much bigger than me."

"Larger than life, you mean."

"Yeah," she smiled shyly. "Plus you went to that feeder workshop."

"Feeder worksho—oh, you mean Lewis Baird's FA Fantasy thing! Look, I've read a few of his stories in *Dimensions,* but I'm not really a fan. I find most of that stuff pretty silly, in fact. I just wanted to see what the guy was like."

"And?"

"Kinda nerdy—like lotsa writers. Into fantasy—like lotsa fat admirers. But he didn't strike me as the sort of guy who'd take it all too seriously."

"And what about you?"

"Well, fantasy's fun. But it pales in comparison with the reality of a beautiful woman like you." Paul grabbed her hands across the table and squeezed them lightly. "I wish I could erase your every doubt, but I guess that'll take some more time. So, to answer your original question: No, I think you're perfect, just as you are."

He watched the emotions play across her expressive face. She finally nodded, returned his hand squeeze, then sat back to finish off her drink. "So what do we want to do this afternoon?" she asked, smiling.

EPISODE SIXTY-THREE

Dear Rachel—
   What a pleasure it was to receive your thank you letter. And, of course I remember you! While misspent years may blur my memory, how could I forget your charming self in a mere six weeks?

   I am most flattered, but also even a bit embarrassed by your kind words. It's so sweet of you to credit me for your upbeat outlook. But please don't paint me in mythic proportions—don't forget even rabble-rousers are human.

But I'm most excited to read the affirmations you've written. It's a wonderful list to live by. Each and every day, emBody your uniqueness, direct the strength of health in Self, and strike a crippling blow at the mentality of Negative People.

Have you chatted with your folks yet about the candy incident? I believe your non-involvement, but the longer you don't assert it, the longer the real tamperer goes unidentified. Those candies were a call for help from someone, and you know the pain of no one caring to listen.

I'd love to come and speak to your school some time. I thank you for even thinking to ask. But the rest of this year is pretty well booked. Maybe next year?

Keep me posted! Here, thinking Positives about you,

Anne Reynard

"So does the Beast finally have the satellite dish off?"

"The beast's name is Molly, Lis," Jenny chided, "it's an Elizabethan collar, and she's been a whole lot less beastly since the surgery."

"Too doped up on painkillers, I bet. Wait 'til she gets back full use of her legs—and jaws!"

"Ha. Ha."

Lissa pulled a pesto bagel from the kitchenette toaster oven, juggling the halves between immaculately manicured fingers, and dumped them on a paper towel. Jenny slid a container of goat cheese across the table, along with a plastic picnic knife, then took a sip of decaf.

"Well, you're the one who internalized the poor dog's crabbiness," Lissa elaborated. "And I think maybe you owe the bitch an apology." Sliding out a wooden chair, she sat across the table and stabbed a slather of cheese from its tub.

"Paul's atoning enough for the two of us," Jenny grinned. "He's still feeling guilty about not catching Molly's dysplasia sooner. It's pretty endearing, really."

"Sensitive new age guy, eh?"

"SNAG? *Mais oui!*" Jenny shot back. "And I'll thank you to keep your cynical lawyerly thoughts to yourself."

"Nothing cynical here," Lissa protested, putting up both hands. "I just recall a stunning young lady the night of her first RADFAm dance. And a poor schlump with the bad luck to make first Connie-tact there."

"Hey, ma, all that's ancient history." Jenny rose to refill their cafés. "And I haven't told you the latest. Paul's invited me out for a weekend."

"A weekend. That—that man!"

"And a lonnnng weekend," Jenny giggled. "It's all perfectly gentlemanly.

He's reserved two rooms in Starved Rock Lodge for sometime after school lets out. I haven't been out there since high school, and I must have mentioned it in passing."

"All of this is, of course, contingent on whether your harridan boss gives you a lonnnng weekend. Now, you do intend to remember protection," Lissa lectured.

"Jeez, you're worse than my mother," Jenny groaned, retrieving a carton of French Vanilla Coffee-mate from the office fridge. "Let's switch the spotlight off me for a while. Delia still getting calls from ticked-off vendors?"

"Thankfully that seems to have settled down," Lissa answered. "D's phone calls have been much more interesting. A couple of the clothing manufacturers have even approached her about being a local distributor."

"Ooh, that sounds exciting. What does Delia think?"

"She's mulling right now. But think what a great opportunity. Right now InFatuation is the only upstate store to carry even a halfway decent supersized selection. Anything that gets D out of chain store hell would be a plus. And with her talent and experience, I could honestly see Delia running her own boutique."

"Darn right," Jenny agreed. "But in competition with Connie? May God have mercy on her soul."

"SANDRA, EH?" Dex snorted. "Flashback! Visions of Gidget!"

"You're showing your age again, dear." Neeko patted his soapy wrist. "I hope you won't be making that comment around Jackie."

"Why not?" Dex protested from his kitchen stool at the sink. He held a plate under the tap, rinsing off bechamel sauce, then handed it to Neeko. "*Grease* has made a comeback, you know. 'Look At Me, I'm Sandra Dee!'"

His petite wife giggled. "Sorry, you don't look a thing like her. I'm sure that reference will only tend to confuse him. Do you have any idea what our son listens to these days? I can assure you it's not vintage Broadway musicals or your moldy oldies."

"I don't expect him to listen to the music," Dex muttered. "Just to recognize it. It's part of his culture."

"Let us debate the value of cultural literacy another time," Neeko countered. She placed the last plate in the dishwasher rack and slid it in. "We were talking about Jackie's cheerleader girlfriend."

"Are we sure he's really old enough for this dating business? What's she like?"

"Tiny," Neeko told him, ignoring the first question. "And very polite. And no, she's not Japanese."

"I didn't wonder," Dex responded.

"No, but I did," Neeko admitted. Turning on the dishwasher, she nodded toward the kitchen exit. Dex rose, groaning, to follow her from the room. "You know Jackie's been questioning. Teenaging. Manhooding. Finding balance as an American non-WASP." Dex's heart tightened for his transplanted bride. "One can only guess where his journey will take him. For a while, he ardently fought everything he thought you stood for."

"That's one attitude I don't miss, thank God."

"So he's proven he's not his father; now's the time to find out who he actually is."

"You're much too wise for me." Dex enveloped his wife in a bear hug, pulling her against his expansive forefront and kissing her shiny black eyes. She smiled and returned the kiss on his lips.

"Wise on some things maybe, but I've got my blind spots too," Neeko sighed before starting a second smooch. "Your friend Eleanor, for instance."

Dex arched his eyebrows but diplomatically held his peace, choosing instead to savor this loving detente. Up the stairway hall they could hear the tones of something mopey and alternative from Rachel's CD player.

"Romantic music, eh?" Dex teased between snatched kisses.

"It's supposed to sound irksome," Neeko reminded him, "otherwise it can't be any good."

"You're right," Dex sighed, letting his wife go. He looked out the living room bay window, imagining his son with some suburban Heather. "I wonder what sort of music Sandra likes?"

EPISODE SIXTY–FOUR

(E xcerpt—The Winnie Harper Show, *May 14, 1998 telecast—* "*My Boyfriend Says I'm Still Not Fat Enough!"*)

WINNIE: We're back, and we've been talking with diet expert Jordan Lewis about the so-called feeder phenomenon. Jordan, you say you've worked with women whose boyfriends—or husbands—have *actually* tried to pressure them to gain weight. What brings these women to you?

JORDAN: How could they *not* come, Winnie? They've finally realized how sick their situation is. That they'll never be fat enough for their boyfriends. That they've abandoned their own physical autonomy to the demands of another.

WINNIE: Don't all women do that, though, to one degree or another? I know *I've* been in a lifelong battle to keep my weight *down*. And I never feel like I'm thin enough. Isn't this feeder thing just the flip-size—I mean, flip-*side?*

JORDAN: Big difference, Winnie. Dieting to lose weight is a healthy act. Eating to gain weight is an aberrant act, and it's no basis for a healthy relationship.

WINNIE: Well, *any* relationship that's based solely on appearance needs a little work in my book.

(Audience applauds.)

JORDAN: Appearance isn't the issue. *Physical* and *spiritual* health is.

(Louder applause.)

WINNIE: Our next guest is a self-described survivor of a feeder/feedee relationship. Her most recent long-term liaison was with a man she says "force-fed" her into obesity, and she's on the show to describe just how destructive this relationship could be. Let's welcome Valerie to the show.

VALERIE: Thank you, Winnie.

WINNIE: According to Jordan Lewis, you've just left a psychologically abusive relationship. What was it like?

VALERIE: It was—you should excuse the expression—no picnic.

(Audience laughs.)

VALERIE: I was with my boyfriend Ian for over two years. We temporarily split for a while, but at the time I wasn't strong enough to leave him for good.

WINNIE: Yet here you are today.

VALERIE: I just got so tired of the whole routine, Winnie. Ian was always pushing food on me. It was the only thing he'd talk about: "What do you want for breakfast? What do you want for dinner? What do you want me to pick up at the grocery?" It got depressing.

WINNIE: Was he always like this?

VALERIE: Not at first. When we started going out, the whole tone of our relationship was different. "I love you for yourself," not "Change your whole life around for me!" He claimed to be a fat admirer, but turned out to be something worse.

WINNIE: We've got some before and after photos here for the audience. Could you walk us through them?

VALERIE: Certainly. This is me and Ian at the start of our relationship. At the time I was what you'd call a midsized woman. This is me two years later.

(Audience gasps.)

VALERIE: As you can see, I'm far from midsized. This last one shows me six months after I joined Jordan Lewis's program.

(Audience applauds.)

Winnie: You've lost a *ton* of weight! Oh, I'm sorry—I probably shouldn't have put it that way!

Valerie: I'm not offended, Winnie. The fact is, I feel free of an enormous burden.

JORDAN: Yeah, her weight and Ian, too!

(Audience laughs.)

WINNIE: We've had shows in the past with men who purported to be—um—FAs, but this feeder thing is something different, isn't it?

VALERIE: I'd say so. True fat admirers don't go pressuring you to *gain* weight! Ian claimed to be into size acceptance. But he wasn't really because he couldn't accept me for *my* size!

JORDAN: You see a lot of that among so-called "fat acceptance" advocates: "Stay fat and unhealthy/get fatter and even unhealthier!" This is not acceptance; it's active promotion of a sinful lifestyle! Why in this very city there's a so-called size acceptance group, and my sources tell me that its *president* is currently involved in a feedee relationship with a local chef! What kind of message is that woman communicating to the world at large?

WINNIE: It does seem to be a bit contrary to the group's message. We attempted to get Valerie's boyfriend to come on the show, incidentally, but he declined to appear.

JORDAN: I'm not surprised.

WINNIE: But not all men attracted to big beautiful women are like Ian. Our next guest, Greg Dillman, is a long-standing F.A. and the promoter of a local size positive *social* group, Full-Figured Friends. The group holds bi-monthly get-togethers where—and I read from its press release here—"The Large-ly Lovely come to dance and commingle with their Admirers." Welcome to the show, Greg.

GREG: A pleasure to be here, Winnie.

WINNIE: You've been putting on dances for BBWs and their admirers for some time now. Have you come across any men that *you* would label feeders?

GREG: Well, Winnie. I'd be lying if I said that every man who came to one of our dances did so wholly out of altruistic motives. No matter what size you are, you need to be cautious on the dating scene these days. There are a lot of predators out there.

WINNIE: I hear that. But what about these so-called feeders? Are they for real?

GREG: None of the FAs who I call friend fit that description. Yet I've got to admit I've heard horror stories from some of the women who come to my dances.

WINNIE: But from your experience, the majority of men who show up to your events are there to *dance?*

GREG: Exactly. They come to have a good time on the dance floor with tantalizing ladies. That's the simple purpose behind Full-Figured Friends.

WINNIE: Sounds positive to me.

JORDAN: It may sound harmless, but within the soil of "size acceptance" lay the seeds of feederism.

GREG: That's just *(word edited out).*

WINNIE: Mr. Dillman, please, this is daytime television.

GREG: I'm sorry, Winnie, but I get passionate in my love for big beautiful women. And I know that most fat admirers are like me in that we'd never willingly do harm to the gals we love.

VALERIE: That may be, but how do we women know for sure? My Ian seemed to be sincere. He's even been an officer in the same size acceptance group Jordan mentioned earlier. But his idea of a perfect relationship was pretty sick.

WINNIE: How much weight did you gain when you were with Ian, Valerie?

VALERIE: More than a hundred pounds. It got to the point where I had difficulty even getting out of bed!

WINNIE: And he wasn't bothered by this?

VALERIE: Heck, no! If anything, he seemed to be *aroused* by it!

(*Audience murmurs.*)

WINNIE: Turned on by your increasing helplessness.

VALERIE: Exactly!

WINNIE: I must say I have a hard time understanding this. In a moment, we'll be hearing from a psychologist and specialist in eating disorders who'll hopefully shed some light on this disturbing story. But, first, we need to take a short break…

EPISODE SIXTY–FIVE

"So, WHATCHA THINK? This place does have distinct possibilities, right?"

At Delia's enthusiastic entreaty Lissa swiveled to survey the room. "Possibilities" was not the word that instantly sprang to mind, but then she wasn't looking at the place through her lover's eyes. Lissa saw an empty, dark, and criminally dusty storefront; Delia envisioned its "possibilities."

"Imagine rows of dress racks along here," Delia instructed, directing Lissa's sight past Claudette, the too-trim Realtor who'd been guiding them through the world of failed business spaces and newly minted mini-malls. "Registers over here," gesturing, "merchandising displays around all the walls. Lingerie here, clearance there—"

"Clearance? You haven't even opened yet and already you're offering clearance items?" Lissa squinted toward the indicated spot—all she could see was a floor desperately in need of re-tiling. But Delia radiated such hopeful confidence; if only there were a way to market that.

"You know," Delia considered, "if we can do this, it'll be for the long haul. The nearest real plus-size boutique is Connie's, and that's way downtown. We work this right, we'd have a lock on the burbs."

"Granted," Lissa acknowledged, "or at least your local supersized Tae Kwon Do students." She nodded toward the right wall, indicating the business beyond, where occasional shouts and whoops could be heard from an afternoon session.

"Music will mask a lot of that," Delia reassured her, then paced across the room with fleshy arms outstretched, as if already savoring the textures of myriad fashion fabrics just within reach of her fingertips. "I think this is the place," Delia finally decided.

From the doorway, Claudette nodded. "You've made a wise choice," the Realtor agreed. "The entire shopping center has great traffic, plenty of parking, and all the other businesses seem to be doing well."

"So why'd this one go under?" Lissa asked dryly.

Claudette looked uncomfortable for a moment. But Lissa had gotten her through two difficult divorces, and the woman wasn't going to cover anything up. She shrugged and led them to the door. "Domestic dispute," she explained. "Neither side wanted to take responsibility for the shop. You know how that goes."

"Unfortunately, I do," Lissa sighed.

SINCE IT WAS THE FIRST OF THE MONTH, Ian knew exactly where to find Patsy. Every month she did data entry in the billing department at a local telecable affiliate, so he parked himself outside the employee entrance at workday's end and waited in the car for her to come out. She was one of the first to leave. Smartly dressed in a linen jumpsuit, she was chatting animatedly to one of her fellow temps. The bright June sun gave her happy round face a healthy, attractive glow that fled as if behind a cloud when she recognized his car.

Patsy murmured a few words to her companion, then moved alongside Ian's Buick. He reached forward to shut off the radio and nervously smiled up at her.

"I haven't been able to reach you," he opened, "so I thought I'd come by and see if you needed a ride home."

"Cindy's been driving me to and from work," Patsy told him, indicating the waiting co-worker.

"I think we need to talk," Ian said. "I've tried to get you on the phone, but your machine doesn't seem to be working."

"Uh, yeah. It's been a busy week."

"Look, Patsy. I don't know if you've heard about that talk show or not, but I've got to tell you, it's all bullshit. You know what Valerie's like—you can't believe a thing that comes out of her mouth! I don't know why she's accusing me of being a feeder, but there's really nothing farther from the truth."

A distressed look washed across Patsy's face. She quickly glanced back toward her friend, then resignedly turned to Ian. After several deep sighs, she spoke. "I don't know what to believe," she admitted. "I know from experience that I'm not the best judge of men. So while most of me wants to trust you, I'm not sure I can trust myself."

"What can I do?" Ian moaned. "It's only my word against hers."

"I just need time to sort my thoughts out," Patsy replied. "I promise I'll call you once I've thought it through." She smiled wanly, then reached through the window to squeeze his shoulder. "I promise." She turned and headed back toward her friend's idling car.

Ian watched with helpless despair as they drove away.

WHEN KIRK PHONED HER AT WORK asking if she was free for lunch, Misty knew something must be wrong. Kirk knew her routine as well as she did. Since she ran the Isle of View Emporium alone, she typically brown-bagged it on weekdays (though with Joe packing them, the quality of her lunches had definitely soared).

So figuring it must be important, she'd agreed to the lunch date, then spent the rest of her morning obsessing. With Kirk in drama-queen mode she could easily indulge in any number of worst-case scenarios.

"Subway okay?" he asked, breezing through the door fifteen minutes early. "I'm on the clock."

"And Subway is the easiest place you can go to get something vegetarian," Misty surmised. Ever since Brian's last visit, Kirk had become loudly (and occasionally annoyingly) vegetarian.

"You're good, shweetheart," Kirk admitted. "C'mon, my treat."

"Oh, goody. Would you buy me a pack of Sun Chips, too?"

"Only if you hurry. Chop chop!"

"Kirk, dearest," Misty admonished, pulling her ring of keys from the register and grabbing the "Out to Nosh" sign. "This bod was not made for hurrying."

They jounced in Kirk's van to the sandwich shop, which fortunately was not yet teeming with hungry patrons. Misty eyed the paltry fiberglass booths, and Kirk caught her hesitation.

"They've got benches in back," he reassured her. "We could dine al fresco." Misty nodded, so they got in line. "I hear the chapter got some dubious publicity on Winnie Harper's scandalfest recently," Kirk began. "Any major repercussions?"

"Ian's pretty upset," Misty said. "When I talked to him yesterday he was gonna call Lissa to see if there's anything he can do legally. But since the show didn't mention his last name, I doubt he has any grounds. The only people who'd know what Lewis or Val were talking about are folks in the size acceptance community. And they'll all recognize it as the bogus ploy it was."

"There's always some dildo who's ready to imagine the worst, though," Kirk countered. He smiled coyly at the bearded young man behind the counter, then placed his order: a twelve-inch roast beef on white bread.

"Not very vegan," Misty observed.

"Don't tell Brian," Kirk pleaded, pointing out the veggie toppers for his sandwich.

"I won't if you'll tell me why we're here," Misty promised.

"What? I can't take my favorite landlady out for a nice meal?"

"Not without piquing her ever-ready suspicions," Misty replied. She also smiled at the counter boy and made her choice. They silently watched as he built her meatball sandwich, then made their way outside.

"Okay," Kirk began as he handed Misty her sub, chips and a Whipper Snapple. "Here's the scoop. Seems our man Brian—he of the cane and lumberjack chassis—has a wee allergy to cat. Young Elwood's been making life at the Seattle homestead sinusly miserable, so we're considering relocating him back to the Midwest—thus reuniting the blues brotherhood."

"And you want your landlady's permission."

"*Mais oui.* I wouldn't dream of violating our lease." He took a generous bite from his sandwich, then made an appreciative moan. "You know, it's been so long since I've indulged my inner carnivore that even this fake beef tastes heavenly."

"What lease?" Misty wondered. "When did I make you sign a lease?"

"I was speaking metaphorically," Kirk muttered around his mouthful. He stopped to swallow, then continued. "So is it okay?"

"I'm alright with it, if Howland is."

"Are you kidding?" Kirk chortled. "Ever since Jake's come into the house Howlie's been acting like they're buds from the same litter. You should see 'em curled up together. It's beyond cute."

"But does this mean that our Brian won't be visiting anymore?" Misty asked, popping open her bag of chips and offering it to Kirk.

"Not in the least. I'm already buying up stock in Benadryl." Kirk grinned wickedly. "And how are things with Chef Joe?"

"Still wonderful. He's about to be promoted at the restaurant, incidentally."

"What's the next level up from sous chef?" Kirk wondered. "Meat man?"

"Hell if I know," Misty admitted. "It's more money, but it's also more responsibility."

"I.e., less time off," Kirk caught. He took another large bite of his sandwich. "At least that means he'll be able to buy more furniture for the apartment."

"And maybe something for the walls," Misty added, pulling her six-inch sub from its plastic wrapper. "You know, I'm still amazed that our relationship is going strong. I keep expecting to wake up in a hospital bed to find that this entire year has been some extended coma dream."

"Eat your sandwich, Dorothy," Kirk advised her, smiling. "And remember, girl—sometimes, the dreams that you dare to dream really do come true."

EPISODE SIXTY–SIX

DEAR RADFAm NATIONAL—

In light of recent negative publicity on *The Winnie Harper Show*, I feel it is my duty to alert you to another possible problem. Recently our local chapter presented a regional weekend celebration and included—as a part of its activities—a so-called Feeder Workshop by the notorious feeder writer Lewis Baird. I'm sure you're aware of his writing—it's filled with all manner of weight-gain imagery and stereotypes that do little to advance the cause of size acceptance. The man may have an audience among some misguided FAs, but I believe that his work is something that RADFAm should not be endorsing, even on a local level.

It comes as no surprise that this chapter would schedule such a questionable activity. Its president, Misty Shores, is currently "involved" with a chef who has been quite open about his feeder proclivities. Even before he hooked up with Ms. Shores, word has it that he made feeder overtures to other unattached women.

I strongly support size acceptance, so you can understand why I must express my dismay at these inappropriate goings-on. The Baird workshop is only the tip of the iceberg when it comes to misjudgments being made by the present chapter officers.

To most outsiders, size acceptance is questionable at best. We can ill afford this type of public behavior. Perhaps it's time the national office took steps to head off future PR problems caused by such blatant misguidance.

Sincerely,

A Concerned RADFAmite

IT FIGURED THAT ONCE SHE MADE THE DECISION to go with Paul to Starved Rock Lodge, something else would come up. Not surprisingly, that something turned out to be family.

Jenny was teasing Clouseau with a cuttlebone, trying to get him to speak (over the last few weeks he had been growing increasingly recalcitrant, as if in jealous-pet competition with Molly) when the phone rang. Turning down the volume on her Sheryl Crow tape, she cocked an ear toward the answering machine, then dashed to grab the phone when she recognized her sister's voice. "Jenny, are you home?"

"Cassie, I'm in!" she quickly interjected—every time she called, Cassandra started out apologizing for taking up tape space. "I'm just screening calls. It's probably not Emily Post-able, but I haven't had to deal with telemarketers in years."

"Oh, I could never do that," Cass confided. "Real callers might be too intimidated to leave a message. I know I am."

That could explain a lot of the hangups Jenny had been receiving lately.

"I'm just a bad person, I guess," Jenny joked. "They beat all that empathy out of you in paralegal training." She settled into her rocking chair. As soon as she did, Clouseau began squawking from his cage. "So how you doing, Sis?"

"Great," Cass replied. "Finally got my vacation time worked out. I'll be able to come up to see you starting—" And of course she mentioned the same days that Paul was reserving their rooms.

Okay, she'd planned for Cass to come up for a visit, but Jenny had never considered the possibility that her trip would overlap Paul's. She fumbled through the rest of her conversation with Cass making no mention of the conflict, but vowing as she hung up to call her sister back later on the weekend. Then Jenny began pacing the apartment, putting action to her agitation. Sensing her mood, Clouseau started to shriek louder.

"Stifle!" Jenny yelled back, and amazingly the cockatiel obeyed.

She flopped back into the chair, rocking distractedly and staring at nothing until the tape ran out. Then she dialed Paul's home phone. He answered on the first ring.

"My sister was just talking about folks like you," she told the schoolteacher, "picking up your phones without hesitation. I bet you get a lot of calls from siding companies."

"And it's always a such delight to hear from 'em," Paul said. "But I had a feeling this was you. Had the same feeling twenty minutes ago, but I was wrong that time. Did you know I could save up to fifty per cent on all my long distance calls?"

"I'm very happy for you," Jenny replied. Clearly Paul was feeling ebullient, and she hoped she wasn't about to ruin it.

"I called the lodge," Paul informed her, "and was able to get two adjoining rooms on the first try. They'd just had a cancellation, which was a stroke of luck since every other weekend this summer was booked."

"Umm, could one of those have two beds?" Jenny murmured, then recapped her phone call with Cassie. On the other end of the line she sensed Paul mulling over this change of plans.

"The more the merrier," he finally answered with a wry chuckle. "That is, as long as we can have some alone time, okay?"

She didn't know whether to be pleased or disappointed by his reaction. "You're one in a million," Jenny finally decided. From the other room Clouseau squawked in agreement.

IT WAS A SIGN OF BEING BACK in Dad's good graces that Jackie was once more allowed unmonitored monitor time. Occasionally one of his parents would discreetly come by and take a quick peek, but since he was staying away from the adult sites (at least at home), it wasn't really a hassle. With his classes and exercises, he didn't have the time to screw around at the keyboard that much, anyway.

Still, with Sandra sending him emails almost daily, it was his duty to check the computer out at least once a night. Even if he didn't send a response, she'd be sure to ask him about it next day in school. Girls, he was learning, expected some form of followup when they wrote to you.

He was looking over her most recent message—an attachment jpg of the slender teenaged girl sitting at her monitor, Barbie-loaded shelf towering overhead, a bottle of Sobe power drink by her keyboard—when his dad came into the room. Dex cleared his throat in advance warning, giving Jackie time to safely minimize Sandra's picture, then came up behind him.

"Think you could pull up a site for me?" Dex asked.

"I live to serve," Jackie chirped, maximizing his web browser. "Where do you want to go today?"

"Ian tells me that folks are spouting off on some of the size acceptance web boards, so I thought maybe you could take me to some of the sites."

"Haven't been on any of 'em for months," Jackie replied. "So I may be out of date. But I think I saved a couple good sites." He aimed his cursor for bookmarks and double-clicked on a file entitled "ZAFTingather." On the monitor, the home ("Celebrate Your Size!") page appeared. Jackie clicked the icon marked "web board."

"You ever done one of these before, Dad?"

Dex shook his head.

"Well," Jackie began, grateful for the opportunity to be teacher rather than pupil. "Let me tutoriate, then.

"Look at this," he said as he scrolled down to a lengthy thread that proclaimed, "Feeders Bite." They read the opening volley, a heavily capitalized rant that neither mentioned Winnie Harper nor RADFAm (indeed, it was difficult to tell what exactly prompted the writer's screed), then followed along the thread. Three postings in they found the first reference to Valerie's accusations, written by someone calling him/herself "marzbarz."

"I can only hope," marz concluded, "that this Ian person gets a taste of his own sick medicine. FAs like him ruin it for the rest of us."

"I was afraid of this," Dex stated after reading several further castigations of the nefarious feeder who'd just been outed on syndicated television. "Ian must be going postal over this. And I wouldn't blame him."

Jackie said nothing. If you asked him, that Ian had always seemed kind of weird anyway. Back when he was hitting the fat girl newsgroups he'd read more than one story about seemingly innocent fat admirers with their own secret motives. More than likely Dad was simply being naïve because he thought he actually knew what the guy was about.

"This marzbarz sure writes a lot," he saw, following the thread to a veiled reference to the chapter and its "pagan president."

His father sighed loudly and shook his head in disgust. "Enough of this," he finally said. "I'll letcha get back to your girlfriend now."

Jackie knew he was expected to dutifully moan and roll his eyes. "Dad, you make it sound so dorky."

"Part of my job. I'd be kicked of the patriarchy if I didn't make you kids squirm every now and then."

Jackie smiled in appreciation and brought up Sandra's picture as means of showing he had nothing to hide.

"A pretty girl," Dex noted as her picture once more filled the screen. He smiled behind his beard and winked, then left Jackie to his computer.

As his father trudged down the hall, Jackie had a sudden realization—Dex was no novice when it came to web surfing. He was perfectly capable of finding the ZAFTingather website by himself. That he'd asked Jackie to do it instead felt kinda nice.

Weird.

EPISODE SIXTY–SEVEN

"**W**ELL, I'VE GOTTA ADMIT THAT Joan Cusack's subplot was unexpected."

Paul held open the door to Kuppa Joe'a's for the rest of the foursome. Jenny, Misty and Joe accepted his gallantry, then headed for one of the more private tables. The coffeeshop wasn't crowded—Sunday afternoon wasn't peak—but they had enough time for a post-matinee snack before Joe headed off to work. With his recent promotion he was finding it harder to get weekends off. The price of success, Misty sighed.

"I think Joe would've identified with Matt Dillon's character," she said. "'Eat something—you look like a swizzle stick!' Just the type of thing he'd want to say." *Except,* an annoyed part of her couldn't help noting, *he wouldn't be saying it with movie quippiness.*

"Seating was more comfortable than I expected," Jenny noted.

"You're right, there. It was actually size friendly," Misty agreed, settling onto a sturdy wooden chair. "I appreciated that I could raise the armrests to accommodate my substantial sit-upon. I'd sure love to rent the place out for a chapter movie party, though it's too bad they only have adjustable seating in the back row."

"What would we show?" Jenny pondered, grabbing a chair on the other side of the table. "The 'Divine' John Waters?"

"Mmm, that might be a bit too—ahem—outré for some of our members," Misty decided. "Maybe *Sugarbaby?* Or *Baghdad Café?*" Paul and Joe had already headed to the counter to place their orders, so she quickly changed the topic. "Mind if we do some quick chapter business while the boys are away?"

"Not at all. What's up?"

"I received a phone call Friday at the shop," Misty explained. "From National. Somebody's been flooding them with complaints."

"Phone calls? Letters?"

"Yep. Plus faxes and emails. I was half expecting 'em to be about Connie's behavior at the fashion show, but apparently the Winnie Harper fiasco has far overshadowed that."

"Does this happen often?" Jenny wondered. "I mean, National calling the chapter officers?"

"I've been a RADFAmite for eight years," Misty told her. "This is the first time I've talked to anybody from National." She pulled a light brown napkin from its holder and ran her fingers over the fold. "I called Dex last night to ask if he'd had any contact when he was president, and he said no."

"So what's the gist?"

"Oh, they were pleasant enough. The whole point of the call was 'We thought you might want to hear this'—not the least accusatory. Still, I know the National office expects us to make some sort of response to the accusations stirred up by that talk show. Something to soothe the membership."

"Soothe the membership," Jenny snorted. "A few anonymous busybodies gripe and we're supposed to do what? Kick Ian out of the chapter?"

"Not while I'm in office," Misty vowed. "But we can't ignore this and hope it goes away."

"I suppose it merits some sort of action. But what, and how do we approach Ian about it?" Jenny asked. "I mean, this is chapter business, and he's an officer. We've got to bring it up at the next officers' meeting. But how do we do it without hurting his feelings?"

"I honestly don't know," Misty moaned. "S'why I wanted to run it past you first." She glanced over to see Paul and Joe carrying a pair of trays to their table. "Let's talk about it later. I shouldn't have brought it up on our night out."

"No, you should," Jenny reassured her, then turned to flash her sweetest smile on Paul. "Who said chivalry was dead?" she cooed as the teacher placed an iced cap and biscotti in front of her.

"Joe and I were guesstimating how big Emily would be in the *Out* sequel," Paul said.

"Why am I not surprised?" Misty chortled, patting Joe on the rear as he moved to sit down beside her.

"It's what I do," Joe grinned, sliding a plate of tiramisu and a mug of herbal tea to his sweetie.

"Amen to that!" Misty proclaimed, raising her cup in a heartfelt toast.

THE INVITATION CAME BY EMAIL—which should've been a tip-off, but Ian wasn't firing on all cylinders these days. Although Dex had never communicated by computer before, Ian took the invite at face value and drove up to the doctor's residence on Sunday. When Logan's son Jackie opened the door Ian peered over his shoulder, expecting to see the former chapter president.

"Your father's expecting me," he faltered. "Could you tell him I'm here?"

"I could if he was here," Jackie answered politely. "But he's not."

"I guess I'm a little early," Ian realized as he followed the boy into the house. Dex's Bose Wave was blasting something heavy metal and rappy, but Ian didn't pay enough attention to current music to know who it was. (He didn't think it was something Dex would willingly listen to, though.) "Uh, your dad invited me over."

"No, he didn't, Mr. Johnson," Jackie corrected. "I did."

His first impulse was to turn around and walk back out of the house. But Dex's boy was so calm and matter-of-fact that he quickly tamped down this reaction. So he took a seat at the dining room table and waited for the boy to explain himself.

"My sister," Jackie began, "didn't do the candy thing."

Oh, great, the boy was about to confess. Maybe he should've gone with his first impulse after all.

"That's all over and done," Ian said, tacitly offering Jackie permission to admit his complicity. "Nobody got hurt, and as long as the behavior stops, we're not worried about it."

"Rachel told me, and I believe her," Jackie continued. "But it got me thinking about some stuff I'd seen on the web. You know the ZAFTingather website?"

"I know about it, but I haven't been checking the size acceptance sites lately."

"Cause they've been talking about you."

"Pardon?"

"You haven't been surfing the sites because what's been on 'em is so nasty."

Ian didn't need this. "Maybe," he muttered, rising from his chair. "And maybe I need to tell your dad that you've been impersonating him on email."

"Whatever," Jackie replied affably, heading for the stairs. "Anyway, I need to show you something." He started up the steps, turning when Ian didn't follow, and reiterated, "C'mon. I really need your help with this."

Ian felt foolish, but he did follow the boy. In Jackie's room was a glowing Gateway computer.

"See you got your computer privileges back," Ian observed dryly. "Wasn't this downstairs?"

"Mom let me bring it back up," Jackie said as he plopped into his desk chair. "Said it disrupted the harmony of the room. Feng shui, or something like that." He clicked off his Chow Yun Fat screensaver. The monitor was set to a web board. "Somebody sure has been dissing you big time," Jackie explained, and he pointed to a convoluted message entitled "The Feeder Menace." The gist was summed up in the final two sentences:

We don't need sick degenerates like Talk Show Ian giving a bad name to all FAs. It's time the size acceptance community rose in public condemnation of this pervert!

"Cute," Ian observed, visibly shaken. "I used to appreciate the fact that the Web was an uncensored forum, but this gives me second thoughts."

"Check the name of the poster," Jackie urged.

"'marzbarz'?"

"Weren't the tampered candies Mars bars?" Jackie asked as he scrolled through the postings, indicating 'marzbarz's' ubiquity.

"I thought they were Dove bars, weren't they?"

"That was the first batch," Jackie pointed. "The second ones were Milky Ways."

"Which are Mars candies, so what difference does that make?"

Jackie minimized his web browser, then turned to face Ian. "Maybe this 'marzbarz' person was the one who really sent the candies. They're bragging and getting off on it."

Ian considered the boy's words. "Seems kinda farfetched, but anything's possible," he decided. "So what's it to you?"

"Rachel swears she didn't do it, and we were both suspects. I just want to find this guilty jerk before my folks start looking at me funny again."

"Okay." Ian could empathize with that. He turned his attention back to the monitor. "What do you want me to do?"

"You're a computer guy. Isn't there some sorta software that'll let us track 'em down? Some way to follow 'em through their ISP? And if we find out who it is, maybe we could nail 'em!"

And to think, just last year Ian was giving Dex advice on ways to restrict this kid's access to the Internet. Ian laughed and nodded, then actually looked at Jackie for the first time. A slight kid, intense and serious, dressed in jeans and a T-shirt. Kind of reminded Ian of himself at that age.

"Maybe we can at that," he agreed.

EPISODE SIXTY–EIGHT

"**S**O, YOU STILL LOOKING FORWARD to Starved Rock? What a goddess-blest place!" Misty's smile hinted at delighted memories. "Haven't been there since high school—and it'll be simply stunning this time of year."

Jenny smiled back tentatively. "I've never been, but Paul is really excited. Though I do wonder if I belong anyplace called 'starved.'"

"Oh, that's ancient indigenous history," Misty chuckled. "Traditionally it's been a mystic, sacred place for several Plains tribes, and site of a tragic massacre. Lucky you're going with a teacher—"

"Oh no, not another learning experience!"

"Okay, then concentrate on the landscape. All those nooks, crannies and caves would never bring 'starved' to mind. Kinda like me." From her kitchen, Eleanor could see Misty gesturing across her vast contours. "You know, I've really gotta grab Joe for a weekend road trip down there. That lodge menu has always been pretty inspiring, too."

Seated across from Misty at the dining table, Jenny flipped the pages of her legal pad nervously. "I've gotta admit I've been afraid to let myself hope for too much, just so I'm not disappointed. But it was Paul's brainstorm, and I definitely wasn't going to pooh-pooh it, 'specially not yet in our relation-ship."

"Of course not," Misty agreed. "This could be a quantum leap forward for you two."

Back in the kitchen Eleanor idly tuned in on this chat as she set a row of Fitz and Floyd cups around the coffee carafe, opened a package of Archway cookies and arranged them around the tray, then considered the results. All they needed for the officer's meeting to start was Ian, who typically ran fifteen minutes late.

"You're right," Jenny said, "though with Cassie around we're probably gonna be a bit more—um, discreet," she added *sotto voce*, smiling as their hostess laid the tray between them. "That looks wonderful, Eleanor. But, excuse me, do you have any sugar?"

Eleanor examined the tray with a puzzled look on her face.

"How thoughtless of me," she finally moaned. She so seldom used sugar that she'd forgotten this elemental coffee tray component. Her poor George had been lucky on Wall Street with Nutrasweet (one of his few real triumphs), so she'd remained loyal in his memory. She dashed into the kitchen to pull a sugar canister from the cabinet, then desperately looked for the sugar bowl.

"It's okay! Really!" Jenny shouted from the dining room.

"No, no! I'll be back in a second." Rummaging through the Tupperware shelf she found an old plastic sugar container tucked in the back and quickly inspected it. The top was a little dusty, but a run under the tap dealt with that. After wiping it down with a paper towel, she scooped a cup of sugar into the container and then dusted off the counter. "You girls want anything else?" she thought to ask before returning to the dining room.

"We're just fine," Misty reassured her.

Eleanor took another look around the kitchen on the off chance that there was something else she'd forgotten, but she couldn't think of anything. She'd been so distractible lately—more than usual—and it was starting to worry her. Maybe it was about time to get out of chapter politics and let the young-sters do the work.

As an officer she believed in size acceptance and was a longtime financial supporter of RADFAm. But increasingly there were parts of the movement that made her apprehensive. Listening to those two girls talk about "relation-ships," she felt very uncomfortable. Even her friend Lainie—who had a good five years on Eleanor—was like a coed when it came to discussing the oppo-site sex, let alone that interracial thing with Lissa and Delia. When had she become such a fuddy-duddy?

Then there was this feeder business from the Winnie Harper show. Per-haps she'd been keeping her head in the sand, but Eleanor had no idea such behavior existed. It seemed like everything had to be about sex these days. When did the simple act of serving food turn into something so twisted?

And how could such a seemingly nice young man like Ian have anything to do with it? Sighing, Eleanor turned back toward the dining room as the doorbell rang.

"Hopefully that's Ian," Jenny said, measuring out a smidgeon of sugar for her coffee. They all turned to see the man in question come through the door looking more disheveled than usual. Without a word he grabbed a chair and looked at the three women excitedly.

"I think I know," he announced, "who tampered with the candy."

JORDAN LEWIS HAD AN OFFICE on the edge of downtown in a former warehouse turned pricey loft hive. The Jorwel Enterprises reception area was halogen bright, with vast one-way window viewing onto the exercise room. While Lissa waited for the entrepreneur to get off the phone she watched a steroidally challenged behemoth grit his teeth in battle with a Nautilus. She thought he was one of Lewis's bookend bodyguards from the conference, but 'Ahnolds' all looked alike to her.

"Miz Jones?" the receptionist said from behind her counter. Waif thin and crystal blonde, she had one of those voices that managed to sound sweet and condescending at the same time. "He's off the phone now."

"Should I just go in?"

The receptionist tilted her head in the direction of a solid oak door nearby, as if she'd exhausted her vocabulary. Lissa rose and purposefully strode to the office door. Before she could knock Jordan Lewis opened it, interrupting her momentum.

He was decked out in a well-tailored business suit, looking more like a suc-cessful boxing manager than one of the country's best-known exercise gurus. Smiling with his teeth (but not, Lissa noted, his eyes), he stepped aside to invite her into his office.

"Quite a surprise to see you here, Miz Jones," he began, perching on the corner of his desk as she surveyed his sanctum. Behind said desk stood a row of photos featuring Lewis with celebrities who had all successfully fought the battle of the bulge. The display had several noticeable gaps—perhaps reflective of those notables whose victories had also been notably short-term. "What can we do for you?"

"It's what I can do for you," Lissa answered sweetly. She eased her body into a fake Biedermaier chair, crossed her legs and took note of the way the exercise guru's hooded eyes lingered on her calves. "I'll keep this brief, but I would like to alert you to a potential imbroglio.

"A member of your program has been making public accusations about one of my clients, and doing so under the aegis of your organization. We have mounting evidence that this woman is and has for some time been involved in a public and private harassment campaign against certain members of the size acceptance community. The most damning evidence thus far links her to the distributing of tainted candy, via the federal mails, to local members of RADFAm."

Lewis' smile remained pasted to his lips, but precariously. "Evidence, you say?" Away from the public eye his preacheresque cadences had been replaced by a softer tone—more workaday Buppy than avid diet crusader.

"This person has been posting libelous statements on the Internet under a name that connects her to the candy tampering," Lissa stated. "We've been able to clearly track her through her Internet Service Provider. Additional research finds several postings were made from a computer connected to your group's ISP account."

"'A name that links her to the tampering,'" Lewis repeated dubiously. "Sounds pretty tenuous to me. Was anyone hurt as a result of this woman's— um—actions?"

"That would be something for the courts to decide," Lissa returned crisply. "My client feels he's suffered irreparable damage to livelihood and character as a result of her performance on the Winnie Harper show. And it's my personal belief that this woman's unstable behavior will only escalate."

She uncrossed her legs, but this time Lewis was too distracted to pay it any notice. Lissa smugly watched him process what she'd revealed, while maintaining her poker face. *Second time bluffing,* she thought—if this one worked, she'd hit the riverboats.

"Before getting in touch with Ms. Harper's production company," she finally said, "I felt it only fair to bring this revelation to you first. It seemed only right since we made such a connection at the last RADFAm conference."

Lissa smiled and rose, offering her hand. Lewis limply took it, then re-membered to tap into his corporate confidence and returned her firm shake. He walked her to the door.

"And the purpose of your visit again?" he asked, before reaching for the knob. "I just want to be clear on this."

"Again, just to alert you," Lissa replied brightly. "We'll be pursuing this aggressively over the next few months, and you might want to be prepared."

"I'm sure we have nothing to worry about," Lewis answered as they re-en-tered the empty reception area. "But I appreciate your thoughtfulness."

"My client's not looking for financial remuneration. At this time. But I don't know how long he might stay so equitable."

"Understood," Lewis said.

Lissa turned down the hallway toward the elevator, feeling Lewis's eyes watching her progress beyond the shimmering glass-brick façade of Jorwel Enterprises.

EPISODE SIXTY-NINE

WHEN LAINIE CAME TO PICK HER UP Patsy's first reaction was to hide. Run, jump into bed and cover her head. And she might have done it, too, if Lainie hadn't sounded so cheerful beyond her front door.

The reason for all this trepidation was the private premiere of Delia's Dress4Success Shoppe, and Lainie had urged her to attend. "It's a Ladies Only event, with yummy refreshments. Plus Delia's offering a fifteen per-cent discount for RADFAm chapter members. Betcha we'll see lots of friends there." So since Patsy's current temp assignment was beginning to look long-term and she really did need to expand her wardrobe, she swallowed her fear and opened the door.

"Ready?" Lainie bubbled as Eleanor smiled tightly behind her. Lainie was dressed decidedly casual in jeans and white blouse with an embroidered vest that hugged her matronly torso. In contrast, Eleanor was her usual too-tense self, drably clad in petrochemical splendor. Patsy hoped she'd look as self-pos-sessed as Lainie when she reached her age, but she suspected that in Eleanor she saw her future.

"Ready as I'll ever be," she replied, stepping out and checking that her door was locked. "You're sure that none of the men will be there?"

"Positive. Lissa will probably be the bouncer," Lainie chuckled. "And if there's one particular man you're thinking of, I've got it on good authority that he and Paul and Joe are out for a guys' afternoon. So please relax."

As they stepped out into the bright June sun the whine and thunder of weekend traffic from the nearby tollway overpass echoed Patsy's agitation. Relax? Not very likely. She had a sneaking suspicion that the only way to inner peace was to stop waffling and simply break up with Ian.

Eleanor's car was parked in Patsy's unused space at the end of the apartment building. (Hopefully this temp assignment would provide enough extra money to find a nice used car and finally give up the Metro.) The silver-gray LeSabre was an older model, but well maintained, roomy and rife with the combined aromas of pine air freshener and Armor All. Patsy slid into the spacious backseat and pushed a large box of tissues out of the way.

Delia's Shoppe was a half hour away, which gave her plenty of time (when Lainie's stream of conversation allowed, anyway) to imagine possible scenarios with Ian. The store was situated in a recently constructed shopping plaza, catty-corner across the intersection from a Bakers' Square and right next to a martial arts school. A cluster of familiar cars was parked in front of the boutique, where a pear-shaped silhouette was visible through the window.

"Looks like a nice turnout," Lainie noted. "Give a RADFAm woman a fashion bargain shopping opp and she'll jump at it every time."

"Some of our younger members seem to disagree with the fashion part," Eleanor muttered as she activated her electronic key lock. The trio entered the Shoppe.

The crowd inside reminded Patsy of a convention vendor's room, thanks in part to the addition of a large table filled with munchies, punch and coffee by the door. Over a CD boombox Saffire, The Uppity Blues Women, were jauntily bragging about their middle-aged sexual prowess while women of all ages and sizes of large rifled through the brightly colored racks. Delia, smartly dressed and looking proudly businesslike, chatted excitedly with Misty by the cash register as Lissa presided over the refreshments.

"Ladies," the lawyer greeted, careful to avoid spilling punch on her chic batik sarong. "I'm so glad you all came!" She smiled and handed a plastic glass to a midsized girl with pink-tinged spikey hair, then homed in on the threesome. "Lainie, before you dive into the clothing could you please person the table just for a sec? I need to discuss something with Patsy."

With a sinking feeling the younger woman felt like a courtroom character that Perry Mason had suddenly singled out.

"No prob," Lainie replied, and Lissa locked arms with Patsy, steering her across the store toward the back where a small TV/VCR was perched on a stool.

"Didn't know if you'd seen this or not," Lissa began, pulling a remote control from the folds of her sarong, "since I know you've been busy with job assignments lately." She switched on the television and Winnie Harper suddenly filled the nine-inch screen.

"I've heard about it," Patsy gasped, backing away from the television. What was Lissa doing, anyway? "This is the show where Val outed Ian!"

"Nope, that was an earlier episode," Lissa assured her. "This was broadcast yesterday."

Patsy sighed and watched the tiny set. The talk show maven was standing exactly in the middle of the dais and appeared to be reading from a prepared statement.

"Two months ago, we aired a show on the so-called Feeder Phenomenon. We introduced a woman who claimed to have been involved in a feeder/feedee relationship, and she identified a man named Ian as the dominant partner. We have since learned from our good friend Jordan Lewis that this man was in fact a composite figure—several men combined to protect the anonymity of any single person—and that no individual named Ian was involved in a feeder relationship with the woman on our show. We apologize for any misunderstandings that this may have created."

She faced the camera as if to ask audience absolution for this little journalistic faux pas, then the show broke for commercial.

"The rest is devoted to female genital mutilation," Lissa said, clicking off the set. "But I knew you needed to see this."

"What's it mean?"

"Well, it means that Val was lying—and that Winnie Harper doesn't want to get involved in a lawsuit where she comes across as picking on the little guy." Lissa leaned over to unplug the set, then picked it up. "Let's get this back to the cashier's desk," she said. "Delia wants to show some Fashion Show videos." She glanced across the room just as an imperious-looking Connie Donovan made her entrance. "You need to do some shopping, and I'll keep an eye on things."

GLUMLY EYEING HER CLOSET, Cassie sighed and pulled out a slightly faded peasant blouse, tossing it onto the bed beside her suitcase and clothing bag. So much of her life was spent either in jeans or work clothes. Her best outfit was her church dress, which was hardly alluring.

It wasn't as if she needed anything fancy—she was going to a state park, for Lord's sake. But for some reason the sight of all her plain clothes seemed more depressing than usual. Who was she trying to impress, anyway? Not Jenny's Paul, certainly—she wasn't that kind of girl. It was just that every time she saw her sister, she couldn't help feeling dowdy.

What she needed to do was take time from her visit for some city shopping. Visit that new boutique Jenny mentioned in her last email. Or InFatuation. She really should splurge, buy a couple items for special occasions and places. Like Denny's, maybe?

Face it, she lived in a community where dowdy was expected of a single woman her age and size. What difference did it make what she wore? Nobody would notice anyway.

Sighing, Cassie returned to her closet, pulled out a denim blouse and flung it toward the bed without looking. On the radio a Christian rock group was singing about the sinful life they'd left behind. There were times when the thought of her sister brought a less-than-Christian feeling of jealousy into her heart. It wasn't fair—she knew that Jenny, too, had struggled for years as a fat woman—but that couldn't stop her envy.

We're all flawed, she realized as she slid both tops into her clothing bag. But shouldn't fatness be enough of a flaw for any one person?

Cassie had been told often enough that her size wasn't just a flaw but a sin. At moments like this she almost felt overwhelmed by her sinfulness. Gluttony. Envy. What did she think she was doing, foisting herself—-not just once, but twice—on Jenny and Paul?

Zipping up the bag, Cassie carried her luggage to the living room, where she dropped them on the couch. Outside her tiny bungalow she saw kids on bikes, hollering and laughing as they rode through the warm summer evening. Had she ever been that carefree?

She went back to her bedroom and shut off the radio, replacing the music with a Mama Cass tape. Stretching out on her bed Cassie watched the ceiling fan and lost herself in the song's lyrics. When she was younger—decades before she met Jenny—she'd imagined Cass Eliot as her older sister. Not really beautiful, but talented, sharing the same name, living an easy-going philosophy—you gotta go where you wanna go, do what you wanna do.

Her adoptive parents would have dual heart attacks if they knew what she was dreaming, but even now the thought of it was enough to ease her spirit. Go where you wanna go. Do what you wanna do. In its own way this was even more reassuring than Scripture. Maybe it was the harmony, the way all those voices, even that of a fat woman, blended and soared. Like a heavenly choir of tie-dyed angels.

Softly she sang along until the tape ran out. Then she reached up and turned off the bedside lamp, her anxiety temporarily erased.

EPISODE SEVENTY

AT FIRST SIGHT OF PAUL'S GEO METRO Jenny's rump twinged in horror at the prospect of two hours of subcompact crunch. (She bet Connie probably hadn't even tried to get in.) By the time they'd reached the Starved Rock exit any semblance of a graceful vehicular exit seemed extremely unlikely. Certainly not an auspicious way to start the weekend.

But her discomfort was not so extreme that it kept her from enjoying the view along the way. Jenny was used to a flat and uninteresting Midwest, mushrooming with suburban sprawl euphemistically dubbed Heights and Mount. But as they drove down the bluff from the interstate through the river valley she was surprised and enchanted by the vista.

Throughout the journey Jenny had mostly basked in the simple pleasure of riding with an appreciative companion on a nifty adventure. It had been a beautiful June day. Day lilies quilted the slopes in yellow and ochre and orange beyond roads canopied a deep arboreal green. Through the trees you caught occasional glimpses of sandstone juts. This must have been a lot like the wilderness traversed by Pere Marquette. (Professor Paul had, of course, given her a thumbnail of the area's lore along the way.) Except for the profusion of antique/indigenous/collectible/bait shops, of course.

Thanks to summer season interstate construction it took longer than Paul had figured, and they pulled into the lodge parking lot nearly an hour later than planned. As she stood and stretched gratefully Jenny took a quick scan of surrounding cars for Missouri plates, but quickly gave up. She turned to Paul, who was beginning to unload their bags from the trunk.

"Legs awake yet?" he asked apologetically. "The Metro's been a good teacher-salary car, but I think it's time to graduate to more size-friendly wheels."

"The ride wasn't that uncomfortable," Jenny fibbed as she straightened her denim culottes and walked over for her garment bag. Trees obscured most of the lodge beyond, but as they crossed the rock bridge spanning Fox Canyon she saw a giant wooden carving of mutant sunflowers sprouting on a patch of immaculate lawn that fronted one wing. A pudgy looking Hispanic family was sitting cross-legged on the grass under the sculpture. In the midst of the group an equally pudgy cocker spaniel watched their approach suspiciously.

Sprawling along the curve of the road the red cedar-shake lodge loomed massive against the brilliant late afternoon sky, obscuring everything beyond from view. *Boy,* Jenny thought, *those Civilian Conservation Corps guys sure did think big.* They passed a couple of entrances, one to a Great Hall where Paul had recalled family camping trips listening to Indian folklore in front of a humongous fireplace. From the outside Jenny just knew that dead animals figured prominently in the interior décor.

The next door revealed the registration area, and as they checked in they learned they'd arrived ahead of Cassie in spite of their tardiness.

The two rooms were on the first floor, right across the hall from each other. Jenny and Cass's looked north across the river valley (though lush foliage concealed all but a few slivers of blue sky), Paul's onto the parking lot lawn. Jenny dropped her bag on the queen-sized bed nearest the bathroom, hung up her garment bag, checked out the bathroom, then went to meet Paul by the desk.

She was about to sit in one of the comfy chairs near a large cage of finches when she spied a coffee shop on the other side of the lobby. A coffee shop? Maybe this place wasn't so primitive after all. A few minutes later Paul found her examining a bear-festooned evergreen (Misty had asked her to scout out ursine items, mindful of her tenant Kirk's upcoming birthday) and sipping an orange-and-banana smoothie.

"Your sister arrived yet?" he asked.

Jenny shook her head. "Have I apologized enough for inviting her?" she asked.

"Too much," Paul smiled. He reached down and patted her elbow reassuringly; the touch sent a small charge through her body. "Have you checked out the view yet?"

"Nope. I wanted to let you show me, Teach." She moved her hand to stroke his shoulder, smoothing the soft chambray shirt.

Paul grinned and went to choose a snack. Jenny blushed at her impudence, then collected herself as he returned with a chilled latte and carrot-nut muffin. "Shall we saunter, Grasshopper?"

"Sure," she chuckled, and they headed out the north exit.

Behind the lodge a rustic (and uneven) cobblestone path ran abreast of the sandstone bluffs that characterized the park. Feeling wary of the footing (these were, after all, her car-riding shoes), Jenny tossed the last third of her smoothie into the first wastebin they found.

She'd had to admit (at least to herself) that she was a bit concerned about all this up-and-down terrain. Not that she had a fear of heights, but she did have a healthy respect of it. She was reassured by the heavy pole fence between her and the heavily forested dropoff beyond. As they walked the undergrowth thinned and she saw firsthand the splendor that Misty had eulogized as native Sacred Earth—a rare and peerless view for a prairie state.

The cobblestone paths converged outside the rear of the Great Hall into a huge courtyard perched over the valley floor some twenty stories below. The river valley meandered for miles all around, hemmed in on the north by another bluff. As Jenny stepped forward for a better look she was grateful for the substantial rock wall topped with heavy wooden poles. Strategically placed binoculars studded the wall amidst groupings of octagonal picnic tables and lounge chairs, mostly occupied.

The pre-evening sky was striped with vivid clouds, tugged lightly in the late day breeze. Jenny watched as several other couples strolled along the path. Suddenly accepting that this handsome young teacher had chosen her to share this moment, a sense of ease settled over her. Smiling up at Paul, she clasped his hand and, in a typical moment of gracelessness, stepped down wrong on a cobblestone.

"Jen!" she heard from a distance. She fell against Paul, nearly causing him to lose his balance in duet. Dropping his glass, he quickly grasped her midriff with both hands and helped regain both their footing.

"Blast! I'm such a klutz," she moaned.

"But a delightful klutz," Paul responded. Their eyes locked, and that feeling of ease glowed suddenly warmer. That is, until she remembered the voice calling "Jen!" just as she'd tripped. Swiveling her head around she saw Cassie standing in the huge door of the Great Hall, a bulky suitcase at her feet.

"My sister's here," she said, reluctantly separating herself from Paul and waving. "I've got her room key."

"Of course," Paul said, waving as well, and he followed her back into the lodge.

"It's gonna be like this all weekend, isn't it?" Jenny whispered before they got within Cass's earshot.

Paul shrugged noncommittally. "Powwow in half an hour at Great Hall dining hall?" he grunted.

"You're the Chief."

CASSANDRA WISHED WITH ALL HER HEART she could have taken back that single shout. From where she stood it looked as if she'd inadvertently interrupted a major moment between the couple. *A great way to start the weekend,* she thought—*establish yourself as a third wheel from the get-go.* Lugging her wheeled suitcase behind her sister, she wondered once more if this trip was a huge mistake.

"We were starting to worry about you," Jenny was saying as she unlocked their room. "You have any trouble finding the place?"

"Actually, my web map directed me two towns over. Had to double back," Cass explained, doing a quick scan of the room. It was woodsy, yet filled with modern motel amenities; a far cry from the Ozark cabins she remembered as a kid. "Probably should've called the lodge for directions."

"Those maps are supposed to work," Jenny said, "though from what I hear they don't always hold up in non-urban areas." She paused as Cass took the unclaimed bed and hefted her suitcase on top. "Whichever bed you want is okay with me," Jen said. "I just dropped my suitcase here because it was closest."

"I've got no preference either."

Paul's invited us to dinner in the lodge dining room in half an hour," Jenny said, unzipping her garment bag and pulling out a blue linen handkerchief dress.

"I should just stay in and order room service," Cass offered as she flipped on the room's television. Onscreen, improbable policeman Wayne Knight was ogling a leggy blonde model type. "Looked like I interrupted something out there."

"Nonsense," Jenny scoffed. "We've got the whole weekend ahead of us, and lots of scenic moments. Besides, I'm not so sure they do room service here." Unbuttoning her cotton gauze blouse, she quickly stripped and pulled the pale blue dress over her zaftig body. Looking at her sister's young and well-shaped form, Cass couldn't help but feel an unchristianly twinge of jealousy. And then there was that dress!

"You definitely know the right thing to wear," Cass marveled. "Mom and Dad weren't much for dressing up—or encouraging it, either."

"My—our—birth mother wasn't much in that arena either," Jenny told her, pulling a pair of white strap sandals from her suitcase. "I had to pretty much learn on my own." She paused, considering Cass, who had not changed from her driving outfit. "The dress is a bit of a test," she confided. "I wore it to the dance where Paul and I first connected, and I wanted to see if he remembered."

"Would it be good or bad if he did?" Cass joked. "If he's paying that much attention to your wardrobe, it might be he was, well—you know." Once she said it she wondered if she'd stepped over a line, but after a moment of surprise—*she's never heard me make a joke,* Cass realized—Jenny grinned.

"We'll just have to wait and see," Jen decided, turning toward the bathroom with her hairbrush and a toiletry kit in hand.

Perched on the edge of the bed, Cass examined her own reflection, rubbing her fingers through her hair, then stuck her tongue out at herself. Reaching for the end table, she picked up a lodge brochure to read what the area had to offer. Maybe she'd spend Saturday afternoon doing some antiquing on her lonesome. The lodge's directions had to be better than MapQuest.

CAREFUL NOT TO HURRY HER, Paul led Jenny up the wood-railed path back toward the lodge. The trees offered cooling respite from the bright June sun. After hiking for the past hour—along the mostly unshaded River Trail, to the summit of Starved Rock and back down to watch barges as they navigated the locks—it was a definite relief. Still, Jenny was being an undeniable good sport about all the exertion.

"You doing okay?" he asked as they reached a trailside bench. Jenny sat gratefully, then smiled over at Paul as he took a seat next to her.

"Fine," she puffed, "though I hope I won't come off as too much of a wuss if I ask how much further we have to go."

"The lodge is just at the top of these stairs," Paul reassured her. "I didn't want this to be grueling, just scenic."

"That it is," she admitted, watching as chipmunks scampered through the underbrush. "I really enjoyed our trail ride together," she said after a few minutes.

That morning, she'd taken her first "real" horseback ride. "Of course," she'd recalled, "I'd always beg to ride the ponies at carnivals and fairs. But that all ended when I was about nine, when the man refused to let me ride, telling me I was too fat and would hurt his ponies. I was shattered! Mom didn't stand up for me, either, and so I've never saddled up ever again."

Paul, who had owned and trained horses as a teenager, felt a sharp stab of anger and sadness at her loss. "Well, trust me," and he gave her a quick hug. "You wouldn't have hurt that pony, and the guy was just being a jerk. I'm sure that these horses will be more than strong enough, so just let ol' Buck here find you a sturdy, safe steed, okay?"

As they pulled into the parking lot he was happy to note that there were no other riders waiting. Around the corral seven horses waited, saddled and bridled, reins tied to the top rail of the fence. It was a mixed lot, Paul noticed, mostly quarter horse and Appaloosa, the typical bunch of horseflesh you'd find at a public stable. With an eye toward temperament and size, as well as whether the saddle would accommodate Jenny's seat, he finally singled out a muscular chestnut gelding for her, and a flashy overo paint mare for himself.

The proprietor joined them after a few moments, had them sign liability releases, and took the money. "I usually like to take a bigger group," the lanky, weathered cowboy admitted, "but people must be sleeping in this morning, so let's saddle up." After realizing that Jenny's legs simply wouldn't reach the stirrup, Paul led her horse to a tree stump, helped her mount, adjusted her stirrup length and checked the girth, then, resting his hand on her thigh, gave a quick tutorial on equine navigation.

"Looks like you've done this a time or two," the trail boss smiled, then watched with satisfaction as the teacher swung nimbly into his own saddle.

"I never realized how far off the ground a horse's back is," Jenny exclaimed. She gingerly practiced starting, stopping and steering within the corral. But she quickly found her center of balance and, after a couple last cautions from the leader, she pulled her gelding into line behind him, with Paul taking up the rear.

Actually, Paul enjoyed this vantage point. For the next hour he noticed little of the geography, choosing instead to keep his eye on Jenny's lovely landscape. The gentle sway of the horse's walk did delightful things for her rear and torso, though he'd much rather have ridden abreast whenever they broke into a trot. He could only imagine how her lush body was responding to all this vigorous bouncing.

As he'd expected the trail was not terribly challenging for an experienced rider. But Paul could see by the wonder and joy on Jenny's face at each turn and rise that she was enthralled by the adventure. At the edge of a creek the leader called a halt, letting the horses take a drink. Paul pulled his horse alongside Jenny's and reached over to squeeze her hand as it rested on the horn. "Having fun?" he grinned.

"Oh yes," she smiled. "But I'll sure be happy to slide into the hot tub later."

"So will I. It's been too long since I've been on a horse—out of bow-leg practice. A nice hike will straighten out the kinks, though."

Jenny giggled. "I'm afraid I won't even be able to stand up after this, let alone hike."

At that moment the pinto jostled Jenny's gelding, and Paul reached over to steady her. Then he leaned out of his saddle, laid his arm across her shoulders and kissed her deeply on the lips. "Don't ever be afraid. I'll be with you, and I believe you can do anything you put your mind to."

Now, sitting here beside the sun-dappled hiking path and remembering the morning, Paul couldn't help feeling rather smug at the results of their equine adventure. Not only had he helped erase the injustice Jenny had experienced as a child, but hopefully he'd instilled in her the desire to ride again in the future. Although present circumstances prevented him from owning any horses, he definitely looked forward to the prospect of repeating their trail ride as often as possible—not only due to its intrinsic pleasure, but also because Jenny looked really sexy in the saddle. Every sway and bounce.

From the path above a teen-aged boy and girl were walking hand-in-hand down the steps. Heedless of their approach, Paul pulled Jenny close and kissed her. Her body yielded eagerly, pressing breasts and belly and soft upper arms against his torso in mutual passion.

Her deep blue eyes locked with his. He loved their candor, the way they graced her every glance, honestly taking in the world around her. He already longed for another kiss, longed to watch them flutter closed again with desire, but then realized that if he did, it wouldn't stop with just that.

"Um, maybe we should head up and see how your sister fared at the antique shops," he offered, edging back on the bench slightly.

"In a minute," Jenny murmured, pulling him close again.

THE LODGE WAS HOSTING A WEDDING RECEPTION, reminding Jenny of her first RADFAm dance. As they walked back to their rooms she saw the bride and groom readying themselves outside the banquet hall. The bride was dark-haired, young and plump, perhaps not as big as your average chapter member, but definitely a big-boned Midwestern girl, large enough to be buying women's sizes at JC Penny's. The sight reassured her.

She found Cassie sitting on her bed, halfway into a Josephine Fuller mystery that Lissa had lent Jenny. At the foot of the bed was a collection of brown bags with tissue paper peeking out. Looked like Cass had indulged in quite a little bit of shopping.

"Hope you don't mind my borrowing your book," Jen's sister apologized, quickly placing it on the end table between them. "I read the inner dust cover, and it got me interested."

"What do you think of it?" Jen asked. So much of her working life was spent wading through legal briefs, she wasn't sure she could find pleasure in fiction anymore. To be honest, she hadn't even cracked the cover yet. Lissa had raved about the book, though, calling Lynne Murray the first woman writer to actually come up with a fat-positive heroine.

"Some of the characters are a little weird," Cass replied, "but maybe that's 'cause it's set on the West Coast."

Jen nodded, making a mental note to prepare her sister before introducing her to Misty. "Looks like you had a productive shopping expedition."

"Oh yes, it was great," Cass acknowledged, indicating a bag with her toe. "Check that one out."

Slowly pulling tissue from the bag, Jenny revealed a handcrafted wooden angel. The figure was chubby, with pre-Raphaelite blond hair and finely detailed features.

"It reminded me of you," Cass smiled, "so it's my little thank-you present."

Touched by the gesture, Jenny examined the ornament. She couldn't remember the last time she'd been that thin, though she suspected she hadn't reached puberty yet. If she took her contacts out, maybe she could see the resemblance.

"You didn't need to do this," she said, leaning over the bed to hug her sister.

"I wanted to," Cass insisted. "It's no big deal." She colored slightly, then continued. "Consider it pre-payment for my leeching off your fashion expertise when we hit the plus-size shops Monday."

"That's a deal," Jenny agreed. Her sister, she saw, was dressed in a variation of the same getup she'd worn yesterday. For some reason it made her think of how Delia had looked when she was still tied to Connie—frumpy and vaguely standoffish, a total 180 degrees from the stylish businesswoman of today. Delia's shop would be their very first stop on Makeover Monday.

"Paul plans to take us to a nearby restaurant," Jenny said. "You up for something Italian?"

"Casual attire?"

"*Si, Signorina,*" Jenny responded. "But you do realize after Monday that question is taboo for the balance of your visit?"

"Fair enough," Cassie grinned as her sister stepped across the hall to knock on Paul's door.

EPISODE SEVENTY-ONE

AFTER A BRISK SATURDAY at the Isle of View Emporium, Misty was only too happy to close up shop. Bustling between register, office and storeroom while lustily joining Justin Hayward via CD on *The Other Side of Life,* she missed the cheery jangle of front door chimes. But even the fragrance of Karma incense failed to mask the fetid miasma of the newcomer's aftershave. *Greg Dillman,* she groaned without looking, *or someone with equally appalling taste.* A quick peek in the security mirror confirmed her initial fear (damn! Why hadn't she locked that door?), and she hastily rearranged her full face from chagrin to a semblance of smiling welcome as she reached to turn down the Moodies.

Greg was nattily dressed, as if coming from some door-to-door sales pitch—only the attaché case was missing, most likely left in his Lexus. As he negotiated the aisle he reached to absently twirl an astral globe, whose constellations spun manically. Oblivious to the cosmic mayhem of his action, Dillman leaned companionably on the counter, placing a leatherette folder between them.

"Misty!" he opened in hearty salutation. "Been trying to reach you at home all week, but it looks like your answering machine's on the blink. You and José must lead a very active night life." He drummed his fingers on the countertop for emphasis, smearing the freshly wiped glass and setting a dish of crystal points chattering.

"Not really," she answered, gritting her teeth to ignore the bad vibes of his boorish tone and behavior. She locked the register, slipped the day's deposit in her purse, and resolved to decontaminate the Isle's aura tomorrow. "So what's up, Greg?"

"Got a proposition for ya," he offered, proffering his folder. Within Misty saw a small stack of orange cardstock sheets with the legend "BBBonanza" emblazoned at the top. She scanned the text beneath, then re-read it a second time to make sure she understood it correctly.

"A beauty contest?" she gaped. "You want RADFAm to sponsor a beauty contest?"

"Co-sponsor," Dillman corrected. "We'd be splitting it with you, of course. I've got some very interested ladies in my group already. We can set it up for fall, and then have all summer to work up just the right publicity blitz."

"I'm not so sure—"

"Look, didn't the dance do well?"

"Relatively—"

"Well, this is just turning the action up a notch."

"I'm not sure," Misty considered, "the chapter wants to 'turn it up a notch.'"

"You're not gonna let a bunch of fuddy-duddy FemiNazis tell you what to do, are you?" Dillman wheedled. Without the safety of the counter between them he'd probably be standing right by her, jostling his arm on her shoulder. "What can be wrong here? It's a celebration of big and beautiful womanhood! A positive affirmation!"

"For the winners, maybe," Misty reflected.

Greg hoisted his eyebrows knowingly, then pushed away from the counter. "I wouldn't want to prod you into something that'd make you feel uncomfortable," he drawled. "But maybe you could take my proposal to the rest of the group? See if any of them are interested. That Jenny would sure look babe-alicious in sequins—"

He enticingly slid his leaflet toward her, then snapped the folder shut.

"All right," Misty sighed, "I will."

"S'all I'm askin', Beautiful," Dillman said, turning to the door. "Give my regards to the Latin Lothario, eh?"

Misty didn't stir from behind the counter until the entrepreneur passed beyond window sight. Sighing once more, she folded Dillman's leaflet and placed it in her purse alongside the day's take. Scrutinizing the store, she mentally step-by-stepped her usual day-end routine, double-checking for things she might have forgotten. Finally satisfied, she pulled out her keys and locked up. She was running late; Joe would be wondering where she was.

Saturday night at Caspar's—though she couldn't pinpoint when occasional had become habit, she'd fallen into a weekend routine. At each visit both Joe and his boss treated her like restaurant royalty, recommending the night's best offerings and solicitously granting her every whim. It was flattering in limited doses, but she suspected it could wear thin if she stopped by any more often.

As she headed for the Metro, she thought back on her own tentative romantic first steps with Joe, then couldn't help but wonder how the weekend was going for Jenny and Paul.

LOUNGING IN A CHAIR with a bottle of cold O'Doul's, Paul admired Jenny as she glided through the swimming pool. Her two-piece turquoise tankini wavered provocatively in the chlorinated water; when she stood up to invite him back into the pool, it draped and clung sexily, revealing a tantalizing flash of midriff between top and trunks. The sight was so erotic that he finally recognized the allure of those slow-mo movie beach scenes that had always left him cold in the past—the cameramen simply weren't focusing on the right women.

"C'mon," Jenny was calling. But Paul was reluctant to join her—he wasn't sure he could stand without his trunks betraying his obvious interest. How would Jenny react? She seemed infinitely more—what?—sweet, innocent, vulnerable—than Connie.

"Right now I think I'm more in the mood for the hot tub," he finally replied, hastily wrapping a towel around his hips and turning toward the vacant Jacuzzi. "Join you shortly."

As he stepped into the steamy roiling water, Paul suddenly remembered—Jenny had removed her contact lenses in her room after dinner, and then left her eyeglasses poolside on the table by his chair. So she probably couldn't see him clearly, after all. And hopefully none of the other pool residents had noticed anything, either.

Well, now that he'd rushed to shock his excitement away, might as well sit back and enjoy. Finding a seat by a strong jet, he leaned into it and let the water do its work. It'd been a long time since he'd ridden, and though he didn't want to admit it, certain body parts were vigorously protesting the experience.

The discomfort certainly hadn't prevented his randy appreciation of Jenny's charms, though. As she climbed out of the pool and wandered his way he realized that he was fighting a losing libidinal battle. She was flat-out gorgeous.

"You know, if I get in there, I may not want to come out again," Jenny chuckled. "I've got aching areas I didn't even know existed."

"'It's not the years, it's the mileage,'" Paul quoted sagely as she gingerly lowered herself into the tub. "You did very well in the saddle today."

"Sure, I'm a real Dale Evans," Jenny laughed. "But I didn't know you owned horses as a kid." She sat right next to him, hips rippling against his, tank top bubbling joyously. "Here I've spilled my whole life, and you haven't really told me much at all about yours."

"My folks were family farmers," Paul began, "until Dad sold it all to a big agribusiness concern. Once it became clear that neither of my sibs nor I were into farming, he decided to cut his losses and enjoy retirement. Now he and Mom live on the Texas coast. I haven't seen 'em in years."

By the sadness mirrored in Jenny's eyes, he could tell that he hadn't been able to keep the hurt from his voice. But, thankfully, she didn't pursue it.

"Well, I'm sure glad we went riding together, and I hope we can do it again," she announced, intertwining her lefthand fingers with his right. "You're a very good teacher."

"I oughta bring you to my next Performance Evaluation," Paul joked. He raised her hand to his lips, slowly kissing it. She tasted of chlorine. Shifting to face Jenny, Paul was overcome with the urge to hold her and never let go, but he merely studied the play of emotions across her face until she broke the silence.

"What?" she asked gently.

"I was just thinking how utterly lovely you look," Paul explained.

"My makeup's washed off and my hair's all stringy, this suit shows every bulge on my body—and you say I'm lovely?"

"I do," he emphasized, and he leaned forward to kiss her. His early insecurity dissipated as she fervently returned his embrace. Paul felt his skin flush in a way that just a Jacuzzi couldn't stimulate. Moving closer, he pressed her to him, reveling in the sensation and simultaneously sinking into her divine blue eyes. They kissed even more ardently.

As they briefly pulled apart the hot tub's water erupted between them, splashing both their faces. All the more motivation to keep together, Paul decided. They rose in tandem and once more encircled each other with their arms, ignoring the other pool patrons. The whole room seemed to swirl sensually in the steam. They held each other tightly for support. Jenny's eyes danced provocatively as she crushed him even closer.

"You do seem to be enjoying this," she beamed, gazing down the tight gap between them. There was no masking it now.

"Oh, I am, Jenny Taylor. Definitely!"

They silently stepped out of the hot tub, grabbed their towels and headed hand-in-hand to Paul's room.

EPISODE SEVENTY–TWO

OMEWHERE—FROM A FACTOID PARAGRAPH in *Reader's Digest*, perhaps—Cassie had once read that you rarely reached REM sleep in an unfamiliar bed. On the basis of two nights at the lodge, she could believe it. Her second night there she'd tossed and turned the dark away, waking up for good at least an hour earlier than usual. As her eyes adjusted to the early dawn light, she saw that her roommate had not come home.

What was she to make of that? She didn't really know her sister very well, let alone the man that Jenny was apparently sleeping with. He seemed like a nice guy, but then so did Ted Bundy. What was she going to say to Jenny when she returned? Cassie didn't want to come across as a fuddy-duddy or worse, some sort of religious crackpot.

Perhaps she shouldn't have come on the trip, she agonized, rolling out of bed toward the shower. The harsh bathroom glare banished all vestiges of sleepiness. Perhaps she should have waited 'til Jenny had returned from Starved Rock before coming up to visit. The romance had been developing for a while, but was this an okay time to get in the middle of it? she asked herself as shower waters mercifully pummeled her.

Cassie couldn't help wondering what their mother would have thought about all this, though she knew what her foster parents would say—good Christian girls waited until marriage, and even then they weren't supposed to like it too much. But her real mother—the mother who'd had her out of wedlock—that was another question altogether. Had she learned from her mistake? Would she be fearful that Jenny might follow her example?

If only she'd known her birth mother, she sighed, drying herself carefully. Wrapping a remarkably generous towel around her head and torso, she headed back into the bedroom.

This was getting her nowhere, she decided, picking up the Lynne Murray mystery Jen had lent her, hoping it would offer sufficient distraction 'til whenever. She was only half successful. Though she'd become enthralled with the characters and story, she still found herself occasionally wandering into the worry zone. It was a quick read, and she was near the book's finish—heroine Jo Fuller facing the killer who was brandishing a blood-stained knife—when she heard the door unlatch.

"OKAY, DAD, hit refresh again!"

Seated at his Gateway, Dex followed Jackie's tutorial. He still had, the screen told him, forty-five seconds until the online auction ended.

"Wait for it; give it another ten seconds. Okay, now!"

Dex hit refresh once more. No one else had bid on the item.

"Can't relax yet, Dad. Someone could sneak in at the last second. Some of these snipers are really good at it. Okay. Now!"

Another click. They had eight seconds left, he was informed, and no other bids.

"Well, if someone sneaks in now, we just won't have the nanosecs to out-bid 'em," Jackie said, holding up his Swatch so they could both watch the digits pass. When it seemed safe, Dex hit refresh a final time. The auction, he was told, had ended, and he'd won his item—a reprint of a Victorian book from 1878 entitled *How to Be Plump.*

"Okay, maestro, what do I do now?" Dex asked.

Jackie smiled and took a sip of Snapple fruit juice, then indicated the item seller's ID on the screen. Over the computer speakers a live version of Pink Floyd's "Teacher" played, gloomily tuneful.

You can either wait until the seller contacts you or send 'em an email right now," Jackie replied. "But if you wanna build good feedback, it's best to com-municate quick as possible."

Dex gladly followed this advice, dashing off a snappy email with his name, address and online ID, "quackcollktr" (ever since resigning as chapter presi-dent, he'd gotten into medically questionable diet collectibles). Then he swiv-eled his desk chair toward his son. "Done!" he announced. "My first online win." Reaching over, he ruffled the boy's already unruly hair (so unlike his mother's ebony veil, Dex smiled), then rose from his seat. "How should we celebrate our victory?"

"Well, if you're feeling generous, I saw a Lara Croft CD-ROM on sale at Best Buy," Jackie offered.

"Nice try, but I'm not feeling that generous." With mock severity he scru-tinized his son. "Blown your allowance already? This girlfriend business can be pretty expensive."

"Da-ad!"

"Okay, okay, that was unfair," Dex retreated. "I still haven't seen Miz San-dra in the flesh yet, though, have I? When are you gonna bring her over to the house? Or do you two only meet via seventeen-inch monitors?"

"I dunno," Jackie grinned with that peculiar mix of pride and embarrassment characteristic of the freshly dating male teenager. "Some day."

"Alright," Dex grinned back. For some reason the sight brought a tinge of melancholy to his heart. "So just how good a 'best buy' is that game, anyhoo?"

IT WAS HALF AN HOUR DOWN THE HIGHWAY before either Jenny or Cassie found the nerve to mention Paul.

His car was still in sight ahead of them—afternoon sun shimmering brightly across the interstate road between them—and perhaps this kept the discussion limited to shared weekend memories and mundane stuff.

Since it was Sunday, road construction was on hold, and they were making good time, at least so far. Cassie had tuned in an oldies station and was now humming along to the musical advice, "live for today." But tomorrow was all Jenny could think about while Paul's words filled her journey home.

She'd been more than a little nervous returning to the room that morning, but her sister had been wonderful. Looking up from the chair where she was curled, still reading the mystery novel Lissa'd lent Jen, Cass rose and gave the younger woman a hug, heedless of the still damp swimsuit in her hand.

"How you doing?" she'd asked, and Jen had truthfully responded that she felt wonderful. (It was only when she saw Paul again at the breakfast buffet that the ramifications of his words reasserted themselves.) Turning to the closet, she pulled down a plastic bag and tossed in her no-longer-new tankini.

"Want to talk about it?" Cass had offered, watching Jen with a look of concern on her full face.

"Maybe later," Jen had said, and it seemed "later" had arrived. As Cass aimed her car for a gas station exit, Paul's Metro vanished down the road. The two women disembarked—Cassie to the pump and Jenny inside to buy some cold caffeine and nibbles—and when they both slid back into the roomy sedan, Paul was long gone.

"I can't help wondering," Cass began as she turned the ignition, "whenever I see Paul's car, just how comfortable it is. I know I couldn't fit behind that steering wheel without some major readjustments."

"Wasn't bad, really," Jenny answered, "though I had a little trouble finding my legs when we stopped. Compact and I aren't compatible."

"Right on," Cassie chuckled, and Jen could see the real question coming. "Your Paul seems like a right nice guy, though."

"He is," Jen replied, then felt the need to be more affirmative. "But definitely."

"So—um—is he serious?"

"Also definitely," Jen said, and she flashed back for what had to be the thousandth time on the Paul moment—lying on their backs across his king-sized bed, a rustic lamp post beyond the curtains offering the only illumination, Jenny feeling relaxed and warm as she snuggled into Paul's arm—

A perfect moment, a timeless moment—until Paul spoke his heart and mind.

How serious was he? Yes, she loved each moment she spent with Paul. So why did his words send cold panic coursing through her?

"That's not the issue," she finally sighed to her sister. "The question is—how serious am I?"

THOUGH IT COULDN'T HAVE BEEN more than a few seconds, it seemed to take Ian an eternity to get up the nerve to actually press the buzzer. Behind him an Indian mother was bellowing at her two young boys to help her get the groceries out of the car. As the youngest dashed in front of him, arms empty but with a key in his hand, Patsy's voice came over the intercom.

"Yes?" she asked.

"Patsy, it's me," Ian shouted into the weak microphone as he stuck his foot in the door. "Okay if I come up?" A pause long enough for him to hold the door open for both mother and second son followed, then Ian heard the buzz. Fluffing his bouquet, he stepped into the apartment building.

Though the building was four stories (and sans elevator), Patsy had lucked out in getting a first floor three-room. Walking down the hall, the odor of red beans and hocks seeping from one of the other apartments, he saw Patsy peering out of her doorway. Timidly, he raised a small wave.

She was in laundry sorting mode—pink sweatpants and a Rubenesque T-shirt—but it didn't matter to Ian. Just the sight of her was enough to get his pulse skipping faster than the hip hop beat throbbing through the walls across the hall. Her expression was serious but not (as it'd been the last time he'd seen her) fearfully so. Nervously, he handed over his bouquet of carnations.

"Thanks," she said simply, then indicated her open doorway. "Come in."

Ian accepted her invitation, stepping into the kitchen and standing by as Patsy rummaged through the cupboards for a vase. In the living room he saw several piles of sorted clothes on the floor. From the flimsy plastic hangers on the couch it looked like she'd recently bought some new work outfits.

"Misty told me about your fulltime job," Ian began, "so I thought I'd come by to offer my congratulations."

Patsy set the vase in the middle of the kitchen table and pulled out a chair. Ian followed suit. "They're lovely," she said quietly, plucking off a slightly wilted leaf. "I'm glad you came over, Ian." She swiveled her head in the direction of her fridge. "I'm being a lousy hostess—you want anything to drink?"

"No, I'm fine."

They sat in silence for what seemed like an even longer eternity than Ian's time outside the building. Finally, Patsy spoke.

"Lissa showed me Winnie Harper's retraction," she said. "You must feel so relieved to have the truth out in the open."

"It's not like anyone was demanding my impeachment on the front page of the *Trib,*" Ian answered. "Only a few folks knew who Val was referring to."

Patsy looked at Ian from across the kitchen table, a tear forming in the corner of one eye.

"God, I'm sorry, Ian," she moaned, and he rushed off his chair to put his arms around her shoulder. So many nights he'd lain in bed imagining this moment, rehearsing the words he'd say ("No, I'm sorry that your history with men has made you so distrustful.") But now none of them sounded right. Instead he just silently embraced her.

When she finally stopped her sobbing, he bent over and kissed her lips.

"Need some help with the laundry?" he asked.

NOBODY FORGIVES FASTER than a dog.

Though he'd heartlessly abandoned her to the neighbors for three whole days, Molly behaved as if he'd just gone 'round the block. She leapt happily as he came through the door, nearly knocking the softsided suitcase out of his hand. As soon as he deposited his luggage on the couch she was eyeing the leash by the door. Paul took the hint. Walk now, unpack later.

They drove to the park, Molly seated in the passenger's side, nose snuffling through the crack in a previously slobber-free window.

"What would you say to us getting a new car?" he asked her. "Something a little roomier, hmm?" The golden slapped him with her tail, simply happy to hear her master's voice. "You might need to ride in the backseat," Paul continued as he turned into the park entrance. Molly paid no attention to this dire prediction.

Grabbing a pair of plastic grocery bags and the handle of Molly's leash, Paul levered himself out of the Geo. They made their way past the park playground and a row of busy picnic tables. There'd been a rash of stories in the paper about cops ticketing owners for letting their dogs off leash, so Paul held onto Molly. The duo walked around a soccer field and headed for the duck pond. Excited to be out and about, Molly paid no mind to her distracted master, happily pulling him in the direction she wanted to go, barking at the occasional jogger or bicyclist.

Paul, meanwhile, was revisiting the weekend.

It had gone wonderfully, he thought. A dream weekend—until that last night. Jenny had looked so lovely. He had a whole set of mental snapshots to cherish for years to come. Jenny seated in the saddle, looking both scared and delighted. Jenny rising, wet and sleek as a seal, after diving into the pool. Jenny lying next to him in bed—

Clearly, he'd jumped the gun. As they'd nestled, spooning in post-coital warmth, he'd kissed her neck and dropped his bomb. "It wouldn't take much for me to fall completely in love with you."

Though she didn't move a muscle when he said it, Paul could feel Jen inching away. She didn't say a word, but the atmosphere of warmth seemed to suddenly leach from the room. *If only you could treat life like a word processor,* Paul thought, *erase each awkward sentence as if it'd never been written.* He'd been speaking from his heart, but apparently they weren't at the point where he could do that yet. Jenny was pleasant the rest of the weekend, but it wasn't the same.

It wasn't sex that changed a relationship, Paul thought, pulling Molly away from a squawking gaggle of geese. It was the "L" word.

EPISODE SEVENTY-THREE

LOVE EQUALS LONELINESS.

This questionable equation echoed through Misty's head as she watched her PC scroll through its opening rituals. In the background Enya was softly keening. Somewhere in the apartment Schmendrick was hissing and acting territorial with Jake and Elwood Blues. Misty was cat sitting for Kirk, Bri and Howlie—and her own pampered pet was none too thrilled by these Maine Coon interlopers in his apartment. Every time the CD came to a particularly soft passage she heard the flurry of cat feet and occasional furniture collisions. Though the pedigreed Blues Brothers outweighed her motley black and white mongrel-cat by a good twenty pounds, Schmendrick seemed to have them totally cowed.

Joe, of course, was at the restaurant. In these few short months since his promotion she'd learned to feel his absence acutely.

While she'd been unattached she hadn't been bothered by an empty apartment. Not all the time, anyway. Now, when Joe wasn't around she found herself turning on the TV or stereo just to foster the illusion that she wasn't alone. The speed with which we all grew accustomed to human contact was a sign of just how much we needed it. That tribal urge.

Her computer finally booted, Misty opened her new Tarot file. She'd bought the CD-ROM at an office supply superstore, and though she'd always looked down on this sort of techno-mysticism, the price was cheap enough to encourage impulse buying. She wanted to try something she'd never been able to successfully do with her own cards—conduct a reading on herself—and this full-moon night seemed like a good opportunity. Passing through the tinny opening fanfare, she skipped the tutorial and checked her options on the "Select" menu—the "Experimental" deck on a Celtic Cross layout.

Then came the big question—what did she want to find out? Let's see what the cards suggested, she decided, so she began selecting cards from the row at the bottom of the screen without a fully articulated inquiry in her head. Then she turned over the central question card. It showed a caveman huddled over a fire with the logo "Home." She was being advised to contemplate the nature of her living arrangement. That made sense.

As she turned over her second card ("Court—Mother of Air"), the phone rang. She let the answering machine pick up and then was glad she had.

"Greg here. Just wanted to let you know there's no hard feelings for backing out of the Beauty Pageant."

Backing out? She'd never even said the chapter was willing to be involved. Resisting the urge to reach out and grab the phone, Misty took two deep breaths then refocused on the monitor, trying to block out Dillman's babble.

"Got a hotel downtown set for fall. I'll be bringing flyers to the Beach Party next weekend. We need to drum up interest early, though in a lotta ways an event like this sells itself—"

Her background card was "Intuition." Her recent past was "Court— Son of Water" (loving connection and attraction). It all seemed to be connecting in ways she wouldn't have expected from a store-bought PC program.

"We've still got room for individual chapter members to be involved. Right now I'm especially looking for lovely ladies who have musical talent. Not as part of the contest but as part of the pageant—"

A loud clattering suddenly erupted from the kitchen area. Misty rose from her chair to find Schmendrick quivering alongside the dish drainer, three Boston Warehouse glasses rolling on the floor. Jake and Elwood were nowhere to be seen.

"So did the boys finally get wise and gang up on you?" Misty wondered, plucking him from the kitchen counter. "Come with me and see if you can behave for a few minutes."

She carried the cat back to the computer table, stopping to erase Greg's message on the way. Schmendrick curled on the monitor while Misty worked through the rest of her reading. Her final outcome revealed "Court—Mother of Fire." She was being advised to contemplate anima, her creative impulses.

Paw dangling, Schmendrick absently patted at the screen.

She hadn't done anything genuinely creative in ages—partly, she suspected, out of fear of freaking Joe out. Well, maybe it was time to get past that fear.

"I DON'T KNOW. I'm not sure I'm ready for this."

"C'mon. You know you want to—or else you wouldn't have headed for this rack."

"I've changed my mind, Jenny. I've spent enough money already, and besides, I can't see myself ever wearing anything like this."

Cassie fingered the one-piece swimdress for emphasis. As suits went, it was pretty low-key—the scalloped neckline might be a mite revealing and the bright tropical print veered about as far from "normal" (black or navy) as possible. But from the way her sister was carrying on, you'd have thought Jenny was coercing her to wear a G-string and pasties.

"That's okay, Sis. Just thought you'd want something sharp for the Beach Party."

"Well, maybe," Cassie started to cave. "It's just that it's been years since I bought a new swimsuit."

"Which is why you didn't have one for the lodge," Jenny persisted. "We've got to redress this unfortunate situation immediately."

"Redress?"

"Set right. Remedy. You know: Dress again."

The pun got both of them giggling more than it warranted, but at least it put the brakes on Cass's momentary fashion panic. She turned and resolutely carried the swimwear into the dressing room.

Jenny passed the time among the clearance racks and waited while her sister tried on the swimdress. Over the day and through every suburban plus-size store Jenny had come to realize shopping for someone else was much more exhausting than buying clothes for yourself.

Particularly when you had to cajole that someone else into making any purchase.

Was she ever that needy? Jenny wondered. She remembered examining herself in the mirror the night of her first RADFAm dance, practically begging for Lissa's encouragement, and she smiled at the memory. Perhaps it was part of the dues for the Sisterhood of Fat Women, to be the cheerleader for someone else making those first tentative steps into self-esteem.

A hissed whisper ("Jen!"), and Cassie was poking her head through the dressing room curtain to gesture Jenny over. Jenny replaced the crocheted coverup she'd been casually considering and walked over to her sister. Slowly, Cass pulled the curtain open.

"What do you think?"

Though her clothes and posture usually worked to hide it, Cassie had a real woman's figure—a little thicker in the torso than Jenny, but definitely capable of catching an appreciative FA's eye. Jenny smiled and gave her sister a thumbs-up. If she didn't back out at the last minute (something Cassie had threatened to do on more than one occasion already) her sister was going to be a knock-out at the RADFAm Beach Party.

"I think you've found your suit," she said.

"You sure?"

"Never been surer. It really suits you."

Cass beamed shyly as she swiveled to take a fresh look at her reflection. Though she probably didn't realize it, she stood a little straighter as she examined herself. A fresh hairdo and some makeup, Jenny decided, and her sister could be a plus-sized catalog model.

"Well, nothing ventured," Cass shrugged, heading back into the dressing booth. "Thanks, Sis."

"I just calls 'em like I sees 'em," Jenny answered, and went back to the clearance rack. That coverup, she'd decided, would complement her own ensemble. She scrutinized it carefully for flaws until her sister rejoined her.

"Ready to go?" Cass asked. "I could do with some lunch."

They carried their booty to the register, which was being presided over by a sour-looking midsized woman in black. As a regular customer, Jenny remembered her from previous visits, and she didn't think she'd ever seen the woman smile. She was usually inclined to be over-nice when confronted by such a sour mien, but today she wasn't going to let the woman's attitude get to her. Instead she just quietly presented her debit card, then waited while her sister got her plastic card approved.

Cass had noticed the woman, though. "Is she always like that?" she asked as they tossed their sacks into the back of Cassie's car.

"Sour and surly, you mean?" Jenny answered. "She's been that way every time I've come into the shop. On my first visit I thought it was something I said."

"Well, if you hadn't been there, I doubt I'd have stayed long enough to find anything," Cass replied, steering the car toward the nearest strip mall exit. "So unlike that first place we visited with your friend—what's her name?—Delia. I really felt welcome there."

Jenny smiled and said nothing. First time she'd met Delia the woman hadn't been all that friendly either. Still, her sister had a point—you expected plus-sized shops to be a haven from the negativity of a fat-phobic world.

"So which way are we turning? Where are we doing lunch?"

"There's a nice coffeeshop not too far from here," Jenny told her, indicating a right turn with a gesture. As her sister slowly edged out into traffic, doubtlessly irritating the more aggressive city drivers forced to stop and wait, Jenny felt a sudden surge of irrational anxiety. What if they ran into Paul at Kuppa's? She still hadn't talked to him since the weekend, though he'd left several messages on her answering machine.

But what were the odds of his being there? Granted, he still had a week of free time before summer school classes, but that didn't mean he'd be at their regular watering hole. More likely he was out in the park, making up for the lost weekend with his dog.

You'd better figure out what you're feeling, she scolded herself, *cuz there's no way you're gonna be able to avoid Paul at the Beach Party.*

"Left at the next light," she directed her chauffeuse.

EPISODE SEVENTY–FOUR

STANDING BESIDE THE SWINGING DOORS separating kitchen from dining room, Joe caught a glimpse of a large couple being led to their table. The male was middleaged, with the stern look of a successful business type, while his female companion was both larger and friendlier. Bedecked in a plain full-length dress, with long reddish hair tied back, her soft round figure brought a pang to Joe's heart. Though she looked nothing like Misty, she still conjured thoughts of her.

Nothing new there—at least once a day something or someone reminded Joe of Misty. He was spending so much time at work that some days it seemed like these memories were all he had.

Sighing, he turned back to the kitchen—no, with Caspar gone for the night, it was *his* kitchen—as a new table worth of orders came in. Though Caspar had begun to ease up on active food prep, giving his protégé more responsibility, the restaurant clientele continued to flourish. If anything, the last few weeks had been busier than Joe'd ever remembered for this time of year.

He knew his expanding work schedule did not appeal to Misty. But then she was accustomed to working on her own in a shop that never would see the volume of customers that Joe needed to satisfy daily. In a way she was spoiled by the limited success of her business, he thought, slapping two New York strips on the counter to be seasoned. Misty didn't know what it was like to have to cater to a seriously demanding restaurant crowd.

Off to the side, Marlan, one month out of chef school, was preparing a trio of salads. Joe eyed them critically, then smiled at the still nervous kitchen newcomer. He wished he had Caspar's knack for making his workers feel comfortable, but Joe himself was too new in his role to be able to communicate anything but his own nervousness.

"Looks great," he muttered to Marlan and returned to his steaks on the grill. Perhaps, he thought as he flipped them both over, he could come up with a new dessert for the restaurant. Something chocolate. Named after Misty. To show that he still was thinking of her.

"SEATTLE SMOG—a deep rich roast with the feel of the Pacific Northwest.'" Kirk opened the sack and took a deep whiff of the coffee beans, rolling his eyes in fake ecstasy as he did. "You know, I think they actually captured Brian's essence," he pronounced after carefully re-folding it shut. "It's like he's really in the room with us."

"If it's that good, you don't need to brew it," Misty told him. "Just sprinkle a few beans inside your pillow."

"I may do that," Kirk replied, placing the unexpected present on table's edge and patting it affectionately. "Thank you for the gift."

"Just trying to get you in the right mood," Misty said, taking a sip of Tension Tamer tea.

"Bribery, eh?" Kirk squinched his eyes suspiciously. "Whatcha been cooking in your devious brain?"

"How would you like," she opened, "to have your rent reduced by at least a hundred dollars a month?"

"Oh, ho. And who do I have to kill to accomplish this?"

"Nothing so sinister," she answered reassuringly. "Just let me throw an idea your way. I've been thinking of doing some remodeling on this floor. You know where the connection between our two apartments is walled in? It wouldn't take all much to remove the partition—"

"And?"

"Make it into a two-person dwelling for Joe and me," she concluded.

"You want me to move into Joe's apartment upstairs?" Kirk recoiled. "After all I've done to this place?"

"It was just an idea," Misty backed off. "If you're not interested, then that's that."

"Didn't say I wasn't interested," Kirk reopened. "If things keep going the way they have, I might not be long for this state, anyway."

"That good between you and Brian?" she asked, momentarily forgetting her plans and scanning Kirk's face to see if he was joshing or not.

"Better," Kirk smirked lasciviously. "What does Joe think of this little redesign scheme of yours?"

"I haven't told him about it yet," Misty admitted. "Wanted to run it by you first."

"A hundred dollars off, you say?"

"Joe's apartment has a good view of the park," Misty wheedled. "Plenty of inspiring scenery during softball season."

"Let me think about it," Kirk finished. "But before I give you an answer, you'd better ask Joe. And Mist, a word of advice—"

"Yes?"

"Let him think that you approached him first."

HOLDING HIS FRISBEE before narrowed eyes, Ian leaned forward and aimed for the ninth "hole." The bright June evening was perfect for Frisbee golf, and to make matters even nicer, the park course was all but deserted. Ian and Patsy were able to go at their own pace, allowing them time to stop at the conveniently placed benches and hold hands.

Careful to keep his wrist straight (you'd think with all the keyboarding he did, this wouldn't be a problem), Ian aimed for the chain link basket. His orange Frisbee hit the pole and bounced two feet away from its target.

"I always thought miniature golf was the game of choice for RAD-FAmites," Patsy said, standing to take her own shot, "and it looks like I was right." Squinting seriously, she casually tossed her Frisbee, only to see her throw intercepted in midflight by a large furry blur.

"Molly!" a voice shouted from across the playing field. Ian and Patsy looked to see a familiar figure purposefully striding toward them. He reached for the golden retriever, who'd galloped to him proudly with her purloined prize, and took it from her. Wiping the slobbery Frisbee on his jeans, he carried it back to Ian and Patsy.

"Paul!" Ian called, looking for Jenny but not seeing her. "Is this how you make money over the summer? Stealing and fencing Frisbees?"

"I'm no canine Fagin," Paul laughed, as he handed Patsy the Frisbee over a frantically leaping Molly. "My classes go on all year. I get a couple of weeks off in June and August, then it's back to the grind. Not like the Regular Ed teachers who have to lead de-tasseling crews just to keep the money coming in."

"So you're staying busy," Ian chuckled. "Seen Jenny this summer?"

An odd look came over Paul's face.

"Some," he replied, as he clipped a black nylon leash to Molly's collar. "Looks like you're having a decent summer."

"Definitely better than my spring," Ian acknowledged. He reached over and squeezed Patsy on the shoulder.

"Amen to that," she agreed, then returned to focusing on her shot. Paul held the dog back while the Frisbee sailed smoothly over its target and landed several yards beyond.

"I did better with Molly's help," she joked. The threesome-plus-canine walked over to Ian's "ball," and he carefully flipped it into the chain basket. It took Patsy two more throws to accomplish this.

"That's it for me," she sighed. "Have you had dinner, Paul?"

"Molly and I did fast food on the way over." He leaned down and scratched the panting retriever on a silky ear. Ian grabbed the two Frisbees and the trio headed toward the wooded pathway separating that part of the forest preserve from the parking lot.

"We'll see you at the swim party, though?" Patsy pursued.

"Wouldn't miss it," he promised. "You know any of the Northern people?"

"Met Mitchell Christian at the Mardi Gras. Though Misty's been our prime contact," Ian told him. "He was the one who offered his place on the lake for a joint event. They're an actively social chapter. Of course, they don't have other social groups in their area—like Dillman's."

"Can't decide whether that's a blessing or not," Paul confessed. They emerged from the woods and headed across the grass. Before they even reached the lot it was obvious there was something wrong with Ian's car. Amidst a cluster of vehicles its top was tilting at an alarming angle. Ian tore across the lot, letting out a moan when he saw the source of its unfamiliar stance.

Both driver's side tires were utterly flat.

"LOOK, JUST BECAUSE A RESTAURANT is patronized by the gay community doesn't mean the food is any good."

"Yes. But don't you think it's important to be supportive in this day and age?"

"Depends on how hungry I am," Lissa answered decisively. She grabbed a butter knife and started slathering a slice of sweet Italian bread. "There are places I refuse to go into, of course. But I get impatient with the line that everything I do has to be for the 'betterment of the community.'"

"That can get tiring," Delia agreed. She looked around the ersatz Southern California setting and waved to a couple she recognized. "But it doesn't answer my original question—where are we going to hold the reception? That place where Joe Rivera works?"

"Caspar's," Lissa offered.

"It takes a while to get downtown," Delia mused. She took a sip of water, then grabbed a lemon slice from the center of the table, careful not to dip the sleeve of her Sue Brett jacket in the butter. "But maybe folks won't mind the drive from the ceremony. It's—what—a half hour?"

"Up to an hour if the traffic's a bear," Lissa considered. "But it's a good choice. Great food, a banquet room, suitable for all our friends. With some of them, just the idea of attending a lesbian 'wedding' is gonna be a big step."

Their meal arrived, and they paused to separate a few slices of vegetarian pizza.

"You having second thoughts about this?" Delia asked. "Or do you think we should scale back our plans? I mean, not everybody on our list will be completely comfortable with the idea of a formal union ceremony."

Lissa reached across the table and grasped Delia's hands.

"I've never been surer," she told her, raising a hand and bringing it to her lips. "Let's look into having the reception at Caspar's."

EPISODE SEVENTY–FIVE

THE **FURTHER NORTH THEY DROVE,** the more the sunny landscape looked like her neck of the woods—rural and homely, dotted with farms and weather-beaten barns. It was like the urban world that her sister inhabited was only a momentary blip on the map. This, to Cassie, seemed more powerful and lasting.

As they drove Cassie and Jen sang along with her Mamas and Papas tapes (though—due to her age, perhaps—Jenny seemed only familiar with the hits, not the equally rousing album cuts). Cass wasn't as nervous as she'd thought she'd be, driving to this party with her swimsuit under her jeans and T-shirt, meeting Jenny's fellow RADFAm group members, but maybe she was saving her panic for the moment when they actually arrived.

Jenny trailed off mid-chorus and once more pulled out the newsletter map. "We should be nearing the exit," she told her sister, pointing to a highway sign indicating a trio of gas stations a mile away. "We're gonna hafta keep our eyes open. The house is just off one of those country roads that doesn't have a name—just a number."

"Not to worry," Cassie told her. "I'm the queen of country roads."

As it happened, they had little difficulty finding the road to Mitchell Christian's house. It turned west between a knee-high cornfield and some woods. They turned onto the twisty, quarter-mile dirt road where Christian's mailbox heralded the event, gaily festooned with blue balloons and a large red-lettered arrow announcing "RADFAm."

As they bounced along Cassie surveyed the scenery appreciatively, relishing the clusters of wildflowers beside the lane. Ahead a lovely landscaped hill-ock, planted with perennials and topped with a tall flagpole flying Old Glory, hid the final curve to the house. Parked along the circular drive a generous cluster of cars lined up—including a familiar vehicle, Paul's little Metro.

"Isn't that Paul's compact?" Cassie blurted, then immediately wished she could retract her words. All week the mention of Paul Daily had been strange-ly taboo around Jenny. Cass's few attempts at bringing it up had been met with swift verbal feints and subject changes. Unsure how far to take it, Cassie had gone along with Jen's ploy.

She parked as close as she could behind Paul's car and disembarked, the sound of music wafting through the trees. Grabbing a cooler and two wooden lawn chairs, the two women made their way up the drive, Jenny pointing out other familiar vehicles as they went.

"Lissa's here. Don't recognize that one. Looks like Misty borrowed Joe's car for the day. Eleanor's here, too. So's—damn, that's Dillman's car!"

"Dillman?" Cassie asked, swerving to avoid a driveway rut.

"I was hoping you'd be spared him, at least your first time out," Jenny sighed. "He's one of our sleazier specimens—" The driveway meandered to the right, and they finally arrived at their destination: a log cabin ranch house with a spectacular lakefront vista. "Seems rustic is the theme of the day," Jenny observed wryly. *Not so much rustic,* Cassie secretly disagreed—*more like heavenly.*

The sounds of reggae and chitchat grew louder as they followed the arrows around the side of the house. A long cobbled path down the sloping backyard led to a sandy beach and long jutting pier; scattered throughout were clusters of men and women. Most of the latter, Cassie noted, made her look (and feel) like Allie McBeal.

Several women turned to wave at Jenny. Waist-deep in the water, Paul was standing and talking to a thin bespectacled man. The music was playing from a currently unattended karaoke machine supported on a card table. Near a phalanx of Weber grills a very large bottom-heavy blonde was seated, clad in a tropical pattern caftan, chatting happily to a curly-haired gent in a swimsuit and multi-Xed polo shirt. Between them stood a TV tray with a cashbox and two stacks of newsletters.

As they approached the couple Cassie guessed the woman's identity—this had to be the chapter president, Misty Shores. From the way she seemed to be flirting with her sumo-sized colleague, the other had to be her boyfriend Joe. But Jenny hadn't mentioned anything about Joe being fat, had she?

"Misty. Mitchell. I want you to meet my sister, Cassie," Jenny opened, clearing up the mystery. Misty and Mitchell were peers, then, though from the glances Jenny's friend kept shooting toward Christian, it was easy for Cassie to imagine something more involved.

"Jenny told us she was bringing you," Misty responded, a smile creasing her generously chinned face. Her sister had forewarned Cassie that the woman was "a bit New Agey," but the only obvious sign was a primitive looking female figure pendant dangling within her ample cleavage. "Sure glad you could make it. And welcome to our little oasis of size acceptance!"

"It looks—like fun," Cassie grinned tightly, glancing toward the boisterous groups cavorting on the beach and in the water.

"It's still early," Misty confided, as Jenny handed her the money for two tickets. "We're expecting at least twice as many more." She then looked toward Jenny and winked. "Paul's here already."

"So I see," Jenny murmured, a strained smile crossing her face. She then observed more brightly, "Looks as if Ian and Patsy have gotten back together." While they were checking in, Paul and his friend had been joined by a round blonde pixie in a strapless suit. She put an arm around Paul's friend in that universal gesture of girlfriend/boyfriend and hugged him demonstratively. Paul's friend responded with a tender kiss on her lips.

"Good to see," Misty answered. She turned toward Mitchell. "I think I told you about the *Winnie Harper* debacle."

"Not the best publicity RADFAm's ever received," Christian replied. He had, Cassie noted, one those deep, resonant voices she'd always found sexy—sort of like the Tennessee Ernie Ford records her foster parents would play. Not the gospel ones, the more mischievous-sounding country songs. No wonder Misty was making eyes at the man. "Even if it was recanted later. Nobody pays attention to retractions."

"Patsy has," Misty corrected, "and that's the one that matters."

Christian shrugged, and with that diffident gesture Cassie decided to also dismiss him. She hoped Misty's Joe was less pompous than this jerk.

"There's my boss," Jenny was saying, indicating a biracial female couple coming through the French doors leading onto the house's back patio. "C'mon, I've got to introduce you."

"Plenty of changing rooms inside the house," Christian shouted as Cassie let her sister drag her toward the pair. They were, she noted, holding hands. Jen had fortunately prepped her in advance for her boss's—differentness, too.

"Lissa! Delia! Here's the sib!" The two women stopped and waited for them on the patio. Jenny's boss Lissa was a striking mahogany-hued, hourglass-shaped woman. Her "friend" Delia she recalled from the week's shopping expeditions. If memory served, Cass had browsed the swimsuits at Delia's boutique. Both women looked closer to her age than Jenny's.

"About time you introduced us," Lissa chastised. "I swear you've been hiding her all week." She stepped forward and energetically shook Cass's hand. "Jenny been showing you the town?"

"S-some of it," Cassie stammered, finally hit by the full-fledged nervousness she'd been anticipating all day. "She's a wonderful—um—hostess."

"I wouldn't expect anything less of her," Lissa grinned. She turned back to Cass's sister. "Paul's here, you know," she said brightly. From the look in her eyes, though, Cass suspected that Lissa was being a lot less ingenuous than Misty had been.

"We haven't made it to the lake yet," Jenny replied. "Can we sit by you two after we get changed?" she asked, pulling Cassie toward the house.

"No problem," Lissa told them. "Catch you in a few."

They stepped into a rumpus room dominated by a large home entertainment center, passing a plumpish girl in a rather skimpy two-piece. "Where's the nearest bathroom?" Jenny asked. The girl indicated a door on the other side of the room. It was closed, so Jenny knocked.

"Uno momento!" a male voice told them.

"That's okay," Jenny shot back. "We'll find another room to change."

"No need," the handsome figure reassured them as he stepped out. Tall and lean with neatly coiffed hair and a calculatedly unshaven face, he looked like the male lead in a medical drama. "In my eyes, Jenny, you need never change." He flashed his teeth deliberately, and Cassie could have sworn they glinted in the fluorescent light.

"Greg," Jenny deadpanned. "You're looking good, as usual."

"You're looking better," the male model countered, turning his striking eyes toward Cassie. For an instant her legs felt very rubbery. "And who is your captivating companion?"

EPISODE SEVENTY-SIX

WHEN HE NOTICED JENNY AND HER SISTER coming out of Mitch Christian's house, it was all Paul could do to keep from leaping out of the lake and racing over to the blonde paralegal. Even from a distance she looked wonderful—a full-figured beach goddess. But if he'd learned anything from a week of unreturned phone calls, it was that a frontal approach was simply not going to work. Best to hold back, he thought; he'd already frightened her once.

Instead he turned back to Patsy, who was being effulgent about her new fulltime job, billing secretary for a suburban ophthalmologist.

"I used to say I enjoyed being a temp, since it gave me freedom to work when I wanted," she was telling Ian and Paul while picking a piece of lake-weed off her suit. "But now that I've got a job where I'll be eligible for vacation in six months—well, it feels pretty darn good."

"And it means you'll be able to take me out to dinner in a few weeks," Ian teased.

"Hey, that's okay," Patsy shot back as she touched his lips with a wet forefinger. "I've heard about how you FAs get your kicks outta feeding us fat chicks."

Ian stepped back to splash her in response. Instead Patsy turned and swam out toward the diving raft, which held several sunbathing RADFAmites. Whooping, Ian followed in pursuit.

Paul watched the two with a smile on his face. It was a propitious sign that Patsy was able to make jokes about a subject that had nearly destroyed their relationship less than a month ago.

An unexpected something in the lake (leech? piranha?) slid along his calf, so he beat retreat to his beach towel. Jenny, he saw, had hooked up with Lissa and Delia. Forgetting his earlier resolve, he picked up the towel and headed for the trio.

"Paul!" Lissa called happily. "Grab some sand and join us." All three women were seated in sturdy beach chairs. Jenny, he noted, was wearing the same sexy suit as at the lodge. Her sister was nowhere to be seen.

"If that's okay with y'all," Paul said, still standing with towel in hand.

"Sure," Jenny replied as Delia patted the ground reassuringly. Eyes masked by prescription sunglasses, Jenny's facial response was hidden, so he couldn't tell if her visage was as welcoming as her word.

"How's the water?" Lissa asked after he'd lowered himself onto his towel.

"Pleasant," Paul told the group. "I was expecting it to be a whole lot chillier. I'm afraid I've become spoiled by climate-controlled pools."

"Maybe we should check it out then, eh, Delia?"

"I'm game if you are," Delia answered, swiftly springing from her chair.

"Hey, Jenny, why don't you guard the cooler while we're gone?" Lissa yelled over her shoulder as she hustled after her lover.

"Whatever you say, boss lady," Jenny saluted as the two women splashed into the water. "Well," Jenny said, finally turning toward Paul. "That was subtle."

"If you don't want to talk—" Paul began.

"No—no, I do. Really," Jenny answered, taking off her sunglasses and blinking prettily as she met his eyes. "I haven't been very nice to you, or almost anyone else, over the past week. And to be honest, I'm not sure why."

"I wasn't fair to you," Paul offered. "I was coming on a bit too fast."

"Well, you did say what was in your heart, didn't you?"

Paul nodded seriously. She looked so lovely in the summer sun that he had to fight an overwhelming desire to take her in his arms, to forestall this achingly difficult dialog.

"It was true, and it still is," he finally said. "You're an extraordinary, once-in-a-lifetime woman. But I don't ever want you to feel like I'm pushing you. Your friendship is much too valuable for that."

"I'd say what we did that night took us beyond the category of 'friends,'" Jenny told him.

"Then what does that make us?"

"I don't know," she moaned. "You've had a big relationship in your past. I haven't. I'm not sure what we are."

"Well, staying apart won't help us find the answer," Paul said, moving off his blanket to get closer to her.

"I know," Jenny sighed, as he rose to his knees to grab her hand. "You're right." She looked out across the lake, softly squeezing his fingers. "Back—when my mother was still alive—I remember telling her once how I'd come to terms with being single. And I think I may have even begun to believe it. Then you came along and really messed that up."

"And that's a bad thing?" Paul smiled sheepishly.

"It's scary," she admitted.

"Oh." He let go of her hand and dropped back down to the sand. "First time I can ever remember being called scary," Paul said, half jokingly.

"And you call yourself a teacher?"

"By an adult, I mean," he corrected. "Okay, then. So what about 'us'?"

She leaned toward him and gently kissed his lips. "I'm not sure," she told him. "Let's just go where time takes us."

That would do for now, Paul decided.

"LOOKS LIKE A GOOD TURNOUT," Lainie noted as she handed a ten-dollar bill to Misty. Beside her Eleanor Bollen was shielding her eyes and squinting across the beach. She looked like an explorer surveying some strange and opulent land.

"Yes, it is," Misty agreed. "We need to do these duo-chapter events more often."

"We saw Dex's car," Eleanor interrupted. "But I don't see him anywhere."

"He's probably inside," Mitchell explained. "Got a video from the convention fashion show running in the rec room. He may be watching that."

"Neeko's with him," Misty added significantly, and she could see Eleanor deflate. There were days, Misty thought, when she just wanted to take the woman and shake her.

"That's nice," Eleanor mumbled, and she turned back to her friend Lainie.

"Joe have to work again?" Lainie asked.

"Yeah," Misty sighed. "He thought he'd made arrangements, but something came up at the last minute."

"That's too bad," Lainie sympathized. "We haven't seen much of him lately."

"Neither have I," Misty groused. "But let's not dwell on that. It's too nice a day."

Thankfully, Lainie was the type of woman who knew when not to push a topic. "Look," she said mischievously. "Lissa and Delia are actually in the water. Who'd have thought that Lissa would be Back-to-Nature Girl?" She led the crestfallen Eleanor toward the beach, leaving Misty alone once again with Mitchell.

"I had to find a replacement for the weekend, myself," the northern chapter president confided. "And it wasn't easy finding someone who could fit into my costume."

"Costume?"

"I do the Renaissance Faire thing during the summer," Christian explained. "Just an 'umble innkeeper, milady, that's me."

Misty looked the rotund academic up and down, trying to imagine him in innkeeper's garb. Take away the bottle of Snapple in his right hand, and it was a breeze. The image was pretty appealing.

Ever since she'd arrived to help set up the beach party, Misty had found herself attracted to her northern co-leader. Though they'd previously met on more than one occasion, for some reason it was like she'd never seen the man before. Mitchell Christian looked so big and nurturing, so strong and stable, that he drew out impulses she didn't even know she possessed.

His round, clean-shaven face had an open mien that meshed nicely with the deepness of his voice. It was the face of a man who would not be afraid to try new things, but who also knew that he had clear boundaries in the way he wanted to live his life. A life which looked, she thought, so much more adult than Joe's.

And she was acting like a twittery coed around him. She bet he'd confused more than one young girl in his Business Ed classes, had spawned more than one lustful fantasy in the minds of young women who'd believed all their lives that fat was unsexy. But she had to regain control of herself.

"I've always wanted to do a Renaissance Faire," she mused. "Set up a tent with a crystal ball, say. Do you think I could make a convincing medieval gypsy?"

"I think you'd make a lovely medieval gypsy," Mitchell assured her. Misty felt herself flush beneath her caftan. Off by the beach the karaoke was playing a wordless version of "La Vida Loca."

What the hey, she thought, *it's only a little harmless flirting.*

EPISODE SEVENTY-SEVEN

ALTHOUGH SHE'D ORIGINALLY staked out her end of the couch to avoid being seen in her swimsuit by all Jenny's friends, Cassie found herself engrossed by the big-screen TV. Along with two other modest partygoers she was viewing a videotape of the fashion show from last spring's convention. Torn between admiration and embarrassment, she was unable to stop comparing her own fat form with the ones parading proudly around the RADFAm luncheon. Occasionally she'd spy her sister at a table in the background, chatting happily with Paul, totally unaware of the rocky times to come.

Lingerie was now on display—and one of her fellow couch companions gleefully identified herself (apparently, these two weren't quite as modest as Cassie thought). "Oh, baby, baby," her friend giggled as the girl vogued seductively for the videocam. "Does yo mama know you go out dressed like that?" The model playfully punched her shoulder. Her two-piece swimsuit, Cassie couldn't help noticing, was not nearly as provocative as the lacy teddy she modeled on tape.

"My Dillmanwear," the girl—whose name was Sonya—joked. "You should have seen Greggy stand at attention when I modeled it for him later, up close and personal."

"You and Greg were—um—an item?" her friend gasped in mock horror. "You never told me!"

"Oh, just that one night," the teddy girl confided. "Thank Gawd." She paused to take a sip from an anonymous flask. "Of course, these days Connie wouldn't let him off leash long enough for even a one-nighter."

Her friend nodded knowingly. "Wouldn't want to get between Connie and her 'property,'" she replied, accepting the proffered flask. "Greg might act like the King of Studs, but right now he's neutered, and there are simply some women that it isn't healthy to cross."

"Well, he sure ain't royalty," Sonya joked, lowering her voice, "but he's no peon either. Knows how to wield his scepter, I can tell you, but that's all there is to it. I mean, what d'ya talk about in the morning? Besides him, that is."

As they continued to chatter, Cassie surmised that "Connie" must be the woman who'd yanked Greg away from her twenty minutes ago. Just as he was introducing himself she'd swooped down the stairs and spirited him off. With a man as strikingly handsome as that, Cassie couldn't really blame her. Just one glimpse of those male model features and she'd felt like an awkward adolescent again.

"Well, you definitely don't wanna piss off the Queen of the Scene," Sonya's friend declared. "She'd mop the floor with both of us, just for kicks."

"Speak of the devil—there she is," Sonya hissed softly, indicating an imposing figure on the videotape, standing behind a podium and describing the couture. This Connie had been the woman with Greg.

"Think she can hear you on the tape?"

"Well, I don't think she's that powerful—"

The video stopped just as a striking midsized woman was heading for the podium. "That's it for the fashion show," Sonya announced. The two young women rose and Sonya winked knowingly at Cassie. Then they headed for the patio door, leaving Cass alone.

She leaned back on the couch, considering their words. Seemed to her that Jenny had mentioned this Connie person in connection with Paul, but she couldn't quite remember how. Sighing, she steeled herself to join the party. As she rose to follow the girls out the sliding glass door onto the deck, she heard a husky feminine voice behind her. Cassie turned to see a stunning dark-haired figure draped in a brightly embroidered black pashmina shawl over a lowcut shimmering swimsuit. Connie, subject of so much comment, stalked down the stairs with Greg Dillman in tow.

"Hope you weren't paying too much attention to those two little grrlz," she opened, giving that last syllable a sardonic twist as she extended a flawlessly manicured hand toward Cass. "I'm Connie Donovan."

In the background Greg was watching this interaction with a pasty smile on his face. His gaze unaccountably made Cassie nervous.

"I wasn't really listening to them," she muttered in return. "I was just enjoying the fashion show."

"Oh, that," Connie laughed airily. "I must admit that the event was good publicity for my store. I gained several new regulars after that show."

Still holding Cass's hand, she escorted her toward the door. "You're Jenny's sister, aren't you?" she asked conversationally. There was something about the woman's voice that told you she knew so much more than you ever could, and for some reason Cassie found herself mesmerized, wordlessly allowing this familiarity. "I've got to tell you—that girl has brought some much-needed youth to this chapter."

Could she pull free before the woman actually propelled her outside? Nope, no way to do it without being unpardonably rude, Cass decided. So they left the dark safety of the house, emerging into the bright and unforgiving afternoon sunlight.

The beach was much more crowded than it'd been when they'd arrived, but somehow Cass felt less self-aware in Connie's presence. A large bearded man with a tiny Oriental companion walked by. He waved to Connie, but she didn't seem to notice.

"You going to give the karaoke machine a try?" Connie was asking. "We're looking for a BBW with a good singing voice."

"'We'?"

"Connie and I are the brains behind Full-Figured Friends," Greg interjected, then stopped as his fellow brain shot him a look.

"One of the city's other size acceptance organizations," Connie explained, "or maybe I should say 'size celebration.' 3F's latest project is a Big Beauty Talent Contest, and we're looking for some creative people to join us. Greg brought the karaoke machine today so folks could do some impromptu auditions. We really need a first-rate vocalist to sing the contest's theme song—someone who also embodies the ideals of big and beautiful womanhood." She guided Cassie across the lawn, and before Cass knew it the trio had arrived at the music machine.

"What makes you think I can sing?" Cassie asked Greg, who was proffering a mic.

"Greg heard you while you were changing into your swimsuit," Connie confided, grimacing. "Let's just skip over the fact that he was hanging around your bathroom door and get to the important stuff—according to him, you can sing."

"By myself, sure. Or at church, in a choir," Cassie muttered. "But I've never done it in public. Alone."

"A shy fat girl," Connie responded, smiling. Greg's answering smirk left Cass feeling foolish about her initial bedazzlement. "What are the odds? I'd have thought differently, considering that pair you were hanging out with earlier." The brunette cocked her head impishly. "Or perhaps you just don't want to sing for us?" she wheedled.

"Oh no, that's not it," Cassie heard herself protesting. She looked around for her sister, hoping that she might suddenly rescue her from this situation. But Jenny was facing the other direction, engrossed in something Paul was saying. No way would she interfere in that particular conversation.

She examined the machine more closely. It looked like a glorified boom-box cum tiny TV, which was now scrolling lyrics to the accompanying instrumental version of "American Pie."

"What kind of selection does this thing have?" Cass finally squeaked.

"Depends on what you're looking for," Greg winked. At that moment Paul suddenly noticed them and directed Jenny's attention their way. Her sister rose as if to join them, so Cass blurted out the first thing that came to mind.

"Got anything by Mama Cass?"

EPISODE SEVENTY-EIGHT

CASS NERVOUSLY SQUINTED AT THE LYRICS on the too-small monitor as the opening bars began, the mike feeling plastic and sticky in her hand, letters wavering before her on the bright yellow background. *You know the words,* she tried to tell herself. *It's your favorite song. You've sung it hundreds of times.* But at that moment it felt like some obscure national anthem.

All around the beach partiers were cavorting and chatting, oblivious to her impending humiliation. Standing behind the monitor, Greg Dillman and Connie Donovan were silently waiting for their victim to begin. Why had she let them drag her over here, anyway? Her throat felt parched and dry—incapable of speech, let alone song.

But then as the tinny electronic notes approached her opening, Cass summoned her courage and tentatively began to sing.

"Stars shining bright above you—"

MISTY WAS CONTEMPLATING PHONING JOE at the restaurant when Cass started in on her song. The party was in full swing and it didn't look like there'd be that many more newcomers, so it seemed like a good time for a break. But instead, as Jenny's sister haltingly hit the first verse, both Misty and Mitchell rotated in their chairs to watch.

In a way the distraction was welcome—it had begun to feel as if she'd perhaps taken the flirtation thing with Mitchell a tad too far.

Misty's northern compeer took note of Greg and Connie standing by the karaoke and observed, "Looks like Greg's finally convinced someone to audition for the Big Beauty Contest. She sure seems pretty nervous."

"Say nighty-night and kiss me—

"Just hold me tight and tell me you'll miss me."

Nervous was an understatement, Misty thought—Cass looked like she was facing a firing squad. From what she could hear so far, though, the girl's fears were largely unfounded. Cass's voice was pretty, even if her delivery seemed a bit thin. Only the nearest partygoers seemed to even notice she was singing.

"So Greg's been trying to sell the event to you, too?" she asked Mitch, eyes still on Jenny's sister. "I hope you haven't taken him up on it."

"Actually," Mitchell Christian answered, "I thought I'd bring it to the chapter at large, see if folks are interested. A beauty pageant could really be a lot of fun. And hard work."

"It would for you," Misty heard herself warning, "if Greg Dillman is your partner."

Though she wasn't facing him, Misty could tell that Mitch was giving her a questioning look. Perhaps she should've been a bit more diplomatic. She kept her eyes on Cassie, who was gathering both voice and confidence in the song's second verse.

"Sounds like you may have a few issues with the man," Christian pursued. "Anything I should know about?"

Misty paused a few bars to consider her answer. "Not really," she finally hedged. "It's just that Greg can talk a good event, but when it comes time to actually help move the furniture, he's nowhere to be found."

"Warning duly noted," Mitch chuckled. "I think we've got enough bodies to take up the slack. But thanks for the forewarning. It's nice to know what to expect."

"Get any financial agreements nailed out upfront. And in writing," Misty added, willing herself to say no more. At the karaoke Cassie was diving into the song's chorus. In that moment Misty flashed to the night she'd dressed as Cass Elliot while Joe had gone as the chef from a can of spaghetti. She smiled at the memory of him in his noncostume.

She'd call him when the song was over, Misty decided.

"STARS FADING, *but I linger on, dear,*
  "Still craving your kiss—"

Eyes closed, no longer relying on the monitor for the words, Cass was immersed in her song. Keeping the world at bay, concentrating only on the song, she'd somehow managed to banish her initial moments of panic.

Though her parents would have been appalled at the suggestion, it felt almost as if she was channeling every plus-sized songstress—Mama Cass, Ella Fitzgerald—-who'd ever sung these words before her. Even the karaoke machine seemed to have lost its tinny resonance—as her confidence grew it bolstered even the sound of the music behind her.

"I'm longing to linger 'til dawn, dear—"

"YOUR SISTER'S GOT QUITE A VOICE," Paul told Jenny approvingly.

It sounded, he decided, less like the late Mama Cass and closer to one of her contemporaries—Spanky McFarland, the Midwestern folk-rocker who at one time had even replaced the beloved Miz Elliot in a short-term revival of the Mamas and Papas. Either way, Jenny's sister was a surprisingly effective vocalist.

Watching Cassie lost in her song, you could even see hints of the same striking beauty that her sister carried so un-self-consciously.

"She does," Jenny agreed, and Paul could hear the surprise in her voice. "This is actually the first time I've heard it."

All across the beach, partygoers had quieted to hear Cass finish her love song. A few male RADFAmites even appeared to really focus on the plus-sized chanteuse for the first time. Off to the side, Greg and Connie were exchanging knowing glances.

"But in your dreams whatever they be,
"Dream a little dream of me."

Paul and Jenny rose together to get a closer look at Cassie. Without so much as a second thought they clasped each other's nearest hand and hustled across the beach. By the time they'd reached Cass (and she had reached the end of her song), Paul realized what they'd both just unconsciously done.

The Couple Walk.

As the music faded they eagerly led the applause. Across the beach scattered clapping could also be heard. Misty and Mitchell enthusiastically joined the accolade as, out in the water, Lissa and Delia whooped appreciatively.

Cassie looked startled to see them—almost as if she'd forgotten where she was—then beamed at her sister and Paul. Jenny rushed up to the karaoke diva and hugged her in congratulations. Cass looked over her shoulder toward Paul, grinning and whispering something into her sister's ear. Jenny blushed attractively.

Then Greg was swooping down on the two women as they separated. "Jenny," he boomed. "Why on earth have you kept this captivating songbird away for so long? And please don't tell me she's the only singer in the family—I'd love to see you two as a sister act."

I'll bet, Paul thought but didn't comment.

"The only notes I can carry are Post-It Notes," Jenny demurred. "Cass is the talented one here."

"Definitely talented," Dillman agreed, cupping his hands over Cass's hands and microphone demonstratively. Cassie started blushing even more emphatically than her sister.

Looks like she's more than a little attracted to Greg, Paul noted with misgiving. Standing behind her, Connie was smiling with a predatory air. Had she ever looked at him that way? A shiver ran through him, belying the warm summer weather.

"I just like to sing," Cass murmured, her shyness returning. Jenny put an arm across her shoulder protectively, warily eyeing the insurance man. But of course Greg was not going to be that easily dissuaded.

"It's obvious that you do," he pursued. "I could hear it in every note. But I hope this won't be the last time we get to hear your voice. It'd be a shame to deprive others of such a gift."

"Greg's right," Connie interjected, edging into Cass's view, blocking Paul from both sisters. "With your voice, diva-hood is only a few good fashions away. And I know exactly where to find them." She cocked her head in Jenny's direction. "You really must bring your sister to my shop," she urged. "Unless you're worried about Cassie here stealing your thunder?"

"Not in the least," Jenny replied in the same pleasant tone that lawyers reserve for their opponents at the outset of a trial. "Sounds to me like you and Greg have something planned. Care to enlighten us?"

"Oh, it's all still in the works," Greg answered innocently. "But I'm sure you've heard that we're working on a Full-Figured Friends Beauty Pageant. And what's a pageant without a pageant theme song?"

"You have a pageant theme song?" Paul asked, amazed. Who'd ever have guessed that Greg Dillman could turn to be a closet Burt Bacharach?

"Well, the start of one," Dillman assured them. "And if everything comes together, I think I can hear The Divine Miz Cassie opening the pageant with it. What do you say, Cass? You're not gonna let your sister squirrel you away again, are you?"

"Don't worry," Cass answered, surprising both Jenny and Paul with the sudden firmness of her response. "I plan to be around."

EPISODE SEVENTY-NINE

ASPAR APPEARED ACROSS THE ANCIENT, scarred butcher block just as Joe finished frenching the rib tips of a particularly nice pork crown roast. This meaty entrée was to be the centerpiece for a 50th wedding anniversary party, and Joe had been ultra-nervous during the meticulous preparations.

As he'd focused on the knifework his mind had repeatedly wandered back to the celebrants—a comfortable elderly couple who both belied the assertion that there are no old fat people—almost as if they were members of his own family. The idea of such a successful longterm relationship as this couldn't help but get him wondering where he and Misty might be in fifty years.

"You are truly an artist," Caspar reassured him, carefully appraising his work. "Some day, much too soon, you'll head off on your own, and it's just gonna break my heart."

Joe blushed, brushing off his boss's compliment by changing the subject. "So you think the Heywoods'll be satisfied?"

"If they aren't, they're soulless," Caspar declared. He indicated a generous bowl of drunken currant and pecan stuffing to the right. "Misty's on the line—if you want, I can finish getting this ready for the oven."

Joe grinned, leaving his boss to finish preparing the crown roast. The most private phone this time of day was at the reservations desk near the entrance, and he crossed the restaurant, skirting mid-afternoon diners and nodding at a few familiar faces.

As he reached the phone he saw that Jimmy was just arriving for work. "We have to talk," he mouthed at his brother, who shrugged and dashed into the back to retrieve his busboy's jacket.

Late again, Joe sighed. He was starting to regret even bringing Jim into the restaurant. All he did was complain about not being allowed to wait tables yet. "That's where the money is," he'd grouse. And no matter how many times Joe repeated that everyone started out bussing ("Be thankful it isn't dishwashing," he'd mentioned at one point, though Jim's only response had been a scornful "As if I'd take that job!"), his brother remained childishly impatient.

"Joe? You okay?" Misty was asking over the receiver. "I could hear your sigh all the way up here. Without the phone."

"Yeah, just wondering why my older brother still has to be such a kid," he replied. "How's the beach party?"

"You know what these things are like," Misty answered somewhat ruefully. "Greg's been slithering around, trying to drum up interest in that beauty pageant of his."

"What else is new? Attendance good? You having a good time?"

"Wish you were here," she confessed, and Joe could hear her pout over the phone line. "But I'm just being a lonely little girl."

"Never little," Joe joked, "but I understand 'lonely.' I've been plenty busy here lately. Maybe I can talk Caspar into giving me a night off. And the sooner the better."

"I'd sure like that," Misty agreed. "I'm—" Her voice trailed off tentatively.

"What?"

292

"Nothing," she answered sheepishly. "Stop by the apartment when you get off work tonight though, okay?"

"You can count on it," Joe reassured her. The phone clicked off, and he stood considering her words.

"Stop by the apartment." He wouldn't just be "stopping by" if he'd agree to Misty's building renovation plans, to moving into her expanded apartment.

It'd been over a month since she'd first broached the subject—and he'd just been putting off a decision ever since. Why? What was he afraid of? They were already spending most of their free time together, anyway. What was holding him back?

Sighing deeply again, at himself this time, Joe headed back to the kitchen and his golden anniversary roast.

ON THE SCREEN a twenty-something actress Jackie vaguely remembered from one of those chick series his sister liked was slowly tiptoeing down a dark sorority house corridor. Over the theater's THX sound system the growing sound of thunder could be heard—then a loud clatter as something dashed out in front of the camera. The victim-to-be lived up to the movie's title (*Shriek and Shriek Again*) by loudly yelling in terror. Beside him Sandra nearly spilled the last of their buttered popcorn.

"Oops!" she tittered as several pieces flew onto Jackie's lap. He looked over toward Sandy, who smiled back at him. In the movie dimness her face looked even thinner than usual—a trick of the light probably. "Want me to get that?" she whispered flirtatiously, pointing to a solitary kernel left on his lap. Jackie blushed, jerked suddenly and lost the greasy morsel as it rolled off his leg. "Never mind," she giggled, just as the forgotten movie victim let out a second shriek.

Jackie reached into their popcorn box. Though she'd put up a huge protest at the snack stand, it looked like Sandra had scarfed down most of its contents. Grabbing a small remnant, he bit into an unpopped old maid and returned to the movie. Girls could sure be funny about eating, he decided.

Without a word, Sandra rose from her seat.

"Where you goin'?"

"Girl's room," she whispered. "Want me to get you anything?"

"I'm okay," Jackie reassured her, rescuing the rest of the popcorn box. He watched her sidle down the aisle, then turned back to the movie. Onscreen a masked stalker was peering through the trees toward a bikini-briefed coed in her bedroom.

His first official date with Sandy—her parents had driven them to the mall theater, while his folks were off at another dumb fat party. It seemed to be going okay—at least as far as he could tell—the lap joke seemed to be a good sign, though who knows what he would've done if she'd actually reached for his leg.

She was gone through two whole slayings, barely making it back in time for the big showdown between the movie heroine and her slasher attacker. In the dark he could still detect a whiff of cinnamon breath spray.

Why had Sandy taken so long? Jackie wasn't sure he wanted to know the answer.

THE PACKAGE WAS WAITING FOR HIM when Ian got back from the chapter beach party. He was just stopping at home for a quick shirt change—then a dinner date with Patsy—when the parcel ambushed him.

Hidden from street view on the other side of the front door's concrete steps, the box looked large enough to contain a good-sized computer monitor. Standing on the sidewalk, Ian rifled through his memory for any mail orders he might've made, but came up blank. Once he'd lugged the box inside and read the return address label, he knew it was nothing he'd ordered.

A look inside the box confirmed his suspicions.

Underneath the flaps was a bright plastic bag with the legend "Welcome to our newest distributor!" emblazoned across the front. Below, in a finely brushed font, were the initials JLE—the logo for Jordan Lewis Enterprises.

"What the hell?"

Ian lifted the sealed plastic bag. Beneath it was a pile of brochures and booklets, plus several plain-wrapped cartons of packaged food and a small postal scale. Tearing the bag open, Ian inspected its contents. His worst suspicions were confirmed.

"Welcome to our newest distributor!" the cover letter also trumpeted, and went on to describe the benefits of becoming a purveyor of Jordan Lewis's diet line. "You have just enlisted in the anti-fat army. A select group of men and women doing their part to make the nation healthier—and making a great living for themselves in the process!"

Stapled to the letter was a copy of an invoice. The whole thing, he realized, had been billed to his MasterCard: $125 membership fee plus an additional $75 worth of product samples, not to mention postage and handling.

Sickly dropping the pile of papers back into the box, scattering a batch of blank order forms in the process, Ian trudged into the living room and plopped down in the nearest chair.

He sat for a few seconds, considering the speed with which his day could go from exceptionally good to utter shit. There weren't, he realized, many folks who had access to his credit card number, even less with a reason to indulge in such a harassing prank. One obvious suspect remained—his former lover, Val.

EPISODE EIGHTY

AFTER PERUSING THE MENU long enough to memorize it, Lissa gave the elaborately pierced and studded waitress her order. "Grilled portabella mushroom sandwich, please," she told the slender young girl. "Closest thing to a hamburger this place offers," she confided to Jenny once the waitress was out of earshot. "Delia's been bugging me to eat meatless more often. And here I thought I was doing so good, cutting back on fried—"

"There's always the Harvest Burgers if you want a meatless sandwich," Jenny grinned. "They almost taste like meat."

"'Almost' just don't cut it," Lissa groused. She scornfully surveyed the vegetarian restaurant, taking in the ersatz Third World atmosphere—willfully primitive artwork and too-loud Brazilian samba music on the loudspeakers, the tables filled with couples dressed in suburban/academic casual—then lifted her purse off a neighboring chair to retrieve the folder beneath. "I tell you, my ol' mammy didn't raise me to eat like this."

"Well, neither did mine," Jenny agreed. "In my house gourmet dining meant paying fifty cents extra for Stouffer's instead of Swanson's." She nodded toward the manila folder Lissa had opened. "Is that my evaluation?" she inquired nonchalantly.

"Just a few notes," Lissa replied, waving a yellow pad at the young paralegal. "Didn't want to forget anything, after all." She impishly studied the pad for a few seconds while Jenny tried not to squirm too much. Then she slapped it face down on the table and simply stated, "You've been doing great, Jen. Keep it up."

For a moment Jenny didn't know whether to feel relieved or pissed off. She finally opted for the first choice. "That's it?"

"S'all I've got to say about your work, Jen. Every day I feel grateful that you're here to help me. I'd be lost without your expert support."

"Well, that was painless. Plus I get a free meal out of it."

"If you call this a meal," Lissa mumbled, then continued briskly. "But I do have something I wanted to talk to you about, so don't breathe easy just yet." She paused to let the waitress set down their water and a tiny dish of lemon slices. "How are things with Paul?"

Jenny colored slightly. Unfolding her napkin as if stalling for time, she spread it over her white silk skirt and cleared her throat. "Why do you ask?" she finally ventured, knowing that this—not a perfunctory performance evaluation—was the real reason she'd been invited out to lunch.

"Saw you together at the beach party, and it looked like at least you were talking again," Lissa opened. "If you want to tell me to go to hell, do so—but I've gotta ask, what's going on with you two, anyway?"

"Me being panicky," Jenny sighed. "Paul used the 'L' word on our Starved Rock weekend, and it kicked off my fight-or-flight response. I thought that was supposed to be a 'guy' thing. I sure didn't think it could happen to me."

"Oh," Lissa answered. "It's a 'fat chick' thing, too. You're told all your life that if you stay fat you'll never find a person who'll love you—so when the possibility actually arises, it's scary.

"Now I'm gonna bring up my girlfriend, but please don't tell her that I did. For years, Delia tried to deny her heart—she was so terrified of those feelings that she glued herself to the straightest damned woman she knew, Connie Donovan. But you saw what she was like around Connie—bitchy, sycophantic and unhappy. Fear'll do that to you.

"Part of you still believes your mother—that you're simply not 'worthy' of a man like Paul—and that's a dead end. I don't know if you and Paul are 'It' or not. But I know that you're gonna spend the rest of your life wondering, if you do chicken out." Lissa grinned and noticed their waitress approaching with a basket of chips and salsa. "Maybe I shouldn't use the word 'chicken' in a place like this, eh?"

"No, it's apt," Jenny replied. "I know I'm not only being unfair to Paul, I'm also cheating myself." She smiled in thanks at the waitress, then sat back and tapped her fingers together. "So enough with the relationship lecture—is a COLA in my future?"

Lissa chuckled. "It's been a very good year for our little firm," she began. "So I think you'll be pleasantly surprised—"

THE SITE WAS VISIBLE FROM THE TOLLWAY, a faux castle festooned with neon-lit fiberglass banners spanning the parapets that proclaimed *Joust for You.* Joe hit the exit just a little too sharply, the impetus momentarily pressing Misty against the passenger door.

The parking lot was packed, so Joe dropped her off at the canopied entrance, then went off to scout a free space.

Settling onto a gothicly uncomfortable concrete bench, Misty waited and wondered—not for the first time—what prompted this excursion. Joe had sprung it on her late that afternoon. "I'm off tonight, and I've made reservations at a place I think you'll really like. Pick you up at five."

When she'd pointed out that she wouldn't have time to change after work, Joe had simply chuckled and said, "You're wearing one of your 'mystic shopkeep' dresses, aren't you? Believe me, you'll fit in just fine."

It turned out Joe was right—the astrological patterns on her peasant blouse were definitely in keeping with these environs. She might even be, Misty thought, the previously undiscovered sister to, say, Merlin. A young couple scrutinized her closely as they strode toward the towering iron-clad doors, as if trying to figure whether she were some hired castle wench.

"Hey, Babe," she called out to the approaching Joe, tacitly revealing herself as just a fellow customer. Joe sped to a trot and quickly reached her side.

"We've got some time until the show starts," he observed, pulling two tickets from his wallet and handing them to the suitably medieval booth attendant. "Want to wander through the exhibits?"

The "exhibits" turned out to be a series of vendor cases—heavy on the pewter, if you please. The small display of crystals got Misty doing some price and quality comparisons. Gauging the inflationary prices, it was all she could do to keep herself from telling customers "Don't buy that; I've got much nicer pieces in my shop!"

Considering the cost of the tickets, it probably wouldn't be good to embarrass Joe and get them both kicked out. Since none of the merchandise caught her eye, and she had absolutely no interest paying extra to visit the mock dungeon cum torture chamber, Misty convinced Joe to find the line to their designated Great Hall entrance. There they waited, enjoying the spectacle of juggling jesters, dark-cloaked mages and regally robed gentry mingling with suburban commoners in Disney-and-other corporate wear.

"Dinner and a show," they soon enough discovered, was barbecue, served sans cutlery, within a cavernous stadium while displays of equestrian and falconry mastery and smartly choreographed jousting competitions played out for the crowd's edification.

It all reminded Misty of professional wrestling—in suits of armor instead of spandex—though she really did enjoy watching the horses and hawks perform. The stadium seating was pretty uncomfortable, but she'd endured worse. Each time she looked over at Joe, she'd catch him watching her with an intense, unreadable expression.

"You look like you've got something to say," she mentioned at one point between jousts.

"Not yet," Joe countered, which, of course, only served to pique her curiosity even further.

Joe remained his usual reserved self throughout the remainder of the performance. In fact, it wasn't until they were waiting in the parking lot for the crush of cars to move out that he actually asked her opinion of Joust for You.

"It was OK," Misty told him, "though I think you've spoiled me when it comes to good food—that meal should have stayed in the Dark Ages. And I could've done without most of the over-the-top heraldic histrionics.

"In the plus column, the equestrian events were magnificent, and I've always wanted to hunt with a hawk on my wrist. Thanks for the vicarious thrill." She reached over to stroke his thigh lovingly. "But I can't help but wonder—what made you think of this place, anyway?"

"Just thought you might enjoy it," Joe answered. "I heard you talking about Renaissance Faires the other day, so it seemed like a good idea." They drove in silence for a few minutes. "So was it?" he finally asked.

"Yes," Misty decided. "Though next time let me know what you're thinking. Those tickets were pretty damned pricey!"

"Well, I've been working a lot," he responded, "and what's the point of working if you can't spend the fruits of your labor on your Faire Lady Friend?"

Whew, Misty thought. For Joe, that was practically poetic! Smiling, she watched him drive. She felt happy in a way she'd rarely felt before.

They got back home around midnight. As they walked past Kirk's apartment she thought she could hear him on the other side of his door, shushing Howlie and the cats. Unlocking her apartment, she could quickly see why he'd been waiting up. In the middle of the living room, sitting on an end table that Kirk must have moved for maximum effect, sat a large vase of white roses. And beside the vase, resplendent in white ribbon bow, lay a shiny new crowbar.

She turned toward Joe, who had remained in the doorway, beaming. He looked so proud and cherubic, young, yet profoundly sexy. Stepping into the apartment, he grabbed her fleshy shoulders and twirled her toward the wall that currently separated her apartment from Kirk's.

"Are you sure you're ready for this?" he asked, raising her plump hand to his lips and gently kissing it.

"Oh, yes, Joe," she declared wholeheartedly as he circled around for a fuller embrace. "I am!"

EPISODE EIGHTY-ONE

ENTERING THE FOYER of Jordan Lewis Enterprises' suburban Distribution Center, Ian couldn't help but feel uncomfortable. He considered the man a flimflam artist of the lowest order, and now here he was, walking into the Citadel of Dietary Charlatanism. The sounds of chittering keyboards and too-perky processing clerks set his left eyelid twitching.

Shifting the bulky carton in his arms, he slowly approached the reception desk. Seated behind it was an Olive Oyl-ish black woman wearing a formfitting sleeveless summer top. She hoisted a finely etched eyebrow inquisitorially as Ian deposited the carton on her desk.

"This was sent to me in error," he told her. "I'd like to return it and have the bill expunged from my credit card."

The woman examined him suspiciously. "We don't usually get returns 'in error,'" she said. "The agreement clearly states that signing up for a Jordan Lewis Distributorship is a financial commitment."

"I never signed an agreement," Ian replied, working to stay as polite as he could. He pulled the invoice from his sports jacket and spread it on the countertop. "This just showed up on my doorstep."

"Let me see," the receptionist said. Peremptorily snatching the sheet from his hands, she suspiciously examined the document, looking for all the world like someone who had just received an irritating and inconvenient subpoena. "Says here that you signed up. It's got your credit card number."

"I never signed any agreement," Ian persisted. "If you've got it on record, then pull the document, and we'll compare signatures."

"That'll take some real digging," Olive Oyl responded, and you could hear the measure of pride she felt imparting this information. *No need to be pissed at her,* Ian reminded himself. *She's just doing her job, and probably thinks she's doing the world a service in the bargain.* "You have no idea how many orders we receive every day."

"I'm sure I don't," Ian agreed. "But I'd still like to get this expunged from my MasterCard bill." He smiled what Patsy told him was his most winning expression (though every time he accidentally caught himself doing it he thought he looked like he'd just stepped on a nail). The receptionist relented, coyly returning his smile.

"Let me just make a quick copy of this," she told him, before vanishing around the edge of the partition.

"Okay," Ian replied, peering after her into the depths of the clerical pool. Beyond the copy machine he wasn't really surprised to see, seated at a desk and chatting with a coworker, his old girlfriend Val. In an instant, without forethought, he was standing in front of her desk.

A flash of—was that panic?—betrayed her before she could mask her true face. Swiveling her desk chair toward him, she ran an extravagantly well-manicured set of nails through her striped hair, then put on a professionally courteous mien. "Why, Ian, what brings you here?"

"You, Val, as if you didn't know."

Valerie cast a glance toward her coworker, a young collegiate-looking blonde with more earrings than you would have thought possible in her right ear and a diamond stud in her nose.

Great, Ian realized, *Val's playing to an audience.*

"Why, Ian," Val grinned, fanning herself as if fending off an attack of the vapors. "I didn't know you still felt that way about me! Sorry, love, but I'm seeing someone else now. And he gets pretty jealous."

"That's not what I'm talking about, and you know it," Ian hissed. "I'm talking about you signing me up to be a distributor for this boondoggle. It's called credit card fraud, Val. But mostly I'm just getting really sick of your games—"

"'Games'?" Val echoed, looking puzzled. "I haven't the foggiest idea what you're talking about." A tiny smile appeared on the edge of her Fuchsia Mist lips. "But if you're interested in becoming a JLE distributor, I'm sure we can work out a good deal."

Before he had time for a retort, the receptionist was by his side. "Mr. Johnson. You shouldn't be back here." Handing him back his invoice, she turned to lead him away from the clerical area, but not before Ian shot a parting verbal shot:

"No more bullshit, Val. I mean it!"

She smiled and gave him a twiddling wave. Ignoring the receptionist's imprecations, Ian snorted and stormed out the pneumatic door.

JACKIE HAD JUST SOLVED the Mr. Creosote puzzle, clicking the wafer thin mint as his reward and feeling relief at getting through this phase of the Monty Python computer game. (The sequence was not one that he especially wanted his father to walk in on, particularly since its object was the ridicule of a vomiting fat man.) Just as Mr. C. exploded on the monitor his sister entered the room. Jackie noted her presence, then returned to the computer to let the sequence run through.

"Playing the game Davey burned for ya?" Rachel asked, once he pivoted in his chair to face her. "Mom wants you to come down for dinner. Turkey ham/yam teriyaki—your fave."

"Be down in a minute," Jackie grinned, but before she could back out he finally got the nerve to bring up something that had been on his mind for days. "'Scuse me, Sis. Can I ask ya something?"

"You can always ask," Rachel grinned. "May not get an answer, though."

"Well, I dunno. I've just been hearing some things about Sandy, and I was wondering if you might've heard something, too."

His stepsister snorted derisively. "Sure, J-boy; I've got nuthin' better to do than keep track of your little girlfriend. What you worried about?"

Jackie paused, momentarily unsure if he should go any further. *Might as well*, he finally told himself. He knew Rachel—if he backed away now, it'd only arouse her curiosity and maybe bring the whole thing out in front of their parents. He wasn't ready for that yet.

"The last two times we've gone out," he began slowly, "she's disappeared in the middle of things. We went to a movie, and I don't think she even saw half of it. She spends more time in the bathroom than with me."

"She's probably just showing good taste," Rachel joked, but seeing the expression on her brother's face, she quickly turned serious. "She's not meeting anybody, is she?"

"Followed her at Fuddrucker's," Jackie admitted. "She went into the Ladies' Room by herself, came out by herself. I don't think she's gonna be meeting a boy in there."

"You two were at Fuddrucker's," Rachel considered. "Little ol' Sandy have a big ol' burger, did she?"

Jackie nodded glumly.

"And I bet she ate a bucketfull of buttered popcorn at the movies, didn't she?"

A second nod.

"So you're worried that she's booting everything you've been buyin' her, is that it? Don't like wasting your hard-earned allowance on a Little Miss Creosote?"

"Ewww! That's not it," Jackie blurted. He heard his voice crack, and he wondered about the wisdom of being so open with his half-sister. "I've been looking this stuff up on the web. It can seriously mess with your body!"

"I know," Rachel relented, and for a moment she appeared to be staring into some invisible window as she said it. "You're right to be worried." She backed out of the room, looking down the hall, then seemed to come to a conclusion. "I tried it a couple times, you know," she finally said.

Not even a nod this time. Jackie knew better than to even hint that he knew anything so serious about his sister.

"It's not funny like they make it in the movies," Rachel continued. "Not at all." She sighed loudly, then gestured for him to follow her downstairs. "You could ask her yourself, you know?"

"Oh, yeah, sure," Jackie sighed. "We've only been out a couple times. So what am I gonna do? Go up to her in the hall and say, 'Hey, Sandy—you been tickling your tonsils?'"

"Well, I'll ask around, Geekboy, see what I can find out."

"Thanks," he mumbled, pressing the standby button on his computer.

"Don't thank me yet," Rachel told him. "There ain't always a reward at the end of that particular rainbow."

EPISODE EIGHTY-TWO

WHEN JOE ARRIVED TO PICK HER UP Misty was standing behind the counter, examining something in the light. The object was waxy and translucent—nearly as big as her palm—but before he could get a closer look she dropped it into her canvas bag and smiled welcomingly at her paramour.

"Ready to go?" he grinned, leaning over the glass counter to kiss the bewitching young shopkeeper lightly on the lips.

"Well, I don't know," Misty chuckled, indicating the empty store. "A responsible retailer waits for the customers to clear out first." She turned to shut off the CD player, Clannad curtailed in mid-keen, then went over to flip the window sign to "Closed." Joe followed her to the doorway, dawdling as usual to savor the sway of her luscious hips. As she stretched to shut off the over-entrance air conditioner he admired her full calves, revealed as her cotton gauze dress crept provocatively up her legs. Standing back, looking at her, he still had moments when he couldn't believe how lucky he was. *May those moments never end,* he thought.

"What's in the bag?" he asked as he stood on the sidewalk, waiting for her to lock up.

"Soap," Misty replied, pulling the item from her bag. It turned out to be a molded Venus of Willendorf figure with a small solid object—it looked like maybe a star—embedded in the center. "This really nice woman came by today, trying to interest me in it for the shop. Goddess Soap, she called it, and I told her I'd try a bar to see if it was worth stocking. You can lather me later."

"Best offer I've had all day," Joe laughed. He'd been able to park just a half a block away—a good thing, since the midsummer heat and humidity were brutal. After holding the passenger door open he dashed around to the driver's seat and started the car. The A/C had been running, so thankfully it kicked in immediately. As they sat in their parking space, waiting for the traffic to die down, Joe examined the bar of Goddess Soap.

"Don't you worry," he asked, "that something like this could be—what's the right word?—sacrilegious? I can't see soaping myself down with Crucifix-on-a-Rope, for example." He handed back the bagged bar, which Misty casually dropped over her shoulder onto the back seat.

"A religious question from you," she marveled once he'd pulled out into traffic. "I don't think you've ever brought this up before, Joseph."

Keeping his eyes on the belching bus ahead of them, Joe reached into his shirt pocket for a Starlight mint. He offered it to Misty, who deferred, and then tore the cellophane off with his teeth.

"I know you take your faith seriously," Joe explained. "Me, I stopped going to church when I moved out of my mother's place."

"Does your brother still go?"

"Jimmy? If and when Mom can drag him out of bed, but a lot of good it does him." He paused to pop the mint into his mouth, then swerved the Impala around the stopped bus. "But I figure if you and I are gonna be living together, we'd better find out more about important stuff like this."

"Do my beliefs make you uncomfortable?" Misty wondered. "I know they're about as far from a traditional Catholic upbringing as you can get."

"I don't have much to do with any religion," Joe told her. "Traditional or otherwise."

"I guessed as much," Misty said. "But sometimes the issue isn't what a person believes, but if they believe. Does it bother you that my pagan persuasion is generally perceived as, well—profane?"

"Nah, I don't think so," Joe considered, turning from the city street onto an expressway exit. "Does it bother you that I don't really have any at all?"

"Maybe," she admitted, "but it's not a deal-breaker or anything. It's just that my spirituality has helped me get through crazy times when I needed strength."

"Just being with you gives me strength," Joe replied softly. They drove along in silence for a few moments, then he returned to the conversation. "You know you haven't answered my original question."

Misty looked puzzled, then remembered. "Oh, the soap. It's just a symbol, and I'm not bothered by that. After all, cleanliness is next to goddess-liness."

Joe groaned and reached forward to turn on the radio. The Mavericks were moaning in Orbisonesque misery as they arrived at their destination, a massive Home Depot. Astonishingly, Joe found a parking space two cars away from the entrance.

"Hey, the place is putting out the welcome mat," Misty laughed as they disembarked.

"It just knows how much money we'll be spending there on the apartment."

"Probably," Misty acknowledged, and the two headed off to begin their new adventure in home renovation.

OKAY, JENNY ADMONISHED HERSELF, right hand wavering over the desk phone, *you're an independent, modern young woman—you can do this!* As if in rebuttal, a slight mew escaped her lips.

Why was she so nervous? It wasn't as if Paul Daily were an unknown quantity, after all. Determinedly she punched in Paul's speed dial number. He answered in two rings.

"Jenny!" The delight in his voice was gratifying. "Hold on a sec—let me turn down the music."

Over the klunk of the receiver being dropped Jenny tried to identify what Paul had been listening to before he muted it. A male singer was beseeching "don't forget to dance." *Good advice,* she thought.

"I'm back," Paul announced. "What can I do for you?"

"Well," Jenny began. "What's your opinion of drum-and-bugle corps?"

She could practically feel Paul's puzzlement coming through the wires.

"Um," he began. "We don't have a lot of band types in my Learning Disorder/Behavior Disorder classes. But some of my high school friends were in marching band. Why the question?"

"Delia scored a pair of comp tickets to *Blast* at the Ford Center, and Lissa passed them on to me because she refuses to go," Jenny explained. "It's an onstage recreation of brass band music with all sorts of choreography. '76 Trombones' cum *Riverdance.* Once upon a time I told my boss how much I liked drum-and-bugle corps, and that bad girl actually remembered! But like I said, she absolutely refuses to go, so I was—um—looking for someone to go with me." Jenny paused to catch her breath. *Slow down,* she cautioned herself. *You're throwing too much at him at once.*

"Hmm. I think I read a review of that show in the *Trib*," Paul said.

Jen saw Lissa watching outside her office, grinning diabolically as her young paralegal practiced the dating dance.

"Sounds like a great chance to get in touch with my own inner band nerd. I'd love to go with you."

Jen pivoted in her desk chair to give Lissa a thumbs-up. Her boss responded with silent applause, lifted her satchel and waved goodbye as she left for the evening.

"So when are the tickets for?"

"This Friday," Jenny answered. "Hope this isn't all too sudden."

"No-no-no, not at all," Paul reassured her. "I've been trying to get up the nerve to ask you out this weekend myself. You just beat me to it." He paused, the sound of '80s music still playing in the background, then continued. "Is this a date—or two friends taking advantage of freebie concert tickets?" he finally blurted.

"Which do you want it to be?"

"Hey, I asked you first, legal lady," Paul countered. "But if it please the court, let the record show that I'd like to go out on a date with you."

"Then a date it is," Jenny laughed.

"Great!" Paul shouted, and the previously silent Molly suddenly barked in the background. She could just imagine the relief on his face. "Do you want me to pick you up?"

"Sure," Jenny answered. "But I've got to warn you about something. I've been to lots of Drum Corps International competitions in the past."

"And?"

"If it's a particularly moving performance, I cry," Jenny continued. "Used to embarrass my friends and fam, to the point where they wouldn't sit next to me. So I thought I'd better give you a heads-up."

"I've been a Special Ed teacher for so long, nothing embarrasses me," Paul reassured her. "You want to go out to eat first?"

"Gee, you mention embarrassment and eating in the same breath. Sure you wanna be seen in a restaurant with me?"

"I'm sure," Paul snickered, "and you just managed to make me eat my words about never getting embarrassed. Very slick. We'll be downtown, so how about reservations at Caspar's?"

"We don't need to go anyplace that expensive," Jenny backpedaled.

"Don't need to," Paul agreed, "but it should be fun. You got the tickets—I'll take care of dinner."

"Hardly seems equal."

"Okay," Paul conceded. "If you won't compromise your principles, than we'll split the dinner bill."

"Done," she agreed, "and we will make it Caspar's." She leaned back in her desk chair, looking outside at the early evening sky. At that moment she felt like she'd made her first active and positive step in weeks. "So how've things been going with summer school?"

EPISODE EIGHTY-THREE

"**YOU'RE HARDWIRED NOW**," Ian said, crawling out from behind the wrought-iron computer table, a grin of accomplishment on his well-worn face. He rose, wiped his glasses on his T-shirt and gestured proudly toward the newly connected PC. *Boys and their toys,* Patsy thought with a mental chuckle.

Her boyfriend had brought her a used Dell—two years out of date (and thus deadwood to his company) but enough machine for Patsy—and also had gotten her on a cheap Internet Service Provider. It was a tossup as to who was more excited about it, but when you came down to it, she supposed Ian had a slight edge. After all, he knew better than her what she could possibly accomplish with the machine.

"So now we can surf the web?" Patsy asked hopefully as they watched the monitor run through the Windows opening. Ian chuckled and pulled out the metal kitchen chair invitingly. (Since beginning to work fulltime Patsy's first goal had been to upgrade her furniture, but a few relics remained.) Leaning across the chair she lightly kissed his cheek, then took a seat. He handed her the diskette provided by her new ISP.

"We need to install this first," he explained, "but since it's your machine, you should probably do it. Hands on is always the way to learn your way around."

At work they also had Windows, so this task wasn't all that daunting for Patty. Once they got to the browser settings, Ian advised her to put it at maximum security.

"I've been getting a lot of those virus emails lately," he elaborated, "and it's possible that you might start receiving them, too. At least one arrived with a 'marzbarz' webnom."

"Val?"

"Well, she's never owned up to it, but Jackie and I were able to track some early web board postings back to her ISP address. I just wish she'd find a new boyfriend so she could get beyond harassing me." He pointed to a logon icon at the upper right of her browser. "Let's see if y'all is connected," he drawled.

A few quick clicks and she was.

"Once we get you on a DSL, this'll be fifty times quicker," Ian noted, but to Patsy it appeared fast enough. She bet that in time she'd learn to be as impatient as Ian, though.

First thing they checked out was her email—no viruses, just a nice welcome message for her from her ISP—then Patsy wanted to visit some size-related sites.

"What's the name of that spot where you first found Val's postings?" she asked.

"ZaftInGather," he replied, spelling out the URL. The site opened onto a pink, stylized image of a group of fat women standing together in a circle. When she got to the site's Main Board she saw one of the topics of discussion was Greg Dillman's impending beauty pageant.

"Have you read this?" she asked Ian, indicating a particularly indignant posting.

"Don't usually visit this site," he grinned. "It's a bit too—um—estrogen-heavy for me."

"Well, listen up," Patsy said, and she read the post aloud:

"'How can the size acceptance movement ever expect to be taken seriously when it remains silent about practices that can only be considered exploitive by serious progressive thinkers? Is it progress for fat women to be objectified just as easily as their thinner sisters? I, for one, wish that women in our Movement would find it within themselves to stop silently acquiescing to this demeaning ritual. Big is beautiful, but big beauty contests aren't.'"

"More publicity for Greg and Connie," Ian considered, holding up his Mountain Dew can to drain the dregs.

"I guess," Patsy considered, back-buttoning from this controversy toward a less-heated topic. She'd never really questioned the political validity of an event like this. Told for so many years that her size was unattractive, she'd looked to pageants as a positive thing. But maybe the writer had a point, she thought as she examined the poster's name. "Tootsierolla," she muttered aloud. Maybe it was just shadow shock, but that was awfully similar to the webnom they'd just been discussing.

JOE WAS BUSY OVERSEEING the evening's meat delivery when his mother phoned. The call caught him unawares—ever since he'd moved into the same building with Misty, his mother had been reluctant to phone him. "I don't want to disturb you and your girlfriend," she'd say whenever he asked about it. Apparently this fear extended to the kitchen at Caspar's, since she'd also stopped contacting him at work. If he'd known earlier about this beneficial little perk, he would have worked a lot harder at getting a girlfriend.

"Joseph," she began. "Has your brother shown up for work yet?"

"I would hope so," Joe said, still counting cartons as they were wheeled into the cooler. "His shift started an hour ago. But yeah, Ma, he's around."

"You know how your brother is," his mother said. "I don't know—I just had this feeling I should call."

Unfortunately, Joe did know his brother. But he wasn't going to get into that with his mother right now. "Jimmy's been doing fine here," Joe reassured her. He took the clipboard from the delivery guy and initialed it. "Caspar is talking about giving him some tables."

"Oh, I'm so happy to hear that," she gushed. "You're such a good brother, Joseph." In the space it took her to continue he could hear one of the afternoon talk shows in the background. "So how are you and Misty doing?"

"It's going great, Mom," Joe told her. "Misty's taking bids on renovating the place, and we've been scoping out HGTV and all the building supply places for ideas."

"Renovating," she repeated, and with that Joe realized they'd just ventured into a subject area he hadn't really introduced yet. "Um, yes, Mom. We're combining a couple apartments, so there'll be enough space to live together."

In the background the audible gasp from the talk show couldn't have been better timed. To her credit, Joe's mother showed more restraint.

"That's a big step," she finally observed. "But you and Misty are adults, and I'm confident that you've made an informed decision."

This subdued response was almost as disconcerting as her more typical hysterical approach. Maybe all those talk show shrinks were getting through to her.

"You're right, Mom," he said. "We've discussed this one to death. But I know that I'm in love with her, and I'm pretty sure she loves me."

"Is 'pretty sure' enough?" his mother couldn't resist asking.

"It is for me," he declared, deftly steering from this dangerous thread. "Oh, did you want to talk to Jimmy, by the way?"

"No," she backed off. "And please don't tell him I called either, will you? I don't want him thinking that we don't trust him."

Well, maybe we don't, Joe thought of adding, but he figured he'd already thrown enough at his mother tonight. "Okay, then. I love you, Ma."

Soon as he hung up, Joe searched out his brother. He was nowhere in the restaurant, so Joe headed for the back.

Standing by the dumpster, Jimmy was sharing a smoke with the delivery driver. Last he'd heard his brother was on the nicotine patch. But that was none of his business, so Joe cleared his throat and the two immediately cut short their discussion.

"Later," the driver told Jimmy, taking back his smokes and heading toward the step van.

"You want something, bro?" Jimmy asked as he flicked his still-smoldering butt into a convenient puddle.

"Not really," Joe said, holding open the back door. "Ma called. She's as nutty as ever."

"You tell her about your moving plans?" Jimmy asked. The nearer he got to Joe, the less his breath smelled like tobacco.

"It had to come up sooner or later," Joe answered.

"Yeah, but I know you wish it was mucho later," Jimmy laughed.

They both walked through the storeroom, but before they got to the kitchen Joe reached into his apron pocket. "Hold up," he told his brother, tossing him a tin of Altoids.

To his credit, Jimmy didn't try to deny anything. "Is it that obvious?" he asked, popping open the tin and plunking two into his mouth. Two quick bites and you could practically see the peppermint fill the small room.

"It is," Joe deadpanned. "So keep that in mind in the future, wouldja?"

"I will," Jimmy promised, looking his brother straight in the eyes as he did. "I don't want to screw up this time, bro. Believe me."

"I do," Joe reassured him as they both headed back to finish the day's prepwork. But of course that wasn't the truth.

EPISODE EIGHTY–FOUR

CASSIE FOUND THE SHEET MUSIC in a dusty box tucked behind the Christmas decorations. It'd been ages since she'd sung anything secular, so most of it was pretty vintage. But she had to begin somewhere—why not start with what she knew? Pulling out a songbook devoted to *Hot Hits of the Seventies,* she flipped through the pages until she came upon one she liked, the "Theme from Mahogany."

Humming to herself, she returned to the living room and wondered if she still had an actual recording of the song. After hearing a particularly powerful evangelist a couple years back she'd gotten rid of most of her nonreligious music (but never the Mamas and the Papas) in a fit of spiritual cleansing, so it wasn't likely.

With feet firmly planted on the worn braided rug she took a deep breath and sang the first line. *"Do you know where you're going to?"* she asked in a voice so wispy that you could barely hear the question mark.

Hmmm. Why was she being so timid about this? She'd belonged to the church choir for years, had even performed solos, so what was her problem?

"You can do this," she scolded herself, though the words and notes on the sheet appeared more muddled than melodic. She gazed out the window at the bird feeder on her front porch. There she saw the neighborhood squirrel stealing sunflower seeds and effectively keeping every single songbird away. As if sensing her eyes on him the creature turned and chittered furiously at her through the screen. "Hush up, you rat!" she told the distracting little scoundrel.

Closing her eyes, she recalled the excitement she'd felt two days earlier when Greg and Connie phoned to offer her the chance to sing at their pageant. Perhaps it was just the handsome insurance man's phone voice, but at that time she remembered feeling confident and so excited to just be asked. But now about a billion butterflies had taken up residence in her stomach.

"Stop being such a baby," she admonished herself. She looked around the room for her iced tea, found it and downed a large swig. Then she took several deep breaths and started over. This time she made it all the way through the song.

IAN WAS STILL FEELING SMUG after the call to his credit card company ("Yes, Mr. Johnson, the Jordan Lewis charges have been expunged from your account") when he got the call from Greg Dillman. Most other days he probably wouldn't have taken it at work, but he was still savoring the thrill of victory. Hell, right now he could deal with even Greg.

"Ian!" the insurance man opened, as if they were the bestest of boyhood buds, running into each other for the first time in years. "How's it goin', my man?"

Ian grimaced sourly, but since nobody was in his cubicle to see, it was an empty gesture. "Day's been going great so far," he told Dillman. "What do you need, Greg?"

"Not a thing, boy-o. I'm offering you an exceptional opportunity," Greg answered. "Of course you've heard about the Big Beautiful Beauty Pageant that we're putting on in November? —Well, today I'm in the business of recruiting judges. And immediately I thought of you."

"You did," Ian muttered. This was definitely not what he'd been expecting. "And what exactly brought me to mind, Greg?"

"You're an officer in the area's premiere size acceptance group," Dillman gushed. "And you clearly are familiar with the multitudinous charms of breathtaking BBWs. Just seemed natural."

"Well, isn't Mitchell Christian also a RADFAm officer? And isn't his chapter involved with the pageant? And if you really want an established local officer, what about Dexter? He's been doing this a lot longer than I have."

"I'm not sure either of them would present the right image for our judges," Greg wheedled. "We wanna show people that everyday guys can be attracted to plus-sized beauties. Guys like you, buddy boy."

The old Size Acceptance double standard. He doesn't want them because they're fat, Ian translated. Because a portly guy can't be an "everyday guy." He didn't know whether to feel disgusted or amused. "Sure you want a judge who was called a predator on *The Winnie Harper Show*, Greg?"

"Why, my understanding is that the show retracted that allegation," Greg pooh-poohed. "And I don't recall you being mentioned by name. I don't think we'll get any bad press from this. So what d'ya say?"

Ian thoughtfully watched his screensaver for a few seconds. Why was he even considering this? When Val had been working up her little talk show lynch party, Greg had been all too willing to supply the rope.

Still, this pageant thing did have the potential to be a major size-positive event. Sometimes you had to work with dickheads like Greg just to get the good word out.

"Give me a day to think about it," he finally informed the entrepreneur.

CRAMMED INTO THE BACKSEAT of the crappy Driver's Ed car with Sharon, feeling every jolt and buffet, Rachel found herself wishing she were in the back of her father's much-maligned minivan instead. When Dex and The Stepmom first bought the Whackmobile both she and Jackie had given them a ton of grief. But sitting in the back of a no-frills Ford Taurus definitely changed your point of view. Oh, for the comfort of their uncool Dodge Caravan!

"Driver center is vehicle center," Mr. Numan was telling Jeremy, who currently sat behind the wheel. The boy responded with a grunt of concentration as he struggled to follow the orange-coned lanes set up in the empty school parking lot. Last spring—for all of about ten seconds—Rachel had actually considered going out with Jeremy. But the boy was so Nick-At-Night she'd ultimately decided against it.

"Hey," her backseat companion whispered, "so how's your cute little bro doing?"

"Cute?" Rachel scoffed. "When did you turn into a perv, Shar? He's three years younger than you."

"You know what they say about younger men," Sharon giggled. "They're supposed to have more stamina."

"I can't believe you said that," Rachel shot back, perhaps a little louder than she should have, because Mr. Numan craned his head around and gave them both a dirty look.

"Any trouble back there, ladies?" he growled.

"No, Mister Numan," Rachel answered dutifully, echoed by Sharon's "No, sir!"

"Good, because you need to pay attention to what Jeremy's doing. Your turn's next, Miss Logan." He turned back to the aforementioned wheelman and commanded. "Both hands on the steering wheel. Ten and two, Jeremy. Ten and two!"

Rachel pulled out her notebook and began scribbling on it:

Jackie's seeing some 1 in his own class! Tuff luck, girly!

Sharon shrugged noncommittally and then raised an eyebrow in question. Rachel continued writing.

This Sandy chick—blond & tiny—looks like she could star on the WB—

"Don't know what she sees in my brother," she elaborated, whispering to Sharon, who winked and grinned knowingly. She was one of those girls who employed dress and makeup to communicate her mood or message du jour without once breaking character all day. Today, her image was pure Party Girl, like a miniaturized version of one of those sophisticated sluts you saw on cable television. Rachel wondered if she had something going that night, but it wasn't anything worth wondering about too hard. She had better things to do than waste her nights with Sharon's crowd.

"Jackie's cute in a Jet Li Junior sorta way," Sharon said as Rachel slid out of the backseat to switch places with Jeremy. "He could do a lot better than Little Miss Sandy, though. Eating disorders are so TV talkshow."

"Have we been paying attention?" Mr. Numan asked as Rachel got into the idling car's driver's seat.

"Sure we have," Rachel chirped, careful to remember to fasten her seatbelt. First day they got behind the wheel Sharon had tried to start the car before putting on her belt. The lecture they'd received from Mr. Numan had blown half of their first day's session.

The August afternoon was bright, so Rachel pulled down her Ray-Bans and did a quick lookaround. North of the lot some kids were goofing around on the tennis court, but otherwise the neighborhood looked quiet.

"Check your mirror," her instructor advised, and Rachel dutifully followed his instruction. "Last time you were a little timid stepping on the gas," he continued. "Let's see if you can do better today."

"Floor it, girl," Jeremy laughed as she reached for the gearshift.

"Shut up, Jeremy," she shot back. "I didn't say anything when you were driving."

"Ignore him," Mr. Numan intoned. "Just ease off the brake—thattagirl. And you, young man, I'd keep my remarks to myself if I wanted to get a passing grade in this class. That clear?"

"Yes sir," Jeremy mumbled as Rachel pushed her foot firmly onto the accelerator.

"Too much!" Mr. Numan barked as they shot across the parking lot. Looking down, Rachel quickly eased off the pedal. "No!" the teacher reproached her. "Keep your foot on the gas—and your eyes on the road!"

"What?" Rachel cried, just as Ford front bumper connected forcefully with tennis court fence.

EPISODE EIGHTY-FIVE

WHATEVER YOU DO, *don't rush her!*

The phrase had become Paul's mantra over the past few days. *Whatever you do, don't rush her!* It'd played over and over through his head—when he showered, while he ate and walked the dog, when he had a rare quiet moment in class. As he drove through the suburbs to pick her up at the law office he silently chanted it. *Don't rush her!* He'd nearly scared Jenny away once by going too fast. Now, with this second chance, he would not blow it.

Traffic was cooperative, but the parking spot gods were not so generous. Though he arrived at her office building fifteen minutes early, it took all that time, plus change, to jockey into a nearby "compact car only" space. She was just coming out of the building as he stepped from the car, a doubled-up clothing bag swinging in her right hand and a broad smile on her lovely face.

She was more stunning than he'd remembered. August evening sunlight was Jenny's element. In it she glowed with effusive beauty. Dressed in a lilac linen skirt and cap-sleeved duster that hugged her buxom form, her face framed by honey blonde hair styled in an elegant coif, she looked so stunning that he suddenly felt profoundly underdressed. Quickly he rushed over to grab the garment bag, nearly stubbing her open-toed foot in the process.

Calm down, dammit!

"Were you waiting long?" she grinned as he carefully laid her bag across the bottom of his empty trunk.

"Not in the least," he reassured her, and before she could open it herself he'd dashed to the passenger door to escort her into the car.

"Isn't every day I get a gentleman holding the door for me," Jenny teased as she grabbed her lower skirt and eased onto her seat.

"I won't tell the Sisterhood if you don't," Paul confided, carefully shutting the door.

"Cross my heart. So where are we going for dinner?"

"Caspar's, of course. I thought that was the deal."

"Well, I wasn't sure you'd be able to get an early reservation on such short notice," Jenny quickly recovered, though Paul guessed that she'd probably forgotten that part of their phone call.

"Actually, I wasn't," Paul admitted sheepishly. "Would you mind having dinner after the show?"

"Not at all," she quickly replied. "So that begs the question—what are we doing before the show?"

HE DROVE ALONG THE LAKESHORE to a large public parking lot near the pier. Jenny hadn't been on the pier since she was a girl—like many city regulars, she tended to forget the tourist spots. The buildings were just starting to light up, though the day was still too bright to make much of a difference. They walked across the lot for a closer view of the lake; an offshore breeze pushed against them, lightly fluttering her skirt.

Everywhere Jenny looked, young couples seemed to be walking hand in hand.

Tentatively she reached over and clasped Paul's arm. He said nothing, just looked her way, covered her hand with his and squeezed. They approached an outdoor sculpture composed of bright alphabet letters and stopped to gaze out across the lake. For a moment Jenny turned back toward the city skyline. She always forgot how striking it was. Driving in from the burbs you passed through miles of depressing industrial sprawl. It couldn't help but stain your view of the city. But looking at it from the lakefront, you remembered how grand it all could be.

She turned back to Paul. It was easy to take him for granted, too, she thought; he was so straightforward and uncomplicated. What was he doing with a mess like her? He returned her look as if trying to read her eyes. Damn, he was handsome! Too handsome, perhaps, for her? No, that was Mother talking again.

"You look thoughtful," Paul observed. "Want to share any of them?"

"What? No penny?"

"I wouldn't dream of bidding so low."

"You'd be paying just about market value. I was just thinking of how handsome the city looked."

"Handsome," Paul echoed. "I don't think I've ever heard a city called 'handsome' before. Though I suppose it could be."

She grabbed both his hands and backed away, stretching their arms as far as they'd go. Then she slowly and carefully eyed him, from toe to head. Black loafers, light grey twill dress pants, cream polo shirt and a navy blue blazer. His hair was slightly ruffled from the evening breeze, and it was obvious that he'd recently shaved. His eyes crinkled with laugh lines. His jawline deepened mannishly. If she was a girl in some shlocky romance novel she'd probably be swooning at this point, he looked so wonderful.

And you know something? Swooning didn't really seem like too bad an idea when you got down to it.

"Not as handsome as you," she finally said, letting go and moving into the statue's shadow so hopefully he wouldn't see her blushing too much.

"Yeah, well, I don't have any poets extolling my virtues. Guess my shoulders just aren't big enough."

"They look broad enough for me," Jenny flirted, resting her hands on his jacket, as if to measure their width.

Then suddenly they were kissing. Jenny slid her arms around his neck, feeling the delicious friction of fabric between them. They kissed for what seemed like hours, ignoring the other couples and families walking past them on the pier.

Every doubt that Jenny may have felt grew small and surmountable. But she knew that once they separated these doubts would probably gain strength again, so she continued to hold on to her lover. Over Paul's shoulders the sun was just beginning to disappear beyond the cityscape.

Finally, slowly and as one, they disengaged from their lingering embrace.

"Wow," Paul gasped. Jenny quickly swiveled to take in her surroundings—she half expected to find a circle of spectators around them, but the real world didn't work like romantic movies. All she saw was two skateboard kids looking their way as they passed. One of the kids gave them a thumbs up.

"Good to see we got some critical approval," Paul chuckled. Apparently he'd turned to see what caught her eye. "Looked a bit like one of my kids, too."

"We probably should get going," Jenny decided.

"Right," Paul agreed, and they headed back to the car. Once they got to the theater she was gonna need a bit of tidying up in the lady's room, Jenny thought. She wished she had a compact, but since she didn't often wear makeup, she hadn't thought to bring one.

"So was this a good idea?" Paul asked.

"Oh yes," she agreed. "It was."

PAUL'S EARS WERE STILL RINGING when they got to Caspar's. But it was clear from the way Jenny sat enraptured from the first drumbeat and bugle blare that she'd loved the show. Drum and bugle corps may not've been his thing, but he could definitely appreciate the way she appreciated it. If only, he ruefully thought, he could inspire that same expression.

The restaurant was easing into its late night rhythms by now—empty tables and lingering customers, the occasional arrival of aftershow diners. They followed the maitre d' through a bewildering maze of cozy rooms with dark oak booths and tables to an area near (but not too, Paul made sure) to the kitchen. They had the choice of table or booth, so Jenny requested a table—the booths looked roomy enough, but why take the chance? Their waiter, a Hispanic male who could very well be Joe's brother, took their drink orders and vanished through the swinging door.

"Have you been here before?" Jenny asked Paul, examining the rather intimidating menu. He shook his head.

"Don't make it downtown that often," he confessed, himself boggling over the prices on display before him, but not wanting to appear too freaked. "Though I've wanted to come here ever since Joe first told me about it. Got to figure that a guy into feeder fantasies would make an excellent chef."

"You know, I simply don't understand that fantasy, Paul," Jenny admitted. "I mean, here you have real-life flesh-and-blood BBWs—and y'all seem to prefer swapping stories."

"I'm not sure I can explain it. But it's clear a lot of FAs do it—maybe it comes from keeping our preference closeted for so long." He saw the waiter returning with their drinks and decided to steer the conversation into a less loaded arena. "So what did you think of the performance?"

"Still coming down from it," she smiled wistfully. "How about you? Am I right in guessing you weren't totally transported beyond the realms of melodic bliss?"

"Just guess I'm more a rock'n'roll guy," Paul said. "Early R & B, greasy ol' blues, the usual suspects. But I really enjoyed watching you enjoy it."

The waiter deposited Paul's O'Doul and Jenny's glass of white Zinfandel, then asked if they were ready to order.

"Could you give us a few more minutes?" Jenny asked. "I'm trying to decide how long I can go the rest of the weekend without eating."

"If you want, we can forego the Dutch Treat thing," Paul murmured. "I can put it on my card."

"No," Jenny insisted. "I meant in the caloric sense. My finances can handle it. But thanks." She smiled up at their waiter. "Is Joe Rivera working tonight? We'd love to say 'Hi.'"

"I can tell him you're here," the waiter replied. "And you are—?"

"Paul and Jenny from the chapter," Paul filled in. "But if he's busy, that's okay."

"It's settling down," their waiter reassured them. "I'll let him know. Do you still need more time?"

"If it's not too much trouble—"

"No trouble at all," he said. Gliding across the room, he was about to enter the kitchen when its door swung open, revealing a uniformed police officer. Beyond the door Paul could see Joe being restrained by a second policeman.

"Jimmy!" Joe hollered, struggling, and their waiter responded to this cry by swiveling and bolting in the opposite direction. The cop took off after him, and as the door swung closed a ruckus could be heard from the kitchen. "What are you doing?" Joe could be heard shouting. "Let go of me!"

"This," Paul observed as they both rose to see if their friend needed help, "cannot be good."

EPISODE EIGHTY-SIX

BEFORE FIRST OPENING HER SHOP, the very idea of Misty adopting inventory assessment as stress reliever would have made her chuckle. She simply wasn't genetically that organized. But wheeling her stool around the Isles' aisles on a Friday night, checking lists against items on display and cataloging needs (and setting the occasional hex on her fortunately few light-fingered loss-culprits who contributed to those needs), while the Moodies sang about cosmic voyaging—these were moments Misty could keep from missing Joe.

There were times when she worried about this—the dawning notion that she'd begun to anticipate his presence, becoming too comfortable with it for her own peace of mind. She was a grown woman who had, by choice, lived on her own for years, but now that solitary soul seemed a whole different woman. Certainly not her.

Sighing, she considered a wall of health and beauty products she'd have to rearrange to make room for the GoddessStone Soaps she'd ordered. Prominent display? Definitely not in the window.

The ringing of the door broke her reverie. Swiveling on her size-friendly throne to inform the visitor that the shop was closed, she belatedly realized it was Kirk.

"Well, howdy, stranger. Thought I'd find you down here," he drawled. "Seems a shopkeep's day is never done."

Did she note a slight accusatory edge in that last statement? Misty wondered. They hadn't been seeing each other as much since Kirk had moved upstairs. Was he pissed with her or was she just feeling a twinge of the guilts?

"Woman's work is never done," Misty answered, rising to give Kirk a hug. "Surprised to see you staying in on a Friday night."

"Just turning into an old homebody," Kirk replied, hugging her back. If only Joe could hug her as enthusiastically; there were times when he seemed to treat her like a china doll. "Now that I've got Howlie plus the terrible twins to take care of, the old night life has lost its allure."

They broke apart, and Misty once again settled onto her ample stool. "And how are the tiggies doing?" she asked.

"Purr-fectly," Kirk smiled fiendishly, after first leaning over to lower the volume on her CD player. "Though I must admit there are times when I swear I can hear Bri's baby boy crying, 'Where's my poppa?' in that pathetic little mewl of his. Who'd have thought that a bruiser of a cat like him would have such a twinkie little voice?"

"Takes after his stepdad, perhaps?"

"Possibly," Kirk lisped.

"What is the state of e-romance these days, anyway? How are things going between you and Brian?"

"Welllll," Kirk elongated, before finally diving into the matter that had brought him downstairs. "'Between' is exactly what I wanted to talk to you about. 'Between' as in too many miles between. Misty, he wants me to move to the Coast. He plans to make an honest woman of me."

For a moment, feelings of happiness and dismay warred somewhere south of Misty's throat, but fortunately the more positive emotion won out. "Why, Kirk," she said, rising to throw an enormous encore hug around her friend. "That's wonderful news! What are you going to do? When are you going to do it?"

"Well, we haven't set a date yet, but I'd be some kind of fey-fool not to follow my heart." He gulped as the two of them separated. "Jesus, I can't believe I just said that. Calling Rogers and Hammerstein! I'm channeling their fluffy Alpine ingénue! Scratch a cynical poofter, and a mushy romantic will bleed out every time."

"Whoa, Mr. Romance. What about Jake and Elwood?" Misty considered. "Isn't Brian allergic to cat dander?"

Kirk had the panache to look sheepish. "That is a problem. Howlie can come with me, of course. But any chance that roomy new floorplan could shelter twin Maine Coon orphans from storm and canine?"

"It would be one way of forcing you to keep in touch," Misty mused.

"I'll get a special calling card just for updates. Promise," he wheedled.

"Joe's gotta weigh in before I make such life-altering decisions. After all, we've finally started this new apartment project together and I'd hate to—"

But before she could voice that concern her cell phone chirped.

YEARS OF TELEVISION had fostered a distinct image of the archetypal metro police station for Paul, so he couldn't help feeling some small sense of dislocation once he'd entered the real thing. The precinct house was in a suitably ancient building, but the interior was brighter than he expected, and there wasn't a single screaming junkie hooker to be seen. If their friend hadn't been dragged to this place Paul might have felt let down, but considering that Joe was still somewhere on the other side of the counter getting processed, it was more of a relief.

Of course that didn't stop him from trying to take in as many details as possible—the anti-drug posters on the wall (not much different from the ones they had in the counselor's office at school), the desks behind the counter and small personal items that were placed on each one (the Wonder Woman action figure being used as a paperweight on a stack of forms, for instance), and, of course, the weary-eyed uniformed cops.

Left of the counter was a glassed-in radio room. As they'd entered the waiting area the chubby middleaged dispatcher within had aimed a womanly look at Jenny that Paul had learned to translate as *Thank God, I'm not as fat as her.*

But once Jenny had hit the familiar judicial ground of the precinct she became Professional Paralegal Woman, focused on the matter at hand. A definite eyeopener for Paul—it was his first time seeing her at work, and the sight was both impressive and mildly intimidating.

The timbre of her voice had grown more clipped and businesslike. Her smooth face was implacable as she'd announced to the desk sergeant that she was Joe's legal representative and that she wanted to speak with him as soon as they were done with his processing. The desk sergeant had nodded amiably and responded with a pleasant, "Just a few."

Twenty minutes later they'd buzzed Jenny through the gate, leaving Paul alone to continue cataloging real-life cop shop details. "I'll be back," she had smiled grimly before disappearing beyond. Leaning over to kiss him her forefront brushed against him lightly, and damned if he didn't feel excited by this brief contact. "Some swell date," she'd grinned rakishly. "Good thing we held off going to the restaurant 'til after the show."

"Yeah," he'd answered. But when a date's defining moment involves handcuffs—what the hell had Joe gotten them into?

Once he saw Misty coming through the heavy station door, he tamped that unworthy thought down. (Back in the radio room, the female com-officer was no doubt already noting the supersized woman's presence.) Misty looked both frightened and angry, and though Paul would later feel embarrassed for the thought, she looked like the mother from the movie version of *Gilbert Grape* coming to demand her son's release from that Iowa police station. A concerned-looking fellow followed in her wake. Though casually dressed, he seemed far too tidy for the present surroundings.

"Misty." Paul rose to greet her, but she didn't immediately hear or notice him. He repeated her name as she made her way to the counter, and she finally turned to focus in on him. "Everything's okay," he said. "Jenny's inside, meeting with Joe now."

"What's going on? Why's he been arrested?"

"I couldn't tell you," Paul admitted. "All we know is there was some kind of big bust in the back of Caspar's. Joe got hauled in, but for all I know it's just for questioning. Jenny should have the scoop soon enough. She's also been in touch with Lissa, so we've got her legal expertise to call on, if necessary." He had maneuvered Misty toward his place on the bench, and she collapsed into it gratefully.

Misty's companion, Kirk, turned out to be the one who'd driven her there—a tenant in the building, but obviously also a close friend. He wondered what Joe thought of the guy. From the way he solicitously held Misty's hands, it was clear the two had some history.

"So did we ruin your night out?" she finally asked Paul ruefully.

"Not at all. Just a momentary bump in the road."

"I hope so," Misty said. "What could Joe be doing to get himself arrested?"

"Probably nothing," her friend answered. "I'm sure it's all a big misunderstanding."

The words sounded weak to Paul, but he wasn't about to say so. Thankfully, at that point Jenny came into view. As soon as she got within reach she hugged Misty reassuringly, gestured the trio out of desk sergeant earshot, then gave them the story.

"It was a drug bust," she explained. "It was supposed to take place in the alley outside the restaurant, but the suspect dashed back into the kitchen. Joe's brother Jimmy, apparently, was making a little supplemental income on the side. When the cops followed him into the restaurant, Joe was in the way. They've been questioning him to see if he knows anything about Jimmy's activities, but they don't believe he's involved in this. Apparently Joe walked in on the aftermath of a contact several days earlier. Jimmy later told the undercover agent Joe was ignorant about what was going on."

"So he's not arrested?" Misty said.

"Not at this point. But if they wanted to they could hit Joe with interfering with a police officer and several other misdemeanors. I don't think they're gonna do that, though."

"So what are they doing?"

"Typing up his statement," Jenny explained. "I'll go back in and help him through the rest of this process. It shouldn't be more than another half hour." She looked Misty in the eyes and asked, "How you holding up?"

"I'm okay," Misty told them, "but it's probably a good thing that brother of his isn't in sight. I'm really sorry about your night."

"The night's not over yet," Jenny said, winking at Paul before striding back into the precinct. Paul nodded and watched admiringly as his Super Girl went back to work—a full-bodied legal warrior marching off to advocate for her client—as he mentally dubbed her final words across the scene: "The night's not over yet!"

EPISODE EIGHTY–SEVEN

IT WAS HARDLY CASPAR'S, but by the time they'd finally left the cop shop, the only spot Jenny and Paul could find for dinner was an all-night Greek family restaurant just off the interstate. Though she half considered begging off (it was pretty darn late, after all), they hit the Palos Gardens anyway. *At least,* she thought, *it's not Denny's.*

The restaurant was busy for the hour, but not so crowded that they couldn't take table seating over a booth. They both were tired. The fluorescent lighting glared brightly, unflattering, but as they sat across the table from each other, Jenny felt Paul had never looked more handsome.

"Dull night," she finally deadpanned, ripping open a packet of sugar for her iced tea. "But I'm glad we were at the restaurant, or Joe most likely would've spent the whole night at that station. Not just the half we did spend."

"Lucky for Joe that you were there," Paul corrected. "All I could do was cheer from the sidelines. You were really something to watch, though."

"Not too scary, was I?" Jenny wondered, the unwelcome mental image of Kathy Bates with sledgehammer in hand coming unbidden to her mind.

"Not to me," Paul chuckled, "but then I've seen you getting all sentimental over drum-and-bugle corps."

"God, that seems like a whole other night," Jenny moaned. "But it was a great concert. Hope you didn't mind being dragged along."

"Not at all," Paul reassured her. "Great concert plus great company equals great experience." She felt herself blushing and took a quick sip of tea, trying to hide her reaction behind the glass——Big-shot Paralegal turns Quivering Schoolgirl at the drop of a single compliment—but she knew she wasn't fooling Paul. She steered the conversation back to a less loaded topic. "I hope this thing doesn't get Joe in trouble at work, though. Hearing Misty talk about all their apartment renovation plans, they're clearly gonna need both their salaries."

"I think Joe's in solid standing with his boss. But I wouldn't wanna be at any family get-togethers anytime in the near future." Swizzling his water, he thoughtfully watched an ice-suspended lemon slice dip and swirl for a few seconds. "Caspar's has an excellent reputation—both the man and the restaurant—so neither should be tarnished by this, and I suspect that's the worst way it could hurt Joe."

"Misty sure looked upset," Jenny mourned.

"I'm sure you see your share of distraught loved ones every day at work," Paul answered gently.

"Yeah, but it's totally different when it's someone you know. I hope this doesn't get between the two of them. They make such a nice couple."

Paul cocked his head impishly. "You do that, too?"

"Do what?"

"Gauge your hopes on the fact that certain couples look so good together," Paul grinned.

"Doesn't everybody?" Jenny smiled in return. "Heck, sometimes I'll be in the mall, and I'll see a couple, and if one of them's fat just that sight makes me feel good. It's not like I know anything about the relationship—it may be as abusive as hell—but I still put my own spin on it. It's human nature."

"Think anyone seeing us at the concert put the same spin on us?" Paul wondered. He smiled inquiringly, a crooked half smile that asked its own unvoiced questions.

"I hope so," she replied, and just saying it out loud seemed to define some inner place she'd never let herself go before. "At the risk of sounding egotistical, I think we make a rather attractive young couple."

Of course the waitress chose this very moment to make her appearance.

"Don't mind us," Paul told her. "It's just the ol' dating thing."

Their waitress, a fortyish brunette with the loose-fleshed look of someone who'd lost more weight than their body wanted, simply nodded and said, "At least you're sober, which is more than I can say for most folks hereabouts at this hour. Ready to order?"

Paul looked inquiringly across the table at Jenny, and in that moment she knew exactly what she wanted to do.

"You know," she decided. "As good as your menu looks, I think we'd rather go home and see what's in the kitchen cupboards. What do you think, Paul?"

She could see his mind working, considering her spin on these words. *Please don't blow a gasket,* she tried to telepath. *I can't tell you what it all means, either.*

Slowly, in answer, he reached for his wallet and pulled out a twenty-dollar bill.

"Sorry to mess up your table," he apologized to the waitress. "But I guess all we wanted was a couple of drinks."

"Makes no never mind to me," Flo said good-naturedly, scooping the bill up and smiling even further when Paul told her to keep the change. "You two have a good night, okay?"

"I believe we will," Jenny assured her, as they headed into the balmy late summer night.

FOR TWO HOURS since the now-forgotten nightmare had jerked her awake, Cassie had lain in bed, struggling to fall back to sleep. The ceiling fan whirred soothingly, but for once its rhythmic humming failed to relax her. She was feeling too wired—too attuned to the meager weight of sheet and blanket, to the sweaty chafe of one leg across the other as she struggled to find a comfortable position in bed—to just let go and sleep. She kept replaying her last phone conversation with Greg and Connie, wondering if she had the nerve to do what they were pushing her to do.

Performing in public—as the opening act of a beauty pageant (even one as far from the mainstream as a BBW beauty pageant)—was simply not in her nature. What if they laughed at her? She was certainly no beauty, not even a Big Beauty like Connie (or Jenny, for that matter). So what business did she have even walking onstage? Would serve her right if someone did laugh!

The closer the actual event, the more she found herself worrying about it. Listening to Greg Dillman wax on and on about all the good publicity it was going to bring did nothing but boost her already inflated anxiety levels. Tonight they'd discussed the dress she'd be wearing for the opening number.

"I've got just the gown for you," Connie had gushed in what probably had been meant as reassurance. "It'll look gorgeous, just the dress for a broad-shouldered gal like you."

Like a big old heifer like me, you mean, she'd nearly snapped back. But that wouldn't have been in the spirit of a Big Beautiful Pageant.

"I really can't afford any fancy new dresses right now," Cassie had finally demurred.

"Nonsense, this will be on loan from my shop," Connie had insisted. "The program will give the boutique credit, so it all makes for great advertising."

Yeah, Cassie couldn't help wondering, *but what happens if I ruin the dress?*

Sighing, she rolled out of bed and padded into the living room. Without really wanting to watch it, she flicked on the TV for background noise. Turning the volume down to a mutter, she flashed through several channels before coming upon a late-night infomercial. Jordan Lewis, once again hawking his diet wares.

Awhile back one of her coworkers had been a Jordanite. The woman had been pretty obnoxious about trying to sell the stuff, until their supervisor had finally warned her not to bring any more order booklets to the workplace. At first Cass had dutifully tried the pre-packaged meals, but for every one she finished she'd been even hungrier an hour later. When she finally begged off buying anything more from the dealer, the woman had clucked her tongue and said, "Okay, if you really want to give up on yourself—"

If she was her sister, Cassie probably would have fired back a suitably snappy rejoinder, but instead, predictably, she'd said nothing. After two years one stupid ad on television still managed to resurrect the sting of that remark. No wonder she was having night sweats about singing in public.

Remote-surfing away from the hateful Lewis, she settled on an old black-and-white movie—Marie Dressler (hadn't she been Tugboat Annie?) dressed in rich matron's finery, appearing both aloof and comic. Certainly nobody's idea of a "big beautiful woman," but seemingly confident enough in herself to walk across the screen in a dress that announced "I don't care whether you think I deserve to wear this or not!"

Turning the volume way down (it was too late now to figure out what Marie and Jean Harlow were chatting about, anyway), Cassie dragged a crocheted afghan from the back of the couch to cover her legs, bunched a squishy throw pillow behind her head, and curled up on the couch with her eyes on the screen. There she gradually slipped into sleep, lulled by the soft drone of dialog uttered by long dead movie divas.

EPISODE EIGHTY–EIGHT

WHEN HE NOTICED THE CHILLINGLY FAMILIAR CAR parked across the street from Patsy's apartment building, Ian's first thought was *God, has Val actually been sitting out here all night?* He wouldn't doubt it, the way Val had been acting lately.

He could've ignored it, of course, but that didn't seem right somehow. Sighing as he unconsciously straightened out his T-shirt, Ian headed for her battered Buick. Shilling for Jordan Lewis, you'd think she'd have rated a better car by now—maybe like one of those pink Mary Kay models.

The early morning street was quiet. As he walked closer to the car, he could see Val hunched in the driver's seat, hands locked at two and ten on the wheel, as if poised to fire the ignition and squeal off. Her window was rolled down, so she had to know he was approaching.

Damn it, he sure was getting sick of these games.

"Valerie," he blurted within a yard of the car, and she swiveled sharply in response. "What are you doing here?"

"Waiting for you," she said, and she had the good grace to look sheepish about it. Ian flashed on his earlier unsuccessful attempts to meet with Patsy outside her job—back when they were going through a Val-induced rocky period, thank you very much—and the memory was almost enough to spark some sympathy. Almost, but not quite.

Since she was mostly masked by the car door, he couldn't be sure. But from the way the gauze peasant blouse stretched across her upper torso, Ian wondered whether she'd gained back some of her lost weight. He wondered if her bosses were saying anything about that.

"And you want to see me because—?"

"I need to make things straight between us," she explained, opening her door and, in rising from the driver's seat, confirming Ian's suspicions in the process. Her clothing was disheveled and her eyes drooped from a lack of sleep. Leaning back against her car, she stood as if using it alone kept her propped up. A hangover? "I needed to apologize for the way I've harassed you."

"You doing this for some program, Val? A twelve-step type deal?"

She smiled lightly. "No, Ian, this is something I felt I had to do all by myself. Woke up in a panic in the middle of the night, and I couldn't stop thinking of all the shit I've put you through. I don't know what was going on with me."

"Whatever it was, I hope you've got it under control," Ian said. "There's nothing left between us, Val. You've gotta get beyond it."

"I know," she admitted. "But it was easier to stay angry with you than to acknowledge all the fucked-up stuff I was doing. I can see that now, though, and I'm not gonna bother you any more."

Valerie seemed sincere, but he'd reserve judgment for now.

"You seeing anybody?" he asked.

"A guy?" Val answered. "Not at the moment, but there are a couple of men at work who look pretty interesting."

I meant a therapist, Ian thought. But he didn't pursue that out loud—perhaps she'd come to that conclusion by herself.

"Well, I'm glad you've decided to knock off the pranks. Bad enough you were messing with me, but some of your antics really spooked the chapter. That bit with the candies cost us several long-standing members."

Val nodded solemnly, then turned to get back into the car. Safely inside, she seemed to regain some gumption as she leaned out to say, "Well, maybe I need to see a counselor or something—for my own wellbeing. But I'm not the only spooky one in RADFAm."

Turning over the ignition, she started to roll up the window, then paused for a moment to deliver a parting shot before driving away. "Since I didn't have anything to do with that goddamn candy."

THE SOUND OF MUSICAL THEATRE wafting up through the air ducts was the first thing to tickle Joe's consciousness. ("Another Opening, Another Show"? *What show, and who cares?* he grumbled.) It was drifting from the apartment below. Moaning as he hoisted himself onto his elbow, Joe peered across Misty's blanket-shrouded shoulder to the digital alarm clock beyond. It read a quarter to noon, hours past their usual Saturday wakeup.

Stumbling out of bed, Joe slowly made his way to the kitchen, nearly stubbing his foot on a carton packed with Misty's paraphernalia. The main floor of the living room was a maze of boxes, housing former inhabitants of a set of shelves that had to be disassembled to make way for a great big hole in the wall.

Recently he'd been experiencing first apartment déjà vu, back when all storage furnishings were comprised of bricks, boards, and corrugated cardboard file cabinets that made a teeth-gritting sound whenever you tugged open a drawer.

He almost made it to the kitchen before the phone rang. Desperately scanning the living room, he finally uncovered the phone on an end table by Misty's chair. He grabbed it on the fourth ring, hopefully before it woke his sweetie up for good.

The timing could only mean it was his mother.

"Joey?" she opened, right away telling him she was more worried than usual. "I hope I didn't get you in the middle of anything."

"Just making some tea," he told her, carrying the cordless handset into the kitchen to do that very thing. He'd learned to appreciate a variety of teas since moving in with Misty—she had a whole cabinet shelf full of herbal teas in strange looking boxes—so he pulled down a packet of Ceylon something and opened it one-handed. "What can I do for you, Ma?" he asked, setting the microwave to boil a mug of water.

"I was wondering if you knew where your brother was," she quavered. "He didn't come home at his usual time last night."

"No, I don't, Ma," Joe answered, "and I don't think you wanna know either. Jimmy's gotten himself in some really deep trouble this time."

"What are you saying?" Joe could hear the panic in her voice, but under the circumstances there was no way he knew to stem it.

"I'm saying that your son was selling drugs to one of his shady old cronies on the police force—and they caught him in an Internal Affairs sting," Joe shot back. For some reason, the thought of her getting so upset over Jimmy's screwup struck him the wrong way. "Hell, they tried to bust me for it, too. So see if I'm around the next time he asks for help finding a job."

"It must be some sort of a misunderstanding," she rationalized, the sound of her son's agitation perversely calming her down. "Surely you don't think that Jimmy—"

"Mom, I saw him," Joe overrode her. "He was in the alley behind the restaurant, doing business and breaking the law. Where I work, Ma."

"So is he in jail?"

"No, he's not in jail. I was the one who got hauled downtown. My older brother ran away and left me to clean up, just like always. But don't you worry, Ma—he got away just fine. What in Holy Hell was he thinking, becoming a fugitive?"

"Will they come here looking, then?" she squeaked.

"The cops?" Joe considered. That wasn't something he'd thought about before now, but it made sense. "I suppose they will. It's where Jimmy lives; it's the address he put on Caspar's application."

"I don't know if I can handle *la policia* coming to my house," Joe's mother cried. "What am I supposed to do?"

"Let them in, Ma," he said as the microwave dinged. He retrieved his mug and dropped the tea bag in. "Just let them in. You've got nothing to worry about. It's Jimmy's mess, not yours."

"I know, but could you come over? I don't think I can deal with them all alone."

Joe sighed, then looked up to see Misty leaning in the kitchen doorway. Though she was bed rumpled, she still looked roundly beautiful. She sidled up to him and kissed him on his receiver-free cheek, her satiny caftan rustling against his side.

"Tell you what, Ma," Joe said. "I'll call the police station and ask if they need to talk to you. If they do, I'll come over to be with you, I promise."

After he hung up, he quickly gave Misty the score. She nodded, then grabbed him in both arms. "Are you doing okay?" she asked.

"I'm fine," Joe reassured her, "but I'm still really pissed with my asshole brother."

"I can't say that I'd be any more understanding if I were in your shoes. Much as I hate to admit it, there are some transgressions simply too maddening to easily forgive."

"You got that right," Joe agreed, heading back to get the phone book. "Say, what does 'Another Opening, Another Show' come from?"

"*Kiss Me, Kate.*" Misty smiled back sweetly, standing at the counter to put the used tea bag in the compost can.

"Name's not Kate, but I'd be glad to, anyway," Joe grinned back. Placing the phone on its cradle, he bounded back into the kitchen to follow Misty's stage direction to the letter.

EPISODE EIGHTY-NINE

AT LEAST, JENNY LATER HAD TO ADMIT, Molly hadn't pulled a Cujo. The golden's stance was guarded when Paul arrived with company, but once he'd held Jenny's hand and together the two had stroked her silky coat, she'd quickly settled down. Which certainly had met with Jenny's approval.

After their long evening's excitement, neither the paralegal nor the teacher could muster more than a companionable hug and kiss before tumbling onto Paul's bed in their underwear, fast asleep, entwined. This, of course, had forestalled any awkward question of sexual gymnastics, at least on that too-early morning.

Somewhere near dawn Molly had risen from her post at the foot of the bed, laying her head by Paul and whining in his face.

"Don't get up," Paul had whispered to Jen. "I've just gotta take the dog out." She'd felt him roll out, then fifteen minutes later he'd returned, his lanky body warmly nuzzling against hers. (Who'd have thought a frame so thin could generate all that body heat?) They both fell back asleep and didn't rouse until close to noon.

When she woke the second time, Jenny could still feel Paul breathing heavily next to her. Quietly eyeing the bedroom, she took her first full look-around in daylight. Nondescript furniture, a Robert B. Parker cracked open on the dresser, two well-used dog toys on the floor—the only hint that this wasn't the bedroom of any other average guy was the Botero Exhibit postcard stuck in the corner of his dresser mirror.

She'd attended that art show herself, and after studying both his sculpture and drawings, she still couldn't decide if the artist had been elevating his subjects or sneering at them. But plenty of FAs, she knew, found such questions irrelevant. At such times their willful critical blindness was a puzzle to her.

Rolling over and inadvertently disturbing Molly—who'd once again resumed guard duty—she discreetly examined her bedmate. Jenny was hoping for one of those timeless moments when you catch your lover asleep, vulnerable, innocent. But instead he opened his eyes and smiled up at her, sweetly bleary.

"Been awake long?" he rasped.

"Not at all," she reassured him, reaching over to gently stroke his face with her fingertips. "Get some more rest."

She rose carefully, grabbed her purse and quickly donned the blouse she'd tossed across the footboard. Molly heaved herself up to follow into the bathroom, but Jenny said, "Sorry, girl, no peeping," and firmly closed the door. "Not til we get to know each other better, at least."

However she must not have completely latched it, because midway through her ablutions the door was nosed curiously open. Mouth full of toothpaste, Jen suddenly became aware of the big mutt sitting stock-still and eyeing her suspiciously. But hey, she worked with, for and against lawyers, so she was not about to let some canine voodoo throw her.

"Yes, girl," she told the dog, finally free of the mass of cinnamony foam in her mouth. "The pack leader's brought me into your den. And I have no intention of skedaddling any time soon."

"Nice to hear that," Paul chuckled, startling her into almost dropping her toothbrush. He was standing in the doorway, Big Dog boxer-clad, proffering an empty glass coffee pot and smiling most devilishly. "Or was I not supposed to hear that? Did I just interrupt a girl thang?"

"You did," Jenny admitted with aplomb and closed the door in his face. "Now leave us ladies alone, why don't ya?"

"Roger wilco," he agreed from the other side of the door. "Want coffee?"

"Wouldn't turn it down. And who's this Roger?" she quipped, examining herself in the tiny bathroom mirror. Despite last night's events, she looked far more rested than she'd ever have expected. And far happier than she'd felt for awhile. In going out with Paul again she'd made a decision that seemed just as right the morning after as it had when she'd made it.

She only hoped that Paul was feeling the same as her right about now.

Reaching down, she scratched one of Molly's floppy ears. The retriever cocked her head to achieve maximum finger play, then plopped and splayed, belly up, on the floor. At the very least she'd reached some kind of understanding with this part of the family.

HE COULDN'T PLACE EXACTLY where or when the notion had originated, but for days now Dexter had been trying to ignore a foreboding, a niggling, an irritating something on the verge of—what?

Sitting in the rain-battered strip mall parking lot, Eddie Cochran spinning on the Discman ("Ain't no cure for the summertime blues," indeed!), he wondered why this feeling now, of all times. Rachel seemed to have emerged from her sullen stage—getting that learner's permit had clearly been a Big Thing—while Jackie was happy dating his little Gidget. (Okay, he needed to stop calling her that—even in his head—or else it was gonna slip out sometime when he didn't want it to.)

His medical practice was doing quite well, something that hadn't automatically been a foregone conclusion during the days he'd first considered leaving ER freelancing. Socially, there were no big crises in the RADFAm chapter, at least that he knew about. And as for his wife, Neeko—well, Neeko did seem to be the X Factor now, didn't she?

He'd figured that unloading chapter officer duties would put a positive spin on their relationship. Though he'd never given her any reason to be, Neeko'd remained irrationally jealous of the other officers (Eleanor Bollen, in particular), so much so that when chapter members had started receiving those batches of tampered chocolates, there'd even been a moment when he'd imagined—but no, that was all Valerie's doing.

Still, there was no ignoring that Neeko continued acting touchy whenever size acceptance came up. Last night was a prime case in point. It'd been their first full-family dinner all week, and Rachel had been teasing Jackie about Sandy. At one point she'd held up a wilted piece of romaine and joked, "Take this with you on your date, Jackie—that way you won't hafta buy her any snacks!"

Her brother had smiled wanly, but he hadn't gotten angry. It was Rachel, after all, who'd first suggested hooking Sandy up with Anne Reynard. She'd even taken the girl aside the other day and given her the therapist's card. One sign that the girl wasn't too far gone—she had shared the self-esteem counselor's name with her parents.

But Rachel's joke had steered the conversation into rocky areas. There were times Dex thought that married people developed psychic connections. Although he'd never said a word to Neeko about it, there had been a moment when Dex was struck by Anne's strong resemblance to his first wife. And though she'd been nowhere around when he'd reached this revelation, Neeko still got prickly at even a passing reference to Anne Reynard.

Jackie didn't know any of this, of course, so he'd innocently shot back, "At least I'm going on a date, Sis! Maybe you should 'motivate' yourself and talk to your Counselor Lady. See if she can help change your crappy social life."

"Touché, Geekboy," Rachel had chuckled. She wouldn't have been so easygoing a few months ago. And she'd probably have lobbed another retort back at him if Neeko hadn't suddenly snorted, loudly and derisively.

"Anne Reynard," she'd spat, glaring at her dinner plate. "As if any poor child could be helped by her!" Then she'd glanced up at the rest of the family, seemingly startled by her words, and they'd quickly shifted the conversation elsewhere.

When Dex tried to ask later about her dinner outburst, Neeko had skirted the topic. "Eating disorders," she'd scoffed, her back to him as she sat on her side of the bed. "Only Western culture could get so bent out of shape by eating! I'm beginning to wonder if it isn't just another fraud being perpetrated by corrupt impostors. Women like Anne Reynard are no better than patent medicine salesmen."

"Now when we had real concerns about Rachel," Dex had gently reminded, "you weren't so down on the woman."

"Teenaged histrionics," Neeko had sniffed. "S'all it turned out to be. There's an entire profession making big bucks from adolescent behavior that'd probably blow over if it was just left alone. An army of so-called mental health professionals working overtime, subverting us into believing nobody's healthy!"

As suddenly as she'd snapped into it, her voice softened. Then she'd rolled over and hugged him, adding placatingly, "It's not as if this Reynard person were a real doctor—or had gone through all your years of medical training. I'm only saying we shouldn't be giving her more credit than she deserves. She's just a middleaged, midsized woman who can talk to kids."

Twining her long tapered fingers through his chest hair, she'd followed this last with a kiss, effectively cutting the conversation short. Obviously, however, it hadn't resolved the questions still buzzing around in Dexter's mind. Was his wife jealous of Anne now? He still recalled that embarrassing moment with Eleanor during the chapter meeting in their house.

Dex sighed as the disc came to a close, only to see Jackie standing under the awning of the martial arts studio. Engaging the ignition, he honked to let his son know he was out there for rainy day pickup. As he shifted into drive the cell phone began vibrating in his shirt pocket. Pressed by crisp broadcloth against his chest, it ominously demanded that he answer it.

EPISODE NINETY

FIRST THOUGHT: *This is not my bedroom—*

Eyes sticky-shut, not sure if and where dream became reality, Rachel slowly sorted it out. Mattress not hard enough—sheets too scratchy—a shock of cold metal along her right arm—an irritating, itchy pressure in her left hand—muttering TV somewhere nearby providing a ubiquitous modern soundtrack—odors.

No, this isn't home—but somehow familiar? Where? Eyelids fluttering, Rachel struggled to focus on something, anything through the fog. Then she sank back inside herself.

FIRST INCLINATION: Dismiss her denial as pure horseshit, since Val's long, inspired history of truth-stretching rivaled only the most tawdry soap opera. But he also had to admit there was something in her manner—not defensive, but loaded with a sort of righteous scorn—making Ian reconsider her claim. "I didn't have anything to do with that goddamn candy. I like my revenge with more style."

So if not Valerie, then who?

Plunking a disc into the CD-ROM drive (*OK Computer*, always an appropriate choice), he returned to the site where they'd tweaked their first clue. The ZaftIngather Web Board always had decent weekend traffic: A dozen threads down, he found a group of posters responding to something sent by "marzbarz." Looked as if Val'd gone home to indulge in some Internet trolling.

This time Ian's ex had chosen to point a Press-On nail at Greg and Connie's impending Full-Figured Friends beauty pageant.

> If members of the so-called Size Acceptance movement were sincere about their so-called cause, they'd be boycotting and picketing this sexist travesty! How can there truly be acceptance when the same old practices of objectification are supported by a so-called BBW Beauty Pageant?

At least one more "so-called" than the posting needed, Ian decided. But it really didn't tell him anything more than he'd already known. Val was a stirrer-upper, but that didn't mean she was also a candy tamperer. Why deny it now? One possible answer—somehow it no longer fit the woman's screwball agenda to be judged guilty.

But that still brought them no nearer to the identity of the real candy prankster. Sighing, Ian logged off, sat back and pondered, Radiohead still moaning through his Cambridge speakers.

NOT HER BEDROOM?—No, parents' room, looking for car keys.

Neeko'd told her they were on the top of the big old dresser, but no keys. Bedside tables, also clear. Foregoing parental privacy for the promise of behind-the-wheel-time (and perhaps a bit of extra gas money?), Rachel pulls open the top drawer of her stepmom's end of the dresser. Pulling out an old set of keys that she's pretty sure no longer fit any of the extant family vehicles, she reveals a well-handled, multipage photocopy.

A member list of the RADFAm chapter—with names and addresses and email info. Several names are crossed off; others have checkmarks by them, and one, Eleanor Bollen, has an email address penciled in next to her name.

What does all this mean?

Neeko's voice—she's found the car keys downstairs—"Hurry up! Looks like it's starting to rain big time—"

Pushing troubled thoughts aside, Rachel shuts the drawer and rushes from the bedroom.

"So what do you want to show me, Eleanor?" Lainie asked, stirring a blue packet of fake sugar into her decaf. ("Just something I've gotten used to," she'd say whenever asked why she continued to use NutraSweet after officially giving up on dieting ages ago.) She smiled concernedly at her friend, and the gesture was sufficient to push Eleanor into the troubling topic she'd been wishing she could avoid.

"Well, you know I finally got online," she began. "Thanks to Ian, it wasn't nearly as scary as I thought. There are still times when I panic—do I say 'yes, save the normal template,' or how to escape those popup thingies. Too many choices, I guess." The chapter secretary paused for a sip of raspberry iced tea. "And then, of course, there are all those flu bugs on the Internet, you know."

"So I've heard," Lainie grinned, as the Kuppa Joe-a waitress slid two croissants across the tabletop between them.

"Ian got me a free mail account with some kind of protection on it, though," Eleanor continued, "so I'm not too worried about bugs or parasites or whatever they're called. But I have been getting some—I don't know what to call them—bothersome emails the last few days. This last one really concerns me." Reaching beneath the table for her purse, she pulled out a folded white paper and handed it to Lainie. "Go ahead, read it," she urged unnecessarily.

The message was short and nasty.

Some fools may buy your sweet and clueless act, but not me! I've seen the way you cozy up to the men in the chapter—particularly the *married* ones. Keep it up, and next time it won't just be hot coffee that's dumped in your lap!

Eleanor watched Lainie read and re-read the note. She nervously nibbled around her croissant, wondering if her friend would come to the same conclusion she'd reached. Finally, Lainie dropped the letter onto the table, asking the one question that clinched it.

"Have you shown Dex this email?"

Not in bed. Car—she's behind the wheel. It's pouring, and the rain pounds louder than Neeko's words. Every few blocks Rachel steals a look at her stepmother, wondering if she'll get up the nerve to ask about the list in her dresser. Traffic is hectic; the downpour seemingly hasn't made anyone any more cautious.

Coming up on a notorious exurban intersection, Rachel suddenly registers the green light's switch to yellow. Driver's training lessons playing, she takes her foot off the pedal to avoid a skid, ending up nose-first a couple feet beyond the stopline. But the light's red! Rachel hits the brakes and is now fully within the intersection—

Should she back up? She turns toward her stepmother, seeing only a body in the passenger seat. Neeko seems oblivious to her mistake. Nothing like the driving Nazi at school. Rachel shifts into reverse, backing up those scary ten too-far feet and erasing her embarrassment.

Bright lights draw her eyes too late to the rearview mirror, revealing a minivan a moment before slamming into the trunk of their car. In slide-show motion the driver's airbag deploys, the car lurches across the intersection—

And a bellowing semi thunders down from the north.

MOLLY HAD BEEN PATIENT, but she couldn't be put off forever—it was, after all, the weekend. And weekends meant park time. Fortunately the dog had been okay with letting Jenny accompany them on their ritual romp. A quick stop at her place for a change to jeans and capable walking shoes, and awa-a-a-y we go. Running ahead of the couple, stopping every ten feet to turn and coax them along, the golden retriever led her human companions along the wooded park trail.

A good walk, Jenny thought, determined not to be the one who suggested parking on one of the concrete benches that popped up irregularly along their journey. For a woman her size she'd always considered herself fairly fit, but keeping pace with this galloping goof was something else entirely.

Finally the trail opened up onto a picnic alcove and Paul thoughtfully suggested a breather. The area was blissfully empty, so they perched together on a table—Paul placing his windbreaker on the wet wood *a lá* Walter Raleigh—and breathlessly contemplated the beauty around them. The leaves, Jen noticed, were showing their early fall droop. Throughout the damp grass lay scattered hedge apples, resembling irradiated tennis balls. Though scudding clouds had threatened another shower, the sky now shone intense blue through the sparse forest cover.

On her left, Paul had just laid his long arm across her back, draping it companionably on her shoulders, his dangling fingers playing with the ruffled hem of her short sleeve top. Jenny'd always felt uncomfortable about those farmwife arms, but from Paul's unhurried stroking it seemed obvious that he didn't share her bias.

What exactly was this? She'd read all the mags, had endured repeated lectures from Lissa—she knew she was capable of attracting a lover. But now that this had all gone beyond Theoretical and into the Real, she still faced down the surety that it all would be revealed as a more-deserving someone else's storybook fantasy. Would she ever conquer her frigging self-doubt?

And what if she did, and it all went to hell anyway?

Molly suddenly sidled up, hefting an ungainly tree branch in her mouth.

"Duty calls," Paul chuckled, rising from the bench to take the branch and break it down into more manageable lengths. Leaning back, Jenny watched the two as they wrestled with the stick. Paul was so handsome, so sexy. She wished her mother had lived long enough to meet him. She bit her lip at this futile yearning for motherly approval.

At that moment Paul suddenly straightened and turned away to fetch a cell-phone from his holster. "Yes, Ian," she could hear. "Jenny's with me." The words sent a shiver through Jenny, and she felt herself keying up in the same way she had the night before. Anxiously, she watched her lover as he digested Ian's news.

"There's been an accident," Paul finally told Jenny, handing her the phone, then turning to clip Molly to her leash. "Details are still real sketchy—"

BACK IN THAT DAMNED STRANGE BED—emerging from the quicksand of memory and pain-killer hallucination—entire body aching, eyes cringing from the pain of institutional brightness—*Someone else in the room?* Rachel squinted down the bed. There at the foot sat her father and brother. *Poor Daddy! God, you look like crap!*

An involuntary twitch signaled Dex that she was regaining consciousness, so he nudged Jackie and stood up. "Please go tell the nurse," he softly asked her brother, and the boy dashed out of the room. Moving to the side of the bed, he laid his massive hand on her forehead. It felt cool and reassuring, yet scary, all at once. "Rachel," he said. "It's okay. You're okay."

Clearing her scratchy throat, Rachel timidly asked The Question. "Dad. Where's Mom?"

EPISODE NINETY-ONE

THE VAST RANGE OF DRESS RACKS both beckoned and repelled Cassie. Definitely uncharted territory here, as she sought an extraordinary design, beyond merely utilitarian, to transform her into a "Big Beautiful

Woman." *Wish Jenny was here,* she sighed, not for the first time, as she riffled through lacy, sleek and beaded Technicolor finery.

Wandering through this upscale downtown plus-size apparel shoppe, it occurred to Cass that she lacked any real-life friends to share events like this with. For years work and church were her prime foci, neither of which tended to yield the "bosom chum" type of friend she saw on TV, one to discuss private fears and dreams with.

Decades equating "reliable and pious" with "lumpy and unattractive," to now being called on to transform herself into someone totally different (for an audience, no less), and her sole support network was a sister living a long way up north.

Prior to meeting Jenny, Cass's wardrobe had consisted of local Wal-Mart-sensible wares, catalog couture and the occasional gift. Fast forward (via the size acceptance group thing) to her driving to the city, confronting rack after rack of gowns, some almost aerodynamic in design, hugging and thrusting and defying the physics of flab—she couldn't help feeling like a fraud. She imagined that at any minute the supersized saleslady would storm out from behind her cash register, clasp Cass's shoulder in meaty hand and demand she leave the shoppe immediately.

Down the nearby sportswear aisle Cassie watched a plus-sized matron offer advice on jeans tops to a considerably larger teenaged girl. Mother and daughter, she supposed. The sight of the pair, serious yet affectionately considering what looked best on this plump young girl, sparked a deep longing in her heart. She had no recall whatsoever of such mother/daughter moments, no positive bonding memories of being taught to dress her best, no matter her shape or size.

I need some unbiased eyes, was her final decision. She was holding a stunning sequined black gown (priced at nearly a full month's salary, thank you!) against her body, vogue-ing in front of the three-way mirror and trying to envision herself as simply ravishing. But her normal, stolid, peasant reflection miserably returned a jaundiced stare in triplicate. *And some moral support,* she added with feeling, returning the dress to its hook on a display. Soon as she got home she was dialing Jenny.

JOE'S MOTHER WAS EVEN MORE DRAMATIC than Misty'd remembered. Perched on an old ottoman, dressed in a clean but faded muumuu, she moaned deeply each time her larcenous son was mentioned. Which meant that they were in for enough lamentation to fuel a festival of college-rock bands.

"Jimmy telephoned an hour ago," Petra was explaining to Joe, seated on the floor at her feet, patting his mother's hand soothingly. "Said he was going to turn himself in, but he had to make some arrangements first. What do you think he's talking about, Joey? What could he be up to?"

Joe glanced over at Misty before answering. From the angry glint in his eyes it was obvious that he was absolutely incensed at the toll his brother's escapades was taking on their mother—even more ticked off than he'd been at their own grueling police station experience. Maybe Misty should be taking umbrage over Jimmy's blatant betrayal of his hardworking younger brother.

"I don't know, Ma," Joe answered, eyes scanning the room. There was, Misty thought, something different about the place, but she couldn't put her finger on it. "But hopefully he'll find a good lawyer."

"What about the lady who got you out?" his mother asked. "Can she help?"

"She's not a full lawyer, Ma—she's a paralegal. Like a law nurse. Her boss could maybe take it on, but I don't think she does a whole lot of criminal cases."

Even beneath her voluminous muumuu, Misty could see Petra's maternal spine suddenly stiffen. Snatching her hand from Joe's grasp, Mrs. Rivera shook her head and scoldingly announced, "Whatever he may have done, Jimmy is not a criminal!"

Joe ducked his head, rose and thoughtfully walked around the room. He dragged a finger across a display shelf that Misty now recalled had been stuffed with toy collectibles, but which now displayed a simple vase filled with flowers surrounded by photos of Petra's sons from youth to now. The shelf was dust-free beneath a hand-crocheted doily.

"Nobody's calling Jimmy a criminal, Ma," he finally responded. "Just saying that he's gotten involved in a ton of trouble with the wrong kind of people. Maybe one of our friends could help. Maybe he doesn't need or want their help. And anyway, he still knows guys on the force."

"I can contact Jenny," Misty offered, happy to have something to contribute without betraying any personal bias. Pulling open her bag, she grabbed her Wiccan Book of Days, whose back pages listed all her vital info, and went toward the kitchen to call.

"Good idea," Joe muttered, returning to his mother's side. "Ma," he asked gently, "where are all your Beanie Babies?"

"Oh, umm," Misty heard over the ring-through on the handset, "Jimmy was saying how cute they were, so—" But before she caught the rest of these dicey-sounding details, the young paralegal answered.

"Thank God, Mist," Jenny gasped as the psychic identified herself. "I've been trying to reach you. Something awful has happened."

THOUGH IT CAUSED HER DEEP SHAME to admit it, if Lainie hadn't been there when Eleanor first heard about the accident, she probably would have just curled up in her chair and stayed home. As illogical as it sounded, she felt as if she was somehow culpable in this horrible tragedy. As if even by just talking about Dex's wife she'd initiated the event herself.

Did some dark corner of her really want this to happen?

Lainie had scornfully pushed her out of that mental cul-de-sac. "Nothing about this is about you," she'd pronounced as Eleanor weakly tried to beg off joining the other officers at the hospital to offer Dex their support. "It's about helping a friend in need. You had nothing to do with the accident; it was an asshole gear jockey driving too fast for conditions. Now Dex and his kids are gonna need all the friends they've got, and you'd never forgive yourself if you weren't counted there among 'em."

As usual, Lainie was right. They left Eleanor's house and drove to the trauma center. The evening was damp and chilly, the sort of cold that caused more aches than usual in Eleanor's bones. (Night like tonight she could almost envy her friends with disability plates.) But her shiver was as much from trepidation as temperature as they scuttled across the crowded parking lot.

The two older women found Misty and Jenny, along with their two beaus, hunched together in woefully inadequate modular chairs in the ER waiting area. Shame once again washed over Eleanor—she had at least twenty years on every one of them, and here she'd been shying away, a little kid scared of going to the doctor.

Stop it! she scolded. *This isn't about your own childish feelings.*

"Any news?" Lainie asked as Misty struggled up to hug the new arrivals. Pressed into the marshmallow-reassurance of the supersized chapter president, Eleanor almost did feel like a child again for just that moment.

"Don't remember exactly what I told you when I called," Misty admitted once they'd moved apart to sit down. "Ian called a couple hours ago. Dexter had phoned, asking if he could put Jackie up for the night. Dex was pretty incoherent, but Ian caught most of what happened—Neeko and Rachel were in a very serious auto accident. Broadsided by a semi." This news made everyone cringe and mutter, even those who'd already heard it.

"Rachel is in critical but stable condition. Neeko made it through the ambulance trip alive, but died here shortly after."

"And Dex?" Lainie asked.

"He's still with Rachel," Misty said. "They haven't released her upstairs yet, since there are still a few tests to administer."

"Um, how is Dex? Really?" Eleanor pursued.

"Focused on and concerned about Rachel," Misty replied. "Whole time she was unconscious, he wouldn't stop worrying about how she's gonna react when she finds out, when all of this sinks in. Dex gave us her counselor's number, but all we reached was voice mail."

"Oh! That poor young one," Eleanor cried with sure awareness of the suffering, grief and guilt facing the whole Logan family—and above all a man she greatly admired—for a long, sad time to come.

EPISODE NINETY–TWO

RIFLING THROUGH WORK TIES for something appropriate to wear, it became painfully clear to Ian that he didn't have much in the way of grownup clothes. The selection ran toward the novelty: the Beatles circa Sgt. Pepper; Spider-Man swinging from skyscrapers; a Tex Avery cartoon wolf; whole zoo of endangered species wildlife ties—none of these were somber enough for a visitation, he realized. In the end the best he could ferret out was a retro pattern in shades of gray, sorta like something you'd expect to see on a member of the guy chorus in *Guys And Dolls*, but the best he could come up with under the circumstances.

Snagging a Mountain Dew from the fridge, he headed out to pick up Patsy. The evening was dim and damp, but at least it wasn't pouring like on the day of Neeko's death. Over the car radio NPR reporters were nattering indistinctly, but he didn't feel like turning up the volume to hear exactly what they were discussing. Instead he drove silently through the busy city streets, pondering the Fates that would not once, but twice make Dex Logan a widower.

As he let himself into Patsy's apartment he found her seated at the computer. The dark blue linen jacket and matching full-length sheath she was wearing seemed a bit spiffy for mere web surfing. But she looked so sharp Ian didn't mind the incongruity. "Find something interesting?" he asked, coming alongside to kiss her on the nape of her neck.

"Just the usual rabble-rousing," Patsy shrugged, swiveling the monitor so Ian could have a better look. She was scanning, he saw, the ZaftIngather message board where he and Jackie had first found Valerie's agitated "marzbarz" postings. "Seems like Connie and Greg's beauty pageant has caught someone's attention," she observed, pointing out a lengthy message thread headlined "STOP The OBJECTification!"

After scanning the initial sally, Ian recognized words that seemed awfully familiar. "In a climate where size acceptance has difficulty being viewed as anything more than a freak show," the posting concluded, "a so-called BBW Beauty Pageant is THE LAST THING WE NEED!"

"I've read this before," he anounced. "These very same words were in a posting Val sent last year that slammed the RADFAm conference—and its Fashion Show. It appears someone's been doing some copy-and-pasting."

Patsy scrolled up to the author's name. "'Sanity Sister,'" he read. "Well, that couldn't be Val."

Patsy giggled in response, then immediately looked contrite. "This gonna be a problem for the chapter?" she finally asked.

"I wouldn't think so," Ian decided. "That's Greg and Connie's show."

"It just bothers me to see this level of anger," Patsy continued as she rolled her chair back and logged offline. "Probably has to do with the way I was raised. When I read these words, they make me feel twitchy and uncomfortable." She stood, smoothed out her dress, then smiled shyly at Ian.

"Well, when I read something like that, all I can think is it's aimed at the wrong target," Ian frowned. "We waste far too much time sniping at each other rather than focusing on the real problem sources." He stopped, catching himself before tirading further, then stepped forward to kiss his girlfriend. "But enough of that—I haven't told you yet how utterly hot you look tonight."

"Is that appropriate?" Patsy worried. "I'm still not used to dressing this nice. Should I tone it down?"

"Not at all," Ian reassured her, wrapping his arms around her luscious curves and kneeling down slightly to meet her lips. "It's not the dress, it's the sexy lady inside."

"Okay," Patsy demurred, buttoning her linen jacket once they separated and blushing so becomingly that Ian selfishly wished they didn't have to go out that night. "I'll take your word for it."

"You'd better," Ian grinned, leading her to the door. There had been a time, he thought, when she wouldn't have taken his word on anything. They'd clearly come a long way.

JACKIE COULDN'T REMEMBER the drive to the funeral home—or much of the day, in fact—but standing now in the viewing room, mobbed by folding chairs and muttery adults, he felt childish and hyperaware of his surroundings. Off to one side Dad sat, hugging Rachel so hard it was a wonder she could breathe. Considering the bruises weirdly contouring her face, it couldn't feel too good to be leaning into his wall-sized torso. But his sis didn't seem to mind. The Rachel he knew didn't even seem to be there, really—just this battered zombie girl.

Throughout the room Dad's med fellows and a whole bunch of fat people were talking to each other in low tones. Against the far wall was the coffin, but Jackie had been working hard to keep his eyes from straying there. Not yet, anyway. There'd come a point, he knew, when Dad would take his hand and they'd hafta go up for a good long look at the body. Mom's body.

Could he do it? As a little kid he'd felt disappointed that he couldn't attend Grandpa Logan's memorial service—he'd almost Hulked out when they left him with a babysitter that day. But today he'd trade anything not to be here. Not now, not ever.

That Miz Reynard woman was walking down the aisle toward them. Rachel escaped their father's arms and quickly rose to meet her. For some reason the relief on his sister's face at the sight of her counselor royally irked Jackie. *She's not supposed to be relieved,* he thought. *Not today!*

"Sweetie, how are you holding up?" the woman asked, and each soothing syllable tweaked Jackie's irritation. What kind of lame dumbass question was that? What was Rachel supposed to say? And why couldn't the bitch leave his family alone, anyway?

"Okay, I guess, Anne," Rachel was whimpering, and the Reynard lady was nodding sagely, as if accepting this obvious fib. *Must be a pretty crappy shrink if Rachel can fool her,* Jackie fumed as the woman turned to his Dad.

"Dex, I'm so sorry for your family's loss," she said, placing a hand on his shoulder. *Slap it off, Dad!* A voice inside him was yelling. *She shouldn't even be here!*

His Dad had started to say something back, but Jackie was already turning to leave the room. Nearly stumbling over a chair at the end of the aisle, he rushed toward the exit, ignoring his father's call as he fled the scene. He'd reached the hall before bumping into a tall man carrying a paper cup full of water.

THOUGH PAUL HAD VOLUNTEERED to fetch her a drink, Jenny started to feel the need to get something for herself two minutes after he left the room.

Perhaps she was still experiencing the emotional vestiges of her mother's death. But even though she knew most of the folks in the room, she still felt abandoned once Paul had stepped out of view. *You've got it bad, girl,* she chastised herself, but it didn't stop her from ditching Lissa and Delia to go in search of the missing waterboy.

The funeral home was more warren-like than it appeared from outside. Once she left the viewing parlor she wandered through a maze of hushed halls. Why weren't there any funeral directors around to assist the befuddled bereaved? Jenny meandered aimlessly until she finally heard Paul's voice.

She peeked in to see him perched on a sturdy leatherette couch in an empty room beside Dex's son. Though Paul's back was to her, it was obvious from the expression on Jackie's face that the two were engaged in heartfelt conversation. Jenny paused, standing in the doorway, as Paul let the young boy vent.

"I'm not mad at Dad or anything," he was claiming, right foot tapping an agitated rhythm on the shiny parquet floor, "but nobody invited her! Thinks she can just take over the house or something just because my dopey sister's been in therapy. It's a whole lot of shi—crap!"

"'She'?" Paul simply repeated, ignoring the near slip. "She who?"

"Mizzzz Reynard," Jackie sneered, looking about five years younger. "Rachel's counselor."

"You don't like her, then."

"No shit, Sherlock," Jackie snapped, then immediately backpedaled. "I'm sorry," he choked, "I don't know why I'm being such a dick."

"What do you want?" Paul asked softly, in a matter-of-fact tone that managed to avoid sounding either judgmental or touchy-feely. Jenny realized she hadn't witnessed Teacher Paul interacting with kids before, even though it was his day job. Looked like he was pretty good at it.

"What do you want?" he repeated, more gently. From the expression on Jackie's face, it was obvious that he hadn't been asked this question—or at least hadn't heard anyone ask him this question—since Neeko's death.

"I don't know," he finally whispered. He paused, looking not at Paul but into some alternative, saner world, maybe. "That woman just shouldn't be here," he muttered. "Our mother is dead. Why's she gotta look so much like Rachel's mother?"

EPISODE NINETY-THREE

THREE BANKER'S BOXES stretched along the table in front of Jenny, daring her to unstrap their tops and get lost in the contents *("You can check out any time you want, but you can never leave.")*

All part of a pending ultra-complicated accident claim of Lissa's, and while there were times when Jenny enjoyed digging into such details, today she kept mentally replaying Neeko's visitation, and the aftershocks of an accident that actually involved personal friends.

She'd watched Dex suffering behind stoic control, seen Jackie's youthful energy flare with anger. But the Logan her mind kept returning to was Rachel.

When her own mom passed away, the predominant feeling Jenny recalled was an aching sense of guilt—that she'd taken her mother's presence for granted enough to find her irritating, that she'd never taken time to show her mother that she really had been raised right, that there were moments when she'd just plain selfishly wished the woman out of her life.

So is guilt a big part of the tie between child and parent, alive or dead? Is it stronger or weaker when the tie isn't genetic? (Or like Cassie and Alice, genetic-but-absent-by-choice?) And where do you find the guts to cope when, like Rachel, you feel at least partially responsible for that person's death?

Jenny sighed, backing away from the still-sealed boxes, only to see Lissa leaning in the doorway, observing her pique.

"Busy?" her boss asked, and Jenny shook her head. "Then maybe you can give me a hand."

Jenny gratefully followed Lissa to her office. Centered on her desk were two cards, printed on lavender cardstock. Headlining the first was a graphic of two ineptly altered female silhouettes embracing on a beach. Beneath was typed the following announcement, with a date and unfamiliar address:

Our Celebration!
Lissa Jones & Delia Cotton
Wish to express their love and commitment
in a union ceremony!
Please come and share this moment
of personal celebration with us.

The second card, Jenny saw, contained the same legend, but surrounded by a border of vines and roses. "I'm not much for layout," Lissa confessed. "Spent all morning trying to make those clipart silhouettes more—you know, less grotesque, and I've failed miserably. So I quickly pasted the announcement on a second page with the more conventionally 'straight' border. Not sure about either of them, though."

"Okay. So what do you want the announcement to say?" Jenny asked, both thankful for this more fun distraction and eager to help her boss.

"'Y'all come to our wedding, dammit,'" Lissa quipped. "Oh, why'd I volunteer to do this? Delia's the creative one, not me. Want to know how truly pathetic I am? This morning I circular-filed a draft announcing 'Jones picks Cotton'—-and I actually searched a retro postcard site for lift-that-bale graphics! My mama, Lord rest her soul, would've killed me.

"Of course, truth be told," Lissa added, one side of her mouth tilting upwards, "she wasn't all that thrilled about the direction I took in my selection of partners, either."

"Think we ever stop arguing with our parents, here or gone?" Jenny mused.

"You know what they say: 'Only thing more powerful than a parent is a dead parent.' So what d'ya think? Are both these announcements as sucky as I think they are? Or am I just being hypercritical?"

"It's your ceremony," Jenny sidestepped. "The only opinions that really matter are yours and Delia's. I personally like the first announcement, but you know better than me if it really and truly captures the essence of what you want. Uh, need any more help—?"

"No," Lissa grumped. "I said I'd do this, and I'm keeping my promise."

"Okay, Boss-lady," Jenny grinned. "Just stick clear of them ol' 'Cotton' fields, okay?"

"Yas'm, Missy!"

JOE HADN'T HEARD ANYTHING from his mother for several days—not unusual in itself, since she still boycotted calling the apartment for fear of unexpectedly having to talk to "that strange woman"—so he'd decided to stop by her house on this, his first free weekday.

"That strange woman" was staffing the Isle, and even without shop customers she always seemed a bit less "Misty" when he showed up there. (It wasn't something Joe felt comfortable discussing with her yet. Was he like that when she stopped by Caspar's? And what scale could he use to measure "not acting like yourself," anyway?) But he gave Misty a heartfelt squeeze and smooch, then headed out, setting the doorbell pealing.

Over the car radio Mariah Carey was belting an old dance hit. Once there'd been a day when Joe'd have spent quality time fant-up-sizing that promising derriere, but it was truly dull fare when compared to his Misty. He joined in singing, picturing his girlfriend on the dance floor instead—just what he needed to steel himself for a return to the home where he'd been reared, so to speak.

The house was closed and shuttered when he drove up. His mom's car wasn't out and the curtains were drawn. Usually the old woman let every bit of sun that the Midwest weather would offer into her home. What if she's sick, or hurt? He should've called first before coming, should've phoned her himself, anyway, but with all that'd been going on—

This wasn't like him. Clearly his brother's idiotic stunt had unbalanced him far more than he'd realized. Geez, if he could get himself worked up like this, how was his mom holding up?

As soon as she cracked open the front door leaving the chain attached, his worst fears were realized. *Shit, Jimmy's here with her, in the house.* "Mom," he coaxed, "It's just me. Joe. Please let me in, Mom."

She did, of course, and he was shocked to see how old and used-up she looked. Wearing a stained, disheveled housedress that looked as if she'd been sleeping in it, her typically immaculate coiffure haphazardly combed, there were stark dark circles under her eyes and her complexion looked pale and waxy. *Damn you, Jimmy!*

"My Joseph," she gasped, and from the raspy wheeze on the end of his name it was obvious she'd taken up smoking again. Joe could feel a core of anger heating inside—it'd been months since she'd picked up a cigarette. "What a surprise!"

"Where is he, Ma?" Joe clipped. "Is he hiding in the basement? Or is he so stupid to be in his own room?!"

Her flash of alarm at that propelled him down the hallway. On the end table by her favorite chair he could see an ashtray piled with stubbed-out butts next to a half-full pack of generic cigarettes. Without thinking he swept up the pack and stuffed it into his pocket.

"Joe! He showed up just this afternoon. It's all a misunderstanding—Jimmy explained!"

"I'm sure he did," Joe barked, swiveling back to face her. "Just a small misunderstanding—that led to me spending half the night in a cop shop! Don't you realize the risk he's putting you in right now? Mom, you're harboring a fugitive!"

"He's your brother!" she screamed. "And he swears it's all just a big mistake!"

"Yeah," Joe muttered. "His big mistake." And he stomped the rest of the way to the room his deadbeat brother had been calling home for the last three years. Pushing the door open, he shouted, "Hey, bro! What's up, man?"

Flying the coop, apparently, since the window was wide open and Jimmy was not in his room. Dashing around the house, Joe made it to the backyard just in time to see a familiar shape hurdling the chain-link fence. "Damn it, Jimmy!" he shouted. "Get your ass back here!" His brother neither stopped nor turned around to acknowledge Joe's order. One thing the sonunvabitch was good at—running away.

Angrily slamming the screen door, Joe returned to his mother, who stood kneading her hands in the kitchen. "Don't you lie to me, Ma," he started. "How long has Jimmy been staying here?"

She looked up as if to answer him, but began a chest-rattling hacking instead, collapsing against the counter and seeming about to faint. Quickly grabbing a chair, Joe got her seated and then, not really knowing what to do next, rushed to the sink for a glass of water. She waved it off and continued coughing, gasping for a clear breath.

Should he dial 911? Before he could decide the spell grew less severe, so

Joe pulled up a second chair and waited for it to totally subside.

Regardless how Mom might defend his big brother, Joe knew he simply had to call the cops. For all their sakes.

EPISODE NINETY–FOUR

WHENEVER HER EAR CAUGHT that soul-stirring, heart-pounding intro to the Moody Blues' "Ride My Seesaw," Misty fought the urge to crank the store's boombox higher and higher. *C'mon. You're a mature, responsible shopkeep,* she'd tsk herself as her hand itched to slide into the volume zone. *Bottom line, mustn't blast the customers away.*

What friggin' customers? Not even one in more than an hour. The irresponsible Fan-Girl inside coaxed, *who's to scare?*

On the verge of succumbing, a sudden jangle drew her attention toward the entrance. Kirk stumbled in, lugging a large pet taxi that brimmed with two loudly complaining furry felines. "Flashback Fannie," he grimaced as she reluctantly notched the volume down. "Do you own anything less ancient than '75?"

"Mais oui," Misty shot back tartly. "There's 'Sur La Mer' Moodies, and 'Strange World' Moodies, and—"

"Heavy sigh," Kirk sniffed. He carefully set the plastic carrier on the glass counter, then wriggled a finger through the door grate, scratching Fur-Person #1 on the nose. "You are aware there are plenty of creamy Britrock groups doing current work," he lectured. "Blur, for instance?"

"Which one's that?" Misty queried. (A few months ago, Kirk had been on one of his Gotta-Keep-Abreast-Of-The-Zeitgeist crusades and shlepped over a CD stack of Nineties artists. She'd dutifully listened, had recognized that "Wonderwall" song from one of the dances, but otherwise had been unimpressed.) "Those brothers who hate each other?"

"Never mind," Kirk capitulated. "You and me've got more vital things to palaver about. We're just getting back from the vet, who graciously deemed them, if not me, sane and healthy. 'Course vets are docs, and even though Maine Coons run husky, Doc likes 'em lean, so of course he says they could lose a couple kilos apiece. Whatever," he snapped dismissively. "I think they're just perfection."

"Which you would," Misty chuckled.

"Just your irrepressible chubby chaser," Kirk camped, reaching through the beaded curtain to retrieve a stool from the backroom.

"'Chubby Chaser'—that's a phrase I wish the straight size acceptance community wasn't too homophobic to co-opt. Artfully alliterative." Misty grinned. "Playful, bordering on bawdy. I've always waffled on 'fat admirer.'"

"You know, I've long admired your fat, Miz Shores, as well as your waffles," Kirk leered suggestively.

She rewarded him with a coquettish runway turn, catching sight of her wildly tie-dyed form in the nearby three-way mirror. When she'd invited Joe to move in, a minor but niggling concern had been that his expertise as a chef (as well as his love of feeder fantasies) would cause her to gain weight. But to date her size had remained mostly constant, which was large enough, thank you very much.

"It is pretty admirable," she agreed. "Big Mamma Jamma! But somehow I don't think I could ever have tripped your trigger."

"Alas, 'struth. Brian alone owns me—heart, soul, every other organ, too!" Kirk laughed, drumming on the top of the gray carrier. As if in outraged response, Jake—or was it Elwood?—poked a meaty claw through the bars. "But you, however, are the cat's meow, milady, and therefore deemed puss-sitter par excellence."

"Brown nose! Flattery only goes so far." Misty grinned fiendishly. "But I gotta warn you to take an organ inventory on them now, before you leave. Ever hear about the pet rat back in college?"

"Grim story, huh?"

"Positively gothic," Misty assured him. "So when you and the dachsy heading for the airport?"

"Wheels up isn't 'til ten tonight. I planned to drop the cats off around five-ish, then in the spirit of abject gratitude, take both you and Roomie out for dinner."

"Just the one of us tonight, babe. And besides, you aren't ready to experience Joe-as-diner." Misty scowled. "He spends the entire night critiquing the food, the service, even the decor."

"Are you sure he's straight, Misty hon?"

A whuffling sneeze from within the box drew her attention and she peered into the carrier, which seemed awfully small for the gimlet-eyed pair of bruisers eyeing her suspiciously. "Promise me you've written up really clear instructions. Shit! Took me forever to get used to another human padding around the place; Goddess knows how I'll cope with these monsters underfoot."

"Hey, Toots, aren't you supposed to be Cosmic Pagan Lady, attuned to all nature's creatures?"

"Yeah, sure," Misty answered, "as long as Nature's Screechers stay outside, don't trip me, and stop wanking for fish and poultry byproducts."

"Not the feeder, you," Kirk observed, lifting a flyer for the upcoming Triple-F BBW Pageant from the counter. "Bringing your little Latin Lover to this shindig? Or do you plan to keep him home, all for yourself?"

"Honestly, Kirk, I'm really conflicted. Our chapter's not officially involved with the event or anything, but the northern RADFAm chapter is. Remember I told you about their president, Mitchell?"

"What, me forget a yummy-sounding BHM? Professor Teddy Bear? At the beach? Island-print swimtrunks? Way you made him sound, he'd teach Brian plenty about hunkyness."

Misty shot him a quick razzberry, then continued more seriously. "Well, anyway, his group is co-sponsoring the Greg and Connie Show, and I'm not certain it's smart for me to be around Mitch. With or without Joe."

"That's right," Kirk recalled, "you couldn't resist his presidential essence, right?"

"Better than Monica could," Misty shot back, a little more defensively than she'd intended. "But I've gotten past that."

"And since he'll most certainly have more clothes on at the pageant, there shouldn't be any problems, right?"

"No," Misty finally agreed. "No problems at all."

Deja vu time.

The downtown hotel/convention center chosen for the Full-Figured Friends/RADFAm BBW Pageant was the same place Paul remembered from the 3F Post-Valentine's Day Dance. Escorting Jenny and her sister into the building, he thought he recognized one of the younger women—Sonya, was it?—from that night. *You're just here to be supportive,* he reminded himself. *For Cassie, and Jenny.*

Funny, though, that it seemed more unnerving to run into the leather-clad bachelorette than a near-certain confrontation with Connie Donovan. He'd just never quite gotten the hang of ignoring flirting—particularly when it was being done in front of a girlfriend. Connie's overt hostility was easier to handle.

Down the hall they could hear Greg Dillman bellowing orders. Paul and Jenny exchanged knowing glances; Cass appeared too locked in her own private thoughts to even notice. She was clutching her clothing bag so tightly that she was in danger of seriously wrinkling the new dress within, so Jen silently relieved it from her nerveless fingers.

Across the auditorium, which in a few short days would host a pantheon of talented (?) plus-size beauties, the trio saw Greg and Connie berating a hapless hotel staffer over the quality of the lighting in the room. Onstage several women from the Valentine's Day Dance were shuffling around, looking bored.

It was Kathi, far less provocatively dressed than the quasi-dominatrix Paul recalled from the RADFAm Fashion Show, who first noticed them entering the room. She waved happily, and Greg—who always had an eye on the women in the room even while bawling out underlings—abruptly interrupted his tirade to turn his attention toward Cassie, instantly affixing an insincere smile on his face.

"It's our Diva-to-Be," he announced happily, trotting up the aisle to give Cassie a large welcoming embrace that he held at least five seconds too long. Behind him arrived Connie, a forced half-smile on her round face. It looked to Paul that she'd gained a few more pounds since they'd been together. As Greg unhanded his star singer, Connie made a point of moving alongside the insurance salesman and proprietarily pulling him away.

"We've got the new lyrics ready for you," Greg told Cass. "Initially I'd hoped to do something a tad more contempo—Sheryl Crow or Alanis perhaps—but Connie convinced me it'd be better to let you stick with what you already know." He reached inside his jacket, pulling out a folded piece of typed paper. "Here you go."

He handed it to Cass, who nervously scanned the proffered lyrics. But once she'd read through it, she smiled with relief; whatever Greg had suggested was apparently in her repertoire.

Connie, meanwhile, was eyeing the dress bag in Jenny's arms—and the shop label prominently blazoned across it. "I see you brought your own gown," she sniffed. "That wasn't necessary, dear, because I'd already chosen an ensemble for you—one in keeping with the look and theme of the pageant."

"Oh, really?" Cass squeaked. "Nobody told me." Nervously she looked to her sister for support, so Jenny stepped in to mediate.

"We'd love to see what you've picked out, Connie," she said soothingly. "I think it's so much nicer for her to have a choice, don't you? Since this is my sister's first solo performance, of course we all want her to feel and look her best when she goes onstage."

"Of course," Connie cooed. "Wouldn't have it any other way." Releasing Greg, she moved past Jenny, reaching forward to pat Cass's arm, then turned to give Paul the once-over. She still looked stunning, Paul realized, but somehow not as attractive as he'd remembered. "And how are you doing, Paul?" she beamed. "I hope these two aren't monopolizing all your time."

"Not at all, Connie," Paul replied, ignoring the leering wink Greg was shooting him over the heads of the two sisters. Okay, he thought, maybe being around Connie wasn't going to be that easy after all.

EPISODE NINETY–FIVE

"**KITTY-KITTY-KITTY!** Here, kitty-kitty-kitty—"

Joe listened to Misty's wheedling chant echoing through the apartment as she sought an AWOL Jake. Meanwhile Elwood crouched near Joe in the kitchen, munching his way through some dry Iams. (At least Joe thought it was Elwood at the bowl; to be honest, he still got the two burly brothers confused.)

He was beginning to get rather concerned. Misty had never been this worried and anxious before, and all over a cat! Clearly she was taking her feline foster-mom gig seriously, and it bothered Joe to see her so distressed even as the pragmatic guy-part of him wondered what all the fuss was about. After all, weren't cats famous for taking care of themselves?

When Jake had failed to appear last night as usual, Misty's first fear was that he'd somehow gotten trapped within the wall separating their living room from Kirk's old apartment. Joe had crawled on his knees to inspect the unfinished construction, only to realize the gap was far too tight a squeeze for any pudgy feline fanny. (Fur-Father Kirk had obviously preferred his puddies like his partners—very well fed.)

"Kirk's gonna kill me if anything happens to his baby," Misty moaned, joining Joe in the kitchen. After a long sleepless night she'd gotten up early, throwing on the first thing at hand, a supersized T-shirt featuring shadowy lavender feminine figures dancing upon her belly and the slogan "Take back the night" emblazoned across her breasts. Joe never grew tired of how the knit fabric hugged her rich figure.

One big difference between FAntasy fashion and reality, he'd learned since knowing Misty, was that few supersized women dressed the way most FAs wished they would. Outfits that accentuated their bounteous shape (thus catching the fat-admiring eye) were instead co-opted by clothing more "acceptable" to the general public. In Misty's case, this meant a closet full of long flowing dresses, and while she undeniably looked hot in them, there were times Joe dreamed of her wearing something more explicitly provocative.

When she was at home with no immediate intention of going out, Mist often donned a formfitting top or nightshirt that drove him crazy. But if he commented on how pretty or sexy she looked, her reaction tended toward seemingly honest puzzlement and "Oh, my goodness! I'm such a mess right now!" It was as if Misty believed such compliments were obligatory boyfriend shtick.

"Joe?" Misty murmured, coaxing him back to the crisis at hand.

"Hmmm. I just got an idea," he replied, turning toward the kitchen counter—and the electric can opener. Back at cooking school he'd worked parttime in a diner where the neighborhood alley cat was adept at sneaking into the kitchen. The kindhearted owner would use the lure of the whir to announce a treat, invariably bringing the stray out of hiding. So, pressing down the lever for about fifteen seconds, his ploy was rewarded by both cats rubbing against his legs, meowing piteously. Jake was filthy, his fur covered with cobwebs and drywall dust, but he appeared none the worse for his adventure.

"My hero!" Misty cried, grabbing Joe and kissing him enthusiastically as Jake and Elwood purred at their feet.

The hero was about to suggest moving this embracing business to a more comfortable room when the phone rang. "Leave it," Misty suggested coyly, obviously sharing his lusty wavelength, but the answering machine message instantly crushed the mood.

"Joseph—are you—there? Oh God, please—pick up—" The feeble, gasping whisper was his mother's. Groaning, Joe strode to the living room to get the phone.

"Mom? What's wrong?"

"Your—brother—" he heard her sob. "Police came here—they've taken him away—"

"Mom," Joe struggled to keep the exasperation from his voice. "Forget about Jimmy for a minute. Are you okay?"

It was taking far too long for her to answer. "Having trouble—breathing," she finally panted.

"Have you called the doctor, Mom?"

"Called—" she said simply, "you—"

Damn—of course she had! Frantically he gestured to Misty, who was watching with concern from the kitchen. "There's an address book in the top drawer of the dresser," he directed, and she rushed to retrieve it. "Misty's getting the doctor's on-call number, Mom. You need an ambulance?"

"Can you—come?"

"Yes, of course I can, Mom. But it's at least a forty-five minute drive. Should I call 911?"

"I need—you," she wheezed, and with that the line went dead. He glanced up to see Misty standing beside him, battered address book in hand.

"Is everything all right?" she asked worriedly.

"No—and no," Joe growled. "Jimmy got his asshole self busted at Mom's house, and now she's struggling to breathe. There's a ninety-eight percent chance that she's just worked herself into a panic attack. But I'd still better run over and check."

"Want me to come with you?"

"Oh, yes. More than you'll ever know."

THE STAGE SURE SEEMED HUGE—and to Cassie's eye the vast auditorium loomed far beyond, into deep shadows. Across the rows of now-empty seats she envisioned a sea of unfriendly faces, every one whispering and sniggering at her, the awkward fat girl who pretended to have talent.

Jen and Paul had headed out to grab some sandwiches; Greg was off somewhere, most likely berating some hapless flunky whose only sin was being in the wrong place. Though an occasional curious head peered into the room, she felt abandoned in the middle of nowhere, self-doubt her only companion. She just ought to forget about the whole thing and go back home.

"Don't worry, Cassie," a deep voice startled her, and Mitchell Christian ambled onstage, a reassuring grin wreathing his face. He was wearing a navy corduroy sport coat and Dockers style pants, his white dress T still managing to look loose on his looming forefront. "Folks who attend an event like this, they're here because they support and believe in fat acceptance. We all want to see charming, lovely, large women willing to showcase their beauty and talent. It's not about scoring points at someone else's expense." He reached out to take her hand. "Remember me? Mitchell Christian. We met at the RADFAm beach party. You did such a wonderful Mama Cass."

"Not that wonderful," she demurred, recalling her trembling hesitation on the first few bars. The northern chapter president had such kind, gentle eyes—deep green, accented with tiny laugh lines. Gazing shyly up into them she felt her stage fright melt away and she began to relax.

"Well, I don't claim to be a music critic," he chuckled deeply, still clasping her hand. "But you sure sounded good to these ol' ears. Then again," he added, "my music library pretty much begins and ends with Patsy Cline. And Willie Nelson." Mitch dropped her hand to glance at his watch. "Almost twelve-fifteen. Got any lunch plans?"

"Oh, my sister Jen went to Quizno's for takeout." Unbidden, she felt a guilt twinge as she struggled to remember what size sandwich she'd ordered, then sternly caught herself. That shouldn't make any difference at all. Should it?

Since getting involved with this pageant, Jenny had introduced Cassie to a lot of size acceptance sites on the Net. Some flat out denied a link between overeating and overweight; others were much more ambiguous. The only sites to consistently support eating whatever you wanted seemed to have a dubious agenda.

"I see," Mitch replied, his full face displaying clear disappointment. Last time she'd inspired that sort of expression in a man was when she'd refused taking a coworker's weekend shift. Now she almost didn't register his reaction as one of regret.

What would Jen do? she wondered. When it came to the opposite sex her younger sister was far more self-assured. Maybe she needed to slip into Jen's not-nearly-so-sensible shoes for once. Then she had a brainstorm. "But if you're not too busy this afternoon, I could use your eyes."

"Eyes?"

"Well, Connie Donovan's bringing over some dresses for me to try on," Cass began, then hesitated as momentary doubt crept over her.

"And you want an unbiased eye?" Mitch prodded. "Sounds like fun."

"Maybe not," Cass admitted. "See, Connie's been pretty insistent about this, but Jen and I have already picked out something I really like from her friend Delia's shop. The whole situation is—" she paused, the exact phrase deserting her, wondering if she even should have introduced the subject at all.

"Fraught with peril," Mitch offered, smiling as if to say *hey, I know it's scary, but we can handle it.*

"Exactly!" Cass exclaimed with relief.

"Well, fear not, gentle maiden. I'll remain ever steadfast by your side, fending off what slings and arrows Miz Donovan might fling," Mitchell intoned gallantly. "Besides, I'm always up for my own personal fashion show."

The sound of Jenny and Paul's return drew their attention. Peering across the room at the restaurant bag, she realized that they'd bought three six-inch subs. Her ever-treacherous mind niggled, *Now will he think you're denying your size and appetite?*

"I'm no Emme," she replied, turning back to her companion. "Dressing posh is plenty new to me, so I need all the moral support I can get."

"Glad to supply it, Cassie, any time." He winked broadly. "And if you'd like, I'm also ready to offer some immoral support as well."

This response once more caught her off guard, prompting a flush that surged through her entire body. She was being flirted with—what to say? What to say?!

"I'd like 'em both," Cassie finally managed to croak before her sister climbed onstage. Maybe the pageant would turn out to be the least eventful part of her day.

EPISODE NINETY-SIX

I F RACHEL HADN'T POINTED THEM OUT, Dex might've missed the quartet of pickets outside the hotel. Cordoned away from the entrance, the group was not obnoxiously vocal, mainly satisfying themselves with wearing sour faces, brandishing signs ("No Fat-ploitation!" "Fat's Fate? An Early Grave!") and shooting looks-that-kill at every plus-sized visitor entering the building. The protesters were all women, pretty much Amway clones and none much more than middlingweight. Dex thought they all were strangers until the heaviest in the group happened to turn toward him. Valerie, who else?

"Say 'No' to Obeeesity!" she shrilled as Dex hustled his daughter through the ultra-sized glass rotating doors. "Big is deadly, not beautiful!"

"Hasn't she been at our house?" Rachel commented, squinting back as the former RADFAMite grew more hysterical. "She looks familiar."

"Yes, she has," Dex affirmed, "and is." Down a hall to the right he caught sight of Connie Donovan's familiar bottom-heavy form. She was holding court over three pretty plump girls close to Rachel's age—the other pageant usherettes, Dex presumed. His daughter waved to one of them, Kelly Gleasen. Wasn't this the same girl who'd been Goth-garbed at the convention? Today she looked far less vampirey—makeup smartly subdued, dressed in jeans with a lacy lavender three-quarter length T-shirt. What a difference a few months (and maybe a boy) could make.

"There's our girl," Connie cooed and gestured broadly. Kelly's companions, Dex realized, were totally unfamiliar. Perhaps their parents were from the northern chapter? All three girls were watching Connie with that pose of ironic teen detachment he'd learned to recognize from his own two kids. "We were starting to worry that you might not make it."

"Yeah," Kelly chimed in once Rachel had gotten close enough to hug hello. "Rumor had it that the crazies outside'd gotten you."

"As if," Rachel snorted, then turned to dismiss her father. Dex was already ahead of her, though.

"That's the way to the auditorium, isn't it?" he asked Connie. "Think I'll just go commandeer a good seat." He leaned over to kiss Rachel on top of her head. "Do great and have a fun time," he directed as Connie shooed the foursome into a nearby dressing room. Rachel twirled to wink at her father, then disappeared through the door.

She seems to be doing better, Dex decided as he ambled deeper into the bowels of the hotel/convention center. Rachel's time in counseling with Anne Reynard seemed to really be helping. If only his son would talk as willingly to someone, anyone.

Jackie remained stubbornly sequestered in surly adolescent mode. Even though Dex understood his grief over his mother's death, there were times when the boy's mopiness set his teeth on edge. Jackie seemed most pissed when he thought no one else was mourning as profoundly as he was.

The only respite from this recent accusatory silence was news that his girlfriend was returning from an out-of-state trip. "Officially" the sojourn had been described as a visit with relatives, but Rachel opined it was actually inpatient treatment at an eating disorders clinic. "Gidget" was scheduled to come home Sunday, so his son had a pleasant distraction to look forward to.

But that didn't assuage Dex's secret sense of culpability. He honestly wasn't feeling the same level of grief as at the passing of his first wife. He couldn't tell what that meant. Maybe he'd used up his store of deepest despair the first time. Sure, those early days without Neeko had been hell—the gut-wrenching suddenness of it. But his sense of absolute loss hadn't lasted for months like it had with Anne.

No, not Anne, forgawdsakes—what was he thinking? His first wife was Lindy!

Horrified by this traitorous transference, Dex turned away from the auditorium to find a quieter place to collect his thoughts.

HERE WE GO, *Greg Old Son!* (Quickly check reflection in the silvery casing of a stage light. Straighten lapels on tux.) *This is your moment! You're the Host with the Most!* (Stride to centerstage, scan the auditorium—hard to get a good look at the crowd with all these lights—but the audience sounds strong. Wrap both hands firmly around the mike.) *Showtime!*

"Hello, and welcome one and all to our city's first—but certainly not last—Big Beautiful Women Pageant! I'm your host, Greg Dillman, but don't worry—you won't be seeing very much of me up here. This night, this stage, belongs to the Lay-dies!" (Pause through applause and whistles)—*two, three.* "And we've really got quite a selection of talented and lovely Full-Figured Femmes for yer night's entertainment.

"But before we do that, allow me to introduce the three judges assigned the difficult task of deciding just who's the fairest of them all." (Gesture to table placed prominently in front of stage; tick off names.) "President of the northern chapter of RADFAm, the organization co-sponsoring this stellar event with my own team, Full-Figured Friends: Mitchell Christian!"

(Spotlight on Mitchell.) *He's like a kid whose parents are making him wear grownup clothes for the first time. C'mon, smile for the audience, Mitch.*

"FA writer and webmaster of his own size-positive online pay-site, Baird's Beauties: Lewis Baird!"

Seems somebody's learned how to use product since the big convention. Good for you, Lew, but it still won't get ya laid.

"And graciously traveling to our fair city from the CornBelt Campustown, hostess of her own popular weekend blues and jazz public radio show, Lady Plays the Blues: Libby St. Lou!"

Whoa—this lady's buxom with a capital B! Bet she'd really cash in selling jpgs on Baird's site. A good 300-plus—and even sitting, her prow is proud. Sure'd love to surf some air waves with her. Okay, Greg, focus—she'll still be around after the pageant. Applause is petering, so let's get this show a-movin'.

"I don't envy them their assignment tonight—there's gonna be a beauteous bevy of boffo girls out here. No, wait a minute, I do envy that assignment." *Don't wait too long for the laugh. Good, they got it. Now—*

"But before we bring out our contestants, virtuoso chanteuse Cassandra Stewart will now open the show with our pageant anthem, 'A Special Somewhere.'" Give it life, Cassie! (Walk applauding down stage left; smile at Cassie—*looks like a virgin who's just learned about wedding nights*—as she steps into the spotlight; gesture to cue recorded music.) *Oh shit, there's Connie, blowing steam! Forgot to mention her store—damn! Ah, screw her—plenty of time to plug her later. This is my song, my baby, My Show.*

JENNY COULDN'T REMEMBER ever feeling more nervous for someone else than at this very moment. Perched on the edge of her reserved front row seat, she squeezed Paul's hand so tightly that his fingers were probably blue.

Cass looked so alone on that stage, grasping the mike stand as if her only support. Then the musical intro started, tinny and artificial-sounding from too-small speakers, bearing no readily recognizable melody. At the downbeat, without hesitation Cassie opened her mouth and the song was born. In that instant her sister transformed from a meek and unsure figure in an iridescent gown into a proud and beautiful woman shining in the spotlight. The change was astounding—even after watching Cass in rehearsal during the past few days, Jenny was in awe. Her sister had taken control of the stage—and the audience as well.

"There's gotta be a Special Somewhere;
"Where size & weight do not define
"A person's Worth or Self-Assurance;
"Or sizeist attitudes confine—"

Okay, so the words were kinda clunky, and the music—was the theme from *Poseidon Adventure* really a good idea? But that pure crystalline voice added depth and nuance, soaring across and around the auditorium. "She's wonderful," Jenny whispered to Paul, and he nodded enthusiastically. "I wasn't sure—"

But Cassie was wonderful, each phrase as personal and passionate as if plucked from her own experience.

"Full-Figured Friends, let's be united
"In this radiant, shining quest;
"That prejudice shall be a distant
"And long-forgotten darkness—
"We won't be silent anymore!"

It figured that Greg would slip in a plug for his own group, with no mention of anyone else (although to be fair, "RADFAm" was not a name that came trippingly to the tongue). But that didn't matter. What was important was the reality of her large and lovely sister, holding her audience rapt through the final quivering note.

As Cassie stepped back from the microphone to receive her deserved ovation, Mitchell Christian quickly rose from the judges' table, retrieving a vast bouquet of cream and pink roses from underneath. Striding to the proscenium, he held them up to Cassie, who took several seconds to realize what was happening. With surprising chivalry, Greg Dillman appeared from offstage to swoop down and pass the tribute to his songbird. Without taking her eyes off Mitchell she hugged the bouquet, mouthing the words, "Thank you."

Gee, she's got it bad for that guy, Jenny realized, and the thought brought a shiver of joy. The night ahead may be about Greg and Connie's Full-Figured Girlies, but this moment belonged to Cassandra.

EPISODE NINETY-SEVEN

IT WASN'T UNTIL SHE'D SLIPPED OFFSTAGE, out of the dazzling lights and away from the applause, that Cass's jitters reappeared—overlaid by the uncommon rush of success.

She'd done it! Done it really well. Climbing up on a stage, singing from her deepest soul in front of an audience that wasn't at worship, shedding everyday Cassie for Cass. Sure, this huge group was probably predisposed to like her as a large woman. But their enthusiastic response did sound genuine.

"Brava and congratulations, girl! You sounded like an angel, and look like one, too."

It was Delia, the lady from the dress shop, standing alongside a strikingly beautiful black woman who she remembered as Jenny's boss, Lissa. The proprietress moved as if she wanted to embrace her customer, but the rose bouquet Cass still cradled presented a floral obstacle. Cassie quickly scanned the area for a place to lay the flowers down, but there were too many bountiful beauty contestants fidgeting around for her to see farther than a few feet.

"Those could use a drink right about now," Lissa quickly offered, gently taking the bouquet from the evening's diva. "And so could you, I'd say."

She vanished out a swinging door, while the dress shop owner took the opportunity to give Cass that hug. From out of the mists of memory her adoptive parents' voices echoed, piously cautioning against "deviant" women getting too close, but Cass shushed their panicky whispers, tentatively returning Delia's embrace.

"Not too hard," Delia backed off, chuckling. "Wouldn't want to spoil the line of your dress, in case you get called back out for an encore."

"Oh, that's none too likely, not with all those sweet young things taking the stage now," Cass demurred. She'd headed down right, away from the main crush of contestants, and watched the first gal stride down center at Dillman's urging. She looked in her early twenties, a generously chesty mid-sized brunette in a bronze challis bias-draped gown. Over the sound system the karaoke track had been replaced by techno instrumental. Catwalk strutting music, Cass surmised.

"Never mind them," Delia pooh-poohed. "I'd love to get some pictures of you in that design for display at the boutique. Would you be willing to do some modeling while you're in town?"

"Now I know you're teasing," Cass flushed.

"Oh no, my dear. Take a look at the average zaft catalog. The 'plus-size' models are barely plus, if at all. And they're body clones that offer no idea how real customers will carry the style. You know, apples vs. pears? But believe me when I tell you, Cass—you look simply mahvelous in that dress."

"That she does." A nasal riposte slashed through any reply Cassie may have had. Connie Donovan, materializing from behind a drape. "But I'd say it's not the dress, it's the star! If you ask my opinion, I could have proffered several items in my line that would have showcased her assets more—appropriately. But that's just one woman's opinion. I can't blame our little songbird here for selecting a dress that displays so well under stage lighting—as opposed to the true light of day."

Oh no, Cass thought, suddenly wishing she could shrink down and hide away in the folds of said dress. Connie was regarding Delia like a Halloween cat, arching up to swat a rival away from the food dish. At that moment Cass recalled an old movie from her youth, *The Turning Point,* where two former prima ballerinas perpetuated a bitter decades-long feud. If she cringed at watching women lay into each other on film, this was a million times worse. How could things have gone so awful so fast?

"Connie," Delia gushed, stepping back and reaching to retrieve a small lavender vellum envelope from her shoulder bag. "I'd really hoped to get a chance to give this to you personally. Mail just didn't seem good enough." She stepped forward to hand the paper to a poised-to-pounce Connie.

"To celebrate the joy and love in our commitment, Lissa and I are hostess-ing a union ceremony," Delia quickly continued, "and how could I not invite you? We were long-time, special friends, after all."

Connie stopped, visibly deflated, gaping at the envelope that she meekly accepted from her former cohort. "You're getting married?" she was able to finally stutter.

"Not in this state. Yet." Delia mugged. "It's just a simple fam-and-friend shindig declaring our intentions until the real thing comes along. We'd love to see you there. Hey, even bring Greg, but only if you promise to gag him during the ceremony."

Using a long red fingernail and still eyeing Delia a tad cockeyed, Connie slit open the invitation and quickly scanned its contents as if certain that it was all a cheap hoax. Then, re-mustering her composure, the entrepreneuse pasted on a broadly insincere smile as Lissa rejoined her partner. From the auditorium applause signaled that the first contestant had just wrapped up her interview with Greg.

"It's so nice when two people are lucky enough to find each other," Connie crooned, air kissing each of the brides-to-be. "And how fantastic to announce it here, tonight, backstage at my pageant." With that she turned and hustled toward the back curtain. "Gotta go check on the rest of my girls, but I'm so glad we had this chance to connect."

"So you will be able to make it to join us?" Delia pressed, grabbing her Lissa's hand and giving it a demonstrative squeeze.

"Just let me double-check my PDA," Connie countered before ducking from view. "That's a busy fashion season, as you very well know." And with that she was gone.

"You were right," Lissa informed Delia, planting a quick kiss on her cheek. "That thoroughly bamboozled her." The grinning twosome turned back to Cass, who was battling her own giggles at the satisfaction of a stammering Connie. "Think Cass here can react more gracefully when we request the honor of her Gift of Song at our ceremony?" Lissa winked.

"Not sure," Delia chuckled. "Shall we ask and see?"

But before Cass had a chance to prove herself one way or the other, a loud, angry commotion rose from the auditorium. Peering from the wings, they saw a group of women waving placards, brandishing them dangerously and shouting toward the stage. In the spotlight a bottom-heavy blonde contestant wilted, totally unbalanced by the interruption.

"Isn't that Valerie?" Delia guessed, but the name meant nothing to Cass. She pointed to a red-faced figure who rhythmically chanted a slogan, indecipherable from where they stood.

"It is," Lissa noted, just as a figure Cass recognized as Ian, backed up by several other RADFAm members—Mitch included—gathered to escort the dissidents outside. The woman called Valerie responded by swinging her sign at the local chapter officer, but the group was awkwardly packed together, preventing actual connection with her target. From Val's off side Mitchell Christian grabbed the sign, snatching it from her hands. She turned as if about to slap him, then quickly changed her mind. In the audience a camera flashed twice as a pair of city cops appeared in the exit.

"Well, that sure wasn't listed in my program! Quality entertainment, though," Lissa smirked as Valerie, bereft of sign or supporters, was led meekly from the auditorium trailed by the rest of her companions. "Now back to our regularly scheduled broadcast."

POSITION ONE: "The Question—the nature of the issue, even if unconscious to the questioner."

Over the years Misty had experimented with numerous Tarot decks—Marseilles, Rider-Waite, Sacred Circle and beyond—but had never successfully (or the least bit coherently) divined her own pattern.

But the recent addition to her cyber-psi library of an experimental, virtual deck by Expert Software had bonded her electronically with insights that felt genuinely helpful. Gunnar Kossatz's artistry, combined with the accuracy of each card's written descriptions, affirmations and hints frequently amazed her.

While waiting for Joe to return with his mother from the hospital, she decided that now was as good a time as any to seek some of that wise E-sight. Booting up the program, she tried to dampen a smothering panic of being sucked unwillingly into some Twilight Zoney phase of life. And scanning the first card, The Well, did nothing to ease her dis-ease.

"A female in touch with a crystal looks into the structure of a well that gets narrower with increasing depth."

That was definitely her. Her commitment to Joe had resulted in far more obligations than she was sure she could handle. Though Joe's mother was only supposed to visit for a few days—a chance to recuperate from the mild infarction that sent her to the emergency room—Misty's Sight projected something more involved. Something life-alteringly involved.

She clicked her cursor on the second position, The Influence—circumstances that have direct bearing on the issue. For an instant, before revealing the card descriptor, she flashed on Greg and Connie's beauty pageant and wondered how it was going.

"Aeon. The last is also the first. All of life's sequences are one great synthesis on playground Planet Earth."

Hmm. This reading certainly wasn't going to be a cakewalk. Leaning back in her armless swivel chair, sipping ginseng tea laced with organic honey, she contemplated this statement. "Synthesis"—combining and dividing, old and new. The old cosmic giggle. She took a second sip, then moved on to The Background position—events leading to present circumstances, the motions of people involved.

"Choice." Rarely could Misty imagine making choices quite so harmonious as this card's portrayal of celestial alignment. So many recent choices had been thrust upon her—Kirk's decision to follow his heart to the Pacific Northwest, resulting in two furry children *chez nous*. And now Ma Rivera's health issues. Misty thought she might be able to find the positive a smidge more easily if she'd actually been offered true choice.

She sniffed disgustedly at her pettiness, moving on quickly to Recent Past. The image of a cyclone instantly drew her eye.

"The Deep Blue. The lifeboat, serenely untouched by turmoil, symbolizes inner resources available at all times if one cares to dive for them. Meditation is the name of the game."

At that moment, Jake—or was it Elwood?—dove across her left thigh, only to slide off the slippery silken caftan fabric. "Sorry. Don't have much of a lap to offer," she advised the disgruntled orange monster as she hoisted him from the floor. Happily both of Kirk's children were remarkably gentle with their claws, AKA meat hooks. She absently scratched the cat's great apple head while selecting her next virtual card for The Present position. Intuition—and its hint spoke volumes.

"Intuition is our direct link to god, our higher self, or whatever you'd call it. To use it effectively, inner silence is required."

Jake/Elwood lay stretched up her forefront, his purr thrumming sonorously, more seismic than audio. "How'm I gonna get silence with you around, MotorMew?" she chuckled as he bumped his head into her hand, tacitly requesting renewed ear-scratch. On the basis of her last phone conversation with Kirk, her longtime friend would most likely be calling the caffeine capital his permanent home. *Ain't love grand, and call me MeowMa!*

So what were the cards telling her? To actually trust her intuition through all this upheaval? What did she know? What felt true and honest and right?

And what about Joe? Was their love strong enough to maintain balance while facing change?

What the heck. She violated protocol, skipping ahead to the final position, The Outcome. The Desert. (Too bad not the one with two Ss.)

"Watch your desire. You get what you want."

Great. Warning or promise? The description hint brought a slight smile to ease her bemusement. "Sometimes the world appears more bearable with pink glasses on. This is not necessarily self-deception, but quite a valuable change in perspective."

Lifting the cat off her caftan, Misty rose from the computer desk.

Jake/Elwood dashed off to some hidden sanctum in their expanded and refinished apartment. Promising to return to study the rest of her Tarot spread later, she decided to check out Mother Rivera's guestroom again, just to friendly-fy it as much possible.

So for now, at least, this change of focus offered an answer. And after living self-reliant for so many years, maybe Misty was finally ready to accept the synthesis that loving Joe created. Just as long as she got to wear those pink glasses from time to time.

EPISODE NINETY–EIGHT

"ISN'T THAT PAUL, there in the background?" Lissa asked, indicating a blurry figure on the far right of her computer monitor. Adjusting her glasses and squinting closely, Jenny examined the unflattering e-photo heralding the *Weekly Instigator*'s online preview, "Bulging Babes at Big 'Beauty' Pageant!" (Coming out soon in print, the web page promised, via everybody's favorite service station tabloid.)

Somebody must have snuck a small digital camera into Greg and Connie's shindig, because the centerpiece of the pic was Cassie, caught midnote, her mouth open wide, looking for all the world as if she were a fish gasping for air. The website's captioneer had of course distorted the image's actual context. "Feed me!" the headline shrieked.

"Shit, I hope Cass never sees this," Jenny groaned. "How'd you hear about it, anyway?"

"Ian found it," Lissa explained. "Some FAs like cruising the tabloid sites occasionally, looking for attractive fat chick photos. Our resident reprobate discovered it last night. From the looks of things, the *Instigator* is planning a comprehensive photo spread of the whole event."

"Thank God Paul isn't into this crap," Jenny replied, taking off her glasses and wiping them, as if also hoping to clear the offending image from her sight.

"Don't be so certain," Lissa chuckled devilishly. "My own dear Delia has been known to peruse the tabs whenever an actress she likes shows up with a few extra pounds. Just don't tell her I've divulged this eccentricity, though—she'd be embarrassed as hell to know you know."

"Well, I've never seen Paul reading this kind of trash," Jenny mused. "Is there anything we can do to derail this?"

"I really doubt it," Lissa answered, swiveling idly in her desk chair. "It was a public and well-publicized event, one that dear old Val made even more newsworthy by her personal little demonstration. Legally, like it or not, the *Instigator* had every right to be there."

"Sometimes freedom of the press can be a royal pain in the ass," Jenny grumbled.

"Tell me about it," Lissa agreed. She turned toward the paralegal. "Still, you're probably gonna want to give Cass fair warning about this. It'd be far worse if one of her coworkers sprang it on her when she got home."

"Hell, yes," Jenny affirmed. "But I really hate to ruin her vacation. She's been so happy since the beauty pageant. Mitchell Christian's been showing her the sights, and I've been fielding tons of phone calls from other FAs who caught her performance. If only I knew who's giving out my number."

"I'd guess Dillman, and he's probably been selling it," Lissa snorted. "So our talented songstress is enjoying the RADFAm dating scene?"

"For sure. And to be honest, I'm having fun with it, too. The past three nights Cass has come in all bubbly and girlish. We talk half the night away like teens at a slumber party." Jenny smiled at the memory. "Never had a sister or even a close girlfriend I could relate to like that, so it's been really kinda cool."

"If you're worried that giving her the bad news will spoil those sisterhood vibes, I don't think you have a thing to worry about," Lissa said. Behind her the tabloid webpage had timed out, replaced by a screensaver slideshow featuring Delia at the opening of her dress shop. It was hard to believe that it was the same sour-faced harridan Jenny had first met at that RADFAm dance so many months before.

"No, it's not that at all," Jenny replied. "But watching Cass this last week has been like some paperback romance come to life. Mitch is so sweet to her, so gentlemanly. And she's just—blossomed. I'd hate to see anything spoil it."

"If anything does, it's certainly not you but those bottom-feeders at the

Instigator." Lissa paused, then an impish expression crossed her face. "Not to change the subject, but how are things going with your own personal bodice-ripper anyway?"

"Well, we seem sorta stuck lately," Jenny confessed. "Maybe that's why I'm so excited about Cass dating. Paul hasn't done anything spontaneous in ages. Ever since we got back together, it's like he's going out of his way to play it safe with me."

"Gee," Lissa smirked. "Wonder what could possibly possess him, acting like that? Could it perhaps be the memory of you bolting like some feral cat the first time he said he loved ya?"

That sure caught Jenny up short. Just then the screensaver flashed a jpg of her and Paul at some get-together, laughing, sharing some joke she wished she could remember right now.

"I really hate when you're right," she sighed.

ALTHOUGH THEY'D DONE the best they could to prepare convalescent space for his ma, there was no way to fix it up completely at such short notice. There was still so much work left unfinished in the conjoined apartments for the place to look the way Joe had hoped for his mom's first visit.

He'd painstakingly scrubbed all the dust and plaster out of Kirk's old apartment, but every time he walked through it toward the bedroom where Ma Rivera was staying, he'd catch sight of something else that looked out of place. That's the damned thing about emergencies, he thought; they never happen when you're ready for them.

As he got to the half-open doorway of the guest bedroom Elwood darted between his legs, nearly making him spill the carefully arranged lunch tray he was carrying. It was impossible keeping the cats out of Mom's room, though he knew she was none too thrilled by their furry presence. Though she hadn't said a word about it (yet), he had to wonder if she wasn't a little scared of the creatures. Sure, it was okay to have a vast menagerie of stuffed animals lying about, but forget about the real deal. And admit it, those two meaty bruisers could be kinda scary.

Heck, Misty's own Schmendrick, so small and quiet that it was easy to forget he was around, had more than once startled Joe by dashing away from him when he got too close. Fortunately the diminutive Siamese had taken an intense dislike to the Maine Coons, choosing instead to become a storefront kitty, holding dominion over the Isle of View downstairs and leaving the apartment to Kirk's heathens. Three felines in the apartment would doubtless drive Mom into the Queen of All Anxiety Attacks.

At least, he thought gratefully, the dreaded diagnosis had ultimately turned out to be stress rather than the much more worrisome M.I. (Though to hear Ma Rivera tell it, she'd been snatched back from the Reaper's bony grasp just in the nick of time.) Jimmy's escapades had just been too much for her. Good thing his elder bro was now in police custody, because Joe wanted to truly and thoroughly pound his ass.

"Lunchtime," he called after knocking to make sure she was decent. She was sitting up in the guest bed dressed in a pink nightshirt, a copy of *The Daily Instigator* spread across her legs. He always felt uneasy seeing her reading that crap, though there had been times when he was younger that he'd sneak a look at each issue, just checking for any good-looking fat women inside. His mother especially seemed to enjoy when the paper printed some current Hollywood hottie in an unflattering light, but since most of what passed for hotness these days didn't much interest Joe, the point of this exercise was lost on him.

His mother inspected his carefully decorated lunch offering—a simple selection of cheese, celery and carrot sticks, sliced fruit and Jell-O, plus assorted crackers—then looked at her son and sniffed, "Are these crackers sodium-free?"

"Salt-free and fresh out of the box," he said. Though her hasty trip to the hospital had revealed no serious problems, her blood pressure was higher than what the doctors deemed appropriate "for a woman her age." So Joe had assured her he'd hold back on salt while she was their guest. It wasn't all that difficult—he wouldn't be any kind of chef if he didn't know a variety of ways to add flavor—but that didn't stop Mom from asking. "How you doing today?" he queried after setting down the tray.

"Better, I guess. But I'm still so tired." She gingerly picked up a slice of white cheese and examined it, but the next words out of her mouth were not what Joe expected. "I hope you're not too mad at me. Are you, Joe?"

"Of course not, Ma. Why do you say that?"

"Oh, I know I should've told you about Jimmy, should've been more honest and open with you. But your brother swore it was all just a stupid misunderstanding, that he only needed a few days to clear it up. He's never done anything illegal—"

That we know of, Joe groused, but refrained from saying out loud. "Ma, Jimmy's the only one I'm ticked at. He was a selfish idiot, getting you involved in his bullsh—er—nonsense."

"Well, Sweetie, that's what a family is all about," his mother answered in that singsong tone of voice she often fell into when lecturing one of her kids. "We stay involved with each other; we protect each other." She picked up a hunk of celery and nibbled at it. "You're such a good son, Joseph," she finally said, "caring for me like this." Then she turned her full attention to the food, effectively dismissing him.

Joe headed downstairs to join Misty in her shop. He found her schmoozing with a customer, a midsized rather scary-looking type with some kind of tattoo on her forehead. Before he'd actually met Misty he probably would've visualized her as a woman a lot like this one—marginal and kinda crazed, actually.

But his Misty was something else, of course—dressed in a blue and lavender linen duster dress lavishly embroidered with dragonfly designs, her hair pulled back into a fetching style and her full face smiling, she looked so naturally radiant that Joe was struck anew by how lucky he was. He loved casually watching her go about her day, loved the way she gracefully maneuvered her full and gorgeous form around the shop. Just the sight of his super BBLover was almost enough to banish all his unresolved anger over his brother and the way the prick had taken advantage of Mom.

Just then Misty glanced over the shoulder of her customer at Joe, beaming in welcome. And at that moment the rest of his anger melted, forgotten for

now.

EPISODE NINETY—NINE

FROM SPEAKERS HIDDEN throughout the rec room Ray Charles was serenading that lucky old sun, while some anonymous backup chorale ineptly chimed in, muting the ballad's raw impact with Easy Listening ineptitude. *Damn*, Dex muttered. Too bad his present AV toys couldn't just unmix their track, leaving Brother Ray at his best.

Still, sitting at his desk wrapping up the final few memorial thank-you notes, part of him was grateful the recording wasn't any more effective. With each note he'd mentally revisited Neeko's funeral, and while his emotions were more steadily balanced, there was little doubt that the right song would upset his delicate equilibrium. (As well as, he'd discovered over the past few days, all those aromas—ah, jasmine! Mementoes, kitschy yet evocative, and myriad reminders of old irksome quirks, like finding just one more wad of Kleenex tucked between furniture cushions.) Anyway, keeping the station tuned to pre-Neeko oldies had seemed like a smart move at the time.

Sighing, Dex sealed the last envelope and pulled out the sheet of stamps. Not his current Bugs Bunny postage, either—he'd had to make a special trip to the PO for "tasteful" ones.

Maybe he should have had the kids sign these too, he wondered.

Jackie, upstairs and quiet, was most likely Instant Messaging his little Gidget. A whoosh of fall air and slamming front door announced Rachel's return from time out and about with Anne Reynard.

In many ways they seemed to be handling their mother's death better than Dex. Footsteps across the floor above heralded Rachel's approach, and he watched her legs come into view down the staircase.

Her day-trip outfit, Dex saw, was that lowcut jeans/high-riding top combo that flashed her midriff—a piece of teen girl immodesty that never failed to startle him. In his generation even a relatively plump girl like Rachel would have been loath to reveal any such midriff bulge for all to see. These days it seemed less an issue—thanks, perhaps, to the hip-hop influence?

"Hi, Sweetie," he began. "How was your time with Madame Reynard?" Whenever Anne's name came up he couldn't help feeling a distinct twinge of embarrassment over the unprofessional way he mooned for her while Neeko was still alive. No way a professional therapist like her could have anything to do with the father of a client—it violated every code of professional ethics—but from what he'd heard about Jackie's behavior at the funeral, at least one of his kids had picked up on his not-so-subtle infatuation.

"Pretty okay," she replied, picking up an envelope, scanning the address, then quickly placing it back on the pile. "Can I talk to you about something?" she finally added. In answer, Dex patted the chair beside his invitingly.

"I need to tell you what I found the day Mom died. Anne says I should get it off my chest, even if I'm not entirely sure what it all means." She paused to note the look of worried puzzlement on her father's face, then continued. "When we were getting ready to go that, uh, afternoon, I went into Mom's drawer to get the car keys. I found what looked like a list of RADFAm members, with marks by the names of those who received that, uh, bad candy. I don't know for sure why Mom would have that list, but I know what I was thinking the day I found it. I mean, could Neeko be the one responsible for sending out those tampered chocolates cuz, I don't know, cuz she was jealous of Eleanor Bollen, the way she's always coming on to you?"

"Eleanor comes on to me?"

"Oh, jeez, Dad, you're so clueless sometimes! Mom hated it when you were an officer. Every time Eleanor came into the house she was upstairs slamming cupboards and stomping around. Even Jackie knew that something was up between Mom and the RADFAm group. Why do you think he was being so bratty about it all?"

On the radio Ray Charles had been replaced by the Drifters crooning "Save the Last Dance for Me." That song brought back memories of a chapter dance and, at the same time, the lyrics' sentiments flooded his eyes with tears.

At first he was reluctant to let his daughter see them, tempted to turn away. But then he realized how dishonest that'd be. Instead, he gave Rachel a half smile and said, "I've been an idiot." He rose from his seat as a single wet tear rolled down a red cheek and runneled into his beard.

"I don't know what the list means either," he told a sobbing Rachel, now fiercely hugging her father. "Let's go upstairs and take a look at what you discovered, okay?"

"**Boss lady, are we working** our usual Day-Before-Thanksgiving half day?" Jenny asked, framed in the doorway to Lissa's office.

"Why you asking?" Lissa queried in response, eyes still focused on a brief draft that Jenny had routed her way earlier that morning.

"I just received an invitation from Cassie to come down for the holiday. She's apparently invited Mitch and wants to put on a big 'family' spread. I'm invited to stay the night and 'bring anyone I want to bring,' whatever that might mean."

"So," Lissa observed, rolling away from her monitor, "Our Wedding Singer and Sister-Chapter Prez are still news? An item? A thing?"

"A great big, meshed-together thing," Jenny smiled. "Since she returned home he's been driving southwards the last two weekends. Lonnnng drive. But Cass says he doesn't have any classes on Friday afternoon, so he's able to make it to her house by the time she gets off work."

"And Cassie's fine with this long-distance relationship?"

"For now, she's just glad there is a relationship," Jenny replied. "Though from the way she's been talking, methinks she won't be satisfied with this state of affairs forever."

"Understandable," Lissa nodded. "So you're driving down on Wednesday? Planning on bringing along 'anyone you want'? Or are you still feeling that same old ennui with Paul?"

"I don't know," Jenny started, only to be interrupted with the sudden arrival of a high-school-aged boy carrying a handled paper bag emblazoned with the Homegrown Pizza logo.

"Either one of you Miz Jenny Taylor?" he squeaked, appearing reluctant to step over the threshold into Lissa's office. He had the same ready-to-bolt look you saw on the face of many a client about to face that first day in court. Who'd have thought a pair of fat gals could come off so scary?

"I am," Jenny told him, doing her damnedest to sound unthreatening. "But I didn't order any lunch."

"Wha—?" For a second the young man looked befuddled, then he lifted his sack eye level and giggled. "Oh, I get it. This ain't your lunch; that's just the bag. I'm supposed to deliver this to you!" With that he pulled a large gift-wrapped box from the sack and with great ceremony toted it over to the stunned paralegal. Then he swiftly darted back to the safety of the doorway.

"Who's it from?" Lissa demanded as Jenny held the package up to the light, carefully examining the wrapping paper. It was light blue with wavery silver patterns; there was no card to indicate who'd sent the package. "Is it ticking?"

From the doorway, the delivery kid snorted.

"Here," Lissa finally said, sweeping a pile of legal envelopes off her desk. "Put it down and open the damn thing!"

Jenny obliged, but the blank cardboard box under the wrapping gave no indication of its contents either. "Nothing suspicious yet," she said, starting to slice the tape with a letter opener. Inside she found a pile of tissue paper; after carefully separating it, she discovered a small bottle.

It was a souvenir, the kind of cheap *tchotchke* you found in one of those touristy downtown shops—a bottle with a small plastic sailboat inside. Leaning up against the boat were two white slips of paper. It took several minutes for Jen to pry them from the bottle without damaging the chintzy little boat, but as she did, Lissa and the delivery boy asked in unison, "What's it say?"

"Tickets," Jenny read, "for something called Luxury Lake Cruises. 'Dining, dancing and cruising on a 200-foot yacht,' it says. 'Beneath the city skyline.'"

"Really," Lissa chuckled. "Who would have thought that they'd have something like that going on so late in the year?" She paused, then asked innocently, "Does it say who the tickets are from?"

Jenny tossed the tissue paper at her boss.

"We both know who sent these," Jenny accused, "and from the goofy tone you're taking, I wouldn't be surprised to learn you already knew about it."

"Why I haven't the faintest idea what you're talking about," Lissa protested, holding her plump hands up in a gesture of feigned innocence.

"Please tell me that you haven't been spilling the beans to Paul about— what we've been talking about, please—"

"Nope, Paul came to me for some suggestions," Lissa countered, picking up the gaudy paper that had spilled down her forefront, "but this is all his doing. He was the one who picked the city skyline cruise; I wasn't sure there'd be any available this time of year."

"Luxury Lake Cruises," Jenny mused. "Can he afford this on a teacher's salary? Sounds expensive."

"It is," Lissa told her. "But don't tell him I told you so."

"So are you, what, going on this date with Mister Daily?" Homegrown

Pizza asked from his safety point outside the office. They'd almost forgotten he was still there. Lissa pulled open a desk drawer, took out three one-dollar bills and handed them to Jenny, who walked over to the delivery boy.

"Is he your teacher?" she asked, placing the bills in the young man's hand. He flushed as they made contact. She couldn't remember ever having had that effect on a teenaged boy before, and she was truly flattered.

"Mister Daily?" he said. "I got him in the mornings, but I do work study, too. So are you gonna go?"

"Well, there's a good chance I'll say 'yes,'" Jenny smiled.

"Alright, Dude!" the young boy cried. "This is just like something out of a chick flick! And I'm bringin' messages of peace and love!"

"Our own Dan Cupid," Lissa cooed, and Jenny grinned as Cupid colored a second time.

A Luxury Lake Cruise, she thought, and though it might've been silly, just the phrase washed her heart with warm feelings. What was Paul up to?

EPISODE ONE HUNDRED

THOUGH IT WASN'T AS CHILLY ON THE LAKE as he feared it might be, Paul was still worried that the weather would sabotage his Luxury Lake Cruise. When he'd made the reservations two months ago it had seemed like such a great idea. But as autumn had grown progressively colder, the stupider the notion had become. Cruising on Lake Michigan in November? What kind of a brain-dead maroon came up with that idea?

Well, at least there were other brain-dead maroons in the parking lot, he saw as he raced around the car to open the door for Jenny. "Such a gentleman," she smiled, swiveling her full and shapely legs out of the car.

Don't gape, Paul! he scolded himself. *Not if you wanna keep up this gentlemanly façade!*

She grasped his hand and rose, straightening the deep teal chemise skirt that temporarily clung to her soft round hips. A light breeze blew in from the lake, and Paul hastily retrieved her matching velvet jacket from the backseat and helped Jen into it. Savoring the ripe curve of shoulders within the lace bodice as he did, he resisted the urge to squeeze and pull her close. *Too early to jump the gun now, Boy-o.*

Hand-in-hand they crossed the lot to the pier where the cruise's 200-foot yacht was moored. The evening sky was streaked with city-light-dazzled clouds, a not-quite full moon flitting in and out among them. The lamps on the pier reflected onto the vessel, which was taller and far more imposing than he expected. Ahead of them an elegant elderly couple was strolling up the gangplank. Floating softly from aboard, the sound of a dance band playing "Satin Doll" was punctuated by waves gently slapping against the hull.

They stopped at the small ticket booth on the pier to confirm their reservations, then walked to the boat. "Good thing I'm not wearing stilettos," Jenny joked as they navigated up the steep gangplank.

"You own a pair?" Paul asked rakishly, and she giggled at the question. She stopped and thrust her right leg forward, revealing sensible black patent pumps.

"One-and-a-half inches is all I'm willing to risk," she replied as they reached the deck.

"A straight line if ever I heard it," Paul chuckled, and they turned to follow an arrow leading them along the Sapphire Deck promenade to the dining and dancing area. The ballroom was decorated in the sleek demi-deco lines reminiscent of an old Astaire and Rogers musical. Completing the illusion was a five-piece combo playing a soft jazz version of "Blue Moon." The dance floor was at least three times larger than the cramped space of their first RADFAm dance. *S'been a lot of mileage since that night,* Paul reflected but didn't say aloud.

"I'd better warn you," Paul confessed after they'd been seated at a table-for-two next to a large window overlooking the glittering skyline. "It's been quite a few years since those ballroom dancing lessons in junior high."

"As long as they're playing a slow one, we don't need to worry," Jenny reassured him, grinning. As they were handed their menus she took a quick glance at the bill-of-fare and suppressed a gasp. "Are you sure you don't want to go Dutch on this?" she asked for the second time since he'd picked her up.

"Positive," he replied. "Bought enough peanut butter for lunches for the rest of the month. Both creamy and crunchy. I'm doing just fine."

"Okay. I won't push," she promised as she took a more detailed look at the dinner cruise offerings. Maine lobster ravioli? They had to be kidding, right?

She gazed across the table at Paul, who was looking more dapper than a schoolteacher should. When their waiter arrived to ask if they wanted anything to drink, she ordered a merlot just to distract the butterflies in her stomach. Surely Paul had brought her out here for something. What could he be up to?

He gave her that little half-smile that caused his face to crinkle up so handsomely. Was he aware how irresistible it made him look? Part of what attracted her was the fact that he apparently didn't know.

She ordered a princess-cut filet (hearing as she did her mother carping in her mind, "A real lady would choose something lighter!"), while Paul went with the Atlantic seafood duet. They chatted about their respective weeks, watching the city recede as the yacht left the pier, and when the band struck up a slow song Paul asked her if she'd join him on the empty dance floor. She smiled and daintily held out her hand in response.

Their presence on the floor was apparently enough to spur other reluctant couples away from their tables. Hey, if the fat chick can get up and dance, then so can we! As the band worked its way through "Only You," she moved with Paul to the music. The feel of his hands was both comforting and exciting at once. Finally she got up the nerve to pursue her question.

"Paul," she said softly. "I know I probably shouldn't have, but I checked into this cruise on the Internet and know how much you're spending on all this—and, don't worry, I'm not gonna offer to pay my way again."

"Good," he chuckled, "cause if you had, I might've actually said 'yes' this time."

"But," she persevered, "I can't help wondering if some proverbial shoe's about to drop. Why exactly are we here?"

"Do you know how stunning you look?" he countered. "Why wouldn't I want to be out on the town with a woman like you?"

"No. Seriously," she pressed.

"Well," Paul began, "I wanted to do something special on the night I asked—" He paused, and in the space between his words she heard a passing dancer lowly singing along to the melody.

"You know, I've rehearsed this all week, but I still don't know exactly how to do it. I was half hoping the setting would do most of the work for me." He paused again, breathing deeply and pulling her closer into his rhythmic embrace.

"I want us to go someplace new," he continued. "Some place we haven't been. I want to spend as much time as I can with you without becoming irritating or intrusive or boringly familiar. I want to be married to you, but I probably shouldn't say that yet since I don't want you to get skittish. So let's just say that I'd like us to be 'Engaged to Be Engaged.'" He then stopped in the middle of the dance floor, pulled a small felt-covered box from his dinner jacket and opened it for Jenny. Nestled within was a beautiful antique gold ring, set with a startling, sparkling aquamarine—her birthstone and very favorite gem.

"I'd planned to wait until after dessert," he admitted. "Maybe go up to the observation deck and do it under the stars *Titanic*-style. But you asked, so here we are. I'm deeply in love with you, Jenny Taylor, and I can't pretend otherwise."

She stood as if frozen, dumbly staring at him as other couples swirled about them, then wrapped her arms around the man she thought she'd never be good enough to have as a partner, and said, "I wouldn't want you to pretend otherwise."

EVEN THOUGH SHE WAS FIFTEEN MINUTES EARLY for the officers' meeting, Misty was still beaten to the punch by Ian and Patsy. Seated at Kuppa Joe'a's single good-sized round table, the couple was chatting happily over two lattes and a large plate of biscotti. Watching Patsy, who appeared more relaxed and casually glam every time Misty saw her, it was like coming face to face with a living commercial for size acceptance. To measure the Patsy of today against the mousey unkempt fat girl of two years ago was like comparing Emme to Tug Boat Annie.

"Patsy was just telling me that Val has left the state," Ian was saying as Misty approached the table with her cup of white chocolate cocoa. "Apparently she was transferred to a Jorwel Enterprises distribution center out west—Utah or some such. And if the rumor mill's to be believed, she was none too gently urged to take the position. While she's an asset to them as a poster gal for weight loss, her more recent public behavior 'round these parts hasn't endeared herself to the front office."

"So her display of civil disobedience at the pageant wasn't approved by Jordan Lewis?"

"The 'display' probably was," Ian guessed, "but the arrest most likely wasn't."

"That's funny," Misty considered as she blew on her mug. "Didn't Lewis make a name for himself back in the day as a card-carrying member of the civil rights movement? You'd think a man with those kinds of experiences under his belt would consider getting arrested for 'the cause' a badge of honor."

"Times change," Ian shrugged. "There's a big difference between being a young comedian/activist with little to lose, and a business tycoon with a substantial bottom line and edgy investors to consider."

"I wouldn't know," Misty grinned. "I'm merely a humble shopkeep." She snagged a dark chocolate-dipped biscotti just to dial up her cocoa ecstasy, dunked it enthusiastically, and took a rapturous bite.

"Not to change the subject, but how are things with you?" Patsy asked. "Is Joe's mother still recuperating?"

"You could call it that," Misty answered, taking a deep sip of cocoa, willing to go along with shifting the conversation away from Ian's ex. "Joe's with her now, watching *Grumpier Old Men*. I think she enjoys the company, but she's also the queen of mixed messages. One minute it's 'I haven't seen you in hours!' The next she's Peewee Herman going, 'Okay, I'm having fun now;

time for you to leave!'"

She paused as all three saw Eleanor enter the coffee shop, nervously looking around for her fellow officers. Ma Rivera could probably be a lot worse, Misty reflected. At least she had the chutzpah to occasionally sit up in bed and ask for things. She wouldn't drive you crazy, expecting you to instinctively divine what she needed without ever overtly telling you what that was. Perhaps unfairly, Misty suspected that Eleanor would be exactly that sort of patient. Just look how she'd hovered around Dex for all this time, never once coming out and expressing her true desires.

Still, if anyone had told Misty two years ago that she'd be doing the Waltons with her boyfriend's mother on the other side of the bedroom wall, she'd have busted a gut laughing. (The 'boyfriend' part would've been the hardest concept for her to swallow.) But now it had all grown so familiar that whenever Joe wasn't around she felt his absence profoundly.

There'd been a picture postcard from Kirk in today's mail—he'd found a really good job and was settling into his new life with Brian in the Pacific Northwest—and the Kodachrome missive made her miss him, too. So many changes over the past year—most of it positive, but even positive change was accompanied by loss.

She loved being with Joe. He filled a part of her she'd never even realized was empty. But she still sometimes missed the goofier parts of her old single life. Curled in front of the tube, eating micro-ed popcorn and enjoying schlocky old movie musicals with her poofter friend, for instance.

He sure had sounded happy in his postcard, at least. After all the joking about the duality of relationship curses, they'd beaten the odds and amazingly were managing to both be joyful at the exact same time. Miracles were indeed possible, she mused.

"Am I the last one here?" Eleanor panted as she glanced around the room.

"Still waiting on Jen and Paul," Ian answered, so she headed to the counter for a small pot of her usual herbal tea. "No, wait—there they are." And with that the young couple entered the coffeeshop. As they approached the table the first thing Misty noticed was the dazzling glint from a lovely aquamarine ring on the blonde BBW's left ring finger.

"All right," Jen announced, waving a virgin calendar book in her hand. "Ready to plan for next year?"

EPILOGUE

ALTHOUGH SHE KNEW NEARLY EVERY ONE of the twenty or so folks standing in the circle at the arboretum—even Connie and Greg had actually shown up, she saw—Cassie still felt relieved to have Mitch by her side for Lissa and Delia's union ceremony.

She'd been given a handwritten copy of the program over a week ago, letting her know when she'd be singing, but even though she knew what was supposed to take place, her old small-town Christian upbringing still kept warning her to be on guard. Cass had never heard of "handfasting" before. In fact, initially she'd imagined it was something to do with food. She'd learned that the "fasting" part of the ceremony referred to the couple binding themselves one to the other.

Her adoptive parents would really freak if they knew she was taking part in a "pagan ceremony," let alone one involving two women. But as far as Cass was concerned, it felt right to do so. As she'd gotten to know them better, both personally and through Jenny, it was obvious Lissa and Delia truly were in love—and they wanted this celebration to make it tangible. She knew that her church, for one, certainly wouldn't condone it, so why not conduct a service outside of church?

According to Mitchell, handfasting went all the way back to the Druids. "In some cultures," he'd explained in his most professorial voice as they'd driven to the arboretum, "it's done to acknowledge the start of a period of trial marriage, usually lasting a year, after which the couple decides whether they want to seal the deal for good. For others, the act of handfasting is meant to establish a lasting bond." He'd then grinned devilishly. "Some early handfasts climaxed—and that's really *le mot juste*—with the fastened couple 'getting it on' while the rest of the tribe watched. Who needed the Internet back then when you had a good handfast to go to?"

"You're just saying that to make me nervous," she'd scoffed. But now, with the approach of zero hour fast at hand—in this steamy rainforest, dwarfed by verdant foliage punctuated with riotously vibrant poinsettias—these naughty little mental slideshows persisted in intruding on her thoughts. She looked at the table in the center of the circle. There she could see an unlit candle, a small knife, and some mysterious white crystals in a bowl. She hoped, as Mitch told her, it was only salt.

No way she could back out now—the ceremony was about to commence. Misty Shores, bedecked in a billowing cotton celestial-batik robe and matching headdress whose colors flowed from pale lavender to deep violet, was making her way along the path toward the circle of friends. Lissa and Delia followed in her wake, wearing matching dark green linen skirt suits, walking hand in hand.

As they entered the circle the two celebrants went around and cordially greeted each guest—an uncomfortable-looking Greg and Connie; the bearded doctor who'd recently lost his wife (What was his name? Oh yeah, Dexter!); an older woman whom Jen had identified as one of the chapter's current officers, plus a second woman her age (and were they a couple, too?); Ian and Patsy; Paul and her sister, standing on Cass's left; then Mitchell and a few others she recognized from the beach party and pageant. Welcoming each guest in turn (Cass belatedly realized this had proceeded in clockwise fashion), they finally reached Joe, who perhaps broke protocol by blowing a kiss at Misty, who was standing in the middle, waiting.

The moment Lissa & Delia joined Misty at circle-center was the cue to start singing. She was doing it a cappella, but here in this greenhouse grove, surrounded by so many new friends, she didn't feel as nervous as she thought she'd be. The ballad was familiar, one she knew from an old Judy Collins album, apparently Delia's choice:

"What I'll give you since you asked
"Is all my time together—"

As she concluded, both her sister and Mitch squeezed her hands in mute applause. They then all stood in silence, the only sound the bubbling of a waterfall in the background. All three women looked so lovely in the diffused winter greenhouse light, like figures from some old children's storybook Cass had read as a not-so-little girl. Then Misty spoke to the circle of friends, her melodic voice both firm and friendly.

"We gather here this solstice day to bind these two souls together in a ritual of love that is older than all history. Let we who stand in this circle attend of their own free will and accord, in peace and in love. To signify this communion, please join hands all around."

Her sister's soft fingers on her left, balanced with the firm clasp of Mitchell's hand on her right, buoyed Cassie for what was to come.

"We charge this Circle to be filled with Love. May this sacred space be consecrated, and may it be a Guardian and Protection for the work we do this day." Misty paused, then strode within the circle to each compass point in turn, raising her arms in supplication and intoning the names and virtues associated with each direction: North/Earth, East/Air, South/Fire, and West/Water. She then returned to the center.

"When Lissa and Delia first approached me about presiding over their union ceremony, neither one was really familiar with the concept of handfasting. In fact, when I mentioned it to them, Lissa thought I'd said 'ham fest-ing.'" This brought a chuckle from the group, especially Mitch, whose love of telecom toys frequently took him to such gatherings. "But once we discussed the spirit of this tradition they decided it was just what they wanted to do, so together we conceived our own version of the ceremony. Be forewarned, young lovers! That's what happens when you ask the crazy mystic lady to oversee your union." She waited again for the laughter to subside.

"So we've joined here today to acknowledge Lissa and Delia's long-stand-ing commitment, one to the other. No mere year-and-a-day promise as in ages passed, but for 'all our time together.'" With this, Misty drew a creamy length of vintage Belgian lace from a pouch on her belt, gestured the couple to clasp right hands to wrists, and began the bonding, encircling the link with the lace three times and finishing with an intricate bow.

"Handfasting represents a heartfelt vow between two equal partners to be bound, one to the other, through all the trials and triumphs inherent to Life. The cord symbolizes the continuity of life: two ends, each with its own character, yet actually one. The knot symbolizes sacred commitment to this union, for without it the cord easily can come unbound. Today, as Lissa and Delia come together to be joined, they formally demonstrate their faith in each other, and their unity, beyond friendship and love.

"Let us bow our heads. Gentle Goddess, Potent God, vouchsafe the mar-riage of your children, sorrow for sorrow, and joy for joy. Bless them as they take one another to hand and heart at the setting of the year and the rise of the new. With the fasting of their hands, may they betroth their souls."

As Misty progressed through the service Cass glanced around the circle, stopping at her sister and the handsome young FA who was her lover and, hopefully—God (sorry, Misty, not Goddess!) willing—her future husband and Cass's brother-in-law. Since the day Jen and she had discovered their sister-hood Cassie had been exposed to a series of life possibilities that she certainly would never have known if she'd remained an isolated fat woman working and living in her small hometown. How many women were there like her old self, she wondered, still leading solitary lives of quiet self-despair, feeling as if they'd always be unworthy as anything more than someone's portly maiden aunt—or the fat lady down the street that all the kids harassed?

Yet here in what Misty would call a "blessed place" were fat women (and men, she added, looking lovingly at Mitchell) who'd found their own worth and created their own happiness. For all their internecine feuds and missed connections (Mitch was still struggling to get a full accounting of the beauty pageant from Greg), groups like this offered hope to people who might oth-erwise have believed themselves beyond it.

"Let this union endure, without end," Misty was saying, unwinding the lace binding the two women's hands. "Let it grow and prosper for as long as love lasts—and may we each serve as witness to the eternal blessing of their love. Please repeat after me, 'So mote it be.'"

And as the congregants echoed the ancient covenant (from Greg's self-conscious mumble to Mitch's hearty affirmation) and the ceremony continued, Cassie wondered about the future, and for once was excited at her own prospects—for growth and prosperity.

And love? So, Cassie hoped, mote it be.

AFTERWARDS
by Becky

IN 1997 BILL & I INTRODUCED *Measure By Measure* as a serialized soap opera (à la the inestimable Mr. Maupin), developing and honing it over several years and countless hundreds of miles.

My aging, ailing mother was living alone, 50 miles away, and our near-weekly visits offered uninterrupted time for conversation, perfect for exploring this fat-topian fantasy. As longtme supporters of the factual NAAFA (National Association to Advance Fat Acceptance) organization, we'd captured remembrances of friends, conventions and events that helped flesh out our fictional characters with a Windy City flair. Bill and I cherished those scenic sojourns, even as we watched Mom struggle and fail. *Measure* became our creative respite from worry and despair.

And so, my first "thank you" is to you, Mom Fox. I love and miss you, and in my heart I know you loved me too. But out of decades-old vestiges of your childhood size issues sprouted seeds of my own quarter-century of body-hatred. Mom, you were always beautiful in my eyes, size 14 and beyond. I pray now that, in reading this story, mothers and daughters can break the chain of self-loathing and embrace their unique personal power. And maybe then your self-doubts can be exorcised as well.

The size acceptance movement espouses the radical notion that people of all sizes deserve the opportunity for the same rights and opportunities as every other citizen. For over 35 years NAAFA has provided a voice for fat Americans, repudiating the lies, myths and acid assumptions of profit-mongering doomsayers by testifying before Congressional committees on health, successfully boycotting offensive representations of fat Americans, pursuing justice in wrongful sizeist litigation, and promoting public personalities who represent and celebrate the diversity of the human body. Thank you, Bill Fabrey.

Thanks also to *Dimensions* online magazine for providing RADFAm with its first home. Over those many months publishers Conrad & Ruby, fellow NAAFA friends and willing family waited patiently for each installment of *Measure,* urging us to "get it published already!" So here's a gracious hat-tip to Dr. Peggy Elam at Pearlsong Press for her boundless energy, expertise and enthusiasm. Let's do this again!

Finally, my most heartfelt gratitude is reserved for all you short-sighted, small-minded, insensitive clones who took every opportunity to tease, taunt and traumatize me. Thanks for pissing me off enough to negate your curses. So while you were spewing "you're too fat, you can't"s, I found my best friend, published several short stories, did some modeling, presented body image/self esteem workshops for juvenile offenders, embodied Kris Kringle for charity. Made a difference.

Oh, and wrote a hit novel. Which you just bought and read. Thank you, and tell your friends!

JUST A FEW MORE WORDS
from Bill

There's not much I can add to Becky's words except to note that writing and rewriting this book with my lovely wife has been a heady experience. Becky is my Jenny/Misty/Ann, and working with her on this sprawling saga has been elevating, maddening, energizing, and, ultimately, bonding. It took a long time for this book to get finished, but I'm profoundly grateful that we both had that time.

March 2009

ABOUT THE AUTHORS

BECKY AND BILL met at a wedding in 1982, fell first in lust and then in love, and ultimately married beneath the June skies at the Temple of the Trees in Central Illinois.

"I'd been told so many times that since no man could *ever* want a fat girl like me, I might as well reconcile my future as either a spinster or a lesbian. So the first question my mom asked when she learned about Bill was 'Is he gay?' It felt so wonderful to say, 'No, he loves every single curve!'"

Over the subsequent years, Bill and Becky have embraced size acceptance. Individually and in tandem, they have authored romantic and fantasy fiction, as well as critical essays and reviews on body esteem, pop culture and critters.

During the '90s they established a chapter of the National Association to Advance Fat Acceptance (NAAFA) in Central Illinois, and while this endeavor lasted only three years, they both remain committed to promoting healthy body image. Since then, Becky has spoken on size acceptance to classes of college students as well as younger children.

After too many years of frigid winters, humid sweltering summers and bland soybean vistas, the couple packed up their household of books, unicorns and furry four-footed kids in 2007 and headed southwest to the Gila Valley of Arizona. There, Bill is enjoying his role as a family therapist for a child welfare agency, while Becky creates jewelry, designs graphics, and sells items on eBay for their home-based business, OakHaus Designs.

This exciting new locale has welcomed and inspired them both, especially the mountains and natural mineral springs next door. So watch for two of *Measure*'s characters to move out west for future adventures.

ABOUT PEARLSONG PRESS

PEARLSONG PRESS is an independent publishing company dedicated to providing books and resources that entertain while expanding perspectives on the self and the world. The company was founded by Peggy Elam, Ph.D., a psychologist and journalist, in 2003.

PEARLS ARE FORMED when a piece of sand or grit or other abrasive, annoying, or even dangerous substance enters an oyster and triggers its protective response. The substance is coated with shimmering opalescent nacre ("mother of pearl"), the coats eventually building up to produce a beautiful gem. The self-healing response of the oyster thus transforms suffering into a thing of beauty.

The pearl-creating process reflects our company's desire to move outside a pathological or "disease" based model into a more integrative and transcendent perspective on life, health, and well-being. A move out of suffering into joy.

And that, we think, is something to sing about.

PEARLSONG PRESS endorses **Health At Every Size**, an approach to health and well-being that celebrates natural diversity in body size and encourages people to stop focusing on weight (or any external measurement) in favor of listening to and respecting natural appetites for food, drink, sleep, rest, movement, and recreation. While not every book we publish specifically promotes Health At Every Size (by, for instance, featuring fat heroines or educating readers on size acceptance), none of our books or other resources will contradict this holistic and body-positive perspective.

WE ENCOURAGE YOU to **enjoy, enlarge, enlighten and enliven yourself** with other Pearlsong Press books and products, which you can purchase at www.pearlsong.com or your favorite bookstore. Keep up with us through our blog at www.pearlsongpress.com.

Fat Poets Speak: Voices of the Fat Poets' Society
Frannie Zellman, Ed.

FatLand: A Novel
by Frannie Zellman

Ten Steps to Loving Your Body
(No Matter What Size You Are)
self-help by Pat Ballard

The Program : A Novel
by Charlie Lovett

Off Kilter: A Woman's Journey to Peace
with Scoliosis, Her Mother, & Her Polish Heritage
a memoir by Linda C. Wisniewski

Splendid Seniors: Great Lives, Great Deeds
inspirational biographies by Jack Adler

The Singing of Swans
a novel about the Divine Feminine
by Mary Saracino

Beyond Measure:
A Memoir About Short Stature & Inner Growth
by Ellen Frankel

Unconventional Means:
The Dream Down Under
a memoir by Anne Richardson Williams

Taking Up Space:
How Eating Well & Exercising Regularly Changed My Life
a sociological memoir by Pattie Thomas, Ph.D.
with Carl Wilkerson, M.B.A.
(foreword by Paul Campos, author of
The Obesity Myth)

Romance novels and short stories featuring Big Beautiful Heroines
by Pat Ballard, the Queen of Rubenesque Romances:
The Best Man
Abigail's Revenge
Dangerous Curves Ahead: Short Stories
Wanted: One Groom
Nobody's Perfect
His Brother's Child
A Worthy Heir
& Judy Bagshaw:
At Long Last, Love: A Collection

www.ingramcontent.com/pod-product-compliance
Lightning Source LLC
Chambersburg PA
CBHW030355030726
47497CB00002B/352

9 781597 190176